Plentywood, MT
D0478363

SENTINELS OF FIRE

Center Point
Large Print

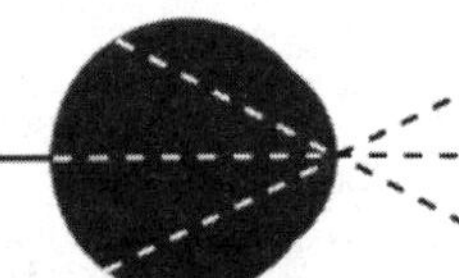

This Large Print Book carries the
Seal of Approval of N.A.V.H.

SENTINELS OF FIRE

P. T. DEUTERMANN

CENTER POINT LARGE PRINT
THORNDIKE, MAINE

This Center Point Large Print edition
is published in the year 2016 by arrangement with
St. Martin's Press.

This is a work of fiction.
All of the characters, organizations, and events portrayed in this novel are either products of the author's imagination or are used fictitiously.

The text of this Large Print edition is unabridged.
In other aspects, this book may vary
from the original edition.
Printed in the United States of America
on permanent paper.
Set in 16-point Times New Roman type.

ISBN: 978-1-68324-166-9

Library of Congress Cataloging-in-Publication Data

Names: Deutermann, Peter T., 1941– author.
Title: Sentinels of fire / P.T. Deutermann.
Description: Center Point Large Print edition. | Thorndike, Maine : Center Point Large Print, 2016.
Identifiers: LCCN 2016034408 | ISBN 9781683241669 (hardcover : alk. paper)
Subjects: LCSH: World War, 1939-1945—Naval operations, American—Fiction. | United States. Navy—Officers—Fiction. | World War, 1939-1945—Naval operations, Japanese—Fiction. | Large type books. | GSAFD: War stories. | Sea stories.
Classification: LCC PS3554.E887 S47 2016 | DDC 813/.54—dc23
LC record available at https://lccn.loc.gov/2016034408

This book is dedicated to the memory
of the nearly 5,000 navy men who lost their lives
at the battle for Okinawa.

ONE

On my very first day aboard USS *Malloy*, a Jap fighter plane came within fifteen feet of taking my head right off before it exploded just above the water on the opposite side of the ship. The captain looked down at me from the bridge wing once all the shooting stopped, shot me a lopsided grin, and said, “Welcome aboard, XO. How do you like your coffee?”

An hour later I thought of a truly smartass reply, but at that very moment, I was speechless and a bit deaf, too. I had literally just come aboard. The bridge messenger, a young seaman who looked to be no more than twelve years old, led me forward along the starboard side through all the guntubs to ascend the weather-deck ladders up to the bridge. We’d gotten halfway up the first ladder when that kamikaze came in out of nowhere, its screaming engine audible above the sudden burst of fire from the midships forties, joined immediately by all the twenty-millimeter mounts. I had been standing underneath a four-barreled forty-millimeter gun mount when the gunners first spotted him. Every gun on that side opened fire. The messenger and I dropped back down to the main deck and huddled under the ladder to avoid the shower of brass cartridges raining down on our heads. The muzzle blasts were so powerful that I couldn't catch my breath, but that was nothing compared to seeing that Jap plane diving right at us, right at *me,* with that big, ugly bomb slung under its fuselage, even as pieces of its wings, tail, and undercarriage were being torn off by the gunfire from *Malloy*'s massed batteries. At the last moment, the pilot lost either his nerve or his head, because the plane pitched up, rolled, and then kited right over the ship before crashing down into the sea, pursued by a sheet of flaming gasoline. A moment later there was a stupendous blast when its bomb went off just a few feet underwater, giving what was left of its pilot one last flight experience and raising a waterspout a hundred feet into the air.

Only thirty minutes earlier, *Malloy* had finished taking on fuel and transferring personnel by midships highline alongside the fleet oiler, *Monongahela.* Once I landed on *Malloy*'s main deck, shed my life jacket, and collected my seabags, I headed forward as the bosun's mates retrieved the highline rig and the ship pulled away from the oiler, accelerating to 27 knots to get clear of the cumbersome and vulnerable underway replenishment formation. It had been a gray, drizzly day, with enough wind to bat the tops off of the waves as *Malloy* threaded her way through all the carriers, battleships, and cruisers of Admiral Raymond Spruance's Fifth Fleet.

Spruance had been conducting air strikes against Formosa and the Japanese home islands for the past three days, trying to reduce what was left of the Jap air forces before the invasion of Okinawa began. The Japs had reacted by throwing kamikazes at the fleet formations, with some success, unfortunately. I'd transferred over to the oiler from the aircraft carrier *Franklin*—the Big Ben, as she was known—where I'd been the gunnery officer, on my way to take over as executive officer in the destroyer *Malloy.* Career-wise, it was a pretty big step. Two days after I'd transferred to the oiler, the Big Ben lost over eight hundred men in a kamikaze bombing attack and was so badly damaged that she had to retire to Pearl and, ultimately, to retirement status in the Atlantic Reserve Fleet.

The captain was back inside the pilothouse by the time I got to the bridge, talking to the ship's Combat Information Center, known as the CIC or Combat, on the tactical intercom, or the bitch-box. He acknowledged my presence with a casual wave, finished his conversation, and then got out of his chair to come shake hands. I introduced myself.

"I'm Connie Miles, Captain," I said. "Reporting aboard for duty, sir."

"Pudge Tallmadge," he said as we shook hands. "Welcome aboard. I'm sorry your predecessor isn't here to do a proper turnover, but he was yanked off to go to command, and that does take precedence."

"Amen to that," I said. "I'll try to hit the deck running."

The captain's nickname, Pudge, must have been strictly an academy thing, because he was anything but pudgy now. Gaunt would have been a better description, with gray hair, light blue eyes with dark pouches underneath, medium height, and a face that looked ten years older than his forty-one years of age. His real name was Commander Carson R. R. Tallmadge III, USN, and he was from the Eastern Shore of Maryland and the Annapolis class of 1929. He'd been in command of *Malloy*, one of the new Gearing-class destroyers, since taking over from her commissioning CO right after that officer had suffered a heart attack in mid-1944.

"Let's go below," he said. He told the OOD—officer of the deck—that we'd be in his inport cabin and to keep the ship at modified GQ, or general quarters, until we got back out to our assigned station, escorting a three-carrier formation. The captain's cabin was just on the other side of the wardroom. Once there he buzzed the duty wardroom steward for some coffee, lit up a cigarette, and then asked me to give him my background.

"Class of 'thirty-five," I recited. "Served in the *West Virginia* for my makee-learn tour, then in

Chester as main propulsion assistant. Postgrad school back in Annapolis, then back to sea in *Houston* out of Norfolk as the assistant gunnery officer. A year and a half of shore duty at the Portsmouth Naval Shipyard, where the EDOs tried to convert me to engineering duty officer. That looked pretty boring to me, so I turned 'em down, which apparently hurt their feelings, because I was sent back to sea midtour to the Big E, again as assistant gunnery officer, right after Pearl."

"You were aboard for Midway, then?"

"Yes, sir. Actually, I was supposed to have gone to *Yorktown*, but that got changed at the last minute."

"That was lucky," he said.

"Yes, sir, I thought so, especially after she went down. Went to *Franklin* from *Enterprise*, this time as *the* gunnery officer. Got off her to come here only days before the Japs got her."

"Lucky again," he said. "That's good. I firmly subscribe to what Napoleon said when he was asked if he preferred brilliant generals or lucky ones. Lucky, every time, he said. Are you married?"

"No, sir, I am not. Almost, once, but then she got cold feet after one of the wives at a ward-room dinner party told her what married life with a naval officer was like: the constant separations; a lot of responsibility but really low pay; the stagnant promotion system; and then some more about the endless separations. She was a bit tipsy, but she was pretty convincing. My fiancée asked me later if that was all true, and I had to admit that it was. That, as they say, was that."

"Sorry to hear it," the captain said. "All of those things are true, or were, I guess. My wife's one of those special women who can live their own lives when I'm gone, and yet make mine worth living when I'm home. About the only thing that's changed is the promotion opportunity: You know, enough people die, the survivors get promoted. You're lucky you and she explored the truth before you got hitched."

"I suppose so," I said. "She was a lovely young lady, but she was pretty clear on what she wanted out of marriage: kids, a nice home, a nice car, and an expanding horizon. This was about the time we were all taking a fifteen percent pay cut if we wanted to stay on active duty."

"Remember it well," he said, nodding. "And we were glad to hand it over, as I remember. It beat going on the bread lines or shoveling dirt for the WPA."

"I wavered," I said. "Almost got out. Madge, that was her name, Madge Warrren, got her father into it. He tried to convince me that a career in banking was a whole lot better than a naval career. Having watched most of the banks fail when I was still at the academy, I wasn't convinced."

"What happened to her, may I ask?"

"She married a banker and became an alcoholic. I guess I was lucky to have dodged a bullet. In a manner of speaking."

"Wow," he said. "Well, speaking of luck, we're going to need as much of that as we can get, and all because we have one of the newer air-search radars."

That was interesting—we'd had two air-search radars on Big Ben, but he was talking as if *Malloy*'s having one was unusual. "Sir?" I said.

"L-day for the Okinawa campaign has been set of the first of April. Operation Iceberg, they're calling it. Gonna be a really big deal, Connie. Upwards of fifteen hundred ships and amphibious craft. A four-division assault, two Army, two Marine, almost 120,000 men, with the entire Big Blue Fleet in support. That's where we and our air-search radar come in. Spruance has ordered up a radar picket line, north and west of the main island of Okinawa. Six destroyers, augmented with some modified landing craft for additional close-in gun support, stationed in a big arc across the top of the island chain."

"I don't remember hearing anything about a picket line for Iwo."

"We didn't, because Iwo is six hundred and fifty miles away from the home islands. Okinawa, on the other hand, is only two hundred and twenty miles. Okinawa is considered by the Japs to be Japanese home island territory. They've got the entire Jap 32nd Army on that island, and the intel people are predicting a bloodbath." He sipped some of his coffee. I noticed his hand was trembling.

"If you were on the *Franklin*," he continued, "then you know that the Japs are on the ropes. For all intents and purposes, their fleet's been destroyed. They've resorted to kamikaze tactics pretty much because that's all they've got. Fleet intel estimates that they don't have all that many airplanes and pilots left, either, especially pilots, so they're making them count."

Well I knew. We'd been the target of all too many kamikazes recently in *Franklin*, and, being the gunnery officer, I knew all about the horror show they could produce. Fortunately *Franklin* had been surrounded by a screen of antiaircraft light cruisers and destroyers, together with the side batteries of two battleships, so it was pretty rare that one got through. "Will this picket line be a formation, Captain?"

"I don't think so, Connie. It looks like we're going to be on our own, stationed maybe ten, twenty miles apart, to create the biggest possible radar coverage."

"One ship on its own? That's a recipe for disaster."

"Do tell. It's one thing to defend against a plane trying to bomb or torpedo a moving ship. Quite another when the plane *is* the bomb. Fleet intel says they'll soon run out of planes. I'm not so sure. I think they're holding back until we actually attack Okinawa. Remember, Okinawa Shima *is* Japan in their evil little minds."

I nodded. I'd heard much the same scuttlebutt on board the Big Ben. The carriers were the queen bees of the fleet and often carried flag officers, which meant that officers stationed aboard a carrier knew more about what was happening in the big picture than, say, officers in a destroyer. Since I was the new guy here, however, it wouldn't do for me to come across as some know-it-all, even if I was to be the second in command.

"Can you tell me about the department heads, Captain?"

"Absolutely, and we're lucky to have four good ones. The whole wardroom is actually way above average. Let's see. The senior one is Lieutenant Jimmy Enright, the navigation officer, sometimes called the ops officer. UCSD grad, headed for law school but came in after Midway. Did one tour on a light cruiser, then showed up for the pre-commissioning detail for *Malloy.* He's bright, a thinker, loves his electronic toys and knows more about them than some of his people. Married, two little kids. Ask him a complicated question and he'll think about it first, then come up with an answer you didn't expect.

"The gun boss is Marty Randolph. Southerner, another lieutenant, academy, 'forty-two, commissioned right after Pearl, pretends to be a good ol' boy but actually stood tenth in his class. Championship diver back at the boat school. Loves his guns and his gunners, and they worship him. Also loves to fight Japs, and his men know that and respond accordingly. He can absorb a tactical situation and split out the main battery on the fly. Not married, but I'm told there is a Southern belle somewhere back home, dutifully pining away amongst the magnolias.

"Chief engineer is Mario Campofino, not an engineer by trade or nature but a very demanding and precise young officer. OCS out of NYU, did one tour in the *Indianapolis* as a makee-learn and then, like you, fleeted up to main propulsion assistant, which, on a heavy cruiser, says a lot. Again, he was part of the precomm detail for *Malloy.* Has a great rapport with his chiefs, whom he trusts, as well he should. But when it comes to running the main engineering plant, he's by the book, all the way. Calm, cool, never loses his temper, unlike the gun boss. Confirmed bachelor, or so he says.

"Finally, Peter Fontana, lieutenant jay-gee, the supply officer. I forget his college, some Podunk U in the Midwest. Supply School, of course, then OCS. Everything tends to amaze Peter, so he's very careful. Going to be an accountant one day if we survive this fight. He's a natural born bean counter. Didn't understand what his real mission was when he first came aboard, but he does now, and he's become really good at it. He oversees the handiest collection of midnight-requisition artists I've ever seen. We go alongside a tender and they will rob that ship blind of all the stuff we're not authorized to have. When they get caught, Peter puts on such a good act of ninety-day-wonder innocence that it is truly amazing to behold. The tender's people know we're guilty, but they're so impressed with this amazingly gullible LTJG Fontana act that they forget to come get their stuff back."

"The goat locker?"

"The chiefs' mess is strong. There are a couple of chiefs whom *I* would not have promoted, but that's just your fleet average situation. *Your* right-hand man is going to be the chief master at arms, Chief Wallace Lamont, a Scottish-descent bantam rooster with the unlikely nickname of Pinky. Red hair, ruddy face, faintly pink eyes. Even so, he's one of those guys you recognize immediately as someone you don't want to piss off. He's half the size of most of the crew, and yet no one crosses that man under any circumstances. Your predecessor depended on him absolutely. He told me more than once that nothing goes on in this ship that Lamont doesn't already know about, and if it's a problem, he's usually already taken care of it."

"Sounds damned useful," I said. "How do I play him?"

The captain sat back in his chair with an amused look. He closed his eyes for a moment. Then he surprised me. "What do you think your job is here, as XO?"

"Run the ship the way you want it run so that you look good."

He chuckled. "Who told you that?"

"Commander Randy Marshal, XO in the *Franklin.* Unfortunately, I understand he died in the big fire."

"Okay," he said. "That's the traditional approach, but these days, out here, it bears no relation to reality, Connie, especially on a destroyer. Let me tell you what's real. In the old days, four-stripers got command by staying healthy long enough to outlive their seniors while not getting caught consorting with goats. That took some time, which meant many skippers were graybeards by the time the war started. I was on one of the cruisers sunk at Savo. Our captain was nearly fifty-five years old. We were utterly ignorant of what we should have been doing that night. The Japs had trained and trained for night engagements with torpedoes, star shells, and some of their cruisers carried up to *twelve* eight-inch guns. We, on the other hand, were past masters at shining brightwork, responding to bugle calls, holystoning teak decks, rigging a taut quarterdeck awning, and steaming in precise formation on any given sunny day. When we got sent to

Guadalcanal we stayed up all night, waiting for something to happen. After three nights of that, we were all zombies, and that's when the Japs came. They tore us to pieces. They sailed by one of our picket destroyers at a range of less than two miles, but everyone on that ship apparently was sound asleep—at their GQ stations.

"We lost *Quincy*, *Vincennes*, *Astoria*, and the Aussie flagship, *Canberra*, all shot to pieces in two quick engagements. I was on *Quincy*, where I learned about swimming at night when the sea itself was on fire. Then I transferred to *Juneau*, where I learned about the Jap Long Lance torpedo. I'm alive today because I was blown over the side when she got hit the second time and the magazines went. Spent the night and the next thirty-six hours in the waters off Savo."

His face reflected some of the horror of those engagements and the trauma he'd experienced. I didn't know what to say. My war had been on carriers. Even when we had been attacked, it had never seemed quite so personal as what the captain was describing.

"Your main job here as XO is to run the ship on a day-to-day basis to the standards I demand. You will conduct daily messing and berthing inspections so that the ship stays clean. You will supervise all the paperwork, the training of the officers, chiefs, and enlisted. You will execute the standard Navy daily routine. You will see to it that someone, including you from time to time, takes stars once a day to confirm our position, even if we can *see* the nearest island. You and Lamont will police the lower decks for minor infractions of naval discipline. You will supervise the department heads in the administration of their departments. You will draft fitness reports for all the officers in the wardroom and ensure the department heads get enlisted evals in on time. And you will spend an inordinate amount of time dealing with all the my-wife-she, my-dog-it personnel problems that three hundred twenty enlisted people can conjure up even when we're eight thousand miles away from said wives and dogs. And that's just your day job.

"In addition to all that, you will be absorbing the *art* of command. The ship, you, and I will face tactical decisions. I'll make the actual decisions and give the orders. You will also make decisions, but you will formulate mental orders. The ship will execute *my* decisions, and you'll get to see how that comes out, and whether or not *your* mental decisions might have been better—or worse. I must see to your education for eventual command, because that's the new Navy. We don't get command anymore by outliving our contemporaries. Nowadays, we get command because commanding officers who live to tell the tale evaluate us and then make recommendations. Admittedly, sometimes we get command because people die in combat and we're the only ones available, but the powers that be are determined to get the system a lot more professional than it was before Pearl Harbor."

I still didn't know what to say, but it all sounded pretty good to me. Even better, the captain was taking the time to explain all this. I nodded.

"Now this is important," he continued, as if what he'd been saying earlier had not been important. "I am afraid. Every day that we press closer to Japan, and they react in their ungodly, barbaric fashion, I am even more afraid. I must not show that, because the crew of this ship, most of whom are under the age of twenty-one, are already scared shitless each time one of those kamis comes out of the sky to kill us all. I have to pretend that I'm shrugging it all off, but when I come down here after an air raid and sit on the steel throne, crapping my insides out, all the pretense goes right out of it. I'm telling you this because you're going to experience it. *Malloy* isn't a forty-five-thousand-ton aircraft carrier, surrounded by two dozen or more heavily armed escorts. When and if, but probably when, they get through and hit us, actually hit us, a lot of people around you are going to die. *You* might die. The ship might die."

He held up his two hands. The shaking was clearly visible now. "I didn't use to do this," he said. "In times past, I was more afraid of screwing up as a brand-new skipper than of anything the Japs could throw at us. Not anymore, XO. I'm sorry if I'm scaring you, but you need to understand this: From here on out, you need to put aside any thought about your career or your professional success as an XO. Where we're going, those things mean nothing. Your job is to get up each morning pretending that you're the owner here, of *everything* that's going on in this ship, and to act accordingly. Between us, we'll try to stay alive."

I stared down at the deck and took a deep breath.

"Well?" he asked.

"What could possibly go wrong?" I asked.

He grinned. "There you go," he said approvingly. "Welcome aboard. Now, go meet the department heads. I apologize again that you're not getting a proper turnover, but it really doesn't matter. *Malloy*'s a good ship and a happy ship. They'll call you XO from day one. That's about all it takes to assume the job. Get each department head to give you a complete tour of his spaces—*Malloy* is no cruiser or carrier, so it doesn't take that long. Get your battle gear together and know where it is at all times. These home-island Japs don't keep gentlemen's business hours."

At that moment, the ship's announcing system broke in to announce that a raid was inbound, many bogeys, and that all hands needed to man their battle stations. *Bong, bong, bong, bong.*

"Like I was saying," the captain said, reaching

for his helmet. I reached for mine, but it wasn't there. Lesson number one.

The next week passed quickly. The ship went to GQ twice daily as a matter of routine, just before sunrise and just before sunset, favorite times for suiciders to make an appearance. I'd moved into the previous XO's stateroom, a tiny cabin with room for a desk, a bunk, and a chair. The only thing I didn't have was a roommate, unlike all the rest of the officers except, of course, the captain. My predecessor had been a heavy smoker, so I asked to have the cabin repainted, turning it from sticky amber to white and smelling now of fresh floor wax instead of stale tobacco smoke. I spent a lot of time touring the ship with the department heads as they showed me their assigned spaces and introduced me to their people. I had lunch in the chiefs' mess, where we mostly talked about morale and the problems of housekeeping endemic to housing, feeding, and cleaning the 320 enlisted and twenty officers embarked, in a ship that was not quite four hundred feet long.

I met Chief Petty Officer Wallace Lamont early on. He was the ship's chief master at arms, which was a collateral duty. His professional CPO rating was gunner's mate. When he found out I'd had two tours in gunnery departments, he positively beamed. Strangely enough, he probably spent more time as the CMAA than as a gunner's mate chief petty officer. *Malloy* had two gunner's mate chiefs, and the junior one, Chief Mabry, took care of the day-to-day duties of being Second Division's CPO. Lamont spent his time adjudicating minor discipline problems, accompanying me on my daily inspections, and generally walking the decks throughout the day and sometimes the night, keeping an experienced thumb on the pulse of the crew.

Chief Lamont turned out to be just the right-hand man the captain had described. Short, feisty, and abrupt, he spoke with a trace of a Scottish burr, an affectation I think he'd developed after making chief eight years ago, to add to his personal mystique. He had come up through the ranks as a gunner's mate and, of course, still was one. The fact that I had been gunnery officer in two previous ships somewhat offset the fact that *Malloy* was my first destroyer. Destroyermen were a proud if a somewhat inbred bunch, and I knew there'd been some comment on the fact that I'd only served in much bigger ships, and yet here I was, sent in as XO. Everyone immediately assumed I had pull somewhere.

I didn't, but there had been some strings pulled to get me into the Naval Academy, courtesy of my parents. Navy people talked of their kids as Navy brats; I'd been a State Department brat. I didn't find out what my folks had really been doing all those years in a seemingly endless stream of embassies until their retirement party in 'thirty-eight. My father, now deceased after his lungs succumbed to years of heavy smoking, never seemed to get promoted. He was always an assistant attaché of some kind—cultural, financial, agricultural—something vague and not very important. My mother worked as a senior secretary in each of the postings, sometimes as the ambassador's personal secretary or executive assistant. I was finishing up my senior year at Western High School in Washington on the day they were given their *despedida*, as it was called, from the U.S. Foreign Service, and I got the day off from school. Instead of going to the State Department headquarters in Foggy Bottom as I expected, we went to the Main Navy Building on B Street, not too far from the White House. There I found out that my parents had been working for the Office of Naval Intelligence the whole time I'd been growing up and, even more surprising, that my dear, sweet mother was the actual intelligence officer, and my father, the guy who never seemed to get promoted, her cover and controller within all those embassies. The director himself awarded each of them a medal for distinguished careers and reminded them that they must never speak about that service, and then we all partook of coffee and cake.

My parents retired to a nice house up in Chevy Chase, Maryland, just outside the District line. I tried once to ask them about what they'd been doing all those years, and all my mother would say was "Typing, Connie, lots and lots of typing." My father just puffed on his pipe and nodded sagely. That was that, and I didn't figure out that they were the principal means by which I got my appointment to the Naval Academy in 1931 until well after I'd graduated. I, of course, thought it was because I was so damned handsome, smart, and, well . . . you know.

The captain had been right—I was addressed as XO right from the start, and there was a subtle but palpable shift in how the enlisted people in this ship interacted with me. As the gunnery officer in the Big Ben I'd been a department head, but not a very important department head, as compared to the air operations officer or the chief engineer. Aircraft carriers had two complements: the ship's company, which ran the actual ship, and the carrier air wing, made up of many squadrons and almost a hundred airplanes that did the business of an aircraft carrier: air strikes, reconnaissance missions, close support of troops ashore, and formation defense. My job had been to manage twelve five-inch caliber guns, sixty of the smaller but still lethal four-barreled forty-millimeter Bofors guns, and 76 Oerlikon twenty-millimeter electric machine guns, most of which were arrayed in guntubs stretching up and down both sides of the 860-foot-long flight deck.

If the pilots did their job, my people stood idle, watching the air show as dozens of our fighters pursued and splashed attacking Jap bombers and suiciders all over the formation, while our escorts, ranging from sixty-thousand-ton battleships to twenty-five-hundred-ton destroyers, filled the sky with black spots of ack-ack and, we hoped, flaming Jap planes. When one did get through all that and head directly for us, my guys could put up a pretty good curtain of ack-ack themselves, and, although it was unnerving to watch one of those planes get bigger and bigger, sometimes already on fire or streaming gasoline vapor from punctured wing tanks, the Big Ben was 860 feet long. If they hit us, supposedly we could take it.

Being the exec in a destroyer, however, meant that things were very different. The executive officer of a warship was next in line for command of the ship if something happened to the captain. The exec went around the ship wearing the mantle of command, all the while knowing that if he ran into a situation that baffled him, he could slip topside for a quiet word with the captain. As a department head, I'd been one of many. As the exec, I was one of two, with the other guy being the commanding officer, as close to a god as was still possible in the twentieth century. Luckily for me, Captain Tallmadge was special. The department heads told me of the first time the captain had, right after the change of command, watched a shiphandling evolution go off the tracks, with the officer in charge of the maneuver royally screwing things up. *Malloy*'s previous skipper would have had a flaming temper tantrum right there on the bridge. Tallmadge had watched things go to hell with obvious but silent dismay. As everyone waited for the explosion, the captain had taken off his hat and thrown it down on the deck in the pilothouse. Then, to everyone's amazement, he got out of his chair and began to chew out—the hat. Called it names, told it how disappointed he was in it, how it had to do better the next time, that this maneuver wasn't that hard, and that there'd be no liberty for that hat until things improved. Then he'd gotten back into his captain's chair, visibly shunning the thoroughly shamed hat, and announced that they were going to try that maneuver again.

It had been theater, and everyone on the bridge recognized that, but it had been most effective. This guy wasn't going to call *you* an idiot—he was going to address the problem, not on the basis of whose fault it was but rather by figuring out how to fix it. As they later learned, the new captain's reaction to any kind of screwup was to tie the incident to insufficient training. Any time he *did* lose his temper, it was the hat that caught hell. People relaxed and began to pay attention to the training, now that no one was chewing their asses as if they'd done something wrong on purpose. It became standard procedure for the junior officers to reveal that they'd made a hash out of something by saying, "I lit off a Hat Dance this morning, all by myself." When I heard that story, I recognized there was a certain genius to it and took aboard the underlying message: Blame the problem, not the people. With rare exceptions, the officers, chiefs, and crew were always trying to do their best.

My second week aboard produced my first lesson in command. The carrier formations were operating to the north and west of Okinawa, sending softening-up missions in against the Japs' aboveground installations on the island. While this was going on, a large air raid appeared midmorning out of densely clouded skies. The CAP fighters—Combat Air Patrol—had been up for an hour, flaming as many of the incoming bombers as they could find, but one of the carriers had been hit and was dealing with a spectacularly big flight-deck fire. We'd shot at some of the raiders, but for some reason our two carriers were not targets that morning. While the raid was still in progress, one of our carrier's Corsairs came past the ship at low altitude trailing a deadly white cloud of leaking avgas. I'd come out to the bridge from my GQ station in Combat when the lookouts first spotted him.

"He's gonna bail out or ditch," the captain said, tracking the wobbly airplane though his binoculars.

Combat reported they had no comms with him. Our gunners had recognized the distinctive gull-wing silhouette and held their fire, but everyone was still pretty nervous and scanning the skies for Japs.

The Corsair banked left and then came back toward the ship in a wide circle. He put his flaps down and leveled off ahead of the ship, going away from us as he settled down close to the sea surface.

"Shall I call away the pilot rescue detail?" I asked.

"No," the captain said. "We're not stopping with an air raid going on. Any kami who sees a ship with no wake will head right for it. Combat will mark and report his position. The carrier who owns him will send some covering planes. Then one of the destroyers will come, but no one is stopping now, XO. Not right now."

At that moment the Corsair hit the water, throwing up a large sheet of white spray, dipping its nose and then settling back on an even keel. Seconds later the weight of that enormous engine tipped it forward again and the plane began to sink. We were perhaps five hundred yards away and closing in on him at 25 knots. I was still dealing with what the Captain had said. Were we just going to drive by and do nothing? Then I saw some of mount fifty-one's gun crew pop out of their mount, wrestling some kind of package over to the port bow.

“Slow to ten knots,” the captain ordered. The lee helmsman reset the engine-order telegraph handles, and the ship immediately began to slow down. Destroyers were handy little ships. The Big Ben would have taken a half hour to slow down that much from 25 knots.

The captain walked out to the port bridge wing as we came past the Corsair, whose tail was now sticking up at a sixty-degree angle. The canopy was open and the pilot was sitting astride the after fuselage, waving at us. The gun crew on the bow heaved an inflatable life raft over the side, smacking it down into the water not ten feet from the sinking plane. The captain waved from the bridge wing, and then we drove right on by. I couldn’t quite make out the pilot’s expression, but I could only imagine what he was thinking. Two minutes later, a Jap Zeke took aim at us from about eight thousand feet, and it took every gun we had to knock him down, and none too soon, either. A second Zeke turned back when we started blasting away at the first one and then apparently saw the pilot bobbing around in his raft two miles behind us. He leveled off and strafed the pilot, reducing the raft to bloody shreds.

When our guns went silent, everyone seemed to be avoiding eye contact with everyone else. The captain had returned to his chair and was staring out the front portholes. I went back into CIC.

Half an hour later, the task force commander

declared the air raid over, and we resumed our assigned station and reset our modified GQ condition of readiness. I went back out to the bridge to speak to the skipper, but he had disappeared into his sea cabin. I took a deep breath and knocked on the door. There was no response. Maybe he'd gone down below? I knocked again and opened the door.

The captain was sitting in his chair with his head in his hands. I excused myself and started to back out, but he told me to come in. There was barely room for both of us in the tiny cubicle.

"I was going to tell you that you got tunnel vision out there," he said. "That's understandable, especially since you've just come from a bird farm. Pilots are everything on a carrier. But if you're the skipper, the *ship's* everything. You must always ask yourself this: Is what I'm about to do or order going to keep my ship safe or put her in unnecessary danger?" He paused to take a deep breath. His red face and shaking hands mirrored my own emotions about leaving that guy out there. "I'm devastated at what happened to that pilot," he continued. "Don't forget, I've been that man in the water, all by myself."

"I understand, sir," I said. "Besides, you were right. Two kamis did come, and they might have sunk us instead of the pilot. It's just, I don't know, a really rotten deal."

"It is, indeed," he said patiently. "That's the

difference between being XO and being the CO. You, the exec, get to observe and learn; I, the CO, get to make decisions like that. My head tells me it was the right decision; my heart is sick about it, and not for the first time. I think I'm getting too old for this stuff, XO, so pay attention. You might be in my shoes sooner than you think."

I had no answer to that, and then he waved me away. He wanted to be alone, and I could well understand that, too. I felt sick.

That night, after we'd secured sundown GQ with no bogeys, I was up in Combat, going over the day's reports with the navigation officer, Jimmy Enright. The navigation officer was in charge of navigating the ship, and also responsible for all the electronic divisions—the Combat Information Center, Sonar, Radio Central. As the Navy stuffed more and more electronic gear into its ships, the second half of his job was rapidly eclipsing the first part. I made some comment about leaving that pilot in the water.

"He probably understood, XO," Jimmy said. "He was safer in that life raft than in some tin can that might be blown in two by a kamikaze. Begging your pardon, but your carrier background is showing."

"I suppose so," I said. "Still—a guy in the water? And we drive by?"

"This'll sound like bullshit, XO, but the tin can Navy is at the sharp end of the fleet spear. The

Japs have to get through us to get a shot at the heavies, and the heavies expect us to keep that from happening. You've read the after-action reports. This carrier was damaged, that carrier was torpedoed, this battleship had two near misses, this cruiser took a kami on the bridge. And, oh, by the way, two destroyers were sunk."

"Like we don't count?"

"We count, all right, because when the heavies lose one of their tin cans, they're just a little more vulnerable than they were before that tin can went down."

"That's a little cynical, don't you think, Jimmy?"

"Maybe, but wait until you see where we're going next."

"The captain mentioned something about a picket line, up north and west of Okinawa?"

"Yes, sir, and I'm thinking it'll take the Japs about one day to figure out who's sounding the alarm when they head down from Japan to strike the amphibs or the supporting fleet units off Okinawa. You've seen what an air raid looks like when the whole carrier fleet is attacked. Now take that same number of Jap planes and focus it on five or six single-ship picket stations."

"Sounds like a real party," I said. "I talked to the captain after what happened today. He's a lot more upset than he let on out on the bridge."

"He's been a great skipper," Jimmy said, "but there are times I think it's starting to get to him.

We were the first ship on the scene after the *Littell* broke in half and went down from a two-plane kami strike. We stopped to look for survivors, and the admiral himself got on the radio and ordered us back to our assigned AA (antiaircraft) station immediately. The skipper got a personal-for blast later, pointing out that he had created a hole in the AA screen by stopping, when there was obviously nothing that could be done for *Littell.* I think they recovered twenty-two out of three-hundred-plus once someone did go back. He was stone-faced for three days after that."

I was appalled at that story, mostly because I'd never heard about the *Littell.* I realized now that my carrier background was showing—every destroyerman out here had heard the *Littell* story.

The following day I had both Chief Lamont and Chief Bobby Walker, the chief hospital corpsman, accompany me on my daily messing and berthing inspection. This was one of the exec's principal duties, a daily inspection of all the berthing spaces, where the crew slept, and the messdecks, where the enlisted took all their meals. Each morning, after dawn GQ and morning quarters, each division assigned two men to compartment cleaning; they swept, swabbed, picked up the trash, hauled full laundry bags to the ship's laundry, polished any brightwork, and generally cleaned up the crowded compartments. My job was to come around at ten thirty in the morning and make sure that that had all been done. Same thing for the crew's dining area, called the messdecks, the galley, and the scullery, where trays and silverware were washed and sanitized for the next meal. Chief Lamont came along as my enforcer. If I saw problems I'd point them out to Lamont, and he would have a quiet word with the compartment cleaners as I headed for the next berthing space.

Chief Walker, an experienced and senior chief corpsman, or medic, was universally called Doc. Some destroyers had an actual medical officer assigned, but if there was a shortage—and with the upcoming landings, there would be a shortage—the tin cans made do with senior medics like Walker. He was a taciturn individual, tall and ruggedly built, with a razor-sharp flattop haircut, who'd served with Marines during the Guadalcanal campaigns of 'forty-two and 'forty-three. He had one assistant, a hospital corpsman second class, and together they formed the medical department, based in what was known as sick bay. On my daily tours he would pay particular attention to the galley and the scullery, measuring rinse-water temperatures, taking water samples from the ship's potable water tanks, and making sure the cooks were keeping themselves sanitary while doing food prep. He held sick call every day right after quarters to deal with runny noses, sore throats, minor injuries, and the inevitable slacker who wanted out of the morning's upcoming evolutions, like refueling detail. He looked at the morning sick call for bad trends: A sudden uptick in sore throats, for instance, meant that the scullery water temperature wasn't high enough.

With the help of these two chiefs, I covered every nook and cranny in the ship during my first week and every week thereafter. I learned where the problem children lived, which compartments were the hardest to keep clean (the engineers', whose daily association with black oil, lube oil, grease, rust, and the bilges made for a genuinely black gang), where the nonregulation coffeepots were stashed, or the laundry bags that hadn't been taken aft, and many other things associated with packing three-hundred-plus men in spaces meant for two hundred. The daily inspections, except on Sundays, were one of the most important things an exec did. Your nose would tell you pretty quick if you were on a ship where the exec did *not* make daily inspections.

The *Malloy* was assigned to a carrier screen, meaning we went where the big ship went, maintaining a specified station on the carrier. We were constantly looking for Jap subs with our sonar, and we stood ready to defend against air attacks, which came just about daily. The carrier formations were vast—up to fifteen big-decks of the Essex class and another dozen or so of the smaller escort carriers. The fleet formation itself covered a circular area of just over fifty miles. There were antiaircraft light cruisers, heavy cruisers, and even battleships, which, now that the Jap fleet had been virtually eliminated from the sea, were used principally as massive antiaircraft gun platforms. Every third day we would go alongside either one of the carriers or an oiler to refuel and replenish food and ammo stocks.

When the Japs attacked from the air, the destroyers would close in around their assigned carriers in a tight circle and put up a sky-full of antiaircraft fire, called ack-ack from the sounds made by the smaller guns firing at any Jap plane who showed an interest in our carrier. The carriers, which had long-range air-search radars, would launch fighters into a Combat Air Patrol screen each morning to stations between Japan and the fleet formation. When a raid was detected, the CAP would be vectored to engage as far out from the screen as possible. The closer the Jap planes came, the more CAP they ran into, with the idea being to grind down the attacking formation to onesies and twosies by the time they got in close enough to target our ships.

I met with the captain each day after morning quarters and caught him up on the housekeeping and personnel issues. He in turn brought me up to speed on the operational events in our immediate future. Captain Tallmadge was a genuinely pleasant man, who took an abiding interest in his people. He was very patient with me. I had come from the carrier Navy with no experience in destroyers, so he took a lot of time to explain how things really worked in the world of tin cans. It was a refreshing change in leadership style; for the most part, my bosses had been somewhat distant, ready to give me the chance to sink or swim in whatever new assignment I was taking on. That was especially true on a carrier, where there were nearly three thousand people milling about at any one time. Tallmadge cared, and the whole crew knew it. Serving in *Malloy* was shaping up to be a pleasure.

Then we went north to the Okinawa picket line.

TWO

April 28, 1945

"XO."

"Yes."

"Morning stars, sir."

"What about 'em?"

The quartermaster of the watch chuckled. "Nautical twilight in fifteen, sir," he said. "You want Mister Enright to take it?"

"I'd love that, McCarthy," I said. "But . . ."

"Yes, sir. Anyway, morning stars."

"Got it," I said. "On my way. Two sugars, please."

"Ready and waiting, XO."

"Captain up?"

"No, sir. Log says he went to his sea cabin at oh one thirty."

I grunted. The captain was a heavy smoker who used all that nicotine to stay up as late as possible. Once he went down, however, he went down. It was one of my jobs to wake him up, which always took some doing. "On my way," I said.

I got up, splashed some water on my face, and put on my uniform khakis. I stared at my reflection in the sink mirror and groaned at what I saw. The fifty-year-old face looking back at me was really only thirty-five. I'd aged fifteen years since we'd gone on the radar picket line. We all had. Even the ensigns were looking old. I went looking for my sea boots in all the clutter in my tiny "stateroom."

The ship was quiet. Reveille was forty-five minutes away. The forced-draft blowers in Number Two Fire Room whined contentedly. The executive officer's stateroom was in after-officers country just forward of and almost on top of number 2B boiler, as the hot steel deck readily attested. Dressed, I stepped across the passageway to the officers' head to pump bilges. There was no time for a shower, and besides, one of our evaporators was on the fritz, so the ship was on water-hours. Rubbing my eyes, I collected my kapok life jacket and helmet and then headed topside to the bridge to take morning stars.

It was still dark when I stepped out onto the bridge, but I could make out the silhouettes of the bridge-watch team. I stopped for a moment to adjust my eyes and listen for any sign of problems. In happier times, the half hour before sunrise was always one of the best things about being at sea. Even in lousy weather, the first sight of the sea in the morning twilight is always a delight. Couple that with the smells of breakfast wafting up from the galley and that first cup of Navy coffee, and all the small terrors of steaming a blacked-out warship at night diminish with each passing moment of rising sunlight out on the eastern horizon.

Not now, though, and not here, some fifty miles north of the Okinawa amphibious objective area. We were aware of an altogether different rising sun up here on the radar picket line, one that came out of the sky in the form of a bomb-laden Jap fighter or bomber, intent on killing us all. I could literally feel the tension, because everyone up on the bridge knew that twilight on the Okinawa radar picket line was no longer anyone's friend. People were scared, and with good reason.

The lee helmsman saw me and announced "XO's on the bridge" to the rest of the watch standers. The officer of the deck, Lieutenant (junior grade) Tom Smithy, greeted me, as Quartermaster Second Class McCarthy handed me a ceramic mug of coffee.

"Morning, XO," Smithy said. "Steaming as before on Okinawa picket station four-Able. LCS 1022 abeam to port, three thousand yards. Comms good. No contacts, air or surface. Gun crews sleeping on station. Visibility unlimited, seas flat, wind out of the northwest at five to seven knots. Barometer is steady at thirty-point-oh-two inches. GQ at zero six forty-five, sunrise at seven fifteen."

"Very well," I said. "Sounds like another great Navy day. I'll be shooting stars on the port bridge wing. Remind me to get the captain up just before GQ."

"Aye, aye, sir," Smithy said and turned back to resume his scan of the horizon. It was nautical twilight, which meant that the horizon would begin to assume some definition as the ambient light slowly grew to the point where it was no longer dark but not quite daylight. It was the kind of light that was good for using a sextant—and also for a kamikaze pilot who had chosen to come in on the deck right before dawn, and that was why the ship would go to general quarters thirty minutes before the actual sunrise took place.

I went out to the portside bridge wing, where McCarthy had set up the sextant, my notebook and chronometer, and a list of celestial azimuths. Normally there would have been a makee-learn ensign on deck, but with the exhausting watch-and-watch routine of the picket stations, six hours on, six off, the captain had decided to suspend navigation training. It wasn't as if we didn't know where we were—forty-nine miles north-northwest of Okinawa—but it was a cardinal rule of the wartime destroyer force that the navigation officer shot stars whenever visibility allowed. Since Jimmy Enright was also the ship's de facto operations officer, I'd begun doing the celestial navigation a couple times a week to spell him. At least once a day, at either morning or evening nautical twilight, I shot stars and fixed the ship's position with an accuracy that not even radar could match. It was an ancient art, and I took pleasure in practicing it.

"Who's up?" I asked.

"Aldebaran, Sirius, Jupiter, Polaris, Vega, and Venus."

"That'll do it. I'll start with the stars, then the fat boy; I'll end with Venus, lower quadrant."

"Aye, sir," McCarthy said as he consulted his Rude starfinder. "Vega should be three three seven, fifty-six point four degrees."

We worked through the list, with me capturing each celestial body in my sextant telescope and then bringing the image down to the increasingly visible horizon, rocking my sextant from side to side to make the twinkling image just touch the horizon, then calling out a mark. The quarter-master recorded the elevation angle and precise time of each observation. Once we had the observations, McCarthy relieved me of the sextant and headed back into the charthouse behind the bridge to set up the plotting sheets.

I stayed out on the port bridge wing to finish my coffee and watch the dawn spread its soft light over a metallic gray sea. I could just make out the silhouette of the LCS off to port. She was out there as an additional surface-search radar asset and AA gun platform. One tried to forget the unofficial nickname for the Landing Craft Support ships stationed with the picket destroyers: "pallbearer," since they often got to pick up the pieces after a kamikaze got through and struck one of the tin cans.

I glanced at my watch: twenty minutes to morning general quarters stations. Gotta go get the skipper up, I thought.

Something twitched down in my subconscious mind. Something I'd forgotten to do? A sound? I'd turned to step inside the pilothouse when I felt and then heard something that hooked my full attention: the rising scream of an airplane engine winding out to redline RPM. Before I could quite grasp what was happening, and awake now like never before in my life, I felt a compression wave as something flashed directly over the ship's mast. Time stood still for an agonizing second as a silvery blur appeared between the *Malloy* and that LCS. Then the OOD slammed the red GQ alarm handle sideways, initiating the *bong-bong-bong* battle stations alarm throughout the sleeping ship. Feeling suddenly naked, I grabbed for my steel helmet even as the LCS exploded in a bright orange fireball with a gut-thumping roar.

"*God* dammit!" I swore, fumbling with my helmet.

One hundred fifty sailors and three officers on the LCS disappeared in a sickening tattoo of booming explosions as all her topside ammo cooked off. A moment later, a boiling cloud of fiery black smoke, dust, and steam produced a dreadful rain of metal and human debris all around where the LCS had been a few moments before. It was clear that she was gone, what was left of her shattered hull already tumbling down into the depths of the Pacific.

The OOD kicked the ship's speed up to 25 knots and executed a sharp turn to starboard. He knew the rules: Move. Move quickly and boldly when the kamikazes came. If you never saw the first one, you weren't going to see the second one, either, who already might be in his 400 mph dive, setting up on a slow-moving American destroyer waking up to yet another homicidal day on the Okinawa radar picket line.

The bridge was filling with the GQ crew. Extra phone-talkers hurried in. The first lieutenant took the deck, while Tom Smithy assumed junior officer of the deck and the conn. Bleary-eyed sailors were squirming into kapok life jackets and fastening their steel helmet straps, while gawking at the deathly pall two miles away. The forward guns trained out to starboard as the director officer atop the bridge searched for the next kamikaze.

"Captain's on the bridge," a sailor announced, and I finally stepped off the bridge wing and into the controlled chaos in the pilothouse.

"I take it one got through," the captain said, tying his own life jacket straps across his chest. He was already wearing his helmet, with the letters CO stenciled in black across the front.

"Felt it before I saw or heard it," I said. "A blur,

then a blast. No radar warning; nothing. I'll go amidships and see about getting some life rafts ready."

"All right," the captain said, climbing into his chair and reaching for his binoculars. "We'll take evasive maneuvers for a few minutes, then pass through the datum."

"Aye, aye, sir."

"XO?" he said. "We're not going to stop."

"All her ammo seemed to go off at one time," I said, still staring at that collapsing plume two miles away. An entire ship—a small one, granted, but still. A dirty cloud of greasy gray smoke was all that was left. "Not likely anybody's still alive over there."

"We'll go see," the captain said. "People survive the damnedest things, but right now we have to get ready for the rest of the bastards."

Jimmy called out another course change and slowed the ship's speed to 20 knots. I headed aft to the boat deck, where the lifeboat crew would be making ready to lower the ship's whaleboat, *Malloy*'s primary motorized lifeboat, to the rail. I knew we wouldn't be putting a manned boat into the water until we *knew* there were no more kamikazes around. Instead we'd drive through the area where the LCS had exploded and kick two inflatable life rafts over the side. If there were any survivors swimming out there, they'd see the rafts. Stopping the *Malloy*, however, was out of the question, as I'd learned that day with the Corsair pilot. This Jap had managed to evade our air-search radar and *two* surface-search radars, most likely by coming in right on the deck. The surface radars should have detected something, which told me that there might be an inversion layer hanging over the ocean, masking incoming contacts. I looked again at the cloud of dirty smoke flattening out over the sea. It was going to be another very long day if this disaster was any indication.

When I reached the boat deck, the lifeboat crew already had the motor whaleboat swung out and ready to launch. I still marveled at the crew's level of training: I'd been aboard for not quite two months now, and everyone in *Malloy* seemed to know his job and when to do it. The chief bosun's mate had come up from Repair Two and was supervising the rigging of two of the ship's canvas-and-wood rafts. Once the captain brought the ship through the area where the LCS had gone down, the deck apes would dump the rafts over the side, but only if the lookouts reported heads in the water. The LCS had been larger than an amphibious landing craft but smaller than a full-sized LST, with a crew of three officers and 150 men. She'd had four rocket launchers, a single five-inch gun, two quad forty-millimeter AA guns, two twenty-millimeter AA guns, and all the ammunition to service that ordnance stowed in deck lockers for quick access. Their original mission had been to provide quick-response naval gunfire support for landings once the big gunships, the heavy cruisers and battleships, had detached from the actual landing operation. They could stay close inshore and deal with all the pop-up targets as the Marines dug the enemy out of their bunkers and caves. When the Japs began to pick off the radar picket destroyers, however, the task force commander had ordered LCSs out to the picket line to augment the line's already slim antiaircraft defenses.

Now that it was full daylight, every man on a topside battle station was scanning the skies for more Japs. There was a layer of thin clouds masking the morning sunlight. I could hear the five-inch gun director training around on its barbette above the bridge, as the director officer examined the indistinct horizon with his optics while down below, in Main Battery Plot, radar operators stared anxiously at their A-scopes, watching for the telltale spike in the shimmering green video display that would indicate a target. Above the gun director, twenty feet higher on the foremast, the bedspring air-search radar antenna made a groaning noise as it, too, scanned the airspace around our assigned station. When the Japs came in a big raid, headed for Okinawa itself or the fleet formations, the radar picket line would usually get plenty of warning. It was the one- and two-plane raids, the ones who were after the radar picket ships themselves, that were much harder to see. I had often wondered why they didn't station the individual picket ships closer together for mutual support.

"What the hell, XO," the chief bosun said, a pained expression on his face as we stared out at the smoky mess that once been an LCS. The bosun was a profane, cigar-chomping, bulky, black-haired Irishman named Dougherty, ruddy faced from years on the forecastles of more ships than anyone else in the crew. Per tradition, he was called Boats.

"They've learned," I said, grabbing a stanchion to support myself as the ship made a tight turn. The bosun seemed to be planted into the steel deck as if he had a gyro somewhere in that big paunch. "Big raids mean lots of metal in the sky. We can see 'em and sic the CAP on 'em. Now they're coming out in onesies and twosies, down on the deck for the last twenty miles. They disappear in the radar sea-return."

"And he went for the LCS?"

"I don't know that, Chief," I said. The boat crews were back on their gun stations, everyone staring skyward, looking for anything. "He damn near clipped our mast. Maybe overshot, went for the LCS as a consolation prize."

"Christ on a crutch," the bosun said. "They never knew what hit them."

"Nor would we," I said. "Part of the charm of the picket line these days."

"We oughta have fifty goddamned destroyers up here," the chief said. "Ain't like there's a shortage."

"Apparently, there is. The landings at Okinawa are bogged down. They've got one destroyer for every half-mile sector of beach on that miserable island. You know the Japs: they're gonna fight to the death, every last one of 'em."

We caught a whiff of sulfurous gun smoke as *Malloy* closed in on the last known position of the LCS. The bulk of the smoke cloud had been blown downwind, but the stink of sudden death and diesel oil remained. The sea was littered with sodden lumps of insulation, shattered wooden crates, some clothes, bobbing steel drums, empty and not-so-empty kapok life jackets, and one lonely life raft that was sadly devoid of survivors.

"Look sharp there," the bosun bellowed to all the men within earshot. "Heads—we're looking for heads. Faces. Anybody swimming, any poor sumbitch raising a hand."

After a minute of steaming through the area, it was plain to see that there were no survivors. The Japs often slung a large, contact-fuzed bomb under a kamikaze's belly in order to amplify the catastrophe of a five-thousand-pound fighter plane striking a ship at 300 miles per hour. Space demons from Mars, I thought. They're not human.

"Chief!" a man shouted, pointing down into the water on the port side. Fifty feet away there was what looked like a head lolling above a kapok jacket collar. The ship's wake had disturbed the water, and a shoulder appeared briefly. As we looked, a dark gray fin cut through the water and bumped the kapok, which is when we saw that that was all there was—a head and a shoulder. A moment later another shark snagged the remains and pulled them down. A wave of frustrated cursing swept through the guntubs. Sharks were every sailor's nightmare.

I felt the ship accelerating and decided to go back up to the bridge. I signaled the bosun to restow the motor whaleboat. There was nothing more to be done here. A mournful silence settled over the ship. There but for the grace of God . . .

THREE

The captain called a meeting in the wardroom later that morning after the ship had secured from dawn GQ, with me and the four department heads, the navigation officer, gun boss, chief engineer, and supply officer. I waited until everyone was there and then called the captain to report that we were assembled. I was a bit concerned when the skipper stepped out of his inport cabin and into the wardroom, waving a hand at the officers to resume their seats. Captain Tallmadge normally presented himself as a pillar of resilience—calm, energetic, and exuding that quiet authority of the born leader. This morning he seemed different. I couldn't put my finger on it, but there was definitely something . . .

"Okay, gents," the Captain began. "What happened this morning was pretty awful. No warning, no radar contact, and a ship and her entire crew gone in the blink of an eye. CTF 58 is asking what the hell happened, and frankly, I don't know what to say. Jimmy—any ideas?"

Jimmy Enright shook his head. The Combat Information Center was under his purview. The CIC contained the radar display consoles, where whatever images the searching radar beams could pick up were displayed as blurry green blobs on a large, circular cathode ray tube. "The ETs tuned the magnetron at twenty-three hundred," he said. "The scope operators reported a lot less clutter. We held the LCS sharp and clear on the surface search. The midnight-to-eight watch standers thought the radars were better than usual. The Freddies"—fighter direction officers—"thought so, too. Still, nobody saw that thing come in on us."

"Captain," Marty Randolph, the gunnery officer, said, "I had the mid-to-eight as the CIC supervisor. We rotated the scope operators every thirty minutes. There was nothing going on. Nothing. The CIC officer and I went over some reporting paperwork, but after zero five hundred everybody tightened up because sunrise was coming. The Freddies were talking to the duty carrier and setting up CAP patrol sectors. The LCS said their search radar was okay, but just okay. They don't have any electronics techs, and we talked about maybe cross-decking one of our guys to sharpen their gear. But it was routine—no indications that a big raid was coming, no reports of a big launch from Kyushu or Formosa. Nothing."

"Yet," the captain said. There were sober nods all around. It hadn't been *Malloy*'s mission to protect the LCS; in fact, the opposite had been true. Still.

"Yes, sir," Marty said. "The bastards got one

through on us. Maybe they're changing their tactics. They know they can't surprise the big-decks down at the AOA as long as the pickets blow the whistle." The AOA was the amphibious objective area.

"Jimmy, how tired are your people?" the captain asked.

Jimmy puffed out a long breath. "They're six on, six off, like everyone else in the crew," he said finally. "We've been up here for just over three weeks, so yes, they're starting to drag their asses. That's why we rotate the scope operators every half hour. You can only stare at that green haze for so long before you start to fall asleep. The men know that, and they're conscientious about it. Somebody sees a guy nod off, we move him."

"Besides," I said, "the watch standers know the kamikazes don't fly at night, so for most of the late night, especially on the midnight-to-eight, everyone's just trying to stay awake and alert, right? That's wearying in itself, and fatigue is cumulative."

The captain raised a hand. "Gents, believe me, I know. I don't think this was a case of our people being asleep at the switch. The Japs are becoming desperate. They fly to Okinawa and see over a thousand ships and amphibious craft. Fifteen hundred, if we can believe our own newsreels. That's more ships than they ever had in their navy. Today they probably have maybe a half-dozen ships of any consequence left and no fuel to run them, which is why they now have pilots willing to crash their planes into *anything* that's American, haze gray, and under way."

He stopped for a moment and rubbed his eyes. "I'm tired," he said. "Everyone's tired. When we ran with the big-deck carriers and the Japs came, we were one of twenty escorts shooting their asses down. We've been in on landings before. We do call-for-fire missions, the Marines or the Army take care of the bloodwork ashore, and then we're off to the next shitty little island. This distant picket duty is different. *We've* never been the targets before. It's always been the big boys, the carriers, the battlewagons, but now the Japs have figured out that they have to get by us to even reach the juicy targets."

"People are scared, too," Mario Campofino, the chief engineer, said. "It was one thing to be part of a whole fleet, but this . . ."

"If it's any comfort," the captain said, "I'm scared, too. Man'd be a fool *not* to be scared. But we're the khaki—we have to set the example. It's only human to be scared of what might happen, like the LCS disappearing like that. On the other hand, we're not exactly helpless. We've got six five-inch, eight forty-millimeter, and ten twenty-millimeter barrels going for us. Our job as the wardroom is to remind the crew of that and then to do everything possible to keep our people sharp and all those guns loaded and ready to fight back. Okay?"

There were nods all around. We recognized the pep talk for what it was, but I thought it was worth doing. I continuously tried to prop people up as I made my daily rounds, inspecting the messdecks and berthing spaces, and sometimes just talking to the men. They needed reassuring, as I did from time to time. I closeted alone with the captain at least twice daily to talk problems and solutions. I would vent my frustrations with our precarious position up here all alone, and he would tell me that we could handle it. Only lately I'd been wondering: Who reassured him? The answer was pretty simple: No one.

The sound-powered phone under the captain's end of the table squealed. The captain picked it up and listened, then told it okay. "The morning CAP is up," he announced. "So now we have some top cover. Go get 'em."

I followed the captain back into his inport cabin just forward of the wardroom mess. The space measured nine feet wide by fifteen long, growing narrower as one faced the bow. It had its own tiny bathroom, or head, at the forward end, a desk and bureau set at the after end, and two portholes, which were currently bolted shut. There was a fake-leather couch along the inboard wall that converted into a pullout single bed. I sat on the couch; the captain took the armchair in front of his desk and let out a long sigh.

"You feeling okay, sir?" I asked.

The captain shook his head. "Actually, no," he said. "I'm sick about what happened to that LCS. I keep thinking we could have done something, even though I know we couldn't. All those people, gone in a flash. And for what? Some Jap pilot dies a 'glorious' death, but it makes no goddamned difference at all as to how this mess is going to come out. They know it, too. They *have* to know it. What is the *matter* with those people?"

I felt the same way. Sick was a good word for it. I wanted to recite the litany of reasons that there was nothing *Malloy* could have done, but the captain already knew all that. As to the Japanese, they were simply barbarians.

"What do you want to say to CTF 58?" I prompted, remembering we were on the hook to answer the admiral's message.

"What I want to say and what I will say are two very different things," the captain said. "I want to say, send more destroyers. Leave those helpless little gator-freighters at the beach where they belong. Hell, send a battleship or six. What else do those overblown tubs have to do, except carry admirals around in grand style? It's not like the Japs have anything left worthy of a sixteen-inch salvo."

Open sarcasm was something new from the captain. In the two months I'd been aboard he'd been Mr. Steady Eddy, the wardroom's stable element when the rest of the officers started bitching and moaning about how the tin cans were being thrown away up on the picket line while entire squadrons of battleships and aircraft carriers steamed back and forth in grand fleet dispositions, ready to refight the Battle of Midway at a moment's notice, even though the great bulk of the Jap fleet already littered the bottom of the Pacific.

"I recommend we tell it like it happened, then," I said. "His message didn't ask for advice, just the facts as we know them. I can gen up a draft pretty quick."

The captain waved his acquiescence. He was obviously in a black mood and just wanted me to go do my job. The sound-powered phone set squeaked.

"Captain." He listened for a moment and then said, "Very well. I'll come up."

He hung up and spoke to me again. "Belay the message—there's a big raid coming in. Radar shows two formations, a big one for Okinawa and a smaller one splitting off and breaking up into pairs."

Those pairs were headed for the picket line, I thought. Here we go again.

I put away my notebook as the GQ alarm went off. I looked at my watch; it was only nine fifteen. It felt like we'd been through a whole day already. I glanced at the captain as I opened the door to go up to the bridge and CIC. He was still sitting there, staring at absolutely nothing. I closed the door gently, so as not to disturb him, which was a bit silly since the passageway was full of men scrambling to their GQ stations outside the wardroom.

I joined the stream of men thumping up the ladder toward the bridge and my GQ station, the Combat Information Center, which was right behind the bridge. I could hear the engine-order telegraph ringing as the ship increased her speed and the OOD initiated evasive maneuvers. Below I heard the sounds of steel hatches being slammed down and repair parties laying out their fire-fighting gear. *Malloy*'s crew was fully trained, so there were no orders being shouted. Everyone knew what to do and where to go, and the ship would be buttoned up in under three minutes, ready for whatever might be headed our way.

The exec's traditional GQ station was aft, at a place called secondary conn, the theory being that if the bridge command team got wiped out, the exec, second in command, would be able to take over from a station a hundred fifty feet aft. Since the advent of the Combat Information Center, however, most execs took station in Combat, where all the tactical information was concentrated and displayed. Some captains were even starting to fight their ships from Combat, although most clung to the tradition of being on the bridge. Our skipper was one of those, trusting his own eyes over what might or might not be true on a radarscope.

"Combat manned and ready, XO," LTJG Lanny King, the CIC officer, reported as I stepped into the dark and crowded space. "We have many bogeys, but none headed directly our way."

"Yet," I said, speaking out loud what everybody else was thinking. Combat spanned almost the entire width of the upper superstructure. There were two vertical, six-foot-high Plexiglas status boards along the back bulkhead, showing what was called the air picture. The boards had a five-foot-diameter compass rose etched into them, with concentric ten-mile range rings expanding from the center, which marked where we were. Contact information on bogeys detected by radar were passed via sound-powered phones to men standing behind the lighted boards, who then marked the range, bearing, course, speed, and altitude of all air contacts within fifty miles of the ship using yellow grease pencils. Because they stood behind the boards, they'd all had to learn to write backward, so that the officers positioned in front of the boards could interpret what they were seeing.

Down each side of Combat were the radar operators, both air search and surface search, sitting at bulky consoles where the green video displays flickered. The entire space was kept in constant semidarkness to make it easier for the radar operators to see their displays. Standing behind the console operators were the two fighter direction officers. The Freddies were fighter pilots who were being given a break from flight duties and who'd been trained to control other fighters by radio and radar. Each morning, all the destroyers would be assigned a section or even two of CAP: carrier fighter planes sent up from the carriers steaming off Okinawa to destroy as many of the incoming Jap planes as possible before they could reach their bomb-release or suicide-dive points over the American fleet.

I stood in the middle of the space, right next to a lighted table where the surface picture was plotted. The table, called a dead-reckoning tracer or DRT, contained a small light projector underneath its glass top. The projector was slaved to the ship's gyro, and thus whenever the ship moved, the projector moved with it under the glass, projecting a yellow circle of light with a compass rose etched onto it. That way we saw a true picture of what the ship was doing. Plotters, men standing around the table wearing sound-powered phones, would then plot the positions of surface contacts, both friendly and enemy, onto a very thin sheet of tracing paper taped to the glass top. The result was the so-called surface picture: what we were doing, where our escorting ships were and what they were doing, and where any bad guys were within range of our guns.

The air and surface plots meant that there were lots of men speaking quietly into sound-powered phones, both making and getting reports, but to my ears it was all just a routine hum. After three years of war, my brain had learned to tune out the routine and repetitive reporting and listen instead for the sounds of immediate danger, indicated by words such as "closing fast" or "inbound" or "multiple bogeys," or that great catchall "oh shit." Combat was the nerve center of the ship in terms of war-fighting. In addition to the surface and air pictures, the sonar operators had a console in one corner, meaning that all three dimensions of what we might encounter, air, surface, and underwater, were displayed in this one space.

If Combat was the brain, then the gun directors and their associated weapons represented the fist. *Malloy* had three twin-barreled five-inch gun mounts, all of them controlled by a large analog computer down below the waterline in a space called Main Battery Plot. There were two gun directors, one that looked like a five-inch gun mount without any guns, mounted one level above the bridge, and a second, much smaller one, at the after end of the ship's superstructure right behind the after stack. The forward director had its own radar, which would feed range and bearing information down to the computer, which in turn would drive the five-inch gun mounts to train and point at the computed future position of incoming targets. The after director was a one-man machine, without a radar, but it could be optically locked on to incoming targets as long as they were very close. It could control the lesser guns, the multibarreled forty- and twenty-millimeter anti-aircraft batteries.

In practice, however, these smaller guns were usually controlled by human pointers and trainers, who concentrated on keeping the stream of projectiles being fired by their guns streaming just ahead of and slightly above an incoming plane. The five-inch could reach out nine miles under director control, but by the time the forties and twenties got into it, the Mark One eyeball was the director of choice. The forties and twenties were for the close-in work, the last ditches of defense. Earlier in the war, Jap bombers would only have to get within a few vertical miles to release their bombs and then turn away. Nowadays, however, the Jap planes *were* the bombs, so there wasn't much of a fire-control problem when a kamikaze came, because he came straight at you. It was simply a matter of how much steel-clad high explosive you could put in his way that determined whether or not he arrived in one piece and killed the ship or did a flaming cartwheel into the sea.

"Station Six-Fox reports she's taking bogeys under fire," Lanny announced.

“Distance?” I asked. I scanned the plotting boards. Six-Fox was the *Waltham*, another radar picket ship. She was an older, Fletcher-class destroyer, with five single-barrel five-inch guns.

“Fifteen miles southwest, XO,” Lanny said. He pointed down at the plotting table. “Right here.”

“Our radars are not picking up Six-Fox’s bogeys,” one of the Freddies said. “Our CAP says the Japs’re coming in on the deck this time. Zeros, it looks like.”

Just like this morning, I thought. I picked up my own sound-powered phone handset, switched to the combat action circuit, and called the captain at his station on the bridge. The captain’s talker, Chief Petty Officer Julio Martinez Smith, answered.

“I need the skipper,” I said.

“Um, we thought he was in there with you,” Smith said. Chief Smith was another CPO who worked for me; as chief yeoman, he was the ship’s secretary, or chief administrative petty officer.

Shit, I thought. “Thank you,” I replied, as if it were perfectly normal for the CO not to be at his station during GQ. I hung up and left Combat, going back down the ladder to the wardroom and through it to his inport cabin. The wardroom was set up as the main battle dressing station, with the chief corpsman and his assistant waiting there with all their medical gear spread out on the table. They were surprised to see me in the wardroom at GQ, but I didn't have time to explain why I was there. I knocked twice on the skipper's door, opened it, and found the captain the way I'd left him, sitting in front of his desk and staring at nothing. He looked up, obviously startled when I poked my head in.

"*Waltham* under attack from low-fliers," I reported.

"They are?" the captain asked. "Go to GQ. They'll be here next."

"We *are* at GQ, sir," I said. "I've been in Combat. I thought you were already out on the bridge."

The captain appeared to be confused. He shook his head. "Must have fallen asleep," he said. "*Damn!* I'll be right up. How far away is *Waltham*?"

"Fifteen miles southwest. Our radar doesn't hold her bogeys."

The captain shook his head again. "Fifteen miles—there's no way we can offer mutual support. They're doing this all wrong, XO. We should be in a loose gaggle, but close enough so that all the pickets can support each other."

I nodded. "Yes, sir, and we maybe should put that in our message to CTF 58. Right now, though, I'm headed back to Combat."

"Right, right," the captain said, getting up. "I'll be up in two shakes."

I felt the ship leaning into another turn as the

OOD made random course changes, forcing me to grab the handrail as I climbed the ladder. If the Divine Wind was blowing, you did not steer a straight course and make it easy for them. But what was going on with the CO? He had never, ever flaked out like that. As I opened the door into Combat I heard raised voices out on the bridge and then the engine-order telegraph ringing up more speed.

"Bogeys, bogeys, composition two, low and fast, three-five-zero, sixteen thousand yards and closing!" one of the radar operators announced.

"Designate to director fifty-one," Lanny ordered. I heard the director rumbling around on its roller path overhead while the gunfire-control system radar operators down in Main Battery Plot attempted to find and then lock on to the incoming planes. I wondered if I should go out to the bridge until the captain showed up, but then I heard the captain's voice on the intercom. "We're coming to zero eight zero, speed twenty-five to unmask, XO," he said. "Open fire at five miles."

"XO, aye," I responded. That was better, I thought. Much more like it. The guns could shoot a projectile out to eighteen thousand yards, or nine miles, but they were much more effective if we waited until the planes got into five miles, or ten thousand yards.

"XO, Sky One. Director fifty-one is locked on and tracking."

"All mounts, air action port. Commence firing when they get to ten thousand yards."

Almost immediately the five-inchers opened up with their familiar double-blam sound as they began hurling fifty-four-pound, five-inch-diameter shells down the bearing. Two of the mounts, fifty-one and fifty-two, were firing shells with mechanical time fuzes, set to explode in front of the approaching aircraft. Mount fifty-three, all the way aft, was shooting some of the new variable-time fragmenting shells. The VT frags were equipped with a miniature radar in the nose that detonated the shell if it detected anything solid coming at it or near it.

"Bearing steady, range eight-oh-double-oh, and still closing."

Eight thousand yards. Four miles. The guns were blasting away in irregular cadence now, their thumping recoil shaking the superstructure and stirring a light haze of dust out of the overhead cableways. The forties would join in next, but not until the range came down to about two miles, or four thousand yards. The twenties were good for about a mile. The individual gun captains were all experienced hands and would open up as soon as they thought they could do some good.

"Director fifty-one reports *splash* one bogey," the JC circuit talker announced.

One down, one to go, I thought. It was hell

having to just stand here and wait to see if the guns were going to take care of business. Then the first of the forty-millimeter mounts opened up. They were noisy guns, firing as fast as the loaders could jam four-round clips of shells into their feed slots. One man, the trainer, controlled the direction of fire. A second man, the pointer, on the other side of the mount, controlled the angle of elevation. Both had to lead their targets, making split-second calculations in their heads as to how best to make that stream of white-hot steel heading out over the water intersect with the silvery blob that was coming in right at them.

Suddenly, everyone in Combat felt a shock wave hit the ship, followed by a loud boom.

"*Splash,* second bogey," the talker announced. "Director fifty-one says his bomb went off."

No kidding, I thought. Not that far away, either. Still, we were safe, for the moment.

I felt the ship turning as the captain ordered her brought about so that we would not get too far off our radar picket station. Right now our job was to stay alive, but our mission, ultimately, was to detect any more air raids headed for the fifteen-hundred-ship armada assaulting Okinawa. That meant we had to get back on station. The radar picket stations were designed to have interlocking radar coverage. If one picket wandered too far off station, it would create a hole in the radar screen plan. The Japs could detect where there was radar coverage and, more importantly, where there wasn't any.

We're bait, I thought. We're totally expendable. Jap planes that divert to the picket line don't attack the invasion forces, so the heavies are glad to see them diverting. I felt more than a little helpless stuck here in Combat. On the other hand, maybe it was better to *not* see the Jap bomber that was about to burn us all to death.

"Combat, Captain. What's the raid status?"

I jumped to respond. "Main raid is in a furball with the inner-ring CAP," I said. "No more bogeys coming for us at the moment. *Waltham* hasn't reported in."

"There's a helluva big column of black smoke southwest of us," the captain said. "Bearing two three five. Keep trying to raise her."

That was where the plotting table last held the *Waltham.* I turned to ask Lanny if *Waltham* had an escorting support ship. "Negative, XO," he reported. "She was by herself."

I tried to quash the sinking feeling in my stomach. I was more determined than ever to put something in our report to CTF 58 about needing mutual support on the picket line. They were launching a new destroyer every thirty days back in the States. Surely they could find a few more for the most dangerous station in the Navy.

I decided to go out to the bridge. Once the main attack group had done what they could over

Okinawa, any stragglers that escaped the hordes of CAP would come back out and try their luck with the pickets. We were looking at a lull of maybe twenty minutes.

The sunlight hurt my eyes when I stepped out onto the bridge. The GQ team made for quite a crowd, what with all the extra phone-talkers and the fact that everyone was wearing bulky gray kapok jackets and steel helmets. The captain was in his chair, sipping on a mug of coffee and sucking down a cigarette. There was a rule about no eating, drinking, or smoking at general quarters, but if the captain wanted coffee and a ciggybutt, he got them. Because the wind was abaft the beam, the air smelled of stack gas, overlaid with the stink of gunpowder from the earlier exertions. The five-inch gun crews were out on deck policing the brass powder cans littering the forecastle. The forty-millimeter loaders were jamming rounds into the clips they used to load the forties. There were contrails at high altitude as the outer CAP fighters searched out whatever bogeys were still out there after the main raid. The lookouts were scanning high and low for the telltale black dots that meant another kamikaze was inbound. I walked over to the captain's chair.

"How close did they get?" I asked.

"Not very," the captain said. "I think fifty-three got both of 'em with that new VT frag stuff. You could see the Able-Able common bursts *behind* the planes as they came in—they're black, as you know—but then there were grayish bursts *ahead* of them, and they did the job."

"Still in short supply," I said. "I couldn't get much of it, even on the Big Ben. Maybe next time we go downtown we'll get enough for all three mounts." "Downtown" was the term for going off-line and back to the main fleet formation off Okinawa to refuel, reprovision, and rearm from fleet replenishment ships.

The captain raised his binoculars to study that black column of smoke on the southwestern horizon. "Any contact with *Waltham*?"

"No, sir. Once this raid is over I think we should go over there, see what's happening."

"Send our CAP over to take a look," the captain said. "We can't leave station."

"I think it's time to speak up, sir," I said. "In our report to CTF 58, I mean. A second destroyer on each station would mean each kamikaze would face twelve five-inch instead of six. Surely they have enough to go around."

The captain gave a bitter grunt. "They need the extra tin cans to escort the high-value ships, XO. The carriers, the battleships. Go ahead and say that in the message, I don't care, but them's the facts of life. Plus, in all fairness, the bulk of the raids go there, not here."

The bitch-box spoke. "Captain, Combat."

The captain depressed the talk-switch on the bitch-box. "Go ahead."

"Stragglers outbound from Okinawa. Inner-ring CAP in pursuit, reporting low-fliers outbound in our general direction."

The captain gave me a weary look. I understood, nodded, and went back into Combat. A moment later the captain's voice came over the ship's general announcing system, the 1MC. Its loudspeakers were placed all over the ship so everyone got the word at the same time. "Heads up, people. This time they're coming *from* Okinawa. Five to ten minutes. Search sectors zero niner zero south and west to two seven zero. Low-fliers."

Back in Combat, I asked the Freddies where our own assigned fighters were.

"Loitering at fifteen thousand feet, but they'll be bingo-state in about ten minutes."

Bingo state meant the planes would be down to just enough fuel to get back to their carrier. They'd barely be able to make one intercept on any stragglers from the Okinawa raid, and maybe not even that.

"Reliefs coming out?"

"Not yet, XO. After a big raid like that, they might be late. Especially if the bastards managed to get to a carrier."

Damned if we do, damned if we don't, I thought. "Okay, send 'em home, but have them go via the

Waltham's last position. I need to know if she's still with us."

"Bogeys still inbound," the radar operator called, "but it looks like they're headed for Six-Fox and Niner-George."

"Alert our CAP that they may get some action over *Waltham*," I said. Then I called the captain on the bitch-box to tell him what I'd been ordering up. He said he concurred. I felt the ship turning again. The captain was taking no chances with bogeys inbound, even if they were after other picket stations this time. No straight-line steaming on the picket stations. One of the Freddies was trying to get my attention.

"XO, the CAP has a tally on the *Waltham*. She's DIW and burning aft. We're vectoring our guys against that single bogey inbound on her, but it's gonna be tight—they're outa fighting gas, and our radar is intermittent on that bastard."

"How bad is *Waltham*?"

"Guys said she looks like a surfaced submarine," the Freddy answered.

My heart sank. I reported on the *Waltham*'s status to the captain and recommended again that we head southwest to see what we could do.

"We'll have to get permission to leave station," the captain said. "Any signs of a second big raid yet?"

"Negative, and our CAP has only enough gas to

make one pass at the bogey headed for *Waltham*. If they get into a chase, we'll have no CAP until the next launch cycle. No replacement CAP for either station as of yet. The only active bogeys are outbound."

"All right," he said. "Do this. Send CTF 58 a voice message. Make it a UNODIR. Tell them *Waltham* needs help, we're headed over there, our CAP are bingo, and we hold no bogeys in our sector."

"Aye, aye, sir," I said. I knew the captain really wanted to head southwest and save *Waltham* if he could, but the rules about leaving station were pretty stringent. Hence the UNODIR, Navy radio shorthand for "unless otherwise directed, I am going to do such and such." That put the burden of abandoning *Waltham* on the admiral commanding the picket line and his staffies down in the amphibious objective area. They might well come right back and say no, but usually they'd let a CO sending a UNODIR message take his chances. If he left station and a big raid got through undetected, woe betide him.

I felt the ship turning again and heard the bells for more speed as I drafted a short UNODIR voice message to Commander Task Force 58, our big boss down off Okinawa. I asked one of the Freddies to relay it via the fighter planes that were about to go back to their carrier. If we waited to send it through the regular naval communications channels, it might be two days before the message would even get to CTF 58.

This was another reason there ought to be two tin cans on each radar picket station, I thought. One could go help another ship without leaving a hole in the radar screen.

I scanned the vertical status boards. *Waltham* was indicated on the surface summary plot now as being thirteen miles west-southwest. The air summary plot showed a dotted line originating near Okinawa and headed for *Waltham*, but the line had stopped, meaning *Malloy*'s radar could no longer see what was probably a kamikaze headed for *Waltham*'s station.

He's on the deck, I thought, and nobody can raise *Waltham*. I was about to go out to the bridge to talk to the captain when the ship made a violent turn to port and the forties and twenties opened up. Before I could gather my wits I heard an airplane engine roar close over the ship, followed by a tremendous crash of steel against steel overhead. I ducked reflexively, closing my eyes and trying to make myself small, then realized how ridiculous I must look. I wasn't even hurt. I opened my eyes. Every other man in Combat was down on the deck.

There was a distant boom off to starboard, and then the guns quit firing. All of Combat was filled with a white haze of dust, and the watch standers were looking at each other as if checking to see if they were still alive. Several men were getting up off the deck with embarrassed expressions that probably matched mine.

"My radar is down," the air-search console operator announced in a high-pitched voice.

"Surface search is down, too," a second operator reported.

We were tactically blind, which meant that Combat was temporarily out of business. I went through the forward door, past the charthouse, and out onto the bridge. To starboard I saw a cloud of dirty smoke and steam hanging over the water, drifting aft, maybe five hundred yards away. The officer of the deck eased the ship into a wider turn; everyone else on the bridge with binoculars was anxiously staring out at the horizon. The captain, whose face was a little white, was standing in the bridge wing door.

"Never saw him," he said. "He was so close the five-inch couldn't even fire. Thank God the AA gun crews *did* see him."

"Bridge, Sigs!" came over the bitch-box. The signalman sounded scared out of his wits.

"Bridge, aye," the captain replied.

"Captain, we got a bomb up here. A *big* fucking bomb. It's wedged between the forward stack and the starboard flag bag."

"Clear the signal bridge," the captain ordered, "and yell up to Sky One to get out of there. XO, go flush everyone out of Combat."

If the signalman had accurately described the bomb's location, it was resting on top of the CIC compartment's back bulkhead. The Japs had been slinging five-hundred-pounders on their Divine Wind planes. If it went off now, it would flatten CIC and probably the pilothouse, too. I stepped through the front door of CIC, where everyone was staring at me with wide, frightened eyes. Apparently they had all heard the signalman's call on the bitch-box.

"Everyone out," I said, trying to pretend I was in total control of myself, as if it was no big deal that there was a five-hundred-pound bomb coiled up perhaps twenty feet from us. "Freddies, set up your tactical circuit down in Radio Central; everyone else muster on the messdecks. CIC Watch Officer, go to secondary conn. Come up on the 1JV circuit until the OOD relieves you."

The watch standers, officers and enlisted, all tried not to crowd up at the front door, but I could feel their fear as they hurried past me and headed down below. I really, really, had wanted to lead that charge but knew I couldn't do that. Once the space had been evacuated, I went back out the bridge to report to the captain. He had sent the entire bridge watch team except for one terrified-looking phone-talker back to the secondary conning station, remaining alone on the bridge. He'd ordered Main Battery Plot to evacuate the AA gun stations nestled on either side of the forward stack, then told Damage Control Central to send an investigative team to the signal bridge. Then he got on the 1MC.

"Attention all hands," he said. "This is the captain speaking. We have an unexploded bomb wedged into the superstructure on the signal bridge. We are going to have to figure out how to defuse it and get it over the side. I want all hands to keep away from the base of the forward stack until we figure out how to do that. In the meantime, all hands on topside stations keep your eyes peeled. We never saw that last bogey until he was right on us. Heads-up ball for the forties on that one. Well done. That is all."

Marty Randolph, the gun boss, arrived down in the pilothouse from his station up above in the forward five-inch gun director.

"Did you see it?" I asked him.

Marty licked his lips. "Most certainly did," he said, his voice strained. "Stared at that damned thing for ten seconds, waiting for my first personal meeting with Jesus. It's big, XO. Really big. Wedged sideways. I didn't linger to see if it's ticking or whatever they do."

The captain grinned. "Linger," he said. "Yeah, sure. Okay. What do we know about how aircraft bombs are fuzed?"

Marty said he'd had a class on bomb fuzing back in gunnery school. "Usually there's a wire, hooked to the plane's fuselage or wing, with the other end hooked to the arming switch on the bomb. They drop it, that wire pulls the arming switch. Then they have little propellers on the nose and on the tail. The propellers are driven by the slipstream as the bomb falls. It has to turn a certain number of revolutions before the arming circuit is completed, which keeps the bomber safe from a preemie."

"So when he saw he was gonna miss with the plane, he dropped the bomb, but it didn't have time to arm," the captain said.

"I sure as hell hope so," the gun boss said. " 'Cause if that bastard's armed, there's nothing we can do about getting it over the side."

Four chief petty officers in full battle gear and oxygen breathing rigs came out onto the pilothouse. "Repair Two investigators," their leader, Chief Dougherty, announced. "Request permission to go up on the signal bridge."

"What if I say no, Boats?" the captain asked.

"Well then, God bless you, Cap'n," he replied. The other chiefs grinned. Everyone was trying to be really cool, calm, and collected. I wondered if the chiefs were as scared as I was. Even the captain's little joke had seemed a bit forced.

"Let me go up first," Marty said. "I know what to look for. Those little props are the key to this. I'm assuming they're jammed stopped right now. We can't have them move for any reason." He turned to one of the engineering chiefs from

Repair Two. “Brainard, you guys bring any monkey shit with you?”

Two chiefs dug into their battle dress and produced what looked like oversized toothpaste tubes. The tubes contained a sealant goo, popularly known throughout the navy as monkey shit, which was used to seal everything from small steam leaks to water seals on boats or leaking bridge windows. When exposed to air it hardened into a plasterlike compound.

“I’ll locate the fuzing props and cover each one up with a handful of monkey shit, which should mean they can’t ever move again.”

“Then what?” the captain asked.

“We’ll wing it from there, Captain,” Marty said. “See if we can find out what kind of bomb it is and get some advice from the bomb-disposal guys on one of the flattops on how to safe it out.”

The ship began to turn again. “We still going to see about *Waltham*?” I asked.

The captain shook his head. He looked over at the gyro repeater next to his chair. “Talker, tell secondary conn to steer back east. Tell ’em to execute a broad weave, base speed fifteen knots.” He turned to me. “No, we have to deal with this problem first, I think. No point in going alongside *Waltham* and then blowing up.”

The talker pretended he hadn’t heard that comment about blowing up. He bobbed his head and relayed the message to the officer of the deck, who was standing out in the breeze at the secondary conning station behind the after stack, along with the helmsman and lee helmsman. The ship began another turn.

"Okay, Marty, go on up," the captain said. "Take Dougherty with you. Talk to me on the bitch-box when you figure it out. XO, go below and see if you can set up some kind of CIC on the messdecks, and remind me later that we need to design a secondary CIC, just like we have a secondary conning station."

I went down to the crew's messing space, where the CIC team had assembled. They'd found plug-in points for their sound-powered phone circuits and were relying on Radio Central to cover the air-control and raid-reporting radio links. We were, however, blind without access to our radar screens and, of course, useless to the main formation as a sentinel. When I sat down at one of the tables, Lanny King handed me a message form.

"This is the answer to the UNODIR," he said. "Short, but not so sweet."

The message, which had come from our own squadron commander, Commodore Van Arnhem, based down in the fleet anchorage, was indeed short. Remain on station. Your mission is radar picket. *Waltham* is our problem.

"Well, screw 'em if they can't take a joke," I said quietly. "By the time anybody gets to

Waltham she'll be sleeping with Davy Jones. Maybe if we told them our radars are down they'd let us go over there. Any word from topside on the bomb?"

"Negative. How are we gonna get rid of that thing? Ten guys go pick it up and throw it over the side?"

"You volunteering to lead that working party?"

"Um, no, sir, I am not."

"We'll have to figure out a way that doesn't involve a bunch of people hugging it," I said. "We'll wait for word from Bosun Dougherty. I'll be right back."

I went back up the bridge and handed the message form to the captain, who grunted when he read it. "Blast to follow, no doubt," he muttered. The tone of the message was clear enough. I also knew that the admiral down off Okinawa would sit down when he had a moment and direct our squadron commander to write a personal-for message directly to the captain regarding his UNODIR. Such hate mail was called a blast. The opposite was called an atta-boy. The rule in the Navy was that one blast undid the working value of ten thousand atta-boys at fitness report time. Oh, well.

The gun boss dropped down the ladder from the signal bridge, his hands covered in grayish goo. "The fuzing props were intact but jammed," he announced. "Now they're really jammed. Bomb case is completely intact. It's definitely a 250kg general-purpose bomb. Not smoking, not ticking, or humming, but a nasty piece of work, and it's embedded just aft of the flag bags and the base of the foremast."

"Got any good news?" the captain asked.

"Yes, sir, it didn't go off while I was tickling its fuze."

"And how are we going to get it out of there and over the side?"

"Sea anchor," a gruff voice responded as Chief Dougherty came onto the bridge. He was a large, loud man and a force to be reckoned with both in the chief's mess and about the decks.

"Tell me more, Boats," the captain said.

"We take a mooring line and wrap that bastard six ways from Sunday. Then we pass the mooring line outboard of all superstructure down the port side, and make the bitter end to a big-ass sea anchor. Pitch that over the side, put the helm down to port, and kick her in the ass. The sea anchor will fill and grab and pull that pogue right off the ship."

The captain looked at me. I shrugged. Sounded like it would work.

"How will you rig the sea anchor?" the captain asked.

"Take a twenty-man life raft, weigh down one long side with five-inch rounds, sew some canvas across the net bottom, and set a yoke which we can shackle to the bitter end of the mooring line."

The captain nodded his approval. "I concur," he said. "Make it so. Marty, go see which side will be better, and whether or not we can remove any interference before we try this. I'd prefer not to pull the mast over if we can help it."

"Should we clear this with the boss?" I asked. "Maybe get some explosive ordnance disposal advice before we go yanking that thing around?"

"If we were sitting down there in the AOA next to a flattop, I'd say yes, call the EOD. But right now we're up here all by ourselves in Injun Country, deaf, dumb, and blind, with too many hours of daylight left for the Japs to pay us another visit. Besides, the last time I conversed with CTF 58, he hurt my feelings. Get on with it. I mean, what could go wrong, hunh?"

There were wary grins all around. Everybody standing there, right down to the captain's phone-talker, knew exactly what could go wrong. Dougherty, however, waved away the danger. "Piece'a cake. We'll be set in forty-five minutes."

"Thirty would be wonderful, Boats. I have one suggestion. That bomb should have two hangar fittings on it somewhere, where they hang it on the plane's belly? Instead of cocooning it in six-inch manila, find those points, rig a wire bridle, and make your line to the bridle, not the bomb."

"Aye, sir. I'll get on it, then."

"Where are we in the great scheme of the

Okinawa invasion?" the captain asked after the gun boss and the chief bosun's mate left the bridge. We could both hear director fifty-one training slowly in a circle above us under the control of operators down in Main Battery Plot. The gunfire-control radar was the only radar left operational on the ship right now, and I wasn't quite sure why. It wasn't much of a search radar, but it was better than nothing. I hoped. I told the skipper what we had cobbled together.

"We're up on the HF raid-reporting circuit, and we're guarding the air-control VHF circuits via some creative patching from Radio Central to the messdecks, but basically, we're out of the game until we get radars back up and Combat remanned. Marty's got the director going in radar search on the horizon, but that's . . ." I shrugged again. It wasn't much, as we both knew, but at least they might detect a low-flier.

"Still nothing from *Waltham*?"

"No, sir." Once the midday haze set in, we couldn't even see that smoke column anymore. "She may be talking to aircraft on VHF, but she's not up on the main raid-reporting circuit."

The captain yawned, covered his mouth, and then yawned again. "Right," he said. "Put a request in for some EOD assistance over the normal comms channel. That way we can say we did ask, but we really can't wait. Let me know when they have the sea anchor ready. I'm going to my cabin."

"But, sir, the sea cabin's awfully close to where that bomb is . . . ?"

"My inport cabin," the captain said. "Call me when you're ready to pull that thing off us."

"Aye, aye, sir," I replied. I was surprised by the captain's decision to lay below. We were about as vulnerable to another surprise attack as we could be, what with no search radars manned and no close-by support, and our situation wouldn't get any better until darkness fell. We had a live bomb parked on the 03 level, which, if it went off, would probably flatten most of the forward superstructure, including the captain's inport cabin. I asked him if he wanted me to stay on the bridge.

He shook his head, got up from his chair, and went forward to look out the bridge windows. The chief bosun was up on the forecastle, where he had the entire first division rousting out one of the 350-foot-long mooring lines, while a second crew was modifying one of the floatation rafts with a wire bridle.

Hell, I thought. It might work. We'd have to get all the topside people to muster at one end of the ship or the other before we let that sea anchor take a strain. I saw the lone phone-talker standing in one corner of the pilothouse, as far from where the bomb was as he could get. I told him to unplug his sound-powered phones and go set up outside the captain's inport cabin. If anyone called him on the 1JV circuit with information for the skipper, he was to knock on the captain's door and give him the report.

Then I went below to get some coffee and maybe a sandwich in the wardroom. It was beyond strange to leave the bridge totally unattended in the middle of the hottest war zone in the Pacific, but there was nothing anyone could do from there until that bomb went over the side.

Thirty minutes later, the phone squeaked in the wardroom and I picked it up.

"XO, this is Marty. We're rigged and ready to go. Request permission to attach the bridle to the bomb's hangar hooks."

"Where's the sea anchor?"

"Port quarter, with the mooring line faked outboard of everything down the port side. Chief Dougherty says to begin a slow turn to port once we drop it over the side, and then there's maybe six fathoms of slack before it'll tighten up."

"You're steering from secondary conn?"

"Yes, sir. Engine orders to Main Control via the 1JV. Everything's working."

"Lemme get the okay from the captain and I'll let you know."

"XO—he okay?"

My eyebrows went up. "What do you mean?"

"He doesn't seem himself. Seems withdrawn, distracted, maybe. I don't know, but the other department heads have noticed it, too."

"I think he's just very tired, Marty. Remember

he's the oldest guy on board, and command out here takes it out of a man, you know? Get your people ready, and get everybody away from the midships area, including inside the superstructure. That includes Radio Central."

"Yes, sir."

I found the phone-talker parked in the passageway outside the captain's cabin and told him to disconnect his phones and go aft. He was gone in twenty seconds. I knocked on the captain's door and then stepped in. I was surprised to find the lights off and the captain stretched out on his sofa-bunk, shoes off, lying on his back. He opened his eyes when I stepped into the cabin.

"Whatcha got?" he asked.

"They're ready to try the sea anchor. I came to get your permission and to recommend you go to secondary conn, away from anything going wrong."

The captain smiled. "Like I said before, what could possibly go wrong with this Rube Goldberg operation?" he asked. "You think Marty has a handle on this situation?"

"Yes, sir, I do," I said. "I still wanted to get your permission to proceed and give you time to get topside."

"You have my permission, and I'm going to stay right here."

"You are?"

"Yup. You've been XO here now, what, two months?"

"Yes, sir."

"Then you don't need me out there on deck. I'd be just another spectator, now that we've had to clear the bridge. I want you to run this show. Don't call me for every step along the way: use your best judgment and get the thing done. Have your damage control parties ready to go if that thing cooks off. Otherwise, get shut of it, reman all battle stations, and let's get back up into the radar screen. Call me when it's over."

"I appreciate the vote of confidence, sir," I said, "but I'd feel a whole lot better if you were on deck watching over my shoulder."

"You're in training for command, Connie," he replied. "I'd feel better if the commodore were here, watching over *my* shoulder, but he isn't. That's a part of command you need to get used to. Now, turn to."

Surprised, I nodded, tried to think of something to say, and then backed out of the cabin. I already felt different, even though I knew full well I still had the captain to fall back on. The officer with the most experience. The owner of the whole shebang when things went off the track. Like that UNODIR message: I had wholeheartedly supported doing that, but when the shit-o-gram came back from our squad dog, as commodores were called when they weren't listening, it wouldn't be addressed to me. I wondered if I was being a little bit disloyal. I started aft.

Even after two months, I was still getting used to the scale of a destroyer command. I'd come to *Malloy* from an Essex-class, thirty-eight-thousand-ton, big-deck carrier known throughout the fleet as the Big Ben. *Malloy* was my first destroyer, and the transition from thirty-eight thousand to twenty-two hundred tons had been initially unsettling. Between the ship's company and the air group, there had been nearly three thousand men on board the *Franklin. Malloy*'s full wartime complement was one-tenth of that. In a carrier, you might know most everybody in your department. In a destroyer, you knew everybody, and everybody knew you. I'd never felt conspicuous in *Franklin*; here I felt like I was onstage almost all the time. It had been a big change.

Back on the fantail I found the bosun's crew ready to deploy the homemade sea anchor. There were plenty of hands to help, as all the forward topside gun stations had been cleared out in case that bomb went off. Jimmy Enright, the navigation officer, walked over.

I asked him if we'd heard back from the fleet EOD people. He pulled me aside, away from eavesdropping ears.

"Negative, sir. And based on what I'm seeing on the Fox broadcast, they've got bigger problems than one unexploded bomb down there on Okinawa. That last big raid? That was over a hundred aircraft, and they put three big-decks out of action, hit a battleship, *sank* an escort carrier and three transports. Plus, the Army's apparently getting its ass handed to it on the south end of the island."

"So we are really on our own up here, I guess," I said.

Jimmy shrugged. "Always have been, XO. Here's Marty."

The gun boss walked back to where we were standing. "I've cleared all the topside people out forward, and we're ready to take tension on the bomb."

"How much damage is this going to do when it pulls out?" I asked. I realized then that I was about to make a decision without ever having seen how the bomb was wedged into the ship's superstructure.

"Front half is buried into the deck behind the signal bridge, so the only way to pull it is to twist it out of its hole, warp it between the mast and the forward stack, under the port flag bag, and hopefully over the side without hitting the main deck."

"Hopefully."

"Best we can do, XO. Can't risk getting a damage control party close enough to dislodge it outta there. This way, if it goes, it eats metal, not people."

"Right," I said. Should I go up there, I

wondered, and take a look for myself? Marty was an experienced department head. The captain was giving me the chance to make the big decisions here, so if I went up there it would indicate that I didn't quite trust Marty's judgment. I decided to proceed.

"Warn the engineers, too. If that thing goes off, it might happen at the waterline, and that could open Number One Fire Room to the sea."

"Already done, XO," Marty said. "We're as ready as we're gonna be. I'm not thrilled with this lashup, but we can't have another kami come in strafing and set that thing off where it is."

"Very well," I said. "Proceed, then."

Marty hesitated, as if he were looking around for the captain. I just stood there, which was when Marty realized that the captain was not going to come out and watch. He nodded.

I had the word passed over the 1MC that we were about to pull that bomb off the forward superstructure and all hands should stay well clear of the forward stack. I saw Marty giving the go-ahead to Bosun Dougherty. The chief looked over at me, and I nodded back at him. Then he started giving orders, and the working party picked up the unwieldy canvas-covered, wood-framed life raft, carried it to the port side, stabilized it for a few seconds on the lifelines, and then heaved it over the side. I felt the ship's rudder bite in and the fantail of the ship begin to swing out and away from the bobbing raft. The gun crews behind the after stack were crouched behind their splinter shields to get some metal between them and where the bomb was wedged, invisible from the back half of the ship.

I watched from the very after part of the port quarter, so I could see when that manila mooring line began to tighten up. Right now it was still lying slack on the water, but the raft was turning over as its bridle pulled half of it below the surface, and then the whole thing submerged suddenly, perpendicular to the mooring line, and filled like a kite coming into the wind. The mooring line submerged with it, and then all the slack came out of it with a whipping noise as the raft resisted being pulled against the sea. A moment later there was a tearing sound as steel gave way forward, causing everyone who heard it to wince. There were two loud bangs, a moment of silence, and then more metal being deformed violently, followed by a splash on the port side.

Marty, who'd been watching from the port-side forty-millimeter guntub, gave a thumbs-up. The bomb was gone. Suddenly the life raft, no longer under tension, popped up about a hundred yards from the stern of the ship. I was wondering if that bomb was still attached to it when there came a heavy thump, like a depth charge, followed by a foaming mass of smoke and bubbles. Marty came down to the fantail as the crew cheered. I was wiping the sweat off my face as he arrived.

"Good job, Guns," I said.

"The monkey shit came off the tail propeller just as the bomb went over the side," he announced. "Thought we were gonna get a show after all."

We both looked back at the discolored patch of water behind us, where dead fish were glinting in the afternoon sun. I wondered if the captain had felt that thump.

"Okay," I said. "Have the OOD pass the word to reman all GQ stations, and let's get back to business before more Japs show up."

Then I went forward to inspect the area where the bomb had been. When I got there I saw a problem. A big problem. The departing bomb had torn away the entire bottom section of the air-search radar waveguide as it lurched over the side. In fact, that was probably why the radars had gone down after it hit. We were blind until we could get a new waveguide, and that would require getting to a destroyer tender. Not only that, it appeared that the buckler plates supporting the mast had been ripped off as well. I went over to one of the wire stays supporting the mast and grabbed it with my bare hand. As the ship rolled gently in the sea, I could feel the stay tighten and then loosen slightly. Was that normal play, or were the stays the only thing holding up the mast now?

I could hear the CIC team remanning their

stations below me. Time to get a report off to CTF 58, but first I needed to report in to the captain. I did my normal entry routine, two knocks, then stepped through. The inport cabin was fully dark, and the captain was nothing more than a long lump under the bedcovers, snoring softly. Because of all the electronics equipment, the CIC was air-conditioned, and the ship's architects had kindly attached a small, four-inch vent pipe to bleed some of that precious cold air from Combat's air-conditioning system down into the inport cabin, which was now almost cold. Ordinarily, I would have awakened the CO and told him what was going on and that we needed to get down to one of the repair ships at Kerama Retto, an island adjacent to the main island of Okinawa Shima.

On the other hand, the captain had told me to take care of business. The fact that he was sound asleep at two thirty in the afternoon while the ship was still very much vulnerable to kamikaze attack said it all. The man was simply exhausted.

I withdrew from the cabin and closed the door softly behind me. Then I went up to Combat. There I dictated a message to the navigation officer, describing the bomb strike and reporting that the mast had been compromised and that our air-search radar, our reason for even being here, was out of business. I then requested permission—no more UNODIRS!—to proceed to Kerama Retto for urgent repairs. I sent it to Admiral Chase, who was Commander Task Force 58, with a copy-to our squad dog, Commodore Van Arnhem, as well as to the Service Squadron Ten commodore at Kerama Retto so he would have a heads-up on what we needed. It was entirely possible we'd be sent on to Leyte in the Philippines if none of the repair ships anchored at Kerama Retto had a waveguide. That wasn't an altogether unpleasant prospect. Anything but this. I told Jimmy to get the ship back to our assigned station in anticipation of a relief ship showing up sometime in the next twenty-four hours.

"Still nothing from *Waltham*?" I asked.

"Negative, sir, and we still don't have any CAP overhead. That big strike this morning made a shambles of the flight schedules, apparently. Pray that the Japs shot their wad for today."

"Pray away," I said, "but keep your people on their toes. Brief the gun crews that we have no radar. All those guys—that's a lot of eyes. It'll be better when the sun goes down, but the skipper says it's only a matter of time before those bastards start flying at night."

Jimmy seemed surprised. "But how could they land back at—oh."

I smiled. It was not like they expected to fly home and land.

Jimmy shook his head. "I've lost track, XO. Are we still at GQ?"

"No, go back to port and starboard. If we stay at

GQ all day everybody will be a zombie. Get some people into their racks, and tell the galley—no, I'll take care of that."

Jimmy nodded, then surprised me. "Where's the skipper?" he asked.

"In his cabin, writing up the reports."

He gave me a look that said *Sure he is,* but he didn't say it. I fake-punched him on the shoulder and left Combat. Jimmie Enright was good people and no dummy.

I went out onto the bridge, which was now fully remanned. The ship was already headed back east. Our assigned radar picket station was about eight miles distant. The OOD, Lanny King, had taken the initiative to start us back toward our station, but he was headed straight for that point in the sea. I cautioned him about straight courses. "There's no big hurry, so go fifteen knots, but zigzag while you do it. The last two kamis got in on us undetected, and that's *with* the radars working, okay?"

"Yes, sir, sorry, sir, I forgot."

"Everybody's tired, Lanny. Keep asking yourself: What else should I be doing? And get word to Lieutenant Fontana to come find me."

"Aye, aye, sir."

FOUR

One day later, we arrived at Kerama Retto, one of several small islands off the west coast of Okinawa Shima, where the battle against the Japanese 32nd Army was in full fury. We had approached the anchorage just before dawn from the northwest, and the southeastern horizon had been filled with flashes of artillery and the explosions of battleship rounds in the low hills to the right of our approach. The allied forces had seized all Okinawa's small offshore islands before assaulting Okinawa proper in order to protect their flanks and to set up artillery and logistics bases. The shape of Kerama Retto provided a relatively protected deep-water cove, where the Navy had anchored several repair and replenishment ships. Protected was a relative term: The Japanese had already managed to sneak a miniature submarine into the cove and torpedo an ammunition ship, and the kamikazes attacked frequently. The Ryukyu Islands were the tops of submerged sea mountains, and the drowned slopes of Kerama Retto were already littered with the debris of ships and support craft that had been towed out and scuttled because they were too heavily damaged to be repaired.

Malloy was directed to go alongside USS

Piedmont, a seventeen-thousand-ton ship designed as a floating repair facility. She looked like an ocean liner, with her two stacks and long, covered galleries down each side, but she'd been painted haze gray and was sporting four five-inch single mounts, two each fore and aft. We discovered the *Waltham* tied up on the other side of the *Piedmont.* Her forward superstructure, including the bridge, mast, gun director, forward stack, and most of the CIC spaces, was a tangled jumble of blackened steel wreckage. Mount fifty-two, the second of the two gun mounts on the bow, was uprooted, with its two blackened guns pointed down at the deck below. There was a charred hole deep on her starboard side just abaft the beam, where Number Two Fire Room was located. As *Malloy* maneuvered to cross under the tender's stern, we saw some of her crew out on her weather decks, mostly standing around, as if still stunned by the extent of the damage. Even while tied up to the tender, she was listing ten degrees to starboard.

I wondered how many of the ship's officers had been lost. The captain, watching the gun boss conduct the landing maneuver from his chair, noted that neither the Union Jack nor the American flag was flying anywhere on the ship, which meant they were going to simply scrap her. "They'll salvage whatever they can in the way of critical parts," he said, "then tow her out of here and open all four main spaces to the sea."

Just like that, I thought. An entire ship. I wondered who'd made that decision.

Jimmy Enright made an interesting point. "There's a waveguide on that mast over there," he said. "We only need about ten, fifteen feet of good metal. We need to tell the ServRon Ten people that, before they . . ."

"Good call, Jimmy," the captain said. "Take that for action."

Once the ship was moored alongside the tender, a gangway was lifted by one of her cranes down to the forward camel between the ships and then positioned on *Malloy*'s starboard side. Then our accommodation ladder was lowered to the camel as well. The camel, a fifty-foot-long bundle of telephone poles wrapped in old rubber tires, was tied up between the ships to prevent them from rubbing against each other. A small parade of men came down from the tender, across the planks on top of the camel, and then up the accommodation ladder to our main deck. These were the repair superintendents and the various shop planners who would meet with the ship's department heads to determine what work would actually be done. *Malloy* wasn't alongside for a normal, two-week-long repair availability, just long enough to get our radar working again and the base of the mast reinforced. That didn't mean that *Malloy*'s department heads wouldn't be trying to cadge as much other repair work on balky pumps, shorted electric motors, leaking steam valves, etc., as they could. Beyond the formal repair requests, individual sailors from *Malloy*'s divisions would be sent on board the tender to cumshaw whatever goodies they could from trade-minded crew members. Apparently, a brass five-inch powder case, which could be cut down on a lathe to make a fine ashtray, would "buy" the most amazing things aboard a tender.

I assembled the department heads in the wardroom for the initial meeting with the senior repair superintendent, who was known as the ship's supe. The captain joined us once everyone was there.

"Captain Tallmadge, I'm Lieutenant Commander Weems from ServRon Ten," the supe said. "Our orders are to get your waveguide repaired, the mast stabilized, and then to get you out of here as soon as possible and back on station. Admiral Chase wants all of that done in twenty-four hours."

"Understood," the captain said. "Do you have a replacement waveguide?"

"We do now," the supe said.

"*Waltham*'s?"

"Yes, sir," the supe said. "She's been struck. We have a stripping crew on board, and it looks like there's about thirty feet of good waveguide left. We'll make a splice onto your system. We need to inspect the base of your mast to see how much shipfitter work needs to be done."

"Okay," the captain said. "Does that mean no emergent work?"

The supe smiled. "Your guys can try, Skipper. Officially, no, but . . ." Our department heads all knew the game, and apparently, the less said, the better.

"Then we're done here," the captain said. "My department heads will help your people make it all happen."

"My shop supervisors are already on board," the supe said. "They're waiting outside."

The captain nodded at the four department heads, who got up and filed out. The ship's supe remained at the table.

"How bad was it on *Waltham*?" the captain asked.

"Very," Weems said. "CO, XO, three of four department heads, nine other officers killed, and fifty-seven others missing and presumed lost. A hundred more wounded. Two kamis came at the same time. One did the front end, the other got into the after fire room. Both were carrying bombs, from the look of it. The after-fire-room hit broke main steam lines in both engine rooms. Basically, all the main-hole snipes except for One Fire Room are gone. She's well and truly wrecked, so she's worth more as a spare-parts locker than a fighting ship. Plus, that crew will have to be disbanded—the ones who can are all walking around in shock. There are an unknown number of bodies down in the main spaces, and they're going to go down with her."

"Great God," the captain said, his face ashen. "I guess we were just lucky."

"They told us you pulled the bomb off with a sea anchor?"

The captain told the story. Then I asked if twenty-four hours was a reasonable objective.

"You don't want to be here any longer than necessary, XO," Weems said. "The kamis still attack this anchorage—we're all sitting ducks, when you think about it. All our gun mounts are manned day and night, and we'll need you to keep your forties and at least one five-inch mount ready at all times. Besides, your damage is minor, so they want that radar fixed and then you back on station. Oh, and the commodores will expect a call."

Commodores, plural? Weems saw my expression. "The ServRon Ten commodore, Captain McMichaels, is embarked here in *Piedmont*, and your own squad dog, Captain Van Arnhem, is also embarked. Our poor skipper is camping out in his sea cabin for the moment. I believe your squadron commander is going to shift his burgee to the *Dixie* as soon as she arrives from Pearl. In the meantime, we've got ourselves a great sufficiency of four-stripers."

"Right," the captain said. "XO, I guess we'll need to make two calls. ServRon Ten is senior, so he's first. Then we'll go see Dutch Van Arnhem, my boss. He'll understand. Mister Weems, thank you, and we'll let you get going. Any hiccups, don't hesitate to come straight to me or the XO here."

"Thank you, sir. One more thing—if any of your people can spare some blood, we're in short supply on the hospital deck. It's a bloody mess over there on the main island. If half the stories we're hearing are true, it's black-flag time over there."

Kerama Retto was about twelve miles away from Okinawa, but even now, here in the wardroom, we could all could hear the thump of bombs, the thud of artillery, and the occasional deep rumble of battleship salvos.

There was a knock on the wardroom door. The quarterdeck messenger, a deck seaman, came in, escorting a chief petty officer. "Chief Winant from the EOD to see the captain, sir," the messenger announced.

"Sorry, Skipper," the chief said. "I can come back if you're in a meeting."

"Come on in, Chief," the captain said. "We're just swapping scuttlebutt here. Coffee's over there, and then come have a seat."

The chief's face didn't look to be more than thirty, but his hair was entirely gray and he moved with the care of a man who does dangerous work, in his case explosive ordnance disposal. He got himself a cup, and sat down at the junior end of the wardroom table.

"I heard a pretty interesting story this morning, Skipper," the chief said. "Something about using a sea-anchor to pull a Jap 250 off your signal bridge?"

"We did ask for EOD assist," I said, "but apparently your team had bigger fish to fry down here."

The chief grunted. "You might say that, XO," he said. "Yesterday was about as bad as the day the *Franklin* got it, and I was onboard for that ordeal."

Mention of the *Franklin* holocaust was jarring, even more so because I'd been serving in her for over eighteen months, and I'd never seen this chief's face.

"Yeah, we heard about that one," the captain said. "Were there really seven hundred *killed?*"

"They'll be revising that number all the way home, sir," the chief said. "We hear there are still parts of the ship they haven't been able to get into yet. Personally, I think she's headed for the scrapyard. Then yesterday, we went aboard the new *Yorktown* to defuse two five-hundred-pounders."

"Well, that certainly qualifies as a bigger fish," the captain said. "Our gun boss had had a class on how aircraft bombs are armed." He went on to tell the chief how they'd "safed" the bomb before yanking it off the 03 level. The chief smiled when he heard the story about the monkey shit.

"You guys were lucky beyond belief," he said. "Your gun boss was correct about the little propellers, but those bombs were never meant to be dropped. They were supposed to hit the ship at the same time as the kami."

"Which means?" I asked.

"Which means those kamikaze bombs are fully armed in flight. The arming lanyard had been pulled out manually somewhere south of Kyushu. I can't imagine why it didn't go off, especially when you shocked it again with the sea anchor."

That revelation produced a chilled moment of silence in the wardroom.

"But they said there was no firing pin visible on the front end," I said.

"There isn't one for the kami bombs. They're fired by setback. The pin's inside a tube. The bomb experiences a gazillion-g deceleration when it hits the side of a ship. That little pin slams forward in its tube to complete an electrical circuit, which fires the initiator, which fires the main explosive charge, all in about one heart-beat. Like I said, lucky beyond belief."

"And if it happens again?" the captain asked.

"Believe it or not, you'd have been better off bringing it down to us," the chief said. "One of us has to get inside the safing and arming compart-ment of the bomb, get by the anti-intrusion traps, find and disable the battery bus and *then* immobilize that pin and any backup exploders. Not for the faint of heart, gentlemen."

"I'll pass that on, Chief," the captain said. "On the other hand, would you care to go back to the picket line with us?"

"The radar picket line, Captain? Begging your pardon, sir, but hell, no. That's really dangerous duty."

We all laughed and then set about our day. Marty will shit a brick when I tell him the truth about his great monkey-shit gambit, I thought.

I was grudgingly getting used to the tin can Navy and its propensity to wing it when something had to be done and done right now. That was a trait I'd brought to my first couple of assignments, and more than once it had put me across the breakers with my department head. In the prewar cruiser Navy, appearances were everything, and junior officer initiative not much in demand. It took me some time to conform, and I think my own upbringing had a lot to do with that. My father was one of those parents who let their kids learn the hard way if the opportunity presented itself. He was an intellectual, somewhat aloof, deeply immersed in his work, about which I had no inkling while I was growing up. My mother—very pretty, very sweet, they never saw her coming—would sit down with me to analyze what I'd done to get in so much trouble as a child, and then encourage me to do better the next time but never to quit trying out new things. Now, as a junior lieutenant commander, I was exec in a destroyer, and I knew they'd be very proud. If I lived to tell the tale.

The next morning we sailed out of the fleet anchorage at just past sunrise. The tender repair people had done an amazing job of reconstructing the ship's radar waveguide and reinforcing the mast's foundations. *Malloy*'s crew had done an equally amazing job of "midnight requisitioning" aboard the destroyer tender. As we reached the entrance to the anchorage I was surprised to see two large aircraft carriers anchored close by, one of them showing clear signs of having experienced a large fire on her port side aft. Landing craft and small boats were shuttling between a heavily laden ammunition ship and the carriers, while up on the flight decks, fighters were turning up in the still morning air. Columns of smoke in the distance indicated that another horrible day was well under way over on Okinawa Shima.

Motivated by tales of dawn kamikaze attacks on the anchored ships, the captain ordered 25 knots as soon as we cleared the anchorage and headed back northwest. We were bound to a new vacant radar picket station, forty-five miles north and west, named Three-Dog. We had gone out in a modified general quarters condition, with all guns and CIC stations manned but the ship not yet buttoned up. As Okinawa's smoking ridges subsided beneath the southeastern horizon, the captain summoned me out to the bridge.

"Wanted to debrief you on my call with Commodore McMichaels," he said when I came out from Combat. Captain McMichaels was a senior four-striper, called commodore because he commanded a squadron of ships, in his case, the ships of Service Squadron Ten. The service squadrons had been one of Chester Nimitz's brilliant operational ideas: Gather together as many repair ships, ammunition ships, refrigerated food freighters, oil tankers, gasoline tankers, bulk cargo ships, fleet salvage tugs, and hospital ships, plus all the utility boats, landing craft, floating dry docks, harbor patrol craft, barges, and any other kind of floating support asset that you could find, collect them into a relatively safe anchorage, and thereby create an instant naval base. Ideally they could find an anchorage that was distant enough to be safe from Jap bombers but close enough that damaged ships could get there, one way or another, get fixed, and get back into the fight. If anyone knew what was really going on with the current campaign, in this case, Okinawa, it was the commodore of the service squadron supporting the campaign. The only fly in the ointment for the floating base at Kerama Retto was the fact that they'd failed to stay out of range of Jap bombers.

On the other hand, the Navy was discovering what it was going to be like when we hit the main islands of Japan.

The captain told me that our losses were mounting, both out in the main fleet formations and, of course, on the picket line. From the carriers to the amphibious landing craft, the body count was climbing rapidly, all because of the kamikaze tactic. We'd seen that at close hand.

I asked the captain if the big bosses were mad at us for trying to help *Waltham.*

"I'm not sure they—and I'm talking about the flag officers at Spruance's level—even know we exist," the captain said. "Okinawa has turned into a meat grinder of the worst kind. The Japs know they can't prevail, so they're bent on killing as many Americans as they can before they themselves are all dead. He was telling me about incidents where the Japs had convinced local civilians that our soldiers were going to *eat* them, and then made them jump off of cliffs to avoid capture. Absolute insanity. They're—"

At that moment one of the lookouts called in from the bridge wing that something had happened behind us. As the captain and I went out to see what he was talking about, a deep rumble overtook the ship from the direction of Kerama Retto and we saw an enormous black cloud mushrooming up over the horizon. More fiery explosions followed beneath the initial cloud, pushing whitish yellow fireballs and smoke trails in every direction. It sounded, and looked, like a volcano was erupting behind us. The entire bridge watch team and the gun crews out on deck were all staring aft.

"Something got that ammo ship," the captain said softly.

"Which we just passed at no more than five hundred yards," I said. There was another, even bigger explosion, and now the entire southeastern horizon was being enveloped by smoke from the blast.

"Combat reports ETA to picket station is ten fifteen," a talker announced.

"Not quite two hours," I said, looking at my watch. "I think it's time to button up and get ready for own brand of insanity."

"Air search working?"

"Yes, sir, better than before, actually. We don't have any CAP assigned yet, but they should be up soon, unless of course, that"—I pointed toward the continuing fountain of fire filling the sky behind us—"upsets the flight schedules."

"God help any ships that were close to that ammo ship," the officer of the deck said.

The captain looked at me. We both knew that every one of the small boats, lighters, and landing craft doing the shuttle work between the ammo ship and the two carriers were already part of that enormous cloud behind us. The two carriers had been parked at least a mile away from the ammo ship, but that was still within range of falling projectiles, rockets, and even bombs that had gone up in the initial explosion. The bitch-box lit up.

"Bridge, Combat, many bogeys, two niner zero, range forty-nine miles and closing."

"Okay, XO, lock her down and load the guns."

I went back into the CIC as the sounds of hatches slamming down rang out throughout the ship when the alarm sounded. The officer of the deck put *Malloy* into the familiar broad weave; we weren't on station yet, but the air-search radar was doing what it was supposed to do, and we had already sent the warning down to the fleet formations off Okinawa and in the Kerama Retto anchorage. Two other picket ships had also detected the incoming raid, which appeared to have originated in Formosa.

I took a seat at the head of the dead-reckoning tracer table. I signaled one of the Freddies over on the air-search radar side to come over. "Still no CAP?" I asked.

"No, sir," the jay-gee answered, "but the ready deck is launching. Some big deal happened down in the anchorage and that's got the command net tied up."

"You have no idea," I said. I wondered if those two carriers were supposed to have left the anchorage already to provide air support. Then I relaxed: There were *ten* big-deck carriers assigned to support the Okinawa invasion.

"Bogeys dispersing," the air-search radar reported. "Range thirty-seven miles and still inbound. Looks like some are coming for the picket line."

"Wonderful," I muttered. Except we weren't yet on the picket line. We were still south of it. Maybe they'd go by us. I almost suggested to the captain that we slow down. The plotters around the DRT exchanged fearful looks. I leaned over to the bitch-box and called the bridge. "Captain, Combat. They're definitely splitting up. Thirty-seven miles out. Looks like a couple of them are trying to get east of us. We're going to have some business here shortly."

For a moment, there was no reply. Then the officer of the deck acknowledged my warning, followed by something odd: "X1JV."

I blinked. X1JV referred to the sound-powered phone circuit used usually for administrative matters—calls between offices, not tactical stations. The *Malloy*, like all destroyers, was equipped with several sound-powered phone circuits. The advantage of sound-powered phones was that they did not require electricity, only connectivity. If the ship lost all electrical power, sound-powered phones still worked. The circuits all had names, of course. The JC was the gunnery control circuit. The JA was the combat action circuit. The 1JV was maneuvering. The JX was for communications. The JL was for lookouts. The X1JV connected offices and central stations like the quarterdeck, the bridge, the engineering log room, and Combat.

I reached down underneath the DRT plotting table and turned the handle on a large barrel switch to X1JV. That connected the handset I held in my hands to that particular circuit. Then I selected the bridge on a second switch and cranked the handle. The officer of the deck picked up immediately.

"What?" I asked.

"Captain went below," the OOD said.

"Are you *shitting* me?" I asked before I had time to think. "Head call, or what?"

The OOD blew out a long breath. "He didn't say, XO. He just left the bridge and went down the ladder. I'm guessing he's in his inport cabin."

"Five, maybe six bogeys inbound," the air-search radar operator announced. "Constant bearing, decreasing range. Director fifty-one in acquisition mode."

I was stunned. The captain had left the bridge with a raid inbound? What in the world—

"XO, recommend coming to course zero two zero to bring all guns to bear," the CIC watch officer said. "Range is twenty-six miles, constant bearing, target video is in and out."

That meant the Jap planes were descending. I

wondered for a brief moment how the hell the Japs knew where we were, and then remembered: They were probably homing in on *Malloy*'s own air-search radar beam. I hit the talk-switch on the bitch-box.

"Officer of the Deck, take Combat's course recommendations until further notice. Increase speed to twenty-seven knots."

"Bridge, aye!"

I then reached for the barrel switch again, turning it to the JC circuit, selected the main battery gun director station, and cranked the call handle. "Sky One," the gun boss responded.

"Marty, we've got a six-pack inbound. I think they're homing in on our air-search radar beam, so I'm gonna take the radar down and do a side-step. The big raid's been reported, but we have no CAP, so I'm not gonna make it easy for 'em."

"We're gonna hide, XO?"

"We're gonna try. It's visual from here out. Knock 'em dead, Marty."

"Sky One, aye."

I turned to the CIC watch officer. "Take down the air search. Now!"

There was a moment of hesitation, but then they jumped to it. I called the OOD on the bitch-box. "Come left, head three three zero at maximum speed. Tell main control to make no smoke."

"Bridge, aye."

We all felt the ship thrumming to the pulse of

her twin screws. The lighting fixtures began to shake, and the deckplates in CIC were trembling as the snipes down in the engine-room holes poured it on.

Twenty-something miles, I thought. Forty thousand yards. The five-inch could begin to do effective business at eighteen thousand yards, or nine miles. The Jap planes were descending from eighteen, maybe twenty thousand feet. Now they'd lost their homer bearings. The sky outside was clear but a bit hazy. No cloud cover. We might just get away.

The wake. They'd see the wake, just like those American carrier bombers at Midway had seen that lone Jap destroyer's wake, pointing directly at the carrier formation they'd been so desperately looking for.

"Bridge, Combat. Slow to fifteen knots," I ordered. "Broad weave around base course three three zero."

"Bridge, aye," the OOD responded.

I desperately wanted to go out to the bridge so I could see what was developing, but my GQ station was officially in Combat, the nerve center. This was where I belonged. In a few minutes, the lookouts would see the incoming Japs visually, and then it would turn into a gunnery exercise. Five-inch, forties, twenties, and nothing for the command to do but watch.

Well, not quite. When the kamikaze was finally

visible to the naked eye, the ship had to be maneuvered. You never pointed the long axis at the kami—that gave him three hundred and fifty feet of ship to hit. You turned, presenting the side—that gave him thirty-six feet to hit and all the gun barrels to greet him. Then you'd twist and turn as the pilots tried to line up a better attack position.

I found myself biting my lip as the noise level went up in Combat. Search sector orders were going out to the lookouts: Split the search. High *and* low. That's the way the Japs would attack.

The gun teams knew their business. They also knew what would happen if they got it wrong. By this stage of the war, *Malloy* was a well-oiled machine—But the captain was a damned important part of that machine, and he was . . . where?

More phone-talkers were making reports, sounding like altar boys at the beginning of Mass. I could hear the big gun director overhead turning on its roller path as the pointer searched through his optics for incoming black dots in the sky.

What should I do—*right now,* what should I do? Go find the captain, roust him out of wherever he was hiding, if that's indeed what he was doing? I could hardly believe that was what was happening, but . . .

The JC talker was tugging on my sleeve. Something about asking for the air-search radar to come back up. "Make it so," I responded, almost reflexively. The gun director's radar needed a cue from the larger, search radar as to where to look. My gambit to remove the beacon of their search beam hadn't worked.

Mistake. I could almost hear my mother saying, *Let's see what went wrong here, shall we?* Not now, Mom. It had left us blind at a critical moment. The captain would have vetoed that. "Yes, bring it back up."

A voice in my head was telling me what to do: Go fight the ship. Get your ass out to the bridge wing and join the anxious eyes scouring the late-morning sky. When it finally started, there would be decisions to make: Which way to turn to unmask all the guns and minimize the kamis target? What speed? If we took a hit, then someone had to direct the damage control effort while the surviving gunners continued the air-defense fight.

I could hear the tone of the talkers' voices rising. They were getting scared.

Get out there.

Then I heard director fifty-one stop turning. They were locking onto a target. The kamikazes were here. The forward gun mounts let go with the first salvos.

Get out there, now.

"I'm going to the bridge," I told the CIC watch officer. "Tell CTF 58 we're under attack."

"XO," he said, "where's the—" His voice was drowned out by another four-gun salvo from the forward five-inch mounts. I didn't wait to answer him. Besides, I didn't know the answer.

I went through the door between the charthouse and the actual bridge just as mount fifty-three joined in to deliver a six-gun salvo. All the bridge portholes had been locked in the up position to prevent glass splinters, so I caught the full force of the blasts. The breeze streaming over the bow was blowing gun smoke and bits of paper wadding through the portholes. Startled, I inhaled a lungful of sulfurous fumes and choked on it. I ordered the OOD to come back up to 27 knots in a somewhat strangled voice.

The forward mounts were firing to starboard, so I headed for the starboard bridge wing, where the officer of the deck, two lookouts, and two phone-talkers were already standing, all looking up into a metallic sky as the first black puffs of the timed fuzes began to blossom. I grabbed the captain's binoculars on the way out and started looking for the kami, but he was still too far away. Another salvo let fly, even louder now that I was out there on the fully exposed bridge wing. Mount fifty-three, back on the fantail, was also firing, but to port.

Port? Christ Almighty—were there two of them?

Finally I spotted the black dot out there, maybe

seven miles, slanting down out of the haze, embraced by a sudden succession of black puffs and then suddenly erupting into a gasoline fireball. I stared at the doomed plane as it came on, the ack-ack knocking pieces off it even as it assumed an even steeper dive angle, too steep, much too steep. He was going in, the pilot probably dead, and then he did, a sudden sheet of white water followed by the depth-charge-like underwater blast of his impact-fuzed bomb.

I ran back through the pilothouse and out to the port bridge wing as the forward five-inch mounts swung 180 degrees in unison to pick up the second kami. At that moment the forties joined the fight. I couldn't see the black dot, but I could see where all the tracer fire was going, rising into an arc of phosphorous lines and converging in a second cloud of ack-ack explosions.

Then I saw it: more than a dot now, God help us—stubby wings and that ominous black cigar shape under its belly, much closer than the first one, close enough for the twenties to get into it. Their massed fire created what looked like a veritable highway of tracer fire rising gracefully toward the target and then arcing back down again, because this bastard was coming in on the deck. Half the forty-millimeter stuff was going into the water now, and some of the five-inch shells could be seen smacking the sea and then ricocheting wildly back into the air before exploding.

The kami was into eight thousand yards, and the gun barrels up and down the length of *Malloy*'s port side were lying flat, their rate of fire if anything increasing the closer the kami got, each gun blast flattening the wake along *Malloy*'s port side to a bright yellow sheen. There was nothing more to be done, no maneuvers, speed changes, gun assignments—it was him or us now. I watched in horrified fascination as the Jap suicider got bigger and bigger, seemingly coming right for me up there on the bridge, and then a wing went spiraling away in black fragments and the kami flipped several times before the remaining wing touched the surface and it went in, no farther than half a mile away.

"*Right* standard rudder," the OOD yelled, and the ship heeled to port into a ninety-degree turn to our right. I looked to see why the turn was being made, and then the forward five-inch started firing again, this time slewing over the port bow but at a higher elevation now. A third kami was coming, this one clearly a medium bomber, with twin engines. I could see it without the binocs, but it didn't seem to be coming in all that fast, not like those modified Zeros had been moments ago.

"Baka, *baka!*" someone shouted, just as a yellow flare ignited momentarily under the bomber and something dropped away. It was a baka bomb, a long, torpedo-shaped cylinder filled with high explosive: stubby wings, three rocket engines in the back, and a lone pilot strapped into a tiny cockpit in the middle. When the Zeros came in, even in a power dive, they came at just under 400 knots. This thing came screaming down at 600 knots, which was technically beyond the computing ability of the Mark 1-Able gun computer down in Main Battery Plot. All the gunners could do was to point the guns down the bearing of the baka, which never changed since it intended to hit the ship, and then enter drop-spots to try to force the outgoing five-inch projectiles into the flying bomb's glide path.

The bomber was turning away, headed back to Formosa to load up another one, when out of nowhere a Navy Corsair appeared behind it and shot it out of the sky in another gasoline fireball. There was nothing, however, the Corsair could do about the baka, which slashed through *Malloy*'s forward stack so fast that its fuzing mechanism didn't even feel it. The baka hit the water out on *Malloy*'s starboard side, which the bomb *did* feel. There was an enormous blast, strong enough to whipsaw the foremast and knock most of the bridge team off their feet. I grabbed the portside captain's chair, which swiveled out of my grasp and dumped me on the deck with the rest of them. I could feel the ship's hull vibrating along her entire length from that blast.

When I regained my feet I sensed that the ship was slowing down. Orders were being transmitted over both the bitch-box and the sound-powered phones, but I couldn't hear a thing after all that gunfire. As I looked aft, I saw an enormous cloud of oily black smoke billowing from amidships, laced with bright white steam, obscuring the entire after part of the ship. I'd thought the damned thing had just hit the stack. Then I realized what was happening. The boilers down below used the smokestack for two things: to exhaust the gases of combustion and to draw down fresh combustion air for the burners. With half the stack gone, the boilers were being starved for air, hence all that smoke.

"Ten knots," I ordered. "Slow back down so they can get those boilers off the line."

The OOD nodded and gave the orders to reduce speed. I looked back at that black cloud behind the bridge. It was boiling aft like some kind of incubus. The topside gun crews couldn't remain on station immersed in all that heavy smoke. I reached for the bitch-box.

"Combat, Bridge. Give me a course to put the relative wind on the port beam. We're coming to ten knots. Any more Japs?"

"Combat, aye. Wait one." Then, "No active contacts at this time."

"Main Control, Bridge. Cross-connect the main plant once you get One Firehouse secured."

"Main, aye. Almost there, Cap'n."

I blinked. Captain? Then I understood. Only the

captain used the bridge bitch-box during general quarters.

"Bridge, Combat. Come to zero niner zero for wind abeam."

I looked over at the OOD, but he was already giving the orders. The ship turned, and the cloud of poisonous, oil-laden smoke began to veer off to the starboard side of the ship. That's when I got a look at the forward stack. The baka had hit it almost in the middle. The top half was suspended by a thin hinge of wrecked metal, hanging off the back of the stump. The oily black smoke was coming up through the uptakes, and there were occasional flashes of red fire as some of the oil aerosol embedded in the smoke met fresh air topside and ignited. That was the danger, I remembered. Get enough oxygen down into that remaining uptake space and the entire cloud would ignite in a real crowd-pleaser.

"Main Control, Bridge," I called on the bitch-box. "Once you get those boilers secured, keep the blowers going. Don't let that smoke accumulate in the uptakes."

"Main, aye," a voice answered, sounding just a wee bit annoyed, as in, don't tell us our business. I grinned. I recognized the voice of the chief machinist's mate. The snipes were a proud bunch.

I looked for my battle talker. The captain's battle talker, Chief Smith, looked back at me, waiting for orders. Well, I wasn't the captain, but for right now, I'd have to do. "All stations report damage and readiness," I ordered. Chief Smith repeated that and then began to announce the answers as each battle station reported back.

The smoke cloud suddenly turned to gray and then began to diminish. The Corsair who'd shot down the launching bomber came by at bridge level and waggled his wings. I gave him a thumbs-up from the bridge wing as he flew past. The fighter lofted back up into the air, did a beautifully precise four-point victory roll, and disappeared into the haze.

Jimmy Enright came out of Combat. "Radars confirm they hold no more bogeys. Okinawa AOA reports a big raid in progress, but the picket stations are clear, for the moment, anyway."

"There'll be stragglers," I said. "When they get done down there, whoever's left will come here."

"Let's hope the sumbitches stay down there and do their jobs, then," Jimmy grumbled. "They're supposed to go to Okinawa and die for the emperor, not annoy the picket line." He lowered his voice. "Where's the skipper, XO?"

"Gonna go find out, Jimmy. In the meantime, once the snipes get the main plant cross-connected, go back up to twenty knots and execute a random weave to station. Tell the gun stations to police their brass and get ready for round two in about thirty minutes. Remain at GQ."

"Aye, sir," Jimmy said and gathered in his phone-talkers. A loud screeching noise came from behind the bridge as the top half of the shattered forward stack broke off and rolled across the 01 level and down onto the main deck, smashing the lifelines flat and scattering some rubbernecking sailors, and then went over the side. As I was leaving the bridge I thought I heard one of the younger quartermasters, who looked to be at least fourteen, say very quietly, "Bye-bye."

When I got down to the inport cabin, I hesitated. What the hell was I going to say? How was I going to explain my assuming commandlike authority, if not command itself? More importantly, what was I going to find? Without the first clue, I knocked twice and pushed the door open. The cabin was empty.

It took me fifteen minutes to catch up with the captain, who was by then all the way back on the fantail, talking to the crew of mount fifty-three. The gunners had been taking advantage of the lull to get out of their hot, smoky gun mount, breathe some fresh air, and relax for a few minutes. The junior seamen were corralling the brass powder cases that littered the fantail area. The gunner's mates were collected around the captain, and all of them were smoking, which was not allowed at GQ. The fact that the captain was also puffing away was apparently being taken for an exception. What harm could it do, I thought, as I walked over. There he was, doing a Henry V pep talk before Agincourt.

"XO," the captain said, as if we were meeting at a cocktail party. "I take it we're in the clear for the moment?"

Fully aware that every crewman within range was listening, I had to consider my words. "There's a big raid over the Okinawa anchorage right now," I said. "We may get stragglers, we may not. CAP's up, radar's up, so with any luck, we're probably safe for the next half hour or so."

"Wonderful," the captain said, taking a last drag on his cancer stick and then pitching it over the side. The sailors standing around were all trying to discretely palm their ciggybutts now that the exec was standing there. "I take it we're cross-connected," the captain said. "Can One Firehouse still operate?"

"We're still looking at that," I said. "The forced-draft blowers weren't damaged, but the uptakes are a whole lot shorter than they used to be. That was a baka. Fortunately, it went a bit high."

"Great," the captain said. "Our luck holds. *Malloy* is a lucky ship, isn't she."

"Yes, sir," I said. The ship heeled as the OOD kept her twisting and turning. I looked around the horizon, which was indistinguishable from the metallic gray sea. "If I may have a word . . . ?"

"Keep your eyes peeled, boys," the captain said to the group of sailors around us. "This is when they come out of nowhere."

Then we headed forward, up the starboard side. When we got to the place where the forward stack had taken out the lifelines, we found two shipfitters kneeling on the deck, already welding in new lifeline stanchions. The captain went about ten feet forward of where the welders were scratching their arcs, well away from straining ears.

"You did well, XO," he said. "And how do I know? Because we're still here."

Enough of this play-acting, I thought. "What's going on, Captain?" I asked.

"Beats me, XO," the captain said. "But I'm damned glad *you're* here."

"But, sir—"

"But me no buts, XO. Which were you more scared of: the Japs, or screwing up?"

I didn't answer immediately. The captain had a point: My main concern had been not to make a fatal mistake.

"Thought so," the captain said. "Look, you did very well. I was listening on the JA, the 1JV. You did everything right."

"No, I didn't," I said. "I downed the air-search radar because I thought the bastards were homing in on it. That left us blind until the last minute. That—"

"And that might have worked," the captain interrupted. "But *I* think they're bringing a radar-equipped bomber with them, a multiengine job that hangs back and gives them vectors. Kinda like our Freddies: They're being radar-directed. When you think about it, though, this is a visual game, at least when you get down to the short strokes. Someone sees the kami, cues Sky One onto it, and then you start shooting. Once the forties and the twenties can see where the five-inch are shooting, they get into it. Weight of lead, XO; weight of lead. That's all we got."

"You weren't on the bridge, sir," I said. There, I thought, I said it.

"No, I was not."

"What the hell, Captain?" I asked, softly. "We need you up there. We *all* need you up there."

The captain's eyes lost focus for a moment. I let out a long breath. A sudden blast of low-pressure steam erupted from the truncated forward stack, startling both of us, but then it quickly subsided. A fine, warm mist settled on us as the steam condensed in the early afternoon air. Then we heard director fifty-one's amplidynes propel the director off to the port quarter, where its radar array went into a tight sector search.

"Back to work, XO," the captain said. "You're doing fine."

"Multiple bogeys, low and fast, inbound from astern," came over the 1MC loudspeakers. "Reman all battle stations. Check setting of Condition Zebra. Make manned-and-ready reports to the bridge."

We were standing next to a ladder that went from the main deck up to the midships torpedo deck, from which another ladder led up to the bridge. The captain pointed to the ladder. "I'm going to take one more turn about deck," he said. "You go to the bridge and take charge."

I was totally baffled, but ten years of instinctive discipline took over. Go to the bridge and take charge. Aye, aye, sir.

Up I went. As I climbed the steel steps that familiar feeling of mortal apprehension churned my stomach.

Which *was* I more scared of: the Japs, or screwing something up so bad we lost the ship?

Both, I decided—and whatever had begun to derange our skipper's mind.

"Bridge, Combat. We've lost 'em. Last skin painted at thirty-three miles, bearing two six five true. Estimating four bogeys, but there's weather out there."

"Bridge, aye," I responded. "Watch your surface-search radar, and be alert for a pincer."

"Combat, aye."

It was time to maneuver. "Officer of the deck, come to zero zero zero, speed fifteen. Forward lookouts scan from the bow to the port beam;

after lookouts from the port beam to the stern. We're looking for low-fliers."

The OOD started barking orders to the helm and lee helm. I went out onto the port bridge wing and joined the small crowd with binoculars glued to their eyes. A pincer was the worst case: The Jap formation would split up about twenty miles out, with two planes turning south and two north. After five minutes they'd all turn inbound on *Malloy.* We'd have to split the gun batteries, which would cut the effective fire on any one plane in half.

"Sky One, Bridge," I called.

"Sky One," Marty answered.

"How much of that new VT frag we have out there in the mounts?"

"We've got about a hundred rounds in each mount, XO," Marty said. "Got some from the tender. After that, it's gonna be Able-Able common, mechanical time-fuzed."

"Okay, that's good," I said. "We may have to split out the battery if they divide into two packs."

"Got it," Marty said. "Remember to turn back east again if it looks like a pincer."

"Right," I said. Leave it to Marty to remind me that our current course would present the long axis of the ship to both sections of kamis. That would definitely *not* do. Then I noticed the ship was boring a straight line through the sea.

"Broad weave, if you please. Base course still north."

Then we waited, everyone staring into the bright haze, each man executing the standard AA search with his binoculars: look right, go up, look left, go up, look right, go up, look left, go up, then go down, look right, go down, look left . . .

The radar bedspring array on director fifty-one was doing the same thing in short, jerky movements, while down in Main Battery Plot two fire-control technicians were staring at separate oscilloscopes, where a fuzz of green spikes glimmered across the round screens, looking like a freshly mowed lawn. If the radar found something, a spike would rise up out of the grass, as it was called, and they'd lock onto it. The big amplidyne motors that trained and elevated the boxy director whined and keened in response to the operator's hands on joysticks inside the director. It was an annoying noise. Everyone was waiting for the lock-on.

"Captain's in Main Control," the 1JV talker announced to no one in particular. The officers on the bridge glanced at one another. So that's where he was. Okay: The main plant was operating in a reduced capability mode. Otherwise we'd be making 25 knots or more.

Everyone heard director fifty-one stop searching. The amplidynes went from loud, complaining noises to very small movements. I looked up above the bridge. The director was pointed due west.

Good: no pincer.

The two forward five-inch guns swung out to port, their twin barrels trembling as the computer down in Plot sent minute train and elevation angles to their amplidynes. I was frustrated by the limited range of the five-inch guns. I had served on a light cruiser designed for antiaircraft work, but her guns were six-inch, which could reach out to almost thirteen miles. It didn't sound like much of a difference, but it was.

I jumped when the five-inchers went to work. Everyone did. The sound hurt my ears, and another cloud of sulfurous smoke enveloped the bridge. I still couldn't see anything out there in the haze, but the miracle of radar was working for us. I could feel the ship quiver as all three mounts, fore and aft, got into it, hurling fifty-four-pound projectiles out to where the Japs were ducking and weaving a hundred feet above the sea surface, coming in at 350 knots, each with a five-hundred-pound bomb slung under its belly and each one intent on driving himself, his plane, all its remaining aviation gasoline, and that hair-triggered bomb into our guts.

I tried to think of what else I should be doing as the guns hammered my ears. We were properly positioned to bring all guns to bear, so no more maneuvering. The ship was buttoned up. With only two boilers available we were going almost as fast as we could go. The gunnery department was fully engaged, with ranges, bearings, and angles of elevation passing through all those sound-powered phone circuits. The five-inch gun mount crews were turning and burning, serving the six barrels in a sweaty cycle: dropping the breechblocks, ejecting the still smoking powder can, ramming a new round, ramming a new powder can, raising the breechblock, and closing the ready circuit key.

B-blam.

Do it all again. Wait for the hiss of gas-ejection air. Drop the breechblock. Both gun crews racing each other, sweating hands on each side, humping the big shells out of the hoists and into the hungry, smoking maws of the guns, punch the hydraulic rammer, extract it, put the powder can in, ram again, extract, raise the block, squeeze the ready key.

B-blam.

There, I thought. The variable-time shells were finding something to detonate on. Black puffs, low down on the water. One. Five. Many. Then the black dot, bucking and weaving through the whirlwind of fiery steel fragments, getting lower and lower as some terrified nineteen-year-old Jap fixated on the American destroyer, muttering fervent prayers to his ancestors, and then joining them as a five-inch shell came through the canopy to vaporize him and his plane.

One down.

Then two down, both creating large gasoline fireballs splattering across the sea as the five-inchers kept it going until someone down in Plot released the master firing key.

There was a moment of silence.

Where were the other two? These guys hadn't even made it into forty-millimeter range. Something's not right here.

Then the midships forties burst into action, but on the *starboard* side.

Pincer! God damn them.

Director fifty-one slewed frantically all the way around to starboard, and all three five-inch mounts followed it in big, lurching jumps, but there was no lock-on, and no more time, either. I sprinted through the pilothouse out to the starboard bridge wing in time to see two more Zeros flying no more than twenty feet off the deck, coming in from the east, with bright flashes blinking at us from the twenty-millimeter cannons under their noses. They were too close for the five-inch to engage, so the forties and the twenties took up the slack, streaming several lines of white-hot steel that arced out over the water, higher than the incoming planes, but then settling back into their faces. I felt rather than heard the Japs' twenty-millimeter rounds hitting the forward superstructure. Out of the corner of my eye I saw the lookout next to me fly backward and thump off the bulkhead, leaving a red spray as he slid down to the deck.

The Japs were close, very close, and the lines of tracers from our twenties were converging now, blasting pieces off the planes. The five-inch guns remained pointed at the enemy, but the Japs were so close that the five-inch shells wouldn't have had time to arm. Something stung my right leg just below the knee, and then the single porthole of the captain's sea cabin exploded in a shower of glass right behind me. The two planes were close together now, as if racing, both trailing streams of white gasoline vapor and engine oil smoke, no more than a thousand yards, when *Malloy*'s twenties found that five-hundred-pound bomb underneath the left Zero. It exploded with a yellow-white flash, shredding the plane and upsetting his wingman, causing the second Zero to drag a wingtip into the sea and then disintegrate into a million pieces, half of which ended up clattering all over the decks and bulkheads of *Malloy*. Its bomb skipped twice on the water and, as I took a huge breath, flew sideways over where the forward stack would have been and out into the sea on the other side, where it went off with a thunderous blast two hundred yards away.

All the guns ceased firing, but my ears still rang with the hammering of the forties and twenties closest to the bridge. Behind us, off the starboard quarter, a patch of avgas was burning brightly on the sea. I turned to go back into the pilothouse but stopped short at a scene of significant carnage. There were twenty-millimeter cannon holes everywhere. All the watchstanders seemed to be down on the deck, which was carpeted with blood and shards of glass. Anyone not wounded or dead was attending to his shipmates. Two phone-talkers had been pretty much torn to pieces by the hail of shells, and Ensign Gall, the junior officer of the deck, was slumped under the captain's chair with a fist-sized hole in his throat and an expression of total surprise still on his face. The chart table on the back bulkhead of the pilothouse was smoldering, with whitish smoke streaming out from the drawers where the charts were kept. The helmsman was still at his station behind the wheel, but he was holding his steel helmet in both hands and gawking at the bright shiny furrow carved by a twenty-millimeter projectile across the top of his helmet. The lee helmsman was down on the deck with the bosun's mate of the watch, tending to another phone-talker, who was crying hysterically because his right leg was hanging by a flap of skin at a ninety-degree angle from his knee.

The chief hospital corpsman, Chief Bobby Walker, came out into the pilothouse from the passageway that led back to Combat. His uniform was already blood-spattered, and he was carrying an armload of battle dressings. His feet went out from under him as he stepped out onto the bloody steel deck, but one of the quartermasters caught him just in time. The chief immediately began the process of triage, ordering the able to start handing out and applying bandages to the not-so-able.

Jimmy Enright came out of Combat, trailing a sound-powered phone-set wire. He, too, had blood spatters on his khakis. He stopped short when he saw the pilothouse, which was beginning to resemble an abattoir, with the chief corpsman shouting orders and bloody bandages flying everywhere. Then Jimmy saw me, still standing in the starboard hatchway.

"We couldn't raise the bridge talker," he said, his voice sounding higher than usual. "You need to get that bandaged, XO."

"What?" I replied and then looked down at my leg. My right trouser leg was black with blood, and my right shoe squelched when I moved. I bent down and raised the pant leg to reveal a large gash on the right upper side of my calf. I remembered the sting. Now, suddenly, it hurt like hell.

"Damn," I said. "Well, scratch, right?"

Jimmy grunted, but he knew what I meant: Compared to the bloody mess all around us, my wound was manageable. "Still," he said, grabbing a battle dressing from the pile on the deck. "Put your leg up here."

Chief Walker came over, watched Jimmy's

clumsy attempts to fit the bandage to the wound, swore, and shouldered him aside. I waited stoically while the dressing was applied, along with a healthy dusting of sulfa powder. Then I realized that Chief Walker had probably been all over the ship, looking for wounded crewmen.

"How many?" I asked.

"One radioman dead, along with some of the radios. Rest of the ship is okay, as far as I know. My striker's out checking. Between the bridge and Combat we're looking at a dozen or so. This is the worst." He stood up, examined his handiwork, and nodded.

"Doc," I said quietly. "Seen the skipper?"

The chief, whose face looked weary well beyond his age, glanced up at me. Then he looked around the pilothouse, saw no captain, and shook his head. Two men on the other side of the pilothouse called urgently for the chief. The man they were tending was convulsing, his feet pounding out a mortal tattoo on the deck. The chief let out a sigh and went back to work.

Jimmy stared at the bloody scene on the bridge.

"We done with bogeys?" I asked.

"Nothing on the radar when I came out," he said. "We've got two dead and seven wounded in Combat, two bad, the rest manageable. That bastard shredded us pretty good. One of the Freddies is down, but amazingly, the radar consoles are okay."

"You should have seen that five-hundred-pounder flying over the forward stack, or what's left of it," I said. "I about crapped my trou." I hesitated. "Jimmy, I don't know where the captain is."

I hadn't meant to say that. It just popped out. On the other hand, Jimmy Enright was the senior department head. It was only fair to make sure that he knew what was going on. The man who'd been convulsing suddenly went rigid, blew a bloody bubble from his mouth, and then relaxed with a gurgling sigh. One of the men tending him swore.

Jimmy looked out the front windows. "Should we slow down now, maybe?" he asked.

"Go back into Combat and get me a radar fix on Okinawa; see how close we are to our assigned station. I've got to . . ."

Jimmy nodded. "Right. Go find him. Something's really wrong."

"Yeah," I said. "God damn it. The crew talking yet?"

"No, sir," he said. "They're all too scared. It was like being in the fish barrel in there, when that guy strafed us. Nowhere to go. Shit flying everywhere. Guys screaming, even when they hadn't been hit. Now that I think of it, the ones who *were* hit didn't make a sound."

Jimmy went back into Combat.

"Officer of the Deck," I called. "Secure from

GQ. Set Condition Two. Get damage reports from DC central. Slow to ten knots. Broad weave. Get a DC party up here to clean up the bridge. Get lookouts back on station. There's still two hours of daylight left."

"Aye, aye, sir," a shaken Jerry Morrison replied. I turned to the helmsman. "All engines ahead two-thirds, turns for ten knots. Helmsman?"

The kid with the creased helmet gaped at me. He was trying not to look at all the blood and gore on the deck.

"Put that damned thing down and get on the helm. Broad weave. Now!"

"Broad weave, aye, sir," the kid said. "But, sir? *Jesus!*"

"Jesus, aye," I said, "but we're still here, and so are the goddamned Japs. Broad weave, and you've got the lee helm, too, until someone relieves you."

I left the bridge and went down into the interior of the ship. The effects of the strafing were everywhere. Holes in bulkheads. Light fixtures dangling over mounds of broken Plexiglas. A fire extinguisher had been punctured, blowing white powder everywhere. A scuttlebutt, Navy slang for drinking fountain, was leaking all over the deck from a single round. There were men moving through the passageways now that general quarters had been secured. Many of them looked stunned. You should have seen that five-hundred-pounder, I thought as I headed aft. Shafts of white sunlight streamed incongruously through the outer bulkheads.

I checked the messdecks, after-officers country, and the chiefs' mess and then went out onto the main deck aft, greeting frightened sailors, pretending everything was okay, almost pulling it off until they got a look at my right leg. The bandage was holding just fine, but the lower part of my khaki trousers was pretty well soaked. I found myself trying not to limp.

As I told people they were going to be all right, my mind was fixated. Where was the captain? In his cabin, maybe? I went back inside the deckhouse. Groups of men were still hurrying through the passageways and moving along the main deck, bound on repairs and cleanup. The after repair party was restowing their damage control locker. The ship was down to 10 knots, barely moving over the slate gray sea, heeling from time to time as the helmsman spun the wheel this way and that, executing that random broad weave to keep from being a sitting duck.

"XO," a voice called as I passed the scullery. It was the supply officer, Peter Fontana. The supply officer was known universally as the Chop because of the porkchop-shaped insignia on his left collar.

"Chop, can you feed us?" I asked.

"Absolutely, XO," he said. "Got the cooks and

messcooks turning to. Beef stew and rice. Say the word and we'll open the line. We're done for the day, I hope?"

"I hope to God we are," I said. "But we'll hold chow until after sunset GQ. I'll call you."

"XO?"

"What, Chop?"

The supply officer looked both ways to make sure none of the troops were listening. "The captain? He's down on the forward reefer flats. He's just sitting down there. One of the mess-cranks saw him and came to tell me. XO, what the—"

"I don't know, Chop," I said. "Something's happened."

"He's such a great guy," Peter said. "Gives a shit, you know? Gives a shit for his people, not his career. Please, tell me he hasn't—"

I raised my hand. "Keep this to yourself, Peter. Give me the reefer deck keys and I'll go get him. Meanwhile, I've changed my mind. Be ready to open the mess line in about thirty minutes. It's been a long, sad day, and we're going to be burying people tonight."

I went forward to the main ladder hatchway leading down to the second deck, where the ship's refrigerated storerooms, known as the reefer decks, were. I didn't know what to think. Here we were, alone on the Okinawa radar picket line, shot up enough to scare the shit out of the crew and down to 10 knots. The main steam plant was still cross-connected until the snipes could figure out how to restore the boilers in the forward fire room with only half a stack. And the captain? Had the captain gone Section Eight?

I unlocked the hatch leading into the reefer deck compartment. I swore mentally when I realized that the mess cook had locked the captain inside the compartment, but he was just obeying standing orders. Need to find out who that is, have a word with him, I thought.

The lights were still on, and the captain was sitting on a lone folding chair parked in front of one of the freezers. He smiled vacantly when he saw me.

"Captain," I began, but then I stopped, not knowing what to say.

"I'm okay, XO," the captain said. "It's nice down here. Quiet. Cool. I told that young man to lock the door behind me. Told him I was conducting an experiment. You know, rumor control."

There were two refrigerant compressors at the forward end of the reefer compartment. One was on the line, the other in standby. I sat down on the standby's motor. "Sir," I said. "You've gotta tell me. What's going on?"

"Oh, it's pretty simple, XO," the captain said. "I've lost my nerve. When that GQ alarm sounds, I want to run. That's kinda hard when we're at sea, so I go find somewhere else, somewhere besides the bridge, and I hide. This last attack, I sat down here in the dark and shook like a leaf. Almost pissed myself. Closed my eyes, gritted my teeth, and I think I actually whimpered. How'd it go, by the way? Thought I heard some incoming . . . ?"

How did it go? I tried to control my expression. I gave him a rundown of the afternoon's action. The captain winced when he heard the casualty numbers. Then he nodded, went silent, and stared off into space.

I didn't know what to say next.

"I'm not crazy, you know," the captain said. "I know what's happening. I'm just paralyzed. I think you'll have to relieve me, and notify CTF 58."

"I do *not* want to relieve you, sir," I said. "You're the captain. You know more than the rest of the wardroom put together. I think maybe you just need a rest. I'll get Doc to give you something. We'll cover for you, a day, maybe two, and then you'll be okay. We need you."

"Have you asked to come off station to get down to the hospital ship?"

"No, sir. They don't have any more destroyers who can come up here. We're going to bury our dead and treat the wounded. That's all we can do right now."

"Ask them to send an LCS, or something like that, up with a medical officer and some supplies. They can do that."

I almost groaned. Of course, that was the thing to do. It hadn't even crossed my mind. There was so much I didn't know.

"I'll officiate tonight," the captain said. "Darkness is our friend. I can do that. I know I can do that. But when the sun comes up, XO, you're gonna own it. Understood?"

I had no answer for that except "Yes, sir." The captain got up, dusted off his trousers, and then saw my bloody pant leg. He blinked. "You didn't tell me—"

"A gouge, that's all," I said. "I was lucky. Hurts more than I expected, but it's no big deal, not compared . . ."

The captain nodded. "I was at Savo Island in *Quincy*," he said, almost whispering. "A complete slaughter. I still have nightmares. Then *Juneau*. Did you know I was one of *ten* survivors, out of a crew of seven hundred? We took a Long Lance during that night fight, crawled out with the *San Francisco* the next morning. We were making twelve knots with a broken keel."

He stopped for breath. I held my silence. He wasn't here. He was back at Guadalcanal.

"A Jap sub found us. Two cripples. We were down by the bow, but we were making it. Took one torpedo hit, and goddamn me if it wasn't right where the first one got us, only this time the forward magazines let go. I woke up in the water, with maybe a hundred other guys. They finally found us, too many days later. We were down to ten."

"Ten?"

"Yup. They haven't published that number, have they? No, they haven't. November 1942. I should have gone home after that. Gone back to the Eastern Shore and farmed some chickens. Dug myself a Victory Garden, but no, I asked to stay. Now look at me. I should have turned myself in six months ago, but I remember thinking, this shit isn't over, and I'm not any worse for wear. Went on to XO in a tin can, chasing bird farms with Halsey and Spruance, then got command of *Malloy.* Going from island to island, doing shore-bomb, rescue-plane guard, odd jobs. One more island, one more landing: How tough could it be? Then these kamis . . . It's just too much, XO. Too much. You're gonna have to take it. I'm done. Just didn't realize it until now."

"We'll figure something out, Captain," I said. "In the meantime, I need you to take a turn about deck, with me. People need to see you. Then we'll get the doc in."

"Sure, I can do that," he said, "but how long until sunset?"

The two of us walked the topside decks of the ship for the next forty minutes, seeing and being seen by all the people who were picking up the pieces on the weather decks. The captain did well. Once out in the sunlight, he straightened up and became himself again, greeting many of the crewmen by name while I trailed along. Chief Lamont caught up with us after about five minutes as word got around that the CO was topside. How he heard remained a mystery, but it was one of his skills.

Doc Walker found us on the 01 level amidships and told the captain they were ready on the fantail. Ready for what, I wondered. We walked aft, and went down to the main deck, through the K-gun depth-charge racks, past the quarterdeck, and out onto the fantail. There, laid out in two rows, were our dead. Their remains were in black rubber body bags, and there were six lying out there in the sunlight. Two sailors in dungarees, white duty belts, white leggings, and white hats were standing watch over them, each with an M-1 rifle resting incongruously on his shoulder. As I stood there, Doc took the captain to each one of them, unzipped the bag so the man's face was visible, and then told the captain who the man was, where he was from, and what he was "famous" for within his division. Then they'd move on to the next one.

I later found out that this was where the captain gathered personal details that he would later connect to when he wrote the letters of condolence to their families.

"We'll do it together this time," he said to me quietly as we walked away. "It's your job to draft the letters, and then mine to personalize them. Not fun."

I couldn't think of anything to say to that. That night, right after sundown but while there was still some daylight, we buried our shipmates who'd been killed in the strafing attack. We hadn't assembled the whole crew for the burial ceremony because there were still contacts being reported around Okinawa, but everyone from the after gun batteries stood in respectful attendance, just beside their guns. The captain and I had changed into choker whites; he read the prescribed words and the psalm. The honor guard, three sailors, also in their dress whites, fired a three-gun rifle salute, and then the bodies were consigned, one by one, to the deep. Our honor guard folded the flags, which would be boxed up later and sent home to families, along with the letter of condolence and personal effects. Throughout, Captain Tallmadge had conducted himself with grace, dignity, authority, and absolutely no sign of the mental state he'd revealed earlier.

If he can manage that, I thought, with all the emotion entailed in sliding someone you knew into the deeps of the Pacific Ocean, then we can overcome this problem. I just have to figure out how.

FIVE

The following morning broke hazy, with seas so calm the water resembled one infinite mirrored surface all the way to the horizon. The only movement of air was a faint stirring created by the ship's own movement. We'd gone to GQ just before sunrise, as usual, and were now steaming at modified GQ as long as Combat held no incoming air contacts. The captain had decided to stay up on the bridge, so I had quietly called a department heads' meeting in my stateroom. I got to sit on my bunk while the four of them crowded into the tiny cabin.

I blew out a long breath. "Okay, guys," I said. "As I suspect you all know, there's something going on with the skipper." I looked at each of them in turn. Jimmy Enright, Mario Campofino, Marty Randolph, and Peter Fontana all nodded. Then the sound-powered phone squeaked. I sighed.

"XO."

"XO, Combat. There's an LSMR"—Landing Ship, Medium, Rocket—"coming up from Okinawa, ETA around noon, with a med team embarked. We also now have two sections of CAP assigned. If you hear aircraft engines, it's them headed out for their barrier stations. They'll come overhead for positive ID as friendlies."

"Thank you," I said and hung up the phone. I relayed the word to the department heads. "Now," I continued. "As to the CO. I believe he's mostly exhausted."

"As opposed to Section Eight?" Mario asked.

"He's not nuts," I said. "He's not babbling or doing bizarre things other than hiding when the shit starts."

Jimmy Enright raised a hand. "Begging your pardon, XO, but that *is* bizarre behavior for the skipper of a warship, especially out here. I don't want to sound like a sea lawyer, but I think this situation needs to be reported to the commodore and that you should assume temporary command until we get further instructions."

I sighed again. "You're technically right, of course, but if we do that, they'll simply haul him off the ship and send him home in what, for him, would be total disgrace. I think we owe him more than that and better than that. You all have served with him longer than I have, but my impression is that he's been a singularly good CO."

"XO," Marty said, "what do Navy Regs say? If the CO becomes incapacitated, you already have the authority to relieve him, as long as you report it to the squadron commodore, right? I mean, if you don't, and something happens and he gets killed in his cabin, they're gonna look pretty hard at you."

"What's the word going around the ship?" I asked, dodging his question.

Mario said that there were some rumors, but so far, nothing vicious or alarming. Then he weighed in. "So why don't we simply get the doc to give him something, put him asleep for a coupla days. See how he comes back from that."

"I'd vote for that," Peter said. "We'd all feel like shitheels starting a major flap when it could be simple exhaustion. Remember who we're talking about here—this isn't Captain Bligh. This is our skipper."

"You know what?" Mario asked. "There'll be at least one medical officer on that LSMR. Make sure he sees the captain, talks to him—you know, tell him he has to make a report to the CO on the condition of our wounded? Then if the skipper starts acting strangely, you'll know what you have to do."

"That's part of the problem," I said. "He acts perfectly normal, except when that GQ alarm goes and the kamikazes show up. You all saw him last night at the burial service. Dignified, sad, but reading that scripture like a bishop. He was the only officer that the crew wanted to see doing that."

"But . . ." Marty said.

"Yeah, but. He told me yesterday that he's lost his nerve. I think the scariest part of that was that he knows it and admits it. It's like he doesn't know what to do now."

"Oh, I think he does, XO," Marty said. "If he knows he's lost his nerve, that he panics when the Japs arrive, he should be *ordering* you to assume command, turning himself in to the commodore, and requesting his own immediate relief. You've been in carriers. Isn't that what the aviators do when they can't face carrier landings anymore?"

I hadn't thought of it that way, although the captain had proposed just that. Proposed, not ordered. Marty was right . . . and yet.

I just couldn't bring myself to force that issue. *Malloy* was a fully trained ship of war, thanks mostly to Captain Tallmadge's personal tutelage over the past eight months. It hadn't been that way under the previous skipper, if I could believe the longest-serving department heads. Captain Tallmadge was also older than most of the other skippers in the squadron, having entered the Naval Academy after two years of college. As far as I could see he exhibited none of the careerism that was beginning to infect the fleet as the war against Japan was obviously drawing to a climax, with some overly ambitious officers scrambling to get wartime commands before the opportunity for "glory" disappeared. Everyone knew that there would be no more fleet carrier battles, or ship-versus-ship duels, because the formerly majestic Imperial Japanese Navy was, for the most part, asleep in the deep. The only thing remaining was the invasion of the Japanese home islands, once Okinawa had been taken.

Just prior to my coming aboard, the captain had warned the department heads that Okinawa was going to be different from the previous island assaults. Not only did the Japs consider it one of the home islands, the introduction of the kamikaze as a full-time, planned campaign meant that the Navy was now going to be in just as much peril as all those doughboys tramping ashore.

"It's one thing when a pilot is trying to drop a bomb on you," he'd said, prophetically. "It's quite another when he wants to come aboard and has no intention of ever going home again. This is going to be bad."

So bad, I thought as I considered Marty's words, that our beloved skipper had taken up running and hiding when the guns trained out to go to work.

"Okay," I said. "I'll make the sure the doc who comes in with the LSMR has some face-time with the captain. In the meantime, let's keep this problem among ourselves. We'll meet again tonight after the LSMR leaves. Mario, I need an updated damage report—what's been repaired, what they're working on, and what's beyond our capability. Marty, same deal with the guns and their crews. And remember, gents: We're still very much in Injun Country."

• • •

The LSMR hove into view thirty minutes past noon, pursued by a large cloud of diesel exhaust from engines badly in need of some work. It looked somewhat similar to the much bigger LST: Landing Ship, Tank. Shaped like a shoe box with a blunt bow up forward, her job was to stand offshore and fire barrages of five-inch rockets into the active battle zone. The little ship had not been modified for picket line duty and thus retained almost all of her rocket launchers. The only visible changes had been a few topside modifications to allow temporary berthing for wounded being transferred from the warships to one of the hospital ships or tenders anchored off Kerama Retto. There were large red crosses painted on her sides and main deck, not that that seemed to matter to the kamikazes. The skies over the picket area had been clear of bogeys all morning, with not even any Jap recon aircraft being detected. Everyone hoped the Japs were taking the day off for some reason, but I suspected they were assembling something special for the combined American and British armada surrounding Okinawa.

Doc Walker and I met the doctor, who was first up the boarding ladder, and handed over Walker's summary of the wounded, listed on a triage basis. The doctor, an impossibly young-looking medical officer except for those dark circles under his eyes, scanned the report and then asked to be taken to sick bay so he could set up shop. Four hospital corpsmen came up from the LSMR, which was rubbing and bumping alongside our much larger sides. They brought up several bulky medical kits and bags of replacement medical supplies. Once the med team was on board, the LSMR rumbled away to take up a station a thousand yards from *Malloy*. She had one twin forty and three twenty-millimeter gun mounts, and *Malloy*'s officer of the deck had reminded the LSMR's skipper to keep them manned and ready. That worthy gave the OOD a sharp look and reminded him that the picket line wasn't where most of the kamikazes came to do business. Our OOD, an ensign, was suitably chastened and saluted the offended skipper of the LSMR—a lieutenant.

I took the doctor aside for a moment and told him that our skipper was suffering from what looked like acute exhaustion. He asked me if I wanted him to deal with the ship's wounded or the skipper first. I told him the wounded came first, but that I needed him to see the captain before the team disembarked.

"Acute exhaustion," he said. "There's a lot of that going around, especially on the destroyers up here. How are *you* holding up?" he asked, glancing at the white bandage showing under my torn khaki trousers. Now that I got a closer look at him, he didn't seem so young anymore.

"Better than he is," I said. I pointed at my right leg. "This hurts, but APCs seem to work it down to a dull roar."

He said he'd look in on the CO as soon as he could. I went up forward to meet with the chief engineer and get a status on the main steam plant. They'd been working on a way to relight the two forward boilers with only half a stack, and we were now back to full power available. After that I went to the captain's cabin and briefed him on what was going on. He took it all on board and then asked me about the department heads' meeting he'd heard called over the 1MC. I didn't equivocate. I told him what we'd talked about and how everyone felt. The captain smiled.

"You're a good guy, XO. Thanks for your honesty, and it may well be that I'm much more tired than I thought, but you should know that when the GQ alarm goes, so does my plumbing."

I had no answer for that.

"I think maybe Marty and Jimmy are right," he continued. "I should go topside, write in the log that I'm no longer capable of performing my duties and that I have *ordered* you to take command. That way there's no whiff of insubordination, or worse."

"There's no chance of anybody in this ship thinking about mutiny, Captain," I said. "In fact, we're all trying to cover for you, and that's because we need you and your experience. Each time I make a tactical decision, you very politely say 'That was good, XO,' but then you come up with something that never crossed my mind. I want to stay alive out here. We all do. The longer we're here, the less likely that becomes. *Waltham* was the fourth destroyer lost up here in three weeks. We need you to tell us what to do."

"*Malloy*'s a lucky ship, XO," the captain said. "That's more important in war than any alleged brilliance at the top."

"We're lucky because you've trained us and you always are one step ahead of everybody else when the kamis come."

"Not anymore, XO," he said with a sigh. "Right now I'm several steps *behind* you when I start crapping my trou while trying not to throw up with fear. *You're* ready, XO. I think I'm done. Let's think about the ship, okay? The ship and the three hundred or so souls on board, not as many as we had before yesterday, but still—that's a valuable crowd."

I was trying to formulate an answer when the GQ alarm sounded. The OOD on the bridge came up on the announcing system: multiple bogeys, sixty miles, high, inbound, but crossing.

I didn't want to, but I glanced back at the captain. His face had begun to go rigid, and his eyes seemed to be losing focus.

Great God, I thought. This is real.

"Go," the Captain whispered. *"Please."*

I sighed, put my hand on his shoulder, and gave it a squeeze. Then I headed for the bridge.

"We need to get the med team back on board the LSMR," I said to the OOD as I came out into the pilothouse, donning my battle gear.

"Yes, sir," the OOD said. "We have time?"

"The radar indicates the raid is crossing, meaning they're headed for the main fleet dispositions around Okinawa. Signal that LSMR back alongside, and let's get all those people plus our most seriously hurt out of here. And tell 'em to move it."

The OOD got on the bitch-box to the signal bridge, and moments later we all heard the clacking of the signal searchlight. The LSMR CO must have already figured out why all our topside mounts were suddenly crawling with gunners, because as soon as the signal light started up, he turned his ungainly craft toward *Malloy* with a great burst of diesel exhaust.

"Okinawa med team to the starboard side, on the double. Kamikazes, inbound," came blaring over the 1MC. That ought to do it, I thought. Then I remembered that I'd been supposed to get the medical officer and the captain together.

Decision time: If I did that now, the captain would leave with the LSMR, probably in medical restraints. On the other hand, we hadn't tried the rest-and-respite treatment yet. I hated to solve this problem without even giving the Old Man a chance. I took a deep breath, then went out to the starboard bridge wing, where I could see the medical team and five of *Malloy*'s wounded in stretchers being assembled next to the sea ladder. The LSMR was nearly alongside.

"As soon as they're clear, have Doc Walker come up here. Then go to fifteen knots and start the dance."

"Aye, aye, XO. Bridge is manned and ready for GQ."

"Good. Log all this, please."

I went into CIC to take a look at the air plot. The enemy aircraft were forty miles out now, and it did look like the main blob of radar video was headed south. We had to assume, however, that a few of them would peel off to go kill the nearest picket destroyer.

"The main task force know this is coming?"

"Yes, sir, as soon as we first saw 'em. Extra CAP are being launched, and our own guys are ten miles from first intercept."

"Watch the surface search for low-fliers," I said. "Don't fixate on that big gaggle unless it turns our way."

Jimmy nodded. "Already on it," he said. He looked around briefly and then asked me, "Didn't happen, did it?"

I sighed and shook my head. "Talk later" was all I could muster.

Jimmy grunted and moved away toward his GQ station next to the dead-reckoning tracer table.

"Combat, Bridge. LSMR is away to starboard. Coming to fifteen knots."

I nodded at Jimmy, who acknowledged the message on the bitch-box. Then I went back out to the bridge. As I stepped out, the bitch-box came up with a big surprise.

"Bridge, Sonar. We have a possible sonar contact, bearing three four zero true, range fifteen hundred yards."

What?

I moved swiftly to the bitch-box. "Echo quality?" I asked.

"Sharp, slight up-Doppler, XO. Looks good."

"Bridge, Combat. Intermittent radar contact, three four three true, eighteen hundred yards."

"Low-flier?"

"No, sir, surface—it's gone now."

Periscope, I thought. *Move!*

"Left full rudder, all ahead *flank,* emergency!" I yelled, startling the helmsman and lee helmsman, but not so much that they didn't respond. The helmsman almost torqued the brass helm off its axle. The lee helmsman grabbed the two brass engine-order telegraph handles and pushed them all the way forward to flank ahead, then all the way back to full astern, and then again all the way to flank ahead in a shower of bells. The engineers down below understood that sudden flank speed command and spun the big steam admission valves. *Malloy*'s hull shook with a rumble from astern as the screws dug in and our one and one-half stacks spat out plumes of smoke.

By issuing conning orders, I had automatically assumed the conn. "Steady three four zero," I ordered. "Combat, tell Sonar to prepare for urgent depth-charge attack. Set depth two hundred fifty feet."

"Two five oh feet, Combat, aye!"

We waited for a very long sixty seconds as *Malloy* accelerated. Then the report I'd been expecting came, "Bridge, Sonar, torpedo noise spokes, two niner zero relative."

The ship was deep into a left turn, which should mean those torpedoes would miss astern. Having fired, the Jap sub would be diving hard by now and also turning away. He knew exactly what we would do next. Our sudden maneuver would save us, but the hull and propeller noise of the flank bell would make the sonar useless. We'd have to wing it.

"Slow to fifteen knots. Combat, take us in on your best EP and drop. Tell the boss what we've got."

"Drop on best estimated position, Combat, aye," Jimmy replied.

"Torpedo noise spokes are null-Doppler," Sonar reported. Then, "Torpedo noise spokes are *down* Doppler." Good news: Down-Doppler meant they were going away. Our maneuver had worked. A moment later, two lookouts reported seeing wakes passing behind us. I, along with the rest of the bridge crew, blew out a long breath. Then I remembered that LSMR. Where exactly was—

A thunderous explosion ripped the afternoon air from about a half-mile on our starboard quarter. I ran out to the starboard bridge wing in time to see the fireball that had been the LSMR, loaded to the gills as she was with five-inch rockets—and *Malloy*'s casualties—turn into a red and black ball of fire and smoke from which a few dozen shore-bombardment rockets ripple-fired in all directions. As the huge cloud expanded, there was nothing to be seen of the LSMR. We all stared in awe, shocked by the suddenness of it and the realization that we'd just lost more shipmates.

"Bridge, Combat. Rolling the pattern."

I shook myself out of my dry-mouthed trance and back to the present menace. *Malloy* ran over the best estimated position of the Jap sub and began to roll multiple depth charges off our fantail. The chances of getting the sub were minimal, but it was worth a try, if only to make the bastards go deep and stay deep now that we were hurling five-hundred-pound depth bombs into the sea. I ordered CIC and sonar control to go back into search mode. As long as there were no kamis coming, we'd work this problem instead. The familiar eruptions began astern, each one kicking the ship in the keel, even at two hundred fifty feet.

A sub, I thought. A goddamned sub. We'd all been so focused on the terror from the skies that we'd forgotten all about Jap subs. I told Combat again to get a report out that we had a Jap sub in the picket area, and that the LSMR was gone. As CIC and the sonar team worked together, the OOD followed course and speed recommendations from Combat, while the sonarmen in the back corner of CIC searched the scope for their elusive prey through all the underwater chaos created by our own depth-charge attack and sudden maneuvers.

"No echoes," Sonar reported. As expected.

I called Combat. "Expanding square search around the datum, but stay within three miles of our picket station." As much as I would have loved to kill a Jap sub, the bosses had made it clear: You're an early warning radar picket ship; remain on station. Period.

We settled into the antisubmarine search routine. I kept the ship doing an expanding square sonar search at a relatively quiet speed: going east for a thousand yards, then north for fifteen hundred yards, then west for two thousand yards, and so on. At six thousand yards from datum, we'd reverse it and collapse the square back to our picket station. On a radar screen looking out fifty miles, three miles of ship's motion were inconsequential. Plus, the search meant we were never on a straight course for more than a few minutes.

I stayed on the bridge for the first hour. If we picked the sub up on sonar, we'd drive in and conduct a second depth-charge attack. Chances were, however, that the sub, having scored a kill, would go deep and then creep the hell out of there, lie low for a while, and then try his luck against another one of the picket ships. Just to keep him interested, however, I had the fantail crew roll two or three depth charges at random points and depth settings along the search pattern.

I decided this would be a good time to talk to the captain. The guns were silent, and there was no immediate threat that we knew about, or could find. I told Jimmy Enright I was going below. He didn't ask why, and I didn't say why.

I tried for some coffee as I went through the wardroom, but the pot was empty. I stepped into the forward passageway and knocked on the skipper's door.

"XO," he said as I stepped into his cabin. "Quite a day, wasn't it. Just when you think the Jap navy can't do that, they appear. Like at Pearl."

"We lost the LSMR," I said, "and more of our people, too."

He paled at that news. I wondered if he'd been in here for the whole submarine incident or if he'd gone walkabout topside again.

"I didn't know that," he said. "I heard the depth

charges, listened to the 1JS circuit, but no, I didn't know that." He hung his head for a minute. I suspected he had just realized that he could have been aboard that LSMR. "What happened to the air raid?" he asked.

"Went to Okinawa," I said. "We haven't heard what happened yet."

"Well, besides eavesdropping on the 1JS, I went up to Combat for a while. Gave 'em the shush signal and just sat in a corner. Looked like an effective piece of teamwork to me."

"We probably scared that sub with the urgent attack, but I don't think we did any more than that. The water conditions are lousy out here for sonar."

There was a knock on the door, and then Doc Walker came in.

"XO," he said. "You sent for me, sir?"

I looked at the captain. He looked back at me and then at the doc. "We both did," he said. I gave a sigh of relief and told Doc to come in.

By sundown, there had been no more air raids or sub contacts. We'd run through the best estimated position of the LSMR and found nothing but a small diesel oil slick and a few shattered wooden pallets. No bodies, no survivors. Jap torpedoes were still the most lethal weapons in the war at sea. One full ton of high explosive, running at over fifty miles an hour. They didn't just hit a ship—they punched into her hull, *then* went off, breaking her back.

What had they been thinking down there in the AOA, I wondered, sending up a fully loaded LSMR to the picket line? Then I remembered—the LSMRs down in the amphibious objective area ran around fully loaded as a matter of ready routine. That was why they were there. When the Marines or Army ground-pounders needed precision artillery support, they called their artillery battalion. If they weren't available, they called a destroyer, which could fire with pinpoint accuracy as long as there was a spotter out there in the weeds to correct the fall of shot. When they got themselves backed into deep shit and needed a barrage covering everything in front of them, they called an LSMR. They didn't want to hear *Wait one, I need to go rearm.*

Face it, I thought: Nowhere out here was safe until all the kamis had been destroyed. The initial fleet intel reports had estimated a few hundred operational Jap planes left on Formosa and Kyushu, the southernmost home island. Someone had failed to tell the Japs. There seemed to be an endless supply of the damned things. Everyone had talked of Okinawa as the last stepping-stone before the big invasion. It was turning out to be more like a tombstone.

We set the modified GQ watches and fed the crew as full darkness fell. I got the word out that I wanted the department heads in the wardroom right after eight o'clock reports. Then I went to find the captain. He was still in his inport cabin, actually looking rested and just finishing up his evening meal.

"XO," he said, "I've just taken a handful of little blue pills the doc gave me. From what he told me, I'm going to go night-night for a while."

You're going night-night for about twenty-four hours, I thought, but I wasn't going to tell him that.

"Yes, sir," I said. "It's full dark outside, so there shouldn't be any kamikazes."

"What's our fuel?" he asked.

I didn't know. Once again, he'd come up with a question that I should have had the answer to at all times. Destroyers burned oil at a prodigious rate. It was our responsibility to tell our bosses when we got to 50 percent fuel onboard. They'd either send an oiler to us or call us down to the AOA to refuel by barge.

"I'll find out, sir," I had to admit. That was the old Naval Academy response for situations where a plebe had no idea of what the correct answer was.

"Fifty-two percent," he said with a weary smile, "but I cheated. I just called the snipe."

I sighed. "I should have known that," I said.

"You will, XO," he said. "Once I'm gone."

"You're going to rest for a day or so," I said.

"Then you're coming back topside to run this show."

He gave me a strange look. "Maybe," he said. "Maybe not. In the meantime, get some black oil lined up." He yawned, then smiled again. "That's an order, by the way."

"Aye, aye, sir," I said, bracing up like a plebe and putting a little drama into it. He smiled again, but there was also some sadness there. He knew.

"You've got to get word to Commodore Van Arnhem," he said. "CO incapacitated, XO assuming temporary command. Something like that."

"How will he react to that?" I asked.

"Dutch Van Arnhem is one of the good guys," the captain said. "Longtime tin can sailor, comes across as really stern and gruff, but he's a kind man at heart and smarter than most people realize. Might explain why he's a commodore, what?"

"Why isn't he up here with his squadron?"

"Because Spruance's staff thought he'd be more useful at KR, coordinating logistical support for his destroyers. Besides, what would he do up here that individual COs aren't already doing?"

I wouldn't mind having him here right now, I thought. The captain yawned again, and I took my leave.

I met with the department heads in the wardroom at 1945. The ship was still conducting the expanding square search, but more for the purpose of giving the Combat team something to do. The

Freddies maintained their long-range air search around the clock, but the rest of the troops in Combat didn't have much to do because we all knew the kamis didn't come at night. Not yet, anyway. Two of the big-decks down near Okinawa had some of the new, radar-equipped night-fighters on board, but so far they hadn't been launched. If the Japs surprised us with night missions, we'd surprise them back.

I briefed the department heads on the captain's status and the fact that he'd been given some sedatives. I asked Jimmy Enright if he'd seen the skipper in CIC during the antisubmarine action. He looked surprised. "No, sir. Absolutely not."

"He said he went up there."

"XO, that space is twenty by thirty-six, without all the gear and the whole GQ team. I can guarantee that he did *not* come into Combat this afternoon."

Which meant that either he thought he had gone up there, or he was trying to fool me into thinking he wasn't that far out of whack. Either way . . . I didn't have to say any of that out loud—they all understood.

"XO," Jimmy said, "it's time, especially if he's been sedated by the doc. I recommend you formally relieve him. I recommend we get a message off to the commodore, ask to go down to the anchorage at Kerama Retto for fuel, and—"

"You *recommend?*" I snapped. "If we'd put him

on the LSMR today, like you *recommended,* he'd be dead like the rest of them."

The wardroom went quiet. The four department heads began to study the green felt tablecloth in front of them. I hadn't meant to let fly like that. These four officers were my only allies. Two of them wanted me to become captain, two of them wanted to wait and see what happened, but they were all still fully supporting my efforts to grapple with the problem. It didn't help that the first two were probably right. Even the captain had told me to do that.

"I apologize for that, Jimmy," I said. "I was out of line."

"Hard to argue your point, though, XO," he said ruefully, "but I understand your frustration. So what the hell are we gonna do?"

"Mario," I said, "are we at or close to fifty percent fuel?"

"Close as dammit, XO."

"Okay," I said. "Jimmy, get a fuel request off to CTF 58. Let's secure from anti-submarine stations. It's dark as a well-digger's ass out there tonight, so I doubt we still have a sub problem. You reported both the sub contact and what happened to the LSMR?"

"Yes, sir."

"Any reaction?"

"Roger, out."

Roger, out meant message received, nothing

more, nothing less. Thank you for your interest in fleet defense. Now go away. They must have had a busy day down around Okinawa today, I thought. I was beginning to wonder if we were ever going to take that bloody island. And then Japan itself? Would this goddamned war ever end? What was wrong with these people? Had the whole war been all about just killing Americans?

"Don't request to leave station," I said. "Just send a fuel request. If they send a tanker up here, then they can refuel all the rest of the pickets, too."

"If we have to go down there, then . . . ?"

"I'll deal with that when the time comes. Right now, I need a cigarette and some fresh air. I'm going topside."

"You don't smoke, XO," Marty said, ignoring the incongruity of a cigarette and fresh air.

"Doesn't mean I couldn't use one right about now. Find the doc; tell him to find me."

Thirty minutes later I was standing next to the captain's chair on the bridge. This night was seriously dark. We'd stopped pretending to look for the Jap sub and had resumed a broad weave through the still calm waters north of Okinawa. The bedspring radar array ground away into the night, looking for Japs. The ship was semi-buttoned-up, with enough hatches open to let air get below. Despite that relaxation, we still had two of the three five-inch mounts fully manned up with sleeping gun crews, and the same for the two quad forty-millimeter mounts aft. The galley had put the word out that there would be soup and horsecock sandwiches—the crew's quaint sobriquet for bologna—available all night. The Chop knew that right now, coffee and food were his main responsibilities up here on the picket line.

I wanted to climb into the captain's chair, but naval etiquette was quite firm about that: only the captain got to sit on the bridge. Everyone else stood. That's why they were called watch *standers*. Besides, I would have been asleep in about thirty seconds. Still, it was tempting.

"XO?" The chief corpsman had materialized beside me.

"Doc," I said. "How are our wounded?"

"Hurting," he said. "The four most serious—" He stopped. There was nothing more to be said. The four most serious were communing with the fishes. I motioned that we needed to go out onto the bridge wing to talk privately.

"You saw him," I said. "What's your take?"

"Not qualified to give one, XO," he said. "I'm a hospital corpsman, not a doctor."

"Don't go all sea-lawyerish on me, Chief," I said.

He smiled in the darkness. "Okay," he said. "He's gone around the bend. You left, and we talked for a while after I gave him the injection."

"The injection? He said pills."

"See?" the chief asked. "You know his record?"

"The *Quincy* at Savo, then *Juneau.* Yeah, I know it."

"He should never have been sent to command. I've been a CPO for eight years. As the ship's doc, I work for the XO, but I *talk* to the CO. Two different animals, with two very different jobs. You trying to make a decision here, XO?"

"I surely am, Doc."

"Make it, then. I'll back you up. He's lost it. I love the guy, but he's lost it, and sunrise is only seven hours away."

"I'd hoped that twenty-four hours of oblivion might do the trick," I said.

"He's as likely to come out of that in a catatonic state as normal," the chief said. "Once the fear demon takes over, his subconscious mind will prefer the somnambulant state to full consciousness."

"You *know* this?"

"No, sir, I'm a hospital corpsman, remember? But I've seen my share of shell-shock victims. I was on Guadalcanal, and before I came to *Malloy* I did temporary duty at Saipan. I know what it looks like, and I'm pretty sure that's what I'm seeing."

"I do *not* want to do this, Chief," I said.

"It'd be no different if he'd received a head wound and was incapacitated, XO," the chief pointed out. “For that matter, he’s incapacitated right now, and, like I said, I have no idea of how or *if* he’ll come out of that. Tell you what, you make the log entry, and I’ll cosign it. If there’s a problem later, you can say that you took the best medical advice you could get at the time. Come sunrise, though, we need a captain. These fucking Japs ain’t never gonna quit.”

I nodded. The chief was right: I’d been making too much of a production over this. The Old Man was out of it, however you looked at it. We absolutely did need a functioning CO. I decided I would make the log entry, inform the commodore, and then get back to the present danger, which was, as the doc had pointed out, only hours away. If the powers that be didn’t like it they could shanghai some unsuspecting three-striper and get him up here as soon as possible. I’d welcome him with open arms.

“Okay,” I said. “Let’s go take care of business. You want to check on the skipper one last time?”

“Sure, XO,” he said. “Be right back.”

I stood next to the chart table and opened the deck log. I sat there, trying to figure out what to write down. Then I remembered Navy Regs. I had the bridge messenger go find the duty yeoman and get him to bring me the Book. It was no help. Chapter eight enumerated a lot of things about the commanding officer, but not what to do if he became incapacitated. Pacific Fleet Regulations probably did, but by now I was weary of all this vacillation. The chief corpsman came back to the bridge.

"Sound asleep," he reported.

"If we get attacked at dawn, will he be able to wake up?" I asked.

"I should think so," Doc said. "What I gave him doesn't induce a coma; it just sedates. But when the guns get going, he'll get going, too."

I thought of the skipper's earlier comment in that regard and then made a simple entry in the deck log that said I was temporarily relieving Commander C. R. R. Tallmadge, USN, of command of USS *Malloy* due to his medical incapacitation. I signed, the doc signed, and then I had each of the line department heads come to the bridge and sign as well. Then I went back to my cabin and drafted a personal-for message to Commodore Van Arnhem, our destroyer squadron commander, informing him of the situation, changing the term "medical incapacitation" to "mental incapacitation," and then had the chief radioman send it by encrypted, operational-immediate message.

That ought to get us an oiler up here, I thought, and probably the commodore, too.

SIX

The following morning dawned clear and surprisingly cool, which, unfortunately, made for really good flying weather. I did stars, and then we went to dawn GQ as usual. The doc checked on the skipper, who was still asleep. Doc suggested that we station a trusted petty officer outside his inport cabin in case we had to rouse him for his safety. I told him to get Chief Lamont to take care of that.

We held morning quarters for the first time in two weeks, at which I had the division officers read an announcement to all hands paraded in their divisional spaces that I had assumed temporary command of the ship until the captain could receive medical treatment. Marty asked me what they should call me now. I told them XO. This was a temporary situation until either the skipper came back to us or a new one came onboard. Either way, I'd remain the exec, assuming someone didn't court-martial me. So XO it was to be.

We picked up one lone bogey late in the morning, way out there at seventy miles, which meant it had to be a fairly large plane, probably a multiengine bomber of some kind. He came within fifty miles of the picket line and then loitered out there. Two other picket destroyers picked him up, too. He did not come any closer, however, and when the nearest picket sent some CAP after him, he withdrew to the northwest in the direction of Formosa and went off our screens. Once he left, I summoned the chief corpsman, and he reported that the captain was still asleep, looking unusually peaceful. I was glad we hadn't gone to GQ over the lone snooper, but I was a little worried about what might be coming next.

At noon Radio called me down to Radio Central to receive a personal-for from our squadron commander. He acknowledged my message and then indicated he would be coming north on a destroyer to embark temporarily in *Malloy* sometime today, as a function of the tactical situation.

I felt a spark of professional alarm. The commodore was the captain's boss. All of the radar picket destroyers reported to him. He had spent some time up here when the picket line was established, but a destroyer simply didn't give him and his staff enough command and control facilities to run the show. As the captain had pointed out the night before, there hadn't been much running to do: in each case where a suicider attacked a picket destroyer, the fight turned into a mano-a-mano deal. The targeted ship either got the kami or the kami got them. The commodore would have been a spectator, and since we'd lost four picket destroyers sunk outright over the past three weeks, probably a dead one. So he'd set up shop on the destroyer tender at Kerama Retto, where he could be helpful—tending to logistics, such as fuel, food, and ammo, repairs, replacement ships when needed, search and rescue assets, and medical assistance, like our recently departed LSMR. The fleet anchorage itself was subject to frequent kamikaze attacks, so he wasn't living safely behind the lines but simply staging himself and his staff where he could do the most good for the guys up in Injun Country. My personal-for message had been the exception: He simply had to come up to the line and deal with this problem personally.

We steamed around our picket station for the remainder of the afternoon. Replacement CAP showed up at 1400 from a new carrier. Our usual carrier had been hit and was headed east for repairs. I had Doc check on the CO every two hours, but he was still down and out. We got a second lurker out at fifty miles late that afternoon, followed by a third. Each time somebody sicced CAP on them, and each time they retired out of radar range. Jimmy Enright wondered how they knew CAP was coming for them. The sly bastards were planning something new, and we were all speculating on what was coming next.

What came next was a high-speed surface contact, which turned out to be a Fletcher-class destroyer called the *Cogswell.* The Fletchers had been the mainstay of the Navy's destroyer force from the beginning of the war. They were fast and agile, armed with five single-barrel five-inch mounts and ten above-deck antiship torpedo tubes. The Gearing class, of which *Malloy* was one, were longer and heavier, a bit slower but more heavily armed, trading forty-millimeter AA mounts for those ten torpedo tubes, and had much more modern command and control facilities. If you wanted to get somewhere in a hurry, though, a Fletcher class with a clean hull and four boilers on the line could do 36 knots all day.

We checked the radar screens to make damned sure there was nothing else coming, then set up an alongside transfer by personnel highline. Four bells rang out over the topside speakers, followed by "DesRon Five-Oh, arriving."

The commodore, Captain Van Arnhem, came over first, followed by his medical officer, Dr. Atkinson. I stood amidships to greet him. The commodore was built like a fullback, with piercing blue eyes, a Moses nose, and John L. Louis–sized bushy eyebrows. He'd begun the war as a lieutenant commander stuck supervising ship repairs in the Boston Navy Yard, then escaped to sea in early 1942 in one of the new antiaircraft light cruisers as chief engineer. From there he had commissioned a new Fletcher-class destroyer in 1943 and had been in the thick of it ever since. I met him on the main deck, saluted, and told him who I was.

"Wardroom," he answered as he shucked his life jacket. "Summon your chief corpsman."

As soon as the squadron medical officer was hauled aboard, the highline rig was broken down and the other destroyer cleared away to set up station two miles distant. It felt good to have five more guns in the neighborhood. This all-day quiet was beginning to spook people.

I gathered up the commodore and his doctor, and we headed for the wardroom. When we arrived, we got a surprise: The captain greeted us at the wardroom door, looking fit as a fiddle after his extended nap.

"Commodore," he said. "Welcome aboard, sir. To what do we owe the pleasure?"

The commodore grunted and gave him a phony fish-eye. No destroyer captain ever wanted to have the commodore embarked and constantly looking over his shoulder. "Pudge," he said. "You're looking suspiciously well."

The captain sat down in his seat at the head of the table. The commodore, not known for being a protocol stickler, took a seat halfway down the table. The squadron doctor and our chief corpsman, Doc Walker, went to the junior end of the table.

"Well, sir," the captain said. "Are you embarking? Tired of all the peace and quiet down off Okinawa?"

"I think it might actually be better up here on

the picket line, Pudge. The AOA and the fleet are catching hell. We're losing a ship and a half a day, statistically, and I mean losing. It's not going so well ashore, either. This island is a whole different kettle of fish, as we're all finding out."

He turned to me. "So," he said. "XO?"

I looked right at the captain. "Sir, I made a log entry last night relieving you of command due to . . . medical problems. Do you remember our discussing this matter?"

"Nope," the captain said. There was a longish moment of silence. "What specific medical problems?"

I was more than a little surprised. I also would have thought he'd have reacted with at least some signs of shock: You did *what?* But he was as normal as normal could be, and obviously much refreshed after his long sleep. I felt both relieved and alarmed. Relieved that he was "back," if that was the right term. Alarmed because it was going to look like a major misstep on my part, if not outright mutiny. I plunged ahead. "The fact that you could no longer—"

"Wait one," the commodore interrupted. "Chief Walker, you may be excused now."

"But, sir—"

"Now, if you please, Chief. Thank you."

Doc got up, looked to me for guidance, then left the wardroom, smashing his chief's hat down on his head angrily.

"Go ahead, Commander," the commodore said to me. Commander, I thought. The formal title used to address the executive officer, even if he was still a lieutenant commander. The temperature in the wardroom was cooling by the second. I did notice that the squadron doctor was watching Captain Tallmadge closely, though.

I set forth the circumstances leading to my actions, and the captain started shaking his head about halfway through my tale. "No," he muttered. "Never."

When I'd finished, the commodore turned to the captain. "Pudge," he said. "This is all, what—made up?"

"Never happened, sir. Never. I would *never*—"

At that moment, the GQ alarm sounded. No announcement of inbound bogeys, no unexpected gunfire, just that *bong-bong-bong* that produced a rush of sea boots outside in the wardroom passageway and a clanging of hatches going down. No announcement meant we'd been surprised, and I expected to hear the roar of the guns at any second. My immediate instinct was to get to the bridge, or even Combat. This fiasco in the wardroom would have to wait. I pushed back my chair but then stopped. A familiar look was coming over the captain's face.

"Commodore," he was saying, "I must get to the bridge. You'll understand, of course. I must. I can't, um, stay here."

"Yes, of course, Captain," the commodore said, remaining in his seat. "Go right ahead. This can wait."

"Yes, right, this can wait. I can't imagine, XO, what provoked you to, um, ah, I have to get to the bridge."

"Yes, sir," I said. "Right behind you, sir."

"Yes, right behind me. Of course. Yes. I, ah . . ."

He opened his mouth and then stopped talking. He started looking around, his hands gripping the edge of the table with visibly white knuckles. The ship began to accelerate, the forced-draft blowers from the forward fire room clearly audible as they spooled up. The forty-millimeter mount that was right on top of the wardroom area began to train out. Still the captain didn't move. He looked like a man tied to the railroad tracks who's just seen the approaching headlight. His face was beginning to dissolve. I felt terrible and turned my head away. I didn't want to see this.

"XO," the commodore said gently. "Take charge up on the bridge, if you please."

The doctor was getting up and coming around the table to get to the captain, who was beginning to keen in an unearthly voice, so obviously terrified that he was frozen to his chair. I practically bolted out of the wardroom and hurried topside. I went into Combat and asked them what was coming.

"Nothing that we know about, XO," Jimmy said. "Do *you* know?"

I didn't answer him. Instead I hurried out to the bridge. Everyone was scanning the skies for little black dots. Everyone except Doc Walker.

Then I figured out what had happened. Doc had come up to the bridge and, while no one was looking, had fired off the GQ alarm. Once it sounded, everyone in the whole ship went into automatic, including our terrorized skipper.

"That do it?" he asked quietly.

"Sure did, and I thank you very much. Even so, I hated to see it."

"Had to be done, XO. They get pretty good at deception, some of them. Still, I'll hate to lose him."

Then the bitch-box lit up. "Bogeys, bogeys, inbound, two five zero, range two-oh, triple-oh."

Well, son of a bitch! I jumped to the captain's chair and hit the bitch-box. "Combat, Bridge. Alert the *Cogswell.*"

"They got 'em, too, XO, and now those Jap bastards are gonna get a big surprise."

And so they did. Two Vals, Jap navy dive bombers, came in, ducking and weaving, expecting a lone radar picket, and then discovering that they faced eleven five-inch, twenty-four forties, and a dozen or more twenties. They were both flamed out of the sky in less than a minute. There was such a display of fireworks it almost looked like overkill. Almost. The sudden silence was broken by some muted cheers from the guntubs.

I told the GQ team to remain on station until darkness and then went below to find the commodore. As I expected, he was in the captain's inport cabin. The captain had been sedated again, this time by the squadron doctor. The commodore gave me the high sign, and we left the cabin and went out to what had been the forward torpedo deck, now packed with forty-millimeter mounts.

"Okay," he said, quietly. The forty-millimeter crews were still pretty jazzed up, but they were also busy picking up brass. "You made the right call. For a moment there . . ."

"He's done that before, too," I said. I described the burial-at-sea ceremony. "Commodore, he's been one of the best skippers I've ever had. Caring, knowledgeable, always one step ahead of everything I've done as XO. I did not want to bring this to a head. I—"

"You did what you had to do," he said, stopping my protests, "and you did the right thing. If it's any consolation, my doctor told me before we got here that he might present as totally normal until imminent danger arrived. Sadly he's not the first, either. So, tell me: He still do the hat trick?"

"Yes, sir, but not so very much once we got up here. Every day here is, well, scary beyond words. These bastards want to die. We don't."

"Yep, that's the crux of it. We've never faced anything like this before, certainly not on this scale. I always imagined the days when machines would act like this, you know, pilotless aircraft, aimed at a ship with no risk to anybody but the target ship. This kamikaze business is truly awful, and we're just going to have to kill them all before it's done."

I saw a chance to plug my pet theory about multiship picket stations. "Sir, today? Two tin cans were here when the Japs expected one. It was over pretty quick. Can't we make that the standard picket station configuration?"

He stared at me for a moment and then smiled. "We'd have at least *three* on each station, if we had them, Connie. We don't. And, just for the record, carriers trump tin cans. By the way, Halsey has taken over the fleet, and the first thing he did was double the AA screens around the carriers. Even so, we're *still* sending carriers back to the States so badly hurt they'll probably never come back out here. I hear you. There are simply not enough destroyers."

"How about the LantFleet ships? That's a land war now."

"This is still a *world* war," he said patiently, "and there are still U-boats out there in the Atlantic sinking merchies. The Brits killed two U-boats near Singapore last month, for Chrissakes. Now, admittedly, the Germans are almost done. Any day now, if you believe the Army. Once they quit, then yes, we'll have more destroyers. But first they have to get here—that'll take six weeks just to make the trip. Then they'll have to be trained to PacFleet procedures. They've been hunting subs and doing convoy duty almost exclusively. What's happening now at Okinawa is way beyond *anything* the LantFleet ships have ever seen."

"Well, then," I said, "can we have some fuel?"

The commodore laughed. "That we can do," he said. "I'll leave *Cogswell* here on your station, and *Malloy* can run me back to KR."

"And the captain?"

"That would be you, now, XO," he said. "I've countersigned the log. You own it, for the time being, anyway. By the way, who's your senior department head?"

"Jimmy Enright, the navigation officer. Solid."

"Well, he has to take over as acting XO. You can't be both. And one more thing—it'll be your responsibility to take care of *you.* By that I mean eating and sleeping. Take naps if you have to, but insist that when you're flat exhausted, you get some sleep time. No one else will do that for you when you're in command. Now, get me a signalman."

Once the commodore had given the good news to the *Cogswell*, we set the modified GQ condition watch and steamed southeast to Kerama Retto anchorage. Due to an anomaly in the atmosphere, our air-search radar was able to pick up the large carrier formations to the west of Okinawa at almost sixty miles distance. Sunset was approaching, so I had the ship set general quarters for the last hour of the approach to Kerama Retto. There were no air contacts other than the ever-present CAP, and that was worrisome. The kamis had been coming pretty much nonstop every day for the past month. We wondered if those Jap bombers lurking at the outer ring of the fleet's defenses presaged night attacks, with kamis being vectored under radar control from bombers who stayed out of the fight.

"What's the moon?" I asked the quartermaster.

"Waxing, three-quarters," he said promptly.

That meant good night visibility for night pilots, of both persuasions. The picket line might be a very dangerous place tonight. I hoped *Cogswell* was up to the task; as ever, dusk and dawn were prime attack windows.

We entered the anchorage and went alongside the tender USS *Dixie*, a different ship from the one we'd tied up to before. The *Piedmont* had gone around to another anchorage on the eastern side of Okinawa. We were the outboard ship in a nest of three destroyers, two of which were in pretty bad shape. With our makeshift forward stack and a few dozen twenty-millimeter "portholes" stuffed with rags and monkey shit, we fit right in. The engineers were summoned topside to hump two long black fuel hoses from the tender across the two other ships to *Malloy*'s hungry fuel risers. An ammo barge came alongside during the refueling evolution, and the gun crews spent another hour lifting pallets of five-inch and forty-millimeter projectiles up from the barge, while other teams sent cargo nets full of empty brass cartridges to the barge for return to ammo dumps stateside, where they'd be reloaded. It was almost 2000 before the logistics effort ended.

The captain had been carried off on a stretcher by hospital orderlies from the tender's sick bay, his face concealed by a carefully arranged bedsheet. The commodore had gone with him, after telling me to get *Malloy* back on station as soon as we had our supplies on board. *Cogswell* has an older and less effective radar than *Malloy*, he told me; she was to return to her patrol station outside Kerama Retto upon our arrival on station. I saluted, and he left the ship, without any bell ringing this time. Everyone was too busy moving food, oil, and ammo. All the ship's officers were out and about, acting as safety observers. The crewmen humping the heavy ammo were tired, and this was no time for someone to drop a five-inch shell.

We cast off from the destroyer nest and stood out to sea at 2200. The Chop had broken off some of the cooks from the store-handling party and told them to get some chow going, which allowed us to feed the crew before we got back on station two hours later. *Cogswell* was positively delighted to see us return and left station with all the speed the Fletcher class was capable of, disappearing over the horizon in thirty minutes flat. I envied them.

The radar picture that night remained foreboding. Once every two hours a single blip could be seen way out on the defensive perimeter. Our air-search radar could not determine height, but the Freddies figured that a contact detected out at sixty or seventy miles had to be a high-flier, and also a pretty good-sized plane. Other picket ships were reporting the same thing, a distant shadow contact. None of the pickets had CAP assigned now that it was dark, but at least one carrier down in the task force operating area had night-fighters on Alert Fifteen. We watched and we waited for something to happen.

I met with the department heads after we'd settled in on our picket station. They briefed me on the stores, ammo, and fuel loadout, and I told them I would remain in temporary command of *Malloy* until such time as a new CO was ordered in.

"That going to happen sooner or later, XO?" Jimmy asked.

"Gosh, you trying to hurt my feelings already?"

There were tired grins all around, but I understood the awkwardness of the situation. Temporary command arrangements were always unsettling. If I was "in command," then why weren't they supposed to call me Captain? The term "chain of command" implies clarity and rigidity. A temporary CO was neither fish nor fowl, not that anyone was going to challenge my orders.

"They can always send a three-striper in from one of the staffs out in the carrier task force," I said, "but that would mean yet another temporary assignment. I'm guessing they'll get a seasoned commander from one of the ships that was either lost or disposed of due to battle damage."

"I can just see it," Marty said. "Morning staff meeting on Halsey's flagship. Need a three-striper to volunteer to take command of a destroyer up on the radar picket line. Don't everyone raise your hands all at once."

"Prime duty assignment," the snipe said, continuing the farce. "Destroyer command, lots of gunnery action, tremendous potential to gain major experience in damage control, and maybe even a swim call in the bargain. Anybody?"

"And glory," Jimmy chimed in. "Don't forget glory. As in, glory to God in the highest, and a really good chance to meet Him, too."

"Okay, okay," I said. Dark as the humor was, it was actually a good sign that they could talk that way. Part of it was that we were closer in age and experience to one another than any of us had been to the captain. That's when I realized that I might be "in command," but I was not "the captain." As it should be, I thought.

"Jimmy, you're now acting XO," I said.

Jimmy stared at me. "Wow," he said. "Didn't see that coming."

"Chop, get a steward to change out the linens in the sea cabin."

"Yes, sir, and how 'bout the inport cabin?"

"Collect the captain's things, do an inventory, pack everything up for shipment back to the States. Then make it ready for whoever shows up to take over. And if you can find time, paint it. The new CO might not be a smoker."

The phone squeaked under the wardroom table.

"Yes?" I answered. It was the CIC watch officer.

"Three other pickets are reporting that they can each see a separate snooper, as if the Japs were putting one at the extreme limits of *each* of our sectors. CTF 58 has ordered the night-fighters to come up as CAP."

"Thank you, I'll be up."

I told the department heads what was being reported. "Get with your division officers and chiefs, sort out any rumors as to why the captain had to leave us, and tell them we can expect a new CO shortly. Remind them that that means a change of command, even up here on the picket line. That means materiel inspections of all four departments, an admin inspection, surveys of custodial gear that's missing, the whole nine yards."

"Between raids?" Marty asked.

"Navy Regs, guys. Read chapter eight. It doesn't say 'except during wartime.' Let's get going; hopefully the Japs aren't getting ready to initiate night attacks."

"Why not," Mario said on a sigh. "Nothing else to do around here."

SEVEN

I needed sleep. I remembered the commodore's warning about sleep deprivation and his instruction that it was my responsibility to take care of myself, physically and mentally. Especially mentally, I thought. I still thought there'd been an exhaustion component to what had befallen our skipper, if my own mental fuzziness was any indication, and I still felt bad about all this. Sure, I'd aspired to command at sea—what line officer didn't? But not this way.

I went into Combat to take a look at the air picture. The long-range snoopers were plotted out at extreme ranges, but there were no contacts other than these mystery planes. Comms were good with the picket ships on either side of our station and with the air-raid reporting center down in the carrier formation, and both of the other pickets had some amphibious craft in their area to add extra firepower. I wondered why we didn't.

I went out to the bridge wing. Coming from the red-lighted CIC I was still a bit night-blind, but there definitely was a moon. To make matters worse, there was phosphorescence in our wake, a phenomenon I hadn't seen since the Philippines campaign. Nothing like having a green arrow pointing right at you wherever you went. I was tempted to have the OOD just put the rudder over three degrees and cut a big circle in the sea. I'd been told the Japs had done just that at Midway, putting their carriers into a circle to make it impossible for torpedo-bombers to line up a shot. Unfortunately for them, the circling tactic made it easy for a dive bomber to predict where the ship would be in the time it took for the bomb to reach the target—all they had to do was look at the wake. I told the OOD I'd be in the captain's sea cabin and he shouldn't wake me unless we caught a raid.

The sea cabin was no more than a steel closet just behind the pilothouse. It had a fold-down bed, a fold-up steel sink, and a steel toilet, and measured perhaps ten by six feet, all in. There was a single porthole, now patched with tape, a sound-powered handset next to the bed, and a gyro repeater with a magnifying lens at the foot of the bed. That was it. The OOD could step through the pilothouse door and open the sea cabin door if he had to get to me quickly. With only a single bulkhead between the sea cabin and the pilothouse, I could hear everything being said out there, so if there was sudden excitement, I'd probably hear it.

It felt strange, occupying the captain's sea cabin, but it was necessary. The captain's inport cabin was too far away in terms of getting to the bridge in seconds. I wasn't comfortable with moving my living quarters from the XO's stateroom to the captain's inport cabin. It just seemed a bit presumptuous. Besides, they'd have a new CO up here within a week or so, and then I'd just have to move again.

I lay down on the bed after slipping off my sea boots. I didn't bother taking off my clothes. My life jacket and steel helmet were hanging on a hook next to the door, and it took me at least fifteen seconds to fall asleep, all the noises from the bridge watch seeping through the bulkhead notwithstanding.

What seemed like ten minutes later, the phone next to the bed squeaked. I picked it up. "XO," I said automatically.

"Morning, sir," the OOD said. "GQ in fifteen minutes."

"What for?"

"Morning GQ, sir."

"Good lord—what time is it?"

"Zero six fifteen, sir. Fresh coffee made and waiting."

I hung up the phone, looked at my watch, and confirmed the time. I couldn't remember the last time I'd had what qualified as a full night's sleep in the destroyer Navy. There was a knock on the door and the bridge messenger, a young seaman apprentice, stuck a hand in with a mug of coffee. "Two sugars, Cap'n," he announced.

"It's still XO, but thanks for the coffee, young man."

Jimmy Enright came out once GQ had been set

throughout the ship. There were no contacts, short or long range, but, as we'd learned to our sorrow, that didn't mean there was nothing out there. All hands topside were looking. I finally took up residence in the captain's chair.

"A night with no raids?" I asked Jimmy.

He handed me a yellow sheet off the Fleet Broadcast. He pointed to a news item. Halsey had taken all the carriers to Formosa and struck Jap air bases all over the island. Then they went just south of Kyushu and did more of the same. Japs had been otherwise occupied, apparently. *We* got some sleep.

"*All* the carriers?"

"All the big-decks, and the fast battleships, too. Left the escort CVs to do air support over the Okinawa battlefields and the picket line. I guess Halsey got tired of sitting still and taking all this grief from the kamis."

"That's our boy," I said, "but you know they'll be back."

"Absolutely," he said. "I almost couldn't sleep last night because of those long-range snoopers. That means something."

"I think it means radar-directed attacks at night on the fleet and the picket line, starting with the picket line. We need to talk tactics."

"First and foremost, they have to get night-fighters out early so we can take out those control planes."

"The escort CVs have night-fighters?"

"Probably not," he said. "So until Uncle Bill gets back . . ."

"We snuffies are on our own," I finished for him. "The moon will be even bigger tonight."

"Even so, XO, you can't see a black dot in the dark."

"How much star shell we carry?"

"I'll have to ask Guns. Probably a hundred, maybe a hundred fifty rounds. You thinking of blinding them?"

"Why not? The search radars can see 'em when they're high enough. When they drop down and get on the deck for their run in, they go off the scope. So, when they do that, compute an advanced dead-reckoning position and start firing star shells on that bearing. Then follow up with VT frag. It's worth a try."

"Damned straight," he said. "Lemme kick this around with Marty and the fire-control chiefs. Maybe there's other stuff we can do."

"Okay, and as acting XO, I want *you* to organize the day so that the crew gets a break and some decent chow. If Halsey kicked ass over there, they'll take a day to recover. But tonight, I think we're in for it."

"I don't understand, XO," Ops said. "The intel report said they had maybe five hundred fighters and bombers left."

"They lost their last operational big-deck carrier

late last year," I said, "but if they kept building planes anyway, it may be closer to five thousand."

After a hot shower and a shave, fresh khakis, and a real breakfast, I summoned the department heads at ten. I asked them to bring me up to speed on where we stood in regard to materiel condition—what equipment was up, what was down, ammo, fuel, people, sick list, walking wounded, unrepaired damage, everything. It took an hour and a half. We were in fairly decent shape, considering.

All the guns were fully operational. In peacetime that had never been the case in any ship I'd served in. Funny what constant suicide attacks could do for equipment readiness. We had a nearly full supply of ammo and lots more of that wonderful VT frag. Our reason for being, the long-range air-search radar, was operating in full beam for a change. Some of that was due to the atmospheric conditions, but most of it was due to the twenty-four-hour-a-day attention of the electronic technicians, who spoke softly to each vacuum tube on an hourly basis, I was sure.

We talked tactics to deal with night attacks. The star-shell gambit looked like it might work to disrupt the kamis on their final drive into the ship. A star shell is filled with a burster charge of magnesium and potassium perchlorate in a perforated steel can, suspended from a small parachute. When it ignites, it produces a blindingly white light akin to welding, especially when it assaults night-adapted eyes. They could be fired on time fuzes to burst wherever you wanted them to.

The CIC radio talkers had come up with the idea of searching the frequency bands for the Jap control circuit and then jamming that with a stronger signal of our own. I asked how they could do that. CW: continuous wave. Set up a Morse-code key on that frequency and simply hold it down. Not wanting to dampen their spirits, I didn't tell them that CW operated in the HF (high frequency) band, while air control circuits were all in the VHF (very high frequency) or even UHF (ultra high frequency) bands. I'd let them do it, anyway.

The chief bosun had suggested we tow a line of spare life rafts behind the ship, illuminated with life-jacket lights, which were small, single-cell-battery-operated white lights. The idea was to distract the kami pilot into aiming astern of us. I knew that some of this stuff would be minimally useful but decided that we'd try it all.

Late that afternoon I addressed the crew over the 1MC, introducing myself with "This is the exec speaking." I told them that the captain had suffered a nervous breakdown, and that I was in temporary command until a new CO could be assigned to the ship. I told them about Halsey's strikes on the kamikazes' bases in southern Japan and Formosa. The good news was that Halsey's strikes had probably seriously hurt the kamis. The bad news was that Halsey and the big-deck carriers, along with their precious night-fighters, were still over a day away from us. I told them about the long-range, standoff snoopers who'd been lurking beyond the normal CAP range.

"I think this means that they're going to start night attacks. A big plane, equipped with an airborne radar, will vector smaller planes—Zeros, Vals, Zekes—against the picket ships. Once our night-fighters get back into the area, we can send them after those radar controller planes. But tonight? We're going to have to fight them off on our own. We're going to try some new tactics, star shells, maneuvers they haven't seen, and, if we can find them, jamming their control circuits. In the end, it'll come down to what it always comes down to: See the bastard, fill the sky with hot steel, and pray.

"The thing that's changed is this: The Japs have figured out that as long as *we're* out here on the edge, they'll never be able to get in and surprise the important ships, the carriers, the amphibs and their support boats, and the merchies, that are going to take Okinawa away from them. Remember this, too: Okinawa is not just another island, like Iwo or Saipan. It's part of their homeland. They know we're going to win this thing. Apparently, they've all agreed to die to prevent or delay that from happening. Everyone on our side is trying to help them accomplish that. I wish I had better news, but there it is.

"The supply officer informs me there are ten cases of steaks in the reefers. I told him to break 'em all out and to set up charcoal grills on the fantail. I wish I had some beer to go with them, but Cokes will have to do."

I paused for a moment. "*Malloy* is a lucky ship. We've dodged some big bullets, and that's because you guys know what you have to do to keep us all alive. Enjoy a steak tonight. Your enemy is eating bugs and razorgrass. We *will* beat these monsters. That is all."

I hung up the 1MC microphone and went into the sea cabin. Jimmy Enright came in right behind me. "That was great, XO," he said. "Tell it to 'em straight and they'll relax and polish their guns. The rumors have been . . . interesting."

"I wish Halsey and his carriers were closer," I said, "but there it is. Maybe they raised enough hell to keep those kami air bases out of business for a few days."

"You think so?"

"No, I don't, not with those snoopers out there. I wish we could drive a destroyer out there to where the snoopers have been loitering, radio and radar silent, wait for him to show up, and then shoot his ass down."

"You know, XO, what they really oughta do is station *our* CAP ashore on the part of Okinawa we've already taken. Then they wouldn't be dependent on carriers."

"You're forgetting, Jimmy. We're small potatoes. The admirals and their staffs think carriers and battleships. We're just a voice on a radio saying, 'Hey, down there—look out, here they come.' Like the commodore said, it's hell on wheels up here for us, but most of the kamis are going against Allied forces off Okinawa. And you know what? The Army and the Marines are getting chewed up pretty bad. The Japs have had three years to fortify that island. Tunnels. Prepared positions. Underground artillery parks. They're all gonna die, but they're gonna take a whole lot of American boys with them. There are no soldiers or Marines going to get a steak tonight."

"Yeah, but they can withdraw if it gets too hot. Withdraw, regroup, attack again. Where do we go?"

"We go to general quarters, Jimmy," I said with a smile. "Call me when the steaks are ready. I'm gonna take a nap."

It had been surreal, the smell of charcoal and burning beef. The cooks had tried to form french fries out of powdered potatoes. Disaster, but the crew ate them willingly, if just to support the side, with ketchup in great demand. Dessert, however, had been a special treat. Our Negro night baker, Mooky Johns, had taken it upon himself to bake fresh Parker House–style rolls that afternoon, which he produced on big metal trays on the fantail with butter and jam. I thought there'd be a riot. I never got one. None of the officers did, but the smell of fresh-baked bread and hot butter was almost good enough. Then the sun went down. Fresh coffee was brewed at both the authorized and all the unauthorized coffee messes, and then we all settled in for the night watch and waited for the vampires.

The radio traffic among the other picket ships indicated that everyone else also thought that the Japs were probably coming tonight. There were five other picket stations active that night. Personally, I thought we all ought to get together, form a circle about ten miles wide, and invite the sonsabitches to try their luck. That wasn't going to happen, because our orders were not to lure the Japs into a thirty-gun AA trap. Our orders were to create the widest possible radar coverage fan between all the kamikaze airstrips in Japan and all those lightly armed support ships feeding the carnage on Okinawa. The cliffs around the fleet anchorage at Kerama Retto were crawling with antiaircraft gun positions, but no radars, so they, too, needed a heads-up to get ready and start looking, even more than the big carrier formations. With the main carrier fleet still six hundred miles away, both the amphibs, known in the Navy as gators, and the picket destroyers were fresh out of air support. The smaller, escort carriers were not night-capable, and thus just as vulnerable to kamikazes as we were. The problem was lack of mobility. The support ships off Okinawa were tethered to the battlefield ashore; we picket destroyers were tethered to our stations.

Atmospheric conditions were both good and bad. It was an unusually good night for radar. The air-search radars especially were working well, with little cloud interference or weird ducting effects. On the other hand, there was a bright moon, which would make it easier for the kamis to line up on us, and also easier for lurking Jap subs to get off a shot. Our only defense against subs was to keep moving in a random manner, not necessarily going fast, but constantly changing course in order to frustrate their torpedo data computers. That, and careful scrutiny of our surface search radar screen; with a calm sea, any radar contact within three miles would be cause for alarm.

At 2100 I went into CIC to get a look at the overall tactical picture. The big vertical plotting boards, normally full of bright yellow grease-pencil markings indicating our own CAP stations, were ominously empty. The radarmen who would normally be writing backward on the boards were sitting around on overturned trash cans, smoking and waiting for something to do. I sat down on the three-legged stool at the head of the

DRT that the captain would use when he was in Combat. I started reading the message board, which was a steel medical clipboard on which Radio Central had clamped yellow teletype messages of interest from the general Fleet Broadcast. Some of it was AP news articles from the States. Other messages were operational summaries about the recent raids over Formosa, the latest Western Pacific weather synopsis, or the admin pronouncements originating at Main Navy and the new Army headquarters building back in Washington called the Pentagon. I found myself looking for a message that would indicate when we'd get a new skipper, but there was nothing. Surely there was a three-striper out there in that enormous fleet who'd be jumping at the chance for a destroyer command, but then I remembered the sarcastic play-acting among the department heads the other night, so maybe not.

"Radar contact, three zero zero, range seven-oh miles, composition one or few, *not* closing."

Jimmy gave me a here-we-go look. "Snooper?" I asked.

"Seventy miles," he said. "Means he's high. Not closing means he's waiting for something or he's building his picture."

Or both, I thought. Then the raid-reporting-net talker spoke up. "Station One-Fox reporting a single contact, bearing zero zero five from him, range six-five miles, not closing."

It was the same pattern we'd seen before, lone aircraft loitering high at some distance. Probably analyzing our air-search radar beams to see where the pickets were. I wished we had the means to detect and analyze *their* radar transmissions, because, with four large, 350kw turbogenerators down in our two engine rooms, we could have jammed them.

Over the next thirty minutes three other picket stations reported similar lone contacts. The senior picket destroyer skipper, two sectors away from us, sent out a warning message to the fleet anchorage that we had a possible raid shaping up; I could just about visualize the commodore hearing that and heading up to the CIC on board the tender. He could watch, but he couldn't do anything for us. Hell, *we* couldn't do anything for us. The ship heeled gently into another turn as we wandered in aimless patterns around our station.

"Should we go to GQ?" Jimmy asked.

"Not yet," I said. "Let people get some sleep if they can. Is Marty awake?"

"He's up top, at Sky One."

"Find out what the gun status is," I said. "I'm guessing he's got the gun crews standing easy on station, but confirm that, please."

"Aye, aye, sir," he said and picked up a sound-powered phone handset.

I couldn't see rousing the entire ship just because we had snoopers taking up position out on the edge of the warning area. GQ meant shutting down the below-deck ventilation fans, dogging down all the watertight hatches, breaking out all the damage control equipment from the three repair lockers, and packing every man from every division into cramped spaces meant for much smaller watch teams.

On the other hand, why *were* those bastards lurking out there?

"Jimmy, what are the Freddies doing?"

"Not much, XO. No CAP, nothing to control."

"Do we have a radio receiver that can listen in to Jap freqs?"

"I'll ask 'em," Jimmy said. He came back a minute later. "That's affirm, XO. All you get is jabber, but the Freddies know which frequencies are usually the main Jap air control circuits."

"All right, have them start dialing through those freqs and listening in. I think those distant snoopers are controllers. Right now they're waiting for something, but if they get kamis assigned to them, the jabber ought to build up on their control freqs. Worth a try, anyway."

"Absolutely," he said. I think he was glad to have something to do.

"I'm going up to Sky One."

He nodded and went back to get the two Freddies going on their eavesdropping mission.

I then went up to Sky One, the gunnery officer's GQ station. Marty was sitting on a sound-powered telephone stowage box, cupping a cigarette in one hand and holding a cup of coffee in the other. He was twenty-eight years old and, like the rest of us, looked twice his age. His talker was asleep behind him, propped up against the barbette supporting the main battery director. From Sky One I could look forward over the tops of the forward five-inch gun mounts all the way to the bow. Astern was the number one stack, or what was left of it, then the midships guntubs that had replaced the quintuple torpedo tube mounts, the number two stack, the small, visually operated director platform, then our second AA gun clusters, twenties and forties, and finally mount fifty-three, the after five-inch mount.

The ship turned again, with the heel being more pronounced at this height above the waterline. With some of the forward stack gone, a change in the wind pushed a wave of acrid, eye-watering stack gas across the director platform. The moonlight was uncomfortably bright, but the horizon was lost in the darkness. The seas were like glass, as if they, too, were waiting for something to happen.

"Hunter's moon," Marty said, echoing my own thoughts.

"Unfortunately," I said. "The snoopers are back, but they're staying way out there. I'm trying to decide when to go to GQ."

Marty chuckled. "I think you'll find, XO, if

you take a turn about deck, that just about everyone in the crew is already on station. Only thing left to do is to lock down the hatches and watertight doors. Nobody wants to be caught below decks by a surprise suicider."

"Yeah, I figured that," I said. "I just hate to secure all the ventilation until we have to. The main holes get pretty unbearable."

"Sky One, Combat?"

Marty leaned over to his bitch-box. "Sky One, aye."

"Freddies say they're hearing a lot of jabber on a freq that was dead quiet five minutes ago."

"Okay," I said. "Get that word out on the air raid reporting net to the other pickets. Then have the OOD sound GQ."

The GQ alarm let go a few seconds later, and the familiar sounds of hatches and doors banging shut echoed throughout the ship. I went below to the bridge to get my battle gear on. Then I climbed into the captain's chair and waited for all the manned-and-ready reports to come in. It was almost 2300. Good a time as any, I thought.

I tried to review in my mind what else we could do to get ready for what I thought was coming. The ship was at general quarters. All the stations were manned and ready. Ammo to the trays, the five-inch loaded up with AA common and VT frag, with some star shells handy in the mount. The snoopers were talking to somebody, and that somebody had to be kamis, so why couldn't we see them on the radar?

Because they were coming in on the deck, flat-hatting fifty feet over the water in the darkness and following course orders from the snoopers. God, I'd love some night-fighter CAP about now. I picked up the 1MC microphone and nodded for the bosun's mate to pipe an all-hands.

"This is the exec speaking," I said. "We think the snoopers out there on the sixty-mile fence have received some kamis, and that they're directing them in toward us and the other pickets. The radars can't see 'em, which means they're on the deck, low and fast. They can't see much, either, but they're getting vectors to close with the picket stations. We're going to start circling now, to make it hard for them to line up. Forties and twenties: You see something coming, open fire immediately. We won't have much warning, and the five-inch may not get to play, so—you guys know what to do. Remember what Father Halsey said: Kill Japs, kill Japs, kill more Japs. That's all."

I put the microphone back in its holder and told the OOD to increase speed to 15 knots, put the rudder over five degrees left, and leave it there until otherwise directed. UNODIR, I thought, with a mental grin.

Something caught my eye, way out on the horizon. It was a white light, intense and growing, which then turned yellow and finally red. It was *way* out there, to the east of us, lighting up the underside of a thin cloud deck we hadn't been able to see before. A minute later, as the red light began to fade, we heard a distant rumbling sound.

"Combat, Bridge. Who's east of us?"

"Station Niner-George," Jimmy replied. "The *Murray.* She's zero niner five, twenty, um . . ."

"We just saw a pretty big explosion out there," I said.

"Lost video on Niner-George," he reported in a tight voice.

Twenty miles was at the very end of our surface-search radar's range, even on a good radar night like tonight. Still.

"Officer of the Deck, twenty knots, please. Ease your rudder to left three degrees."

"All engines ahead *full,* make turns for twenty knots. Ease your rudder to left *three* degrees."

The helm and lee helmsman answered up and executed the orders. I was thinking furiously. I'm the Captain. What should I be doing, right *now?* I hit the bitch-box.

"Combat, Bridge. What's the bearing to the snooper in our sector?"

"Three three five, range fifty-five miles."

I punched the button for Sky One. "Sky One, Bridge. Open barrage fire on bearing three three five. Use Able-Able common into a range notch at ten thousand yards until you get a lock-on, then shift to VT frag."

"Sky One, aye," Marty replied. To his credit, all three five-inch opened within thirty seconds, firing deliberately, punching out a stream of projectiles timed to burst not quite five miles from the ship in the direction of what *might* be approaching at 300 knots. Fifteen seconds later, a yellow fireball erupted out on that bearing, momentarily illuminating a terrifying sight: Three surviving Vals, single-engine carrier dive bombers, wingtip to wingtip, on the deck, so low that their props were kicking up roostertails, were clearly visible, coming straight for us. The forties and the twenties got into it one second later, pumping out such a stream of tracers that we almost couldn't see the Vals anymore. The ship's constant left turn was going to mask our own guns' fire, so I yelled for the helmsman to shift his rudder to right-ten. The five-inch continued to fire, probably in local control now, and then I saw VT frag bursts erupting among the incoming kamis, followed by a second fireball, then a third.

The fourth kami, however, was devoted to a stronger god, because he hit mount fifty-one broadside. Going almost 300 miles an hour, he knocked the entire mount right off its roller path and over the side in a flaming ball of erupting aviation gasoline, shattered steel, and body parts. An instant later, the ship shook as the Val's belly bomb went off underwater, creating a bright green bolus of fire in the sea and smacking the hull hard enough to set off the gyro alarms on the bridge.

The guns fell silent. We were still turning. There were two patches of burning gasoline drifting astern. I closed my mouth and took a deep breath. Great *God!*

We were alive. Four Vals had come in low, really low, right down on the deck, but under precise radar control from the snooper. We'd killed three, thanks be to God, but number four had hurt us, and hurt us bad. There was nothing left of mount fifty-one and its ten-man crew except a stark, circular black hole in the forecastle deck, framed by its glistening roller path. The hiss of a ruptured gas-ejection air line made a bright sound in the darkness. There was no wreckage on the forecastle. One moment, a gun mount blasting away at an approaching suicider; the next moment, a clean deck.

The crew of mount fifty-two, just behind fifty-one and slightly above, were leaning out of their hatches, dumbstruck.

We all were. A two-gun, five-inch thirty-eight caliber gun mount had been knocked clean over the side in the blink of an eye.

We were still turning, but to no purpose. I told the OOD to resume the random weave while I tried to gather my wits. The bitch-box spoke.

"Bridge, Combat. What happened?"

Good question, I thought. Then Sky One joined the conversation.

"What happened was that the XO told us to start firing blind down the bearing to the snooper, and that killed three out of four kamis," Marty said. "But mount fifty-one is . . . gone."

It was time for someone to take charge. That would be me, I realized.

I ordered the OOD to slow to 12 knots and maintain the random weave. I told Marty to evaluate any damage to the forward ammunition handling systems. Then I asked Combat for a range and bearing to the snooper patrolling our sector.

"He's still out there, forty-eight miles now, bearing three three five," Combat replied.

I considered our options. There was nothing to be done for the crew of mount fifty-one. They, and their shattered gun mount, were already spiraling down to the bottom of the sea, some nine thousand feet below us. If that snooper loitering out there was a long-range bomber, he could stay there for several hours, just waiting for new kamikazes to report in. Forty-eight miles at 27 knots, we could be underneath him in an hour and a half.

"Combat, Bridge. Bring all the radars down to standby. I intend to go kill that snooper. Give me a course at twenty-seven knots to intercept the center of his orbit, and when we get to within four miles of that EP, light everything back off, lock him up, and shoot his ass down. Sky One, you copy?"

"Sky One, aye."

“Combat, aye, recommend three three zero.”

I told the OOD to follow Combat’s recommendations, and off we went. We were leaving station, and I hadn’t asked permission—but as long as that snooper was out there, he could feed the next wave of kamis and the one after that into our station until we were all dead. The fleet anchorage had been alerted that the Japs were out tonight, but I didn’t think they were really interested in Okinawa. Tonight they wanted the pickets; hence the four-plane formation vectored against us, and probably each of the other stations, as evidenced by that flare of fiery death to the east of us. With a director orbiting outside our range at twenty thousand feet, the kamis could all come in right down on the deck, under our radar envelope, and we’d never see them until they hit us.

Our mission was to provide radar early warning of an incoming kamikaze attack. For that, we were required to remain on station. However, nothing in our orders said we had to stay here until we died, and with the Japs’ new tactic, slavishly staying here on our lone station was tantamount to a suicide mission of our own.

The hell with that.

The gun boss appeared on the bridge. He looked a bit shell-shocked. “Gone,” he said. “Just goddamned gone. The handling rooms, the magazine crews, everybody below decks is okay. All we need now is a new gun mount. Where we going?”

I explained what I had in mind.

"Hell, I can hit him at *twelve* thousand yards," he said. "VT frag, once we lock him up, and he's meat."

"We're going out dark and quiet," I said. "No radar until we think we're pretty close. He'll run like hell once he detects our air search."

"Won't matter," Guns said. "Get me within four miles of that bastard, and we'll take him down." Then he changed the subject. "We never got to try the star shells," he said.

"No time," I replied. "Keep them up in the mounts, though. You'll get your chance. Now, if we go back down to the tender, and they can hoist a gun mount off another, more heavily damaged ship, can we remount one?"

"Hell, yes, XO," Marty said.

"How about battery alignment? Roller-path compensation?"

Marty had forgotten that I'd been doing five-inch guns for years. "Um, I have no idea how we'd do that, XO, but we can and we will." Then his face sagged. "Great God, the whole gun mount crew—wiped off the ship like so many flies."

"Look at it this way, Marty," I said. "If we hadn't been turning, that bastard would have hit us in the forward fireroom. With his bomb. We wouldn't be having this discussion right now."

"What was that big explosion to the east of us?"

I didn't answer him. He closed his eyes. "Okay," he sighed. "You're right, XO. Let's go kill this guy."

And so we did. After a ninety-minute transit, we lit off the air-search radar and found our snooper well within range. Combat passed a fire-control designation to director fifty-one, and the remaining five-inch mounts blasted into action about five seconds later. Fifteen seconds after that we were rewarded by a flaming arc of aviation gasoline streaming out of the night clouds and down into the sea.

"Back to station," I told the OOD. "We're done here."

EIGHT

The next morning our squad dog acknowledged our damage report, and we were ordered to depart station and proceed down to the tender *Dixie* at Kerama Retto. The big-deck carrier formations were almost back in the area, so we had CAP during the transit. We'd learned that *Murray* had been hit by three Vals in waterline strikes almost simultaneously. She'd rolled over and sunk a minute later with the loss of all but thirteen souls. One other picket had been badly damaged by a similar night-strike and was being towed to Kerama Retto. Two other pickets had been attacked but had managed to fight off the suiciders with little damage. There were no air contacts as we started down, so I retired to the captain's inport cabin and began to write the letters to the families of the men lost when mount fifty-one was blown over the side. We'd searched the area of our picket station at dawn, while still at sunrise GQ, in the scant hope that someone might have made it out of the sinking gun mount, but found absolutely nothing. We'd now lost enough people that the empty seats on the messdecks were becoming alarmingly noticeable.

I ground out the letters over a two-hour period as we wove our way south and east. There was a basic format, and then, with the help of the men's division chiefs, I interjected personal details wherever I could so that the families wouldn't think we'd mimeographed their letter of condolence. In each case, I was careful to use language suggesting that their loved one had been killed instantly and suffered a minimum of mortal anguish. The truth was, of course, quite different. That plane had hit the mount broadside with enough energy to lift it from its roller path and smash it sideways right over the side in the blink of an eye. The mount would have been buttoned up for GQ, which meant there was no way out for any of them. Some of the men would have been killed outright at the moment of impact. Some of them, however, would have discovered that they had no chance whatsoever only when the remains of the gun mount passed through the first few hundred feet of depth on the way to the dark oblivion of the Pacific Ocean bottom and imploded.

If this keeps up, I told myself, we all might soon join them. It would come down to how many kamikaze pilots and planes the Japs had left, and apparently that number was a lot bigger than all the king's intel officers had known. For the first time in my naval career, I experienced the helplessness that any individual feels in the face of the sheer, overwhelming power of war at sea in the face of strong odds. The radar picket destroyers needed some protection, but Halsey wasn't going to bring the picket line back into the protection of the fleet formation. We had become the equivalent of a seaborne tripwire.

I felt like one of those tethered goats the Indian Raj princes used to put out in the jungle so that their royal hunting guests could get an easier shot at a tiger. I didn't much like that analogy and wondered if other people in the ship were having similar feelings. Everyone supposedly loved Bull Halsey's bombast toward the Japs, but not for the first time I thought of inviting him to come up to the Okinawa picket line for a little overnight campout.

The phone squeaked. "KR in sight; we've been signaled to go alongside the *Dixie.*"

"I'll be right up," I said.

We moored alongside another badly battered destroyer, the *Billingham*, which had been smashed from one end to the other during an attack on the carrier formation just before they left for that two-day strike mission up north. No part of her waterline was visible, and her main deck was only about three feet from the water. We could actually smell her as we nosed in alongside, a horrible reek that combined burned flesh, leaking fuel oil, spent high explosives, and saltwater-soaked debris. Our guys stared with horror at the sight of her. Chief Dougherty suddenly ordered five of our people to jump our mooring lines over to

Billingham's deck, because those zombies standing there didn't seem to know what to do with the heaving lines we'd thrown over.

From my perch on the bridge wing I looked up to the bridge of the tender and saw the commodore. I saluted him, and he saluted back, shook his head, and stepped back into the tender's pilothouse. I could just imagine what he was thinking: Left the XO in charge and look what happened. Wait till he found out about our leaving station to kill the controller aircraft, I thought. Oh, well, what was the worst he could do: Send me back to the picket line?

Once we got tied up to *Billingham* I went below to change into clean khakis for my arrival call on the commodore. I had the casualty lists from last night and a summary of our battle damage, which, beyond the loss of a third of our main battery, wasn't all that bad. I'd told the snipes to scrounge some fuel, and Marty to see if there was some more VT frag to be had, one way or another.

"They gonna send us back like this?" Marty had asked.

"Absolutely," I told him. "The radar works, and we can move. Unlike this wreck we're tied up to."

I'd known the exec in *Billingham* and wondered if he was still alive. Her bridge and CIC area were mangled and burned beyond recognition. A small crowd of *Dixie*'s repair department engineers was gathered amidships around five massive, gasoline-engine-driven water pumps. Oily black seawater was pulsing over the side from five hoses that snaked up out of the flooded main machinery spaces below.

The commodore met me at the gangway, which was unusual. We exchanged salutes again, and then he offered his hand.

"You survived a very bad night, Connie," he said. "Well done. We've lost *Murray*, along with two ships that were with Halsey up north. That doesn't include *Billingham* here, and she's probably going to be a strike. I want to know what you did and how you did it."

Careful what you ask for, Commodore, I thought. We walked forward along the port side of the tender toward the series of ladders that led up to the staff offices. I was just about to step up onto the first ladder rung when what sounded like a gunshot cracked the morning air. I spun around just in time to see a second manila mooring line, made up between *Billingham* and the tender, tighten up like an overstrung guitar string and then part with a punishing noise, its bitter end slashing back against the side of the tender hard enough to make a dent. Then a third, and a fourth. Men everywhere on the weather decks of the tender and down on *Billingham*'s main deck were taking cover as line after line parted, the ruptured ends whipping back, tearing down stanchions and lifelines, bowling over at least two deckhands, and even thrashing the ship's motor-whaleboat. Oil- and water-soaked figures began to swarm topside from below decks, pursued by a boiling foam of fuel oil, seawater, and other debris erupting from *Billingham*'s wrecked main machinery spaces.

Then I figured it out: *Billingham* was sinking, and then I remembered that *Malloy* was moored to *Billingham.*

Our Chief Dougherty figured it out just about the same time as I did. I saw him grab a fire ax off the forward superstructure bulkhead and begin whaling on the nearest mooring line. Several other of *Malloy*'s deckhands followed suit, chopping frantically at the brown manila lines with fire axes and even their personal bosun knives when the lines tightened up and began to pull *Malloy* over into a starboard list as *Billingham* began to settle.

The commodore swore, but there wasn't a single thing either of us could do but watch. *Malloy*'s mast began to lean in at an alarming angle as *Billingham*, like some decorous and much-abused old lady who'd lost control of her plumbing, simply went down alongside the tender. Our people got the last of our mooring lines cut away just as *Billingham*'s decks came awash. *Malloy* righted herself with a jerk and then, with no mooring lines, began to drift away from *Billingham* and the destroyer tender. The gangway between the tender and *Billingham* rolled off the camels and into the water, and then, with a great whooshing sound from the remains of her stacks and all those gaping holes in her main deck, great sprays of dirty seawater geysered up into the morning air as *Billingham* sank out of sight alongside the tender into two hundred fifty feet of water.

Just like that, she was gone.

I looked across to *Malloy*, which was definitely drifting astern now. Our main engines had been secured when we moored, but the boilers were still producing steam for the electrical generators, so I knew she'd be able to get back alongside. Someone on *Malloy*'s bridge ordered the bosun to let go the starboard anchor, which he did with a single sledgehammer blow to its pelican hook. The six-hundred-foot chain ran out in a great cloud of rusty dust and then jerked to a stop when the anchor hit bottom. *Malloy* continued to drift astern as the anchor chain rose again and then stopped with a visible jerk. At that depth, almost the whole chain had roused out of the chain locker.

One deck below where we were standing, people from the tender were throwing life jackets and life rings down into the water for the few, too few, men paddling around where *Billingham* had been a minute earlier. Then fuel oil began to erupt like the mudpots at Yellowstone, burping gouts of black oil into the survivors' faces and eyes even as they struggled to grab onto life rings and kapok jackets bobbing nearby. Within seconds, most of the men in the water were blinded by the oil, unable to see the life jackets three feet away from them. Some men from the tender went over the side and dropped the twenty feet into the water to help the struggling survivors. It was awful.

Well done, I thought, until I remembered *Billingham*'s depth charges. Great God, I thought. In all the shock and confusion following the battle damage, had anyone remembered to safe their depth charges?

No, they had not. The tender rocked as the first of the depth charges went off, practically alongside but, fortunately, at depth. Still, they produced the all too familiar mountainous eruptions right alongside, blowing seawater, fuel oil, and the ragged remains of *Billingham*'s survivors and their rescuers into the air again and again until all twenty of her depth charges had gone off and there wasn't a single survivor down there in the sea. The water between the tender and *Malloy* glimmered with a thousand dead fish and, tragically, many other things too horrible to mention.

Then it got really quiet. I felt literally sick to my stomach. I looked over at the commodore, whose mouth was open and whose face was ashen. I didn't know what to say or do. Neither did he.

They were all dead. Everyone who'd survived

Billingham's bloody thrashing up on her picket station was now either entombed in her carcass or bobbing around down there alongside the tender, pulverized by her own depth charges and so coated in fuel oil as to be indistinguishable from the other bits of buoyant wreckage still popping up onto the surface. Then the tender's GQ alarm sounded, followed by that all too familiar warning: Many bogeys, *in*bound, man all gunnery stations.

"I need to get to my ship," I said to the commodore.

"And do what?" he asked. His expression was unfathomable.

I grunted at him. He had a good point.

"We've got more guns than the tender," I said. "Or we did, anyway."

"Go to it, young man," he said. "I'm going to lay up to my cabin and cry."

I took off down the port side of the tender's main deck, looking for a way to get over to *Malloy*. There wasn't one, and, besides, there was no time left. I heard the thump of distant five-inch guns from other ships in the anchorage, followed by the screaming of airplane engines being over-driven to certain mechanical destruction in their power dives, followed by the blasts of even more five-inch, everywhere throughout the anchorage. They were joined by massed anti-aircraft guns up on the surrounding hills. Smoke generators on the beach lit off, blowing huge, billowing clouds of white smoke to obscure the ships in the anchorage.

I stopped running. There was nothing I could do but watch. The kamikazes fell out of the sky like so many demons, dropping straight down like the German Stukas had done in those newsreels from back in 1939 over Warsaw, engines howling as they hit their red lines and beyond, five-inch flak bursting all around them, sometimes near them, then *in* them, through them, converting the kiting planes into bright fireballs, and then a sudden slash of green water, followed by a dirty explosion as their underslung bombs went off.

Malloy, anchored, was spouting flame from one end to the other, five-inch, forties, twenties, and probably even some potatoes. The rate of fire was so heavy that the ship literally disappeared from view.

I felt the tender take a hit, forward somewhere, lurching heavily, not like a destroyer but with a soggy response to the nasty insult of a five-thousand-pound kami crashing into a seventeen-thousand-ton ship.

I sat down on a set of bitts, my face in my hands. The world had gone berserk. I was beyond being scared. I was just . . . there. The sound and the fury all around me, guns blasting, planes crashing, the sea erupting on every side, *things* flying through the air all around me, spattering the decks and whining through the air like hot steel hornets, and I just sat there.

It was quite a show, I'm sure, but I think I missed it. And then it was over.

I dimly heard the tender's 1MC summoning damage control parties to the forecastle, and then the dismaying urgent calls for medics. I looked over at *Malloy*, still anchored right where I'd last seen her. She'd stopped shooting. I could see Marty up on Sky One, talking frantically into his sound-powered phones. There were people out on deck, calmly policing brass. I waved at them. They did not see me.

I'm going mad, I thought.

Just like the captain?

Oh, shit, I thought.

No. No. No. It was just an air raid, and apparently it's over. My ship would gather herself, light off her main engines, and come back alongside as if nothing had happened. If she was still there, well, then, nothing *had* happened.

Me? I still owed the commodore my arrival call.

As the tender's GQ repair parties swept past me, headed for the forecastle to deal with whatever had happened up there, I stood up, pulled myself together, and went to find the commodore. I hoped he had some coffee, or maybe even some whisky.

Captain Tallmadge had admired the commodore.

He'd told me that Captain Van Arnhem was married to a Southern lady who had inherited a large plantation in central Georgia. They'd met at a midshipmen's ball in Savannah, fallen in love, and married as soon as he had met the statutory two-year wait following graduation, during which new ensigns were forbidden by law to take a wife. They apparently had an arrangement: She would live on the plantation while he pursued his naval career. She would raise their two daughters there, and he was free to come home as often as he could. She would travel occasionally to see him, but she'd made it clear from the outset that her primary duty was to the preservation of their thousand-acre farm. I remembered thinking at the time that this was an odd setup for a marriage, but Captain Tallmadge had informed me that it was not that uncommon, especially once the Depression set in with a vengeance. Naval officers were hanging on to their jobs by their teeth, enduring pay cuts just to stay on active duty, dodging "hump" boards, where the Navy convened committees to decide who had to go so that the Navy stayed within dwindling force-level limits, and generally keeping their heads down. The farm must have been a pleasant refuge from all of that whenever the Van Arnhems could manage time together there. I knew from personal experience in four wardrooms that married middle-grade officers in the Navy had a tough time. Van Arnhem seemed to have found a practical way of handling it. I was looking forward to getting to know him better.

"You left station?" the commodore asked.

"I did," I said. "I wasn't just going to sit there and wait for that bastard to collect a new set of kamis and send them at us. Think of it this way, Commodore: The kamis are coming out of Kyushu in southern Japan and Formosa. That's a long trip, especially at night. They get there, with just enough gas to do their one-way mission, expecting to check in with a controller. He's not there. Now what? Turn south in the darkness and hope to find something? More likely they ran out of fuel and died in the ocean. Besides, there was no fleet formation to warn. Just us targets. We went balls-to-the-wall for ninety minutes, lit off the radar, found that bastard, killed him, then hustled back to station."

He gave me a long, authoritative look, which then wilted. "Right," he said. "This will stay between us Injuns. But explain something: Why didn't he see you coming?"

"I don't think they have an active radar," I said. "I think they've been homing in on *our* air-search radar beams. They just listen, do a direction-find on our emissions, and establish a bearing. They don't need a range—they know we're forty, fifty miles above Okinawa. So they tell the kamis to fly that bearing and look out the window. We turned all our electronics off and then ran up the last known bearing of the controller aircraft. When we lit off again, there he was, fat, dumb, and happy until we killed his ass. After that, no more problems in our sector."

"How'd you get the first three?"

"We assumed they were coming directly from the controller aircraft, so I had the five-inch open a hit-the-notch barrage fire on that bearing, pretty close to the surface. Had no idea there would be four aircraft, but they flew right into it. All but one."

The commodore looked at me. "Pretty damn good," he said. "You've been around guns, haven't you?"

"Yes, sir," I said. I gave him a quick synopsis of my naval career. "And now I need a five-inch mount."

"Fresh out of those," he said. "Had one, actually, but it just sank. Besides, there's no way we could do an installation and a battery alignment out here, swinging on the hook. But I think we can get you a quad forty. They're self-contained mounts and all they need is 440 volts. Better than nothing."

I nodded. One could never have too many quad forties. "We are going back, then?"

"Yes, of course," he said. "We're down to three

radar pickets, not including *Malloy.* I think last night convinced even the fleet staff that they need to beef up the CAP protection, especially with this radar-controlled tactic."

"How's it going ashore?"

"Backward," he said matter-of-factly. "Three days ago the casualties outnumbered the total number of reserves on the island. That's not sustainable."

"We have to win it, eventually. Their forces aren't getting any bigger."

He sat back and lit up a cigarette. "We *will* take Okinawa," he said. "Like you said, we can resupply, they can only hunker down and die. If it were me, I'd stabilize the front lines and starve them out."

"So why aren't we doing that?"

"There's a timetable for the invasion of the main islands. We need the Okinawa airfields so that fighters can go all the way with the bombers coming out of other bases. They're already flying some missions from the northern part of the island, but we need the whole thing."

I thought about that. "If Okinawa is this hard, what's Japan itself going to be like?"

"This, times ten," he said. "God, it's been a lousy day. I need a drink. Fancy a whisky?"

I very much did. He broke out a bottle from his desk safe and poured a generous measure. We then went through some of the admin details of getting replacements for my losses and the tender's plan for craning over a quad-forty mount the next day.

Finally I mustered up the courage to ask him about the captain.

He sighed. "Pudge is on the way back to the States, and that's going to take a while. My doctor saw him before he went ashore, to be lifted back to Guam."

"And?"

"Gone," he said. "No one home. Sits there with a bemused expression on his face, but there's no one home. Doc says he might come out of it, maybe when he's back with his wife and family, stateside. But . . ."

Now I wanted another drink. Hell, I wanted the whole bottle.

"Someone coming in to replace him?" I asked.

"Ready to be relieved, XO?"

"God, yes, sir."

"Sorry to disappoint you, young man. In fact—" He got up and went to his desk. He picked up a piece of paper and a small black cardboard box. He stood in front of me and gestured for me to stand.

"I have here your promotion to full commander, date of rank from the day you assumed command of *Malloy*, signed by Bull Halsey himself. Take those collar devices off."

In a bit of a daze, I reached up and unpinned

the gold-colored lieutenant-commander oak leaves from my shirt collar points. He pinned on the silver oak leaves of a full commander. He shook my hand and then went into the bedroom area of his cabin, returning with an officer's cap with scrambled eggs.

"This is my spare," he said. "You can replace it when, and if, we both survive this ungodly mess. In the meantime, you are now the commanding officer of USS *Malloy.* In other words, there's no one coming to replace Pudge."

"Couldn't find any volunteers?" I asked with as straight a face as I could.

He glared and then laughed. We both laughed. It was all we could do. I told him about the little parody around the wardroom table.

"Will I get an exec?" I asked.

"We'll try," he said. Then we both felt a bump as something came alongside the tender with perhaps a little more force than necessary. *Malloy* was back alongside.

"That would be Marty Randolph," I said. "He will never make a ship handler."

"Then go train him some more," he said. "Captain."

I blew out a long breath. Captain.

"And for God's sake, stay alive, please. I'm supposed to be a destroyer squadron commodore, but at this rate, I'm down to a division minus."

"We have a unit commander's cabin in

Malloy," I said. "This Injun right here wouldn't mind a little adult supervision."

"And I'd be honored to come aboard, Connie, but Halsey has other ideas. The theory is that I can do more good down here than I can do floating around up there. Okinawa isn't just an Army-Marine versus dug-in Japs slog anymore. It's mostly about logistics: fuel, bullets, bombs, and beans. The Japs are down to what they had stashed in their tunnels when we got here. We, on the other hand, can keep bringing more stuff to the fight. That's probably not evident to the soldier in his foxhole, but it's certainly evident to Imperial Army HQ back in Tokyo. Beans, bullets, and replacements are what's going to win this thing. That tells me that the kamikaze war is going to intensify."

"Someone needs to tell the Army to win it soon," I said. "We're fresh out of foxholes up there on the picket line."

NINE

The crew of a destroyer is a perceptive bunch. The moment the quarterdeck OOD, Ensign McCarthy, spied my brass hat and those silver oak leaves, he said something to the petty officer of the watch. A few seconds later, there were four bells and the words "*Malloy*, arriving" echoing over the ship's topside speakers. That single announcement changed everything, as I knew it would. I was no longer XO. I was *Malloy.*

I sent for Jimmy Enright and told him to assemble all officers in the wardroom, where I briefed them on what had happened.

"Look," I said, "this is kind of unusual. The aviators fleet their execs up to command in their squadrons all the time. If you're an aviator, being selected for XO means you're going to become the CO. The destroyer force rarely does this, but these are unusual times." I stopped, tried some coffee. I was a full commander after only ten years in the Navy. Somebody either thought very highly of me or realized that I probably wouldn't survive to present a problem later, when regular promotion cycles returned.

"The battle for Okinawa is going . . . badly. That's the only word for it. Our guys are having to dig them out of their rat holes Jap by Jap, cave by cave. Our guys want to stay alive. Their guys *want* to die with honor for some so-called emperor who started all this shit. Our guys have resorted to using flamethrowers instead of rifles. It's that bad."

"Sounds like the picket line," Jimmy Enright said.

"Yes, it does," I said. "Last night, well, I guess we were lucky, if you can call it that. Four Vals coming in under radar control. Not one—four. We got three of them, but if we hadn't gone after that controller aircraft, I'm not sure we'd be here today."

"That was your idea, XO," Marty said. "Sorry, sir. Captain."

I think that was when it really hit me. I wasn't XO anymore. I really was the owner.

"There are supposedly eight picket stations," I said. "Last night we had six ships. Now we have only four tin cans left to fill them. You all saw what happened to *Billingham* today."

I looked out at the ring of extremely sober faces around the wardroom table.

"That was heartbreaking," I said. "There's no other word for it. But we'll win this battle, if 'win' is the right word. We will take Okinawa, and all those Japs out there are going to be annihilated. On the grand scale, it's simple math: We can keep bringing more troops, more ammo, more ships, more supplies in every day. The Japs are making do with what they had when we showed up. *Nothing's* getting through to them. No food, medicines, ammo, people. Nothing. They're all going to die, and they're apparently ready to do that. We will prevail, but the cost has every level of command wondering how *we* can keep this up, and we haven't even begun the invasion of Japan itself."

I stopped to let them think about that.

"Most of you have known me as XO. That's a special position in a warship, the guy with all the authority of the captain, but lacking that final degree of ownership, of *ultimate* authority. You're going to have to make that jump. I'm the captain now. Jimmy Enright is the XO."

I paused to think about what I'd just said. "*I'm* going to have to make that same jump. *I'm* the captain now, not the XO. I didn't ask for this. I kept waiting for them to send in a new skipper. They didn't. They made me skipper, so now I'm going to act differently. I'm going to distance myself from the day-to-day camaraderie in the wardroom. Jimmy is taking over as XO." I paused for another moment. This was harder than I'd expected.

"This will sound a bit conceited, but I have to say it. You could kid around with the XO. You don't kid around with the CO unless he starts it. There's a reason for that: When extremis arises, there has to be one officer whose orders are executed without question. If he happens to be your buddy, then you might question what he says. If he's the captain, you do what he says. That's why officers eat separately in the wardroom, and why we don't call the enlisted men by their first names. Truth is, this separation, however artificial, makes things easier once the serious trouble starts.

"That said, the truth is we're all in this lovely little fire pit together. At some point, the Japs over there on Okinawa are going to give up, do their ritual suicides, and maybe some of them might even surrender. Once the home islands cease to hear from the defenders of Okinawa, they're gonna know it's over. Here. That's when I think the kamis will stop coming here, if only because they'll be saving them up for the really big show.

"Our objective is to stay alive until that moment when they write off Okinawa, as they've had to write off Iwo, Saipan, Guam, Tarawa, Truk, Guadalcanal . . . After that, we'll see.

"The other night we opened a blind barrage on the bearing of where that controller aircraft was and killed three out of four kamis who were coming specifically for us. We need to do more of that kind of thing, and we need, *I* need, everybody thinking about tactics. What can we do to screw them up? We all feel we're in a desperate position up there on the picket line because we're effectively tethered, but I think the Japs, for all their *banzai* bullshit, are feeling the same thing. They *know* it's almost over. They know goddamned Halsey actually is going to ride the emperor's white horse down the main drag in Tokyo. They know they're finished, in China, Southeast Asia, everywhere. Their fleet is gone. Our bombers have begun burning their cities to cinders. They *know.* They *have* to know. Which means we are dealing with a cornered animal. A *fierce* cornered animal, which means they are at their most lethal, and if we know anything about the Japanese, lethal is absolutely their stock-in-trade.

"So you guys have to help me to help you to stay alive. We can't retreat or otherwise run away, so we have to outthink them. We have to outwit them. We need to stay up late and get up early, every day, until this business is over. Any questions?"

"Still two sugars?" Jimmy Enright asked.

"Absolutely," I said with a grin, "XO."

He tried to grin back but didn't quite pull it off. I made a mental note to formally split out his responsibilities as navigation officer with the next-senior guy in his department, Lanny King, the CIC officer. How? Hell, I'd tell the XO to make it happen, that's how.

Our new quad-forty gun mount was a hand-me-down from the USS *Pawley*, a tin can that'd been running with the carriers until a kami missed one of the flattops and careened lengthwise down *Pawley*'s port side, cleaning house in a spectacular fashion. Her hull was intact, as was her main plant, so she was bound for one of the larger anchorages in the rear just as soon as the tender's shipfitters could build her a temporary bridge and pilothouse. We were going to scavenge her starboard-quarter quad forty, one of the few guns left intact along her superstructure. The tender's welding gang cut the mount off the 01 level aft on *Pawley*, and then one of the tender's large cranes lifted the entire mount up and over the back of the tender and down onto our forecastle, where the same welding team fastened it to our main deck in a fiery display of sparks right over the roller path of the late departed mount fifty-one.

We were going to be one funny-looking destroyer, I thought as I watched the welders burning steel. Still, a quad forty was better than nothing. Its rounds were one-third the size of the five-inch, but there were four barrels, it had a higher rate of fire, and that mount could flat create a cloud of metal fragments close in, which was where the kamis finally had to quit jinking and turning and settle into that final, lethal glide path. I was glad to get it. We could store forty-millimeter ammo down in fifty-one's magazine spaces, but we'd have to figure a way to get it up to the actual gun crew. All the ammo-handling machinery for mount fifty-one had been extracted from the handling rooms like the root of an excised tooth when the mount went over the side. I was thinking about that until I saw the gun boss arrive on the forecastle to examine the installation.

No longer my problem, I reluctantly told myself. Technically, anyway. This was Marty Randolph's problem, and he was fully capable of solving it. *My* problem was making sure that we didn't forget to ask for more forty-millimeter ammo, now that we had a third mount. I'd already asked the commodore for some more people to make up our losses, but he'd come up empty. He said the carriers were sucking up all the replacements coming out from Pearl. I'd said something silly like "How do they think we're going to defend them if we can't man our own guns?" He'd replied that the carrier people didn't think about us at all. Period.

I realized I knew that. When I'd been gun boss in Big Ben, destroyers were simply little gray things out there on the horizon, zipping here and there and either shooting at something or coming alongside for fuel and begging for ice cream.

In the end we did get more forty-millimeter ammo craned down to us from the tender, but in turn, we had to relinquish most of mount fifty-one's ammo. Marty tried to hang onto mount fifty-one's VT frag ammo, but those VT frag rounds were still in short supply and some bean-counter knew where every one of them was hiding, even after the chief gunner's mate had told the tender's people that we'd shot it all up. That declaration had produced a wizened warrant officer with zero sense of humor who said he would need to come aboard and take a physical inventory, if we pleased. I quickly dispatched Marty to put out that incipient fire, because I did not want the tender's people to know what *we* had been stashing in the other two five-inch magazines. Sometimes the damned bean-counters were as big a threat as the Japs. The warrant came to see me to complain that my people were fudging the ammo logs. I told him he was welcome to come up to the picket line and count the brass. I'd even speak to his skipper about it. He seemed to lose interest after that.

They got a fuel barge alongside at 1530, and while the fuel was being loaded on board, Marty and I joined the tender's chaplain and wardroom in holding a memorial service for everyone who'd perished that morning when *Billingham* suddenly sank alongside. The commodore and his small staff also attended. The tender had lost eighteen people, and nobody seemed to know how many of *Billingham*'s crew had still been aboard helping the tender's engineers when she gave up the ghost. Both her captain and the exec had been killed during the attack. There'd been no one picked up out of the water alongside, alive or dead, and there was still a large oil slick streaming to the surface not far from the tender. If that continued, the tender would have to shift anchorage to keep her own main condenser inductions free of Navy special fuel oil.

As I listened to the chaplain's words, I realized I'd become numb to the loss of so many people. I suppose it was because I knew, once we had completed refueling, that *we* were going back up there. I would never have said that I didn't care about the tender's losses or *Billingham*'s dead, but the simple fact was that I cared only about *my* people and *my* ship. I still felt somewhat out of place with my new, if borrowed, brass hat and those silver oak leaves on my shirt collar, but it had been interesting to observe the transition that had begun in how my own officers and men acted around me. When the service was over, I asked the commodore for permission to shove off and return to station. He took my hand and said he'd pray for our safe return. He meant it, too. The commodore and Pudge Tallmadge were cut from the same cloth. Now Tallmadge was on his way home, his good and generous mind wrecked. The commodore had gone up to his cabin to weep for what he'd just witnessed. I think that disturbed me more than anything else up to that point in our Okinawa experience.

Three hours later we resumed our radar picket station as a glorious sunset spread over the western horizon. There were now only three destroyers stationed north of Okinawa because the fourth had been sucked up unexpectedly by the Big Blue Fleet to replace *Billingham.* The big difference was that the fleet was back, with sixteen carriers operating to the west and north of Okinawa, flooding the skies with CAP. The Freddies reported that night-fighters were going to be launched every four hours throughout the night and that they were going to be stationed way out, for a change—eighty miles instead of forty. The Freddies also reported that they had a new, additional duty: to delouse all aircraft formations coming back toward the fleet from advanced positions. Apparently a Jap fighter had fallen in astern of two Navy fighters and followed them back to their carrier, before then attempting a suicide attack, so now every returning section of CAP would get special scrutiny by the picket station Freddies. I found myself amazed at how electronics were taking over the battle for our survival.

Radio Central brought me a message forwarded by the commodore summarizing the current situation on the Okinawa battlefield. After reading that, I summoned the department heads and then waited in the captain's cabin for the call from our now formally appointed XO, Jimmy Enright.

"Captain, we're ready."

I came out of the captain's cabin—my cabin

now—went into the wardroom, and sat down at the head of the table. There was no more who's-in-charge scene-setting to be done. The navigation officer was now the exec, and Jimmy had stepped up handsomely to that position.

"Okay, gents," I began. "There's only three of us left up here on the radar picket station: us, the *Daniels*, and the *Westfall.* The *Thomas* left to join a carrier group. The good news is that we have night-fighters available to go after those controller aircraft, if and when they show up. The bad news is that none of them have shown up, so nobody knows what's coming next."

"Didn't like that nasty surprise last night, did they," Marty said.

"I told the commodore about that," I said. "He was actually pleased. Said we had to do more wildcat stunts like that. But there's a hitch: In the next few days there are going to be some fifty transports and cargo ships arriving at KR to resupply the Okinawa beachheads. More troops, ammo ships, hospital ships, everything. The Jap's 32nd Army lines are holding around something called Shuri Castle, but it's turned into a dark-alley knife fight out there in the weeds. From here on out, the side with the most stuff is going to prevail."

"Okay, then," Marty said. "For the Japs, holding is losing."

"Then the end is in sight," Mario offered.

“Think of a cobra, run over by a car,” I said. “It’s out there in the middle of the road, writhing in agony. Who volunteers to walk right up to it, cut its head off?”

Nobody.

“Right,” I said. “The commodore thinks that, for the next couple of nights, the Japs are gonna throw everything they’ve got at Okinawa. They’ve got nothing to lose now, except, of course, the war. At some point, some Jap general staff decision maker is going to say, ‘Enough. Okinawa is lost.’ We now need to get ready for what’s coming. Until then *we* have to survive long enough for them to make that decision and knock this shit off.

“So here’s what I want: Until further notice, Chop, I want food available around the clock. Open galley line. If someone’s hungry, I want him to find food at any hour of the day. Marty, every gunner on station until I say otherwise. Guns loaded, crews looking. Sleep when and where you can, head calls as necessary, but I want half of every gun crew awake at all times. Jimmy, I want your CIC people on port and port—night and day, until further notice. They can nap behind the status boards, but I want them right there.

“As I said earlier, there are only three destroyers available for the picket line now. The big dogs are keeping all their destroyers close aboard, but since the fight for Okinawa is all concentrated in the south, there’s apparently a sudden surplus of small support ships, so they're gonna send each picket station three amphib support ships—LCS, LSMR, L-whatever's available."

Marty began to shake his head.

"I know," I said, "but look: The gators have guns. We keep them close in. The kami who's expecting one target now has four, all of which are shooting at him. Law of averages, gents—enough gun barrels unloading in the kami's direction, we just about have to knock him down."

Jimmy Enright gave me a look that said, we all know the fallacy in that logic. If the Japs are making their last stand on Okinawa, their commanders back in Japan aren't going to send just one kamikaze. Mercifully, he kept quiet.

So there we were: one partially maimed destroyer, promises of a small gaggle of amphib gun platforms, and the knowledge that the next few nights were probably going to bring the battle for Okinawa to a climax. As I'd said before, all we had to do was stay alive until the Japs wrote Okinawa off their books, the way they had so many island bastions before. The question was: how long would that take?

The department heads were looking at me expectantly. I wanted to finish up with something profound, something hopeful and perhaps even memorable. I drew a blank.

"All we can do is our best," I said. "So let's go do that."

TEN

It was one in the morning, and still no Japs. No nothing. The radars were displaying only light green scope snow and our own CAP, prowling their stations at eighteen thousand feet. I got tired of looking at them. USS *Daniels* was east of us about twelve miles; USS *Westfall* was east of *Daniels*, some twenty-five miles away. I told Jimmy I was going up to Sky One to get some fresh air. As I walked out I saw Jimmy reaching for a sound-powered phone handset, probably to alert Marty that the skipper was headed his way. I smiled in the darkness. As a junior officer I'd done the same thing, many times. The sound-powered phone network was like a set of jungle drums, never entirely silent until the shooting started, then all business. Otherwise, the captain of a ship couldn't go ten feet without some talker muttering a heads-up into his mouthpiece. In a way, it was rather comforting.

I found Marty up on the director level sitting on his favorite sound-powered phone storage box and smoking a cigarette. I realized I was probably one of a very few nonsmokers on the ship, and there were times when tobacco had its appeal. Marty started to stand up as I came on deck, but I waved him back down. His JC talker was awake this time and sitting on his own box. We nodded at each other. The crew of director fifty-one was perched on top of the director, their feet dangling over its steel sides, escaping the hot confines of all the machinery inside. It was almost totally dark outside because of an overcast layer, and I'd had to wait a few minutes to fully night-adapt my eyes.

"Where are they, Marty?" I asked.

He shook his head. "This is scarier than when we see them coming," he said.

"You got some star shell ready?"

"Yes, sir, mount fifty-three is loaded with star. Fifty-two with VT frag. Fifty-one . . ."

"Is gone."

"Yes, sir. Any more news from Oki?"

"The American commanding general was killed this afternoon by an artillery barrage," I said. "A Marine general is in charge now until the Green Machine can get another general in."

"Maybe the Marines can get this thing done, then," he said.

"The Army is nobody's second team on this one, Marty," I said. "Every grunt out there in the weeds has a Jap by the throat. I swear, reading the sitreps, this whole fight is getting personal."

"Certainly seems that way when the kamis come here," he observed. "What's the big picture, Captain?"

I blew out a long breath and stared out over the

water. For some reason I remembered a fragment out of Virgil, something about a wine dark sea. Nope. This one was just dark, and fresh out of witchy Phoenician queens unraveling a silken thread to delineate the extent of the kingdom's principal city. The little flotilla of Landing Craft Support ships that were supposed to be out there hadn't shown up yet.

"This campaign," I said, "for *this* island and its airfields, is all about what's coming next: the final assault on the Japanese home islands." I was aware of the enlisted men in range of my voice: the director crew up on their steel box, the JC talker, the signalmen who'd gathered in the darkness behind us just because the captain was there.

"Our commodore thinks that the entire nation of Japan, all of its people, and there are millions, will turn into kamikazes once the Allies actually attack the sacred homeland. We're going to need a miracle to pull that one off."

Marty nodded in the darkness. I couldn't think of anything else to say, so it went quiet up there on the 03 level. Then Marty surprised me.

"Sir," he said, "where you from?"

"The Big Ben," I said, but even as I said it, I knew that wasn't what he was asking.

"No, sir, before that. Way before that. Where are you from, if it's okay to ask?"

I walked over to the port side of the director platform and called down to the bridge watch for some coffee. The bridge messenger popped up the ladder a moment later with a ceramic messdecks mug. Two sugars, too. Every watch station in the ship with a coffeepot apparently had the word: two sugars, and a clean mug, if possible.

I went back to where Marty was perched on his box and leaned against the forward bulkhead. There was a light breeze at my back as *Malloy* cut through a calm sea at 15 knots, still weaving like a drunk every few minutes.

"I was a State Department kid," I said. "My parents were both Foreign Service officers, and I don't believe we ever did have a hometown. I was born in Washington, D.C., and we lived all over the world as I was growing up. I went to a variety of schools as a kid—local Catholic academies in South America, British comprehensives in London, a French *lycée*, a German *Gymnasium* for my junior year of what we call high school, you name it. Finished up back in D.C. My father had some connections, which is how I managed to get an appointment to the Naval Academy in 1931. So, where am I from? Nowhere and everywhere, I guess."

"That's very interesting, sir," Marty said.

I then told my little audience about my naval career up to the point where I'd been gun boss in Big Ben. Marty asked if I had a family, and I told him no, that my fiancée had handed me a Dear John letter early in the war once she realized it was going to be a long haul. The white-hats listening in the dark knew all about those. Now, having been in the Navy for only ten years, I was already a three-striper and in command instead of having a wife and family. Before the war that achievement often took twice as long, meaning that promotion beyond lieutenant commander required someone ahead of you to retire or die. That, in turn, meant there weren't many officers in the professional career pipe leading to command when war broke out in the Pacific. Wartime attrition over the past three years thinned it out even more; I was a prime example. That said, I still halfway expected that we'd get a message one day informing us that a Commander So-and-So was inbound to take command. On the other hand, we were on the Okinawa picket line, and as the department heads had parodied the week before, maybe not. The commodore had told me that Navy casualties, both on the picket line and out in the main fleet formations, were keeping just about even with Army casualties ashore on Okinawa. That was a very new and disturbing statistic, and the kamikaze tactic deployed on a large scale accounted for damned near all of it.

"Sky One, Combat. Captain up there?"

"Go ahead," I said.

"We have an intermittent surface contact, bearing three three zero, range twelve miles. Quality poor, comes and goes."

Twelve miles was just over the visible horizon, so this was probably one of those radar "ghosts" the operators talked about, small splotches of video on the screen that sometimes painted bright and then disappeared, but I wasn't going to take any chances. The last intermittent radar contact had been a Jap sub periscope.

"Tell the bridge to increase speed to twenty knots and widen the weave, in case that's a sub."

"The range is twelve miles, sir," Combat said, meaning way out of torpedo range.

"And that could be the radar mast on an I-boat," I replied. "He might not stay at twelve miles, and he's free to maneuver. We're stuck here on station."

"Aye, aye, sir. We'll watch it."

I felt the breeze increase as we came up to 20 knots from 15. The twists and turns of the broad weave became more pronounced. I really wished that we'd had the ability to search passively for electronic signals, like the Japs apparently did. I'd love to have known for sure if there was a Jap radar shining out there. It had taken them three years to appreciate the importance of electronics in this war, but now they seemed to be catching up fast.

"Sky One, Combat. Contact has disappeared."

"Right, I'll be down."

I went back down the ladder to the level of the pilothouse and then went into Combat. Jimmy

Enright was there, along with the CIC officer, Lanny King. Both of them were staring at the surface-search radar display. There were no contacts, other than *Daniels* out to the east of us. Then there was one, but not in the same place as the first, apparently. We all saw it at the same time.

"What's that?" I asked.

"New skunk," the scope operator announced. "Much better video, too. He's out there, though, thirteen miles. Last one was twelve miles, but over here." He pointed at a different mark on the scope, where he'd marked the original contact using yellow grease pencil. This contact was almost due north of us.

"Put director fifty-one on that bearing," I ordered. "See if they can pick it up, too, and report to the air-raid net that we're getting unknown surface contacts."

Lanny jumped to carry out my orders. I knew that twelve miles—twenty-one thousand yards—was way out of our gun range, but the fire-control radar had a beam the size of a pencil lead. If it could gain contact, that would prove that his little blip of video was real and not some radar anomaly being generated by the much larger surface-search radar beam.

I could hear the various phone-talkers muttering quietly into their mouthpieces. Something's going on. Heads up. The Word, getting around the whole ship, and more efficiently than if we'd held quarters and read them the news.

I went out to the bridge and slipped into my chair. The bosun's mate of the watch made the ritual announcement. "Captain's on the bridge."

We waited while we tried to figure out what was out there. The five-inch director couldn't find anything. Then Jimmy Enright had an idea. "Bridge, Combat. Request permission to vector our section of night-fighters over that contact."

"Can their radar see something on the surface?"

"No, sir, but we can fly them right on top. They might be able to see what's out there."

"Give it a shot," I said, but I wasn't too hopeful. There should have been a big moon up, but there was enough cloud cover to blot out the usual ambient light over the sea. On the other hand, if there was one of those monster Jap battleships out there, the planes might see that. After the terrifying surprise they achieved at Leyte Gulf, we'd learned to expect anything and also to respect them.

I thought about more coffee, but my stomach said no. Five minutes later Combat reported that the two radar-equipped Corsairs were descending for a low pass. Combat still held that piece of low-grade video out there, still at twelve miles, moving very slowly to the east. I considered firing some five-inch star shells at maximum range, but with two fighters out there on the line of fire, that could cause an accident.

Then the junior officer of the deck, Ensign Lang, jumped sideways to get his hands on the centerline alidade, a small telescopic eyepiece mounted over the dimly lighted gyro repeater. I was about to ask him what he was doing when I saw it, too: a flare of red light way out on the horizon, right on the bearing of our mystery contact. I lifted my binoculars to see it, but it had already gone out.

"Bearing, zero zero five," Ensign Lang called out.

"Bridge, Combat. The fighters are reporting a rocket, headed our way."

I'd been looking right over the bow at that red flare. We hadn't encountered rockets before, but if it was headed our way, we needed to turn hard to present the gun battery.

"Officer of the Deck, come right with full rudder to zero niner zero," I ordered. "Flank speed twenty-seven knots."

The officer of the deck gave the orders as we all stared out to port, looking for anything. Director fifty-one's radar array was nutating, making tiny little movements of the beam, up, right, down, left, up . . . searching frantically for something, anything, headed our way.

"Bridge, Combat. We have a—"

Before Jimmy could finish his sentence, something roared overhead from port to starboard, making a sound like steam escaping from a lifted safety valve, and thundered off into the night to the south, away from us. No one on the bridge saw anything, but everybody heard it and ducked just the same. Then the bitch-box erupted again.

"Bridge, Combat. Crowder Two-Niner reports a second rocket. One of the pilots says it's a submarine, a *big* submarine, launching these things. They're gonna try to strafe it."

"Captain has the conn," I shouted. "All back full, emergency!"

The lee helmsman jumped to it, pulling the two arms of the engine-order telegraph straight to back full from ahead flank, then all the way forward, and then all the way to back full. The snipes got the message and opened the astern throttles at the same time as they closed the ahead throttles. The ship began to tremble as the turbines and their massive reduction gears were dragged down to stop in one direction and then began to spin in the opposite direction. I now knew what we were facing, incredible as it seemed: A Jap submarine was firing baka rocket planes at us.

There was nothing the guns could do. From twelve miles out, a baka could be on us in just over sixty seconds. It was a piloted rocket, though. Surely they had been taught to lead their targets, which would usually be moving ahead at 27 knots during an engagement. I was counting on that, and I hoped that by backing down hard, we'd make the pilot of this 600 mph flying bomb miss ahead, especially if he was having trouble seeing us. We also weren't helping him see us by firing every gun we could at him, because it would have been pointless.

Seconds later, another roar of escaping steam flashed over us, in front of us, actually, and then came a tremendous explosion in the water off to starboard as the baka went in and its warhead torched off. By now *Malloy* was gathering speed in the astern direction, kicking big sheets of white spray over the fantail. The gun crews must be thinking the bridge had gone nuts. So what? It had worked—but how were these things seeing us? Then I realized what the answer was: They'd been fired by the submarine down the bearing of our own radars. The baka pilot didn't have to see us: He simply had to fly his rocket-propelled bomb in whatever direction his mother ship had fired him.

"All stop," I ordered. "All ahead standard. Make turns for fifteen knots."

The forced-draft blowers wound down and then immediately back up as the snipes reversed the throttles once again.

"Bridge, Combat. Crowder Two-Niner reports another launch flare. They're going in for a strafing run, but they can't see the sea surface."

"Break 'em off, then," I ordered. "They're kidding themselves."

A third baka. A piloted rocket plane, going so fast our gun system couldn't even compute a solution even if it did manage to lock on. Some young pilot, vintage three weeks of training, had his hands on two primitive controls: direction and elevation. He was coming at us at 10 miles per minute from only twelve miles away. There wasn't any way we could fire at him, but maybe we could blind him.

"Sky One, commence firing *star* on bearing zero one zero. Rapid continuous. Burst at five thousand yards."

Marty must have been thinking the same thing, because mount fifty-three way back on the stern opened immediately, blasting out successive two-gun salvos as fast as its crew could load them. Five thousand yards was short range for star shells, which meant their parachutes would probably be ripped right off when the bursting charge let go. Star shells were meant to be fired high and long, with the projectile arcing over and then slanting down as it blew off its end-cap, deployed the chute, and then ignited its white-phosphorous load. With luck the star would burn for almost thirty seconds as it descended, by which time the next shell was bursting above it. My hope was that the pilot, with night-adapted vision, would be blinded by all the pyrotechnics exploding above him as he came screaming toward us. The downside was that we would be perfectly illuminated by our own star shells.

The first four stars burst just as I thought they

would, streaming out into the darkness trailing white-phosphorous sparks and a burning chute in the direction of the incoming baka. Half the crew was trying to see this thing when we heard that frightful sound of the rocket engine blasting right in front of the bridge windows, so close that its right wing struck the port corner of our pilot-house and tore out every porthole from left to right in a whirlwind of flying glass and ruptured steel. Moments later, a big boom from way off on the starboard side indicated that the baka had gone into the sea.

"Bridge, Combat. One of the Crowders hit the water. His wingman is reporting that they were trying to strafe that sub. He doesn't know if they hit him or not. We've lost the surface contact."

"Captain, aye," I said mechanically. "Do we need to initiate search and rescue?"

"Sir, the other pilot said his wingman flew it right into the water at three hundred knots. Not survivable."

Great, I thought. Now we'd lost a CAP as well as the front of *Malloy*'s bridge. If the sub had submerged, it was probably over, until the next sub, of course. The Japs had figured out a way to stuff three bakas into some kind of watertight hangar on a submarine's deck, surface, launch them, and then dive the hell out of there. This would make for an interesting intel report.

I got down out of my chair, brushing shards of

glass and a lapful of metal filings off my trou. There was a fresh breeze blowing in through all the missing portholes. The front bulkhead looked like an open zipper. Air-conditioning on the bridge, at last.

Would this never end, I wondered. I looked at my watch. It was only 0145, not that the arrival of daylight would mean safety, but at least we could see the sonsabitches. Invisible rocket-bombs coming out of the dark at near the speed of sound was getting on my nerves.

"Broad weave, OOD," I said and then went into Combat to help with the reporting. I wasn't sleepy anymore.

Two hours later, it happened again. This one was scarier than the first three, happening almost in slow motion as I was sitting in the captain's chair on the bridge. The red flare on the distant dark horizon as some kind of booster lifted a baka into the night, headed straight for us. Everyone on the bridge was trying frantically to spot the incoming suicider. I wanted to get up out of my chair, to grab binoculars and stare into the night sky, to detect anything our gunners could lock onto, but I couldn't move. Then came the escaping steam sound, rising in intensity as the baka began its dive, actually seeming to slow down as it came in front of the pilothouse windows, from left to right, its right wing slashing a long cut across the front of the bridge, its pilot looking right at me as he went past, bucktoothed, ferociously slanting eyes, just like in all the war bond posters, grinning like a death's head . . .

I sat up in the sea-cabin bunk with a strangled noise in my throat, covered with sweat. My insides churned, and I barely made it to the steel commode in time. As I flushed the pot I wondered if anyone outside in the pilothouse had heard me in there. I'd never had nightmares before, not even bad dreams. This one had been a doozy, and I felt sick for the next fifteen minutes, staying on the commode just in case. I looked at my hands in the dim red light from the pelorus mounted above my fold-down bunk. "Now who has shaking hands," I muttered. A vision of Pudge Tallmadge holding up his trembling hands flashed through my mind. He had a sympathetic smile on his face.

What are you scared of, I asked myself: the Japs trying to kill you or making a mistake in front of the crew and everybody?

Captain Tallmadge had warned me, hadn't he: *I am afraid,* he'd said. *I didn't use to do this, shake like this.* Forget your career and your promotions and all that stuff: up here it's life or death, and more often than not, death. Whole destroyers folding in half and going down like a diving sea bird, both ends flashing high and then sliding out of sight with half their crew still inside, wondering what was happening until they heard main bulkheads collapsing and the sea roaring in like Niagara. A destroyer moored safely to a tender suddenly giving out what sounded a lot like a ship-sized death rattle and then sinking right out of sight, with mooring lines popping like gunshots everywhere and crewmen frantically spilling out of her like so many drowning bugs, unaware of the depth charges at the back end counting the pounds per inch of sea pressure before . . .

"*Stop it,* for Chrissakes," I said out loud. *You can't do this. Think about your crew, the nearly three hundred high school graduates of last year's class. You don't think their guts aren't churning when they're out there, on deck, face-to-face with these vampire aircraft coming straight at them, on* purpose? *Just stop it.*

I got up off the commode and washed up. I checked the time: 0410. I'd gotten two hours, which was more than a lot of people in the ship. I picked up the phone and called the OOD, who was only about ten feet away.

"I'm up, and I'm going below for a shower and clean clothes. Tell the Japs to stand down for the next half hour."

"Aye, aye, sir. Will do."

"And get ahold of Mooky; see if he can make fat-pills for breakfast."

"Absolutely, sir."

ELEVEN

By daylight the damage to the front of the pilothouse didn't look that bad. There was a slash in the metal, as if some giant had taken a paring knife to the horizontal row of portholes across the front. The shipfitters actually found the wingtip from the baka bomb in a twenty-millimeter guntub on the starboard side. They were able to weld some plate over the gash, so now there was no reason for us to make a trip back down to the duty destroyer tender. Not that they would have let us leave station anyway.

With the air picture quiet after dawn GQ, I met with the department heads. The officers had made short work of the wardroom's ration of morning fat-pills, otherwise known as hot cinnamon rolls.

"Close calls last night, gents," I began. "We got lucky when the first baka couldn't find us, we backed down on the second so he missed ahead, and we blinded the third one. That almost backfired on us, because we solved his where's-my-target problem for him."

"I can't believe these things have a man in them," Peter said. "Flying a rocket?"

"Even better," Jimmy Enright said, "we think they launched from a surfaced submarine."

"I'm waiting to see if they think we've gone

looney-tunes up here when that report gets in," I said. "The question is, what can we do to protect ourselves if they come back?"

"I vote for learning how to submerge, like that sub did last night," Marty offered.

"I think we should request an additional section of CAP," Jimmy said. "Have them patrol an area ten miles north of us, but at five thousand feet instead of fifteen thousand. Their radars can't see things on the surface, but they'll see that red flare. They could drop flares of their own and then go down and strafe that bastard."

"Put that in an op-immediate message to the commodore," I said. "They'll need time to change out the night-fighters' weapons load. One problem, though: We let them take the first shot."

"Maybe patrol our station in a big circle?" Marty asked. "We can't generate a firing solution on a baka anyway, and certainly not at night, so it doesn't much matter if the guns can bear or not, but going that fast, the baka pilot probably can't turn that thing if his target is constantly turning."

I nodded. That, too, would probably work, or at least make it a lot harder for the baka pilot. One thing I'd noticed at dawn GQ was that the cloud cover had blown off. Tonight might be clear, with our mortal enemy, the moon, shining in full splendor. We needed to do something.

"We'll try it," I said. "In fact, maybe start doing it now. There's nothing to say that sub can't surface in daylight, shoot one or two, and go back down."

Then Chop surprised all of us. "Could we get the task force to send one of the Jeep carriers up here with a couple of destroyers?" he said. "You know, form a hunter-killer group like we did in LantFleet, and go hunt down that sub? He has to be hanging around here somewhere."

I'd forgotten Peter had done his first tour in an Atlantic Fleet destroyer, where the problem was the Nazi U-boat, not kamikazes. "So far they haven't been willing to spare even a fourth tin can for the picket line, Chop, let alone a carrier," I said. "That could work, though. That has to be a pretty big submarine to be able to carry three bakas. Or maybe even more."

What I didn't say was that Halsey and his staff were less than receptive to suggestions from mere tin cans out on the edge of the huge task force formation. The phone interrupted us.

"Large raid, many bogeys, Captain. They look to go past us, but . . ."

"Do it," I said, and the GQ alarm sounded seconds later. "We'll pick this up when the raid's over," I said, getting up to go get my battle gear.

"*If* we're still here," I heard Marty mutter.

I went into Combat to see what was shaping up. All three picket ships had detected the massed formations of Jap bombers and fighters that were coming toward us from their supposedly badly damaged bases in Kyushu. According to the air-raid net, three big-decks were spitting off CAP as fast as they could unfold their wings. The on-station CAP might be able to disrupt the incoming formations, but there looked to be several dozen Jap planes inbound, so this was going to be a three-alarm air battle.

I got on the 1MC and briefed the crew, telling everyone to be alert for the inevitable low-fliers. Having said that, I realized it had been unnecessary. "You don't need to be told that," I said, my voice echoing strangely over the top-side speakers. "You guys know your business. Everybody says *Malloy*'s a lucky ship, but I think you make your own luck because everybody does his job in a superb fashion. Keep it up, and we may just get to sail away from this fire pit. That is all."

I climbed up into my chair on the bridge and waited, like everyone else. It was a clear day, with a little haze but not much. My head itched under the straps of my steel helmet liner, but I didn't even think about taking it off. With sunglasses on I was able to watch surreptitiously the expressions on the bridge watch team's faces, which ranged from bravado to thinly masked fear. The bosun's mate of the GQ team was one Robert Hanks, nicknamed Slim Bob, undoubtedly because of his Buddha-sized belly. Slim Bob stood at the back bulkhead of the pilothouse, legs spread in a stance reminiscent of Lord Nelson to accommodate a nonexistent heaving main, one arm behind his back and the other perched on his expansive front porch, that hand firmly gripping his silver bosun's call, which was slung around his neck with an ornate white lanyard made up of a hundred different sailor knots. His round red face was set in an expression of supreme indifference.

The officer of the deck was Lieutenant (junior grade) Barry Waddell, six foot three, skinny as a rail, and permanently hunched forward to avoid hitting his head on various objects mounted in the overhead. He was a Dartmouth grad, OCS, and reportedly a serious scholar of English literature. He was the ship's first lieutenant, in charge of First Division, the bosun's mates. Chief Dougherty, of course, was the real first lieutenant, having eighteen years of seamanship experience in destroyers, but there had to be a division officer, and Barry was it. He looked like a scholar and nothing at all like what one would expect from that admiring sobriquet "destroyerman." Here he was, though, out on the Okinawa picket line and very far from Hanover, New Hampshire, watching out the empty portholes through binoculars that were bigger than his scholarly hands as we bored a large, continuous, three-degree right rudder circle in the water while the CIC team vectored fighters toward the approaching Jap formations.

"Bridge, Combat. Possible low-fliers, bearing zero niner zero, range twenty miles, closing, fast, composition two, maybe three."

"Where's our CAP?"

"Diverted to the main raid, Captain. We're on our own until they get more planes up."

Situation normal, I thought.

"Officer of the Deck, steer due north, speed twenty knots, narrow weave."

Our circling stopped as *Malloy* steadied up on a northerly course to present all our guns to the incoming Japs. The main battery director slewed off to starboard and began searching the horizon. Twenty miles, forty thousand yards, two, maybe three planes headed in, 300 miles per hour, 5 miles per minute, we had four minutes to find them, lock on with radar, open fire, and knock them down before they came through the ship and killed us all.

"Sky One, Captain. Open fire as soon as you have a solution, even if they're out of range."

"Sky One, aye."

A minute later our two remaining five-inch gun mounts slewed out to starboard, slaved their servos to the electronic orders rising from Main Battery Plot, elevated, and began shooting. Their most effective range was six to eight miles, but that was for computed, accurate, killing fire. The guns could actually throw shells farther, out to nine miles. Against a surface target, that would have shells falling all over the place, but with these new VT frag shells, anything that disrupted that little proximity fuze's cone of radiated energy would trigger a blast, and it only took one to knock a plane out of the sky. That possibility was well worth the expenditure of ammo, especially when the bastards were aiming to crash on board.

I felt my insides clenching when the five-inch started up, but I was determined to sit in my chair and let my people do what they did best: fight the ship. I swiveled the chair to starboard and searched the horizon for those black puffs that would indicate that the shells were seeing something worth detonating over. There was more haze now, or more than I had noticed before. I thought about maneuvering, executing a weave or a zigzag to confuse the approaching suiciders, but, being a gun-hand, I knew that the best chances for a hit came from keeping the ship steady on course and speed, reducing the variables of the fire-control solution on those of the approaching targets. Pray there wasn't an I-boat out there, refining a torpedo firing solution.

The twin barrels of mount fifty-two continued to hammer away, elevated at about twenty degrees. Hot shell casings were clanging around the forecastle as the crew inside the mount labored to feed those two hungry guns.

There: black puffs, and then a bright flamer, a

black dot careening out of the sky and cartwheeling across the water in a boil of blazing avgas and white water.

I moved my binoculars right, then left, looking for more black dots, more puffs. Couldn't see any, but then I could. A whole constellation of black puffs, and then another fireball, this one going straight up into the air, looping over, and sheeting down into the sea, followed by an impressive mountain of white water as its bomb went off. I wanted to cheer, but the guns were still shooting, and now the forties had joined in.

At this point I *really* wanted to get out of that chair, get out to the bridge wing to urge on the massed barrels of *Malloy*'s broadside as the twenties joined in, and then I saw it, a black dot, no, a real silhouette now, stubby wings, pieces being chewed off by our guns, that big, ugly bomb seeming to wiggle from side to side as we tore the plane to pieces, until finally one of our shells found the bomb itself. The plane and its bomb dissolved in a white flash, close, so very close, and then came a clatter of debris flaying the sides of the ship, followed by a thunderclap that shook the bridge. It was strong enough to break windows, if we'd still had any.

The guns stopped shooting. Unfortunately my ears did not stop ringing. I was dimly aware that the bitch-box was trying to tell me something.

"Say again, Combat?"

"High-altitude bogeys, possibly bombers, two seven zero, range thirty-seven miles, composition four. We've just received CAP and we're vectoring them to engage, but the plot shows these guys're on a course to overfly our station."

"Captain, aye," I said. "Officer of the Deck, right three degrees rudder and increase speed to twenty-five knots."

I heard the director slewing around to the west, looking for the incoming Japs. As we began to execute a wide circle, the director would have to keep moving in its effort to achieve a lock-on. If they were high-altitude bombers, a circle was the best maneuver. If they were kamis, well, it was anybody's guess. As I thought about it, I realized the Japs would probably not employ conventional high-altitude bombing tactics against a destroyer-sized target. A carrier, maybe, but a tin can? The chances of their getting a hit were minimal.

So what, then? Overfly your target at eighteen thousand feet and then execute a vertical dive? A conventional dive bomber would allow room for a pullout, but a *kami?* He'd come straight down, and that would make for another impossible fire-control problem, with us having to shoot straight up. Four Jap carriers had learned that the hard way, at Midway.

I keyed the bitch-box. "Combat, Captain. Lay out a five mile wide figure eight on the DRT and issue conning instructions to the bridge to maintain that track."

"Combat, aye."

I then called Marty up on Sky One and explained to him what I thought they were going to try. He confirmed my own intuition—there was no way that we could engage a vertical diver.

"So we have to make him miss, Marty," I said. "He'll be coming down so fast he'll be skinning his paint off, but that won't allow him any time for reacting to a sudden maneuver. Here's what I want: *You* guys start looking low for the usual kami low-flier tactics. You can't do anything about the vertical divers, but they may also be a distraction. Sector searches, coordinate with Combat, and let me worry about the high-fliers."

"Sky One, aye," Marty said. For once, he sounded a bit uncertain. I was glad he couldn't see how uncertain I was about any of this.

Then I got on the 1MC. "This is the captain speaking. We have a high-altitude raid inbound. Our CAP is after them. They're either conventional bombers or kamis. If they're kamis, they're going to try a vertical dive attack. You'll see we've gone into a figure-eight pattern to make it really hard for them to hit us, but here's the thing: I think they're a diversion. While we're all looking up, the real kamis are going to attack from low level, right on the water, just like they always do. So everybody topside look low. Let the CAP take care of the guys way up there, but let's not get caught by some low-flying sneaky bastard. That is all."

"Bridge, Sky One."

"Captain, aye."

"We could take those high-fliers under fire, Captain. They're in our computer's range."

"We've got CAP up there, Marty," I said. "Let's not go shooting down any Corsairs."

"Sky One, aye."

"Look down, look flat. Bring your director radar down flat on the sea surface."

"Sky One."

The officer of the deck turned in my direction and surprised me. "Thanks for telling us what's going in, Captain," he said, his voice tight with fear. "It helps."

I nodded. What I didn't want to tell him or anyone else was that this looked like a pincer effort: high-fliers coming in from the west doing suicide dives while low-fliers came boring in from the east or the north, on the deck, skimming the waves, hiding in the sea return of our own radar displays. I felt that familiar coil deep down in my belly. My steel throne beckoned, but I shut it out of my consciousness. The ship heeled as we reversed the constant turn to start the other leg of the figure-eight.

Think, I told myself. What else should we be doing? The figure-eight maneuver would make the vertical-dive planes strain really hard to get a hit. If they did hit us, we'd be finished. They'd punch right through our unarmored ship, from the 01 level right down through the keel, and we'd be open to the sea and gone in minutes.

Don't think about that, I told myself. What *else* should we be doing?

"Bridge, Combat. Our CAP is engaging. Two Corsairs, reporting four Bettys. They've flamed one, and now it's a furball."

"Captain, aye. Watch your *surface*-search radar, Jimmy. Watch it hard."

"Combat, aye, and now two Bettys flamed."

Then I heard director fifty-one stop its rumbling search and steady on a bearing to the north. Moments later both five-inch gun mounts swung out and began firing. I felt a momentary surge of elation. I'd been right. Then it hit me: The figure-eight might help with a high-diver, but it would mask our own batteries if we got skimmers.

"Bridge, Combat. Third Betty flamed, but number four has disappeared. They're looking."

"Captain, aye." They're looking, but probably not in the right place. This was either going to work or it wasn't. I got out of my chair and went out to the engaged side, where clouds of gun smoke and bits of burned wadding were streaming over the bridge wing as mount fifty-two blasted away at some unseen target. I wanted to look out to the north, where the guns were firing, but instead, I looked straight up, and, great God Almighty, there he was. I think my heart stopped. The OOD looked up when I did and yelled, *"Oh, shit!"*

Black circle, glinting windscreen, knife-thin wings, two engines, in a slow spiral but a screaming dive, coming right for us, coming right for *me,* and there was nothing I could do about it but watch in morbid fascination. A moment later he slashed into the sea not a hundred yards from our port side, unable to turn tightly enough to intercept our figure-eight, and leaving nothing but a small line of white froth where he went in. I held my breath, waiting for a close-aboard bomb blast, but nothing happened, and then I lifted my head to see what the guns were working on.

Two black dots were coming in low, not twenty feet off the sea surface, jinking from side to side through a virtual hail of tracers and a forest of shell-splashes and VT-frag detonations from the five-inch, forties, and twenties, raising white and green waterspouts all around them.

"Steady as she goes," I yelled into the pilot-house so that the guns wouldn't have to be constantly training because of the figure-eight.

Then, by God, the two kamis collided. One jinked right, the other left, and they smashed into each other and then both went into the sea at several hundred miles an hour, cartwheeling for nearly a quarter mile before all the wreckage stopped splashing down. The guns quit, and I could hear cheers and jeers from the nearby guntubs. I heard a second sound and looked over to see our Dartmouth scholar feeding the fishes over the port bullrail. He'd been that scared, and I wanted to tell him I knew exactly how he felt. I wasn't sure how many people had actually seen that Betty go in. I turned away and relaxed my hands, which had been gripping my binoculars so hard that they were cramping.

"Bridge, Combat. Sonar's reporting a wide noise-spoke abaft the beam, possible deep explosion?"

"Tell 'em it's okay; that was the missing Betty."

"It *was?*"

"He came straight down, just barely missed us. You can call off your CAP search now."

"Combat, aye," Jimmy answered, his voice sounding just a bit weak. Then I saw something ominous to the northeast of our station: a rising column of dense black smoke blooming up over the eastern horizon. I called Combat and confirmed the bearing matched the station of the next picket destroyer over, USS *Daniels.* Combat tried to raise them but received no reply. I asked if they'd been attacked by high-fliers, but Combat had no information; *Daniels*'s CAP was being controlled on a different radio circuit to avoid mutual interference. I told

Combat to keep trying, but it sure didn't look good. We also tried to raise the *Westfall*, who'd been stationed farther east, but received no response from her, either.

Will this never end? I wondered. Again.

TWELVE

Early that afternoon we received a message indicating Commodore Van Arnhem was coming up to the picket line on another one of those high-speed Fletchers. There'd been no more raids after the high-altitude bombers, but Combat was reporting that the big morning raid had done some real damage off Okinawa. Apparently they'd heard from CAP aircraft that when they got back to the carrier formation, many of them had had to go find alternate decks to land on. I wondered if the Fletcher-class destroyer coming up from Kerama Retto would be staying, because we'd been unable to raise the *Daniels* all morning. We'd vectored two Corsairs over her station, but they could find no sign of her or even of any wreckage. At the least there should have been an oil slick if she'd been sunk. An hour after we first saw the smoke column, *Westfall* had reported seeing it, too, so we now knew she was still with us.

I didn't want to think about the *Daniels* just disappearing like that. They'd promised us pallbearers, but no small craft had materialized as yet, so if she'd been sunk, there were people in the water and no one to pick them up. I wondered if we really were down to just two ships on the six-station picket line.

The commodore arrived at 1500 and, since the seas were flat calm, requested a boat transfer. When he and two staff officers came up the sea ladder I found out why: He had luggage; he was going to break his burgee in *Malloy*. I sent a wardroom steward scurrying up to the unit commander's stateroom to make sure everything was in order as I took the commodore to my cabin for a quick coffee. The Fletcher class, USS *Morrow*, took off in a southwesterly direction, back toward her fleet formation station. I wanted to suggest she go east and find *Daniels*, but she was gone before I had the chance to bring it up to my boss.

"This morning was pretty bad," the commodore said, once we'd settled in my cabin. "We got the first indication that the Japs have been holding back some veteran fighter pilots during this kamikaze campaign. Our pilots had become used to shooting newbies out of the sky with one arm tied behind their back, but this morning we lost a fair number of CAP, and then came the kamis."

"I think we lost *Daniels*," I said. Then I told him about the high-flying Bettys, the pincer attack, and their new vertical dive tactic.

"Bastards *will* not quit," he said. "The only good news is that the Army's reporting cracks in the Shuri line. The Japs are running out of ammo and troops, and our guys are making some progress, finally. The bad news is that somebody told the Jap *army* about kamikaze tactics."

"Oh, great," I said.

"They're determined to bleed us. If it were me, I'd stop right where we are, consolidate the front lines, and starve the bastards out."

"Well, I, for one, am glad you're here."

He gave me a knowing look. "Getting a feel for what Pudge was going through?" he asked.

I nodded. "I've had it easier than he did. I wasn't there for swim call at Guadalcanal or Savo. I think I have more reserves than he did, but . . ."

"That's why I came up," he said. "It made all the management sense in the world for me to coordinate logistics, repair, replacements—ships, people, five-inch mounts—from a tender in KR for eight ships, but the real fight is up here. Finally I went to CTF 58 and told the admiral I didn't have anything to do because all my ships were getting picked off one at a time."

"If you could have seen that Betty coming straight down on us this morning," I said, "you might want to rethink that. There was no way we could even shoot at it."

"But you made him miss," he said. "Tell me about that."

I did, and then he wanted the story on a submarine launching bakas. Apparently that report had met with some incredulity at the fleet staff level.

"They need to talk to the aviators who saw it, then," I said. "We never saw more than a red flare out there on the horizon and then the bastard was on top of us. The pilots saw a sub, which they told our Freddies was a really big sub. Unfortunately there wasn't much they could do to it at night, and one of them actually crashed trying."

"Right," the commodore said. "New tactics, though. That's worrisome. I got your message about changing the loadout on some night-fighters, but the fleet staff said no. There are too few of them, and . . ."

"And the carrier defense comes first, yes, I know."

He shrugged. "How useful are the gator gunships up here in terms of adding to the defense?" he asked.

"Not very, in my opinion, except in the performance of their *un*official mission."

"As pallbearers, you mean?"

"Yes, sir."

"A most unfortunate choice of terms, isn't it," he said with a sigh. "Halsey heard about it and had a fit."

"How nice for him," I said. "We have a different perspective up here on the picket line."

He raised a finger. "Don't get uppity, Connie. As Halsey himself would tell you, for every kami that comes against the picket line, twenty come after him and his carrier."

"Him and his *fifteen* carriers, plus his several dozen battleships, cruisers, AA cruisers, destroyers, and, what, five hundred fighters to protect them? We have . . . armed landing craft and two CAP, if any? Maybe that's why we're down to two pickets, Commodore."

He raised his hands. "I know, I know. One of the reasons I came up here. I need to see for myself, and try to help formulate some better tactics, like you've been doing. Figure-eights, circles, backing down, shooting star at them—all unheard-of, but they worked." He changed the subject. "So there's still no sign of *Daniels*?"

I shook my head. "They apparently didn't go for *Westfall*, so it's just the two of us."

"Okay, let's go over to *Daniels*'s station right now, twenty-seven knots. We owe her that much. In the meantime, my staffies and I are going up to Combat and talk to your radar people and the Freddies."

"Aye, aye, sir," I said, getting up. "I'm still glad you're here."

He grinned. "You're just saying that because you think I brought my Scotch bottle with me."

"Did you, sir?"

"Hell, yes."

"There is a God."

One of the benefits of having the commodore embarked was that we could leave station without asking for permission. As it turned out, it was worth the trip. We discovered 185 survivors of

Daniels drifting in seven life rafts and six floats, nearly eight miles east of her assigned station. Why they'd been so far off station remained to be discovered. The survivors had seen our two Corsairs searching west of them, but, as too often was the case, the Corsairs never saw them, probably because of their huge engines. Corsair pilots were the first to have to depend utterly on the landing signal officer when coming aboard a carrier because, at the critical moment of catching the arresting gear, they could no longer see the flight deck. *Daniels*'s skipper had survived the sinking; her exec, who'd been headed aft to look into a problem with the after forty-millimeters' power, went down with the ship, along with most of the people who'd been below decks.

They pieced together what had happened while floating around in their rafts, waiting for someone besides sharks to show up. Their CAP had mixed it up with a single Betty and reported downing it almost immediately. They'd missed three others, because fifteen minutes later, while *Daniels* was in the process of shooting down another pair of Zekes coming in on the deck together, just like ours, the two Bettys had hit her amidships doing a vertical power dive from eight thousand feet and cut her right in half. The forward section of the ship, with its high mast, the bridge, director, radars, and heavy gun mounts up on the 01 level, had capsized immediately, turned upside down, and gone out of sight in less than a minute. The back half, from just forward of the after stack to the stern, had floated until the third and final Betty hit her on the after forty-millimeter gun platform and cut what was left of her in half again. Everything was gone in under two minutes. Bizarrely, because there'd been no bombs going off, just the pure impact of a ten-ton plane hitting the unarmored decks of a destroyer at 400 miles per hour, there'd been no fire or other explosions, so if you'd survived the planes' impact, you were able to go over the side and into a raft. There were almost no injuries among the survivors. They were either okay, albeit still in shock, or gone to the bottom with the pieces of their ship.

By then it was nearing sundown, so the commodore directed his new flagship to take *Daniels*'s survivors to Kerama Retto, where we could also rearm and refuel. The skipper of the *Daniels* was one of the people still in a state of shock. He sat on the couch in the commodore's cabin and kept saying, "we never even saw them," over and over again. I didn't envy what he would have to undergo in the weeks ahead. He was so upset that he'd even refused the offer of "medicinal" Scotch from the commodore. Who could blame him: He had lost nearly half his crew in the blink of an eye. In accordance with the stark traditions of naval command, "lost" was the operative word. His professional peers would always see him as the captain who lost his ship and half his crew. There were times when Captain Tallmadge had implied that if we were sunk, he planned to sink along with the ship. That seemed to be the only way a captain could erase the sin of losing one's ship. I said something along those lines to the commodore as we hustled down to KR.

"That shouldn't be news, Connie," he said quietly from his chair on the port side of the pilothouse.

Gulp.

Refueled, rearmed, and having transferred *Daniels*'s survivors to the tender, we steamed back to our station north of Okinawa right after sundown. I heard from Jimmy that Rear Admiral Chase, the fleet air-defense commander, had fanged the commodore over the radio for leaving station without permission. The commodore had referenced a UNODIR message he'd sent upon recovering the *Daniels*'s survivors and then hung up the radio handset.

"What priority did he use on that UNODIR?" I asked.

"Routine," Jimmy said, and we both smiled. That message would eventually get to Admiral Chase, but probably not for a few more days. Word was circulating on the sound-powered phone circuits that the commodore had muttered,

"Screw 'em if they can't take a joke," before leaving Combat. The crew was beginning to warm up to Dutch Van Arnhem, and so was I.

Our station had been changed because there were now only two radar pickets, *Malloy* and the *Westfall.* I still could hardly believe that Halsey's enormous Third Fleet, which had begun Operation Iceberg with seventy-seven destroyers, couldn't spare one lone tin can to bolster his early warning radar coverage by 33 percent, but apparently they couldn't. I didn't voice these sentiments to the commodore, however. I knew his thoughts on the matter, but I also knew that there were limits as to what could be voiced aloud. Fair enough. I was a very junior commander, USN; William Halsey was a very senior fleet admiral with five stars. Still, we were depending on the Japs' continuing to attack from the north and northwest. Based on some of their tactics the previous night, I thought we were relying overmuch on assumptions.

The commodore and his two staff officers, one an operations specialist and the other an air-defense expert, met with me and the four department heads after dinner in the wardroom. There'd been no more raids that day after the morning's activity, so we all expected it to be an interesting night. As we sat down, the bridge called and said that a small flotilla of fifteen LCSs and LSMRs was approaching from

Okinawa. They were asking for stationing instructions. I was about to instruct them when I remembered I wasn't the senior officer here anymore. I passed the news to the commodore, who said to order them into a protective ring around Malloy at a distance of two thousand yards.

The commodore's operations officer, Lieutenant Commander Al Canning, had an interesting idea. "For the whole time the picket line's been up here, it's been in the same place. Ships might occupy different stations, but the Japs know where those stations are. Why don't we move them tonight?"

"First tell me how you guys think they're locating our ships at night," the commodore said.

"We think they home in on our air-search radars," Jimmy said, echoing my theory. "And we can't turn them off because that's why we're here in the first place."

"So they take a passive bearing on a radar beam and fly down that bearing?"

"Yes, sir, like when they came at us out of the east. They can come from any direction, because they know where we are. If they come in on the deck, the air search can't see them, but they can still home in on that radar signal like a beacon."

"You think the individual planes are equipped with this kind of gear?"

"If they're flying a section of two or three, which is usual, then only one has to be equipped," I pointed out. "The other two just have to keep station on him."

The commodore turned to his operations officer. "So if we somehow could move the ring of stations *and* bring the ships together, maybe we could do the same thing: leave one air-search radar up to suck 'em in, silence the other ones, and maybe we could surprise *them* for a change."

"Even better," Marty said, "bring each ship's radar up at odd times, but between those times, move the ships whose radars are off. If they've got something out there, say, a submarine or a controller aircraft, who builds the picture of where the pickets are and then sends that dope to the incoming kamis, we could get them to fire kamis at vacant stations at night. They only have enough fuel for one-way trips, which means they'd go into the sea instead of us."

"I like the sound of that," the commodore said. "We'll never convince the big dogs to let us leave station, but they didn't say anything about moving ships around within the stations, even if we're down to only three."

"Two," I interjected.

The commodore blinked, then nodded. "Two, right."

"It's possible," I continued, "that some of these suicider planes have their own radar. It wouldn't have to be too sophisticated if they're given the initial bearing to their targets. I've heard our own submariners talk about Jap antisub planes having radar, but they're usually multiengine jobs, not fighters."

The commodore threw up his hands. "If that's true, then what're we doing here?"

"Well," I said, "let's suppose one or more of them does have a functional radar that'll tell 'em how far we are in front of them. What if we take *all* the pallbearers that CTF 58 just sent up and assign them to one destroyer. Make him the one who has his radar on. As they approach, their radar sees thirteen targets, not one lone destroyer. Then when they get here, they run into thirteen floating gun batteries instead of one. They never said anything about not moving the gators, either . . ."

The commodore nodded. "Concur," he said. "Al, put a plan together. We'll send it off to CTF 58, but not until we get the ships in place."

"Routine precedence, Commodore?" Canning asked, innocently. Everyone grinned.

"Carrier pigeon, Al. With a busted wing."

There were four small kamikaze raids between sundown and midnight, aimed at Kerama Retto for a change. Because of our warnings, nine kamis in all arrived to a basin obscured by artificial smoke and a warm welcome from the gun emplacements on the hills surrounding the anchorage, as well as from the assembled logistics ships and the smaller amphib gunships. Night-fighters had cut the original eighteen-plane raiding force in half again, based on warnings from the picket destroyers, but they had to break off once they approached the defensive gun circles the Army and the Marines had put up on those hills. All nine who made it to KR were shot down without achieving anything. Congratulations all around, but, as the commodore noted, this was yet another tactical change. Someone in Tokyo had finally recognized that it was the American seaborne logistics train that was going to defeat them.

While we listened to the air-raid reporting circuit during the KR attack, Radio Central brought up a message. Halsey was taking the Third Fleet carrier striking forces north and west again to hit Jap air bases along a big arc ranging from Formosa to the southeastern coasts of Honshu Island in Japan proper. It was another good news, bad news deal: The good news was that Halsey was going up there to reduce the numbers of planes available for kamikaze missions. The bad news was that we were not going to have any night-fighters while the big-decks were away. Halsey had left four escort carriers behind to protect KR and the picket line, but the smaller carriers did not carry the precious night-fighters.

At 2330, the 1MC quietly announced midrats. Individuals from the gun stations were cycled in groups of two or three through the messdecks for sandwiches and a mug of hot soup: midnight rations, or midrats, as the sailors called them. Most of the officers grabbed some soup and sandwiches in the wardroom, but everyone was careful to leave no station completely unmanned.

The commodore came in for some chow just after midnight. He and his two staffies had restructured the picket line as per our brainstorming session earlier. *Malloy* was now in the center of the overall picket line arc, fifty-five miles, not forty, north of Okinawa. Three hours earlier, starting at 2100, and while *Westfall* was still thirty miles away, *Malloy* and *Westfall* alternated bringing their air-search radars into standby for thirty minutes at a time, during which *Westfall* made five-mile position adjustments and then came back up on the air, each time moving closer and closer to *Malloy.* She was now ten miles from us. Our personal swarm of amphib gunships continued to match our movements, more or less. Station-keeping was not an art much practiced in the gator Navy. Each time we took our radar down, our weary radar operators got to take a short nap, as did the Freddies. They'd simply slump at their consoles and give in to what they'd been resisting all night. Otherwise, just about everyone on board, along with half the engineering department, was awake and wondering what the Jap devils would come up with next.

At 0130, as I was beginning to nod off in my chair on the bridge, we found out.

"Bridge, Combat. Holding six to eight bogeys, bearing three three zero, range sixty-five miles, inbound. There's something flying out ahead of them, something larger."

"Our radar or *Westfall*'s?"

"Our radar, Captain. *Westfall* is currently radar silent."

"Alert the pallbearers, and *Westfall*. Tell her to stay radar silent. Plan to light her off when they get to thirty miles. Inform the commodore."

"Combat, aye."

The commodore's two staff officers were standing watch-and-watch in CIC, four on, four off. The commodore was in his cabin. The one on duty would call him, but I still had to make sure that they did. I called back to Combat and told them to tell the boss what I'd ordered them to do. Once again, I'd forgotten that I had a unit commander embarked.

The word was already going out over the sound-powered phone circuits, GQ in five minutes. I'd found that telegraphing the GQ alarm made for a better setting of all the watertight and firetight doors and hatches throughout the ship. It gave people five minutes to wake up, gather their wits, and head for their GQ stations, instead of falling out of their racks in a panic when the alarm rang, scrambling for shoes, life jackets, and helmets, and then pounding through passageways and up ladders in the dark. The phone-talkers alerted people on their circuit to go into each berthing compartment and rouse the petty officers, who then roused the sleeping crewmen, and then everything went better. Another Pudge Tallmadge innovation.

By the time the commodore came up to the bridge, GQ was as good as set throughout the ship. He commented that he hadn't heard the alarm, and I explained *Malloy*'s system. Then, just to make sure, we did sound the general quarters alarm. The manned-and-ready reports came in in quick order.

"Bridge, Combat. We've got something new."

My heart sank. "Go ahead."

"There's a band of radar interference opening up on the air-search scope," Jimmy said. "It's like someone's painting a ring around us, out at about forty miles."

"That's chaff," the commodore said from his chair on the other side of the pilothouse. "They've got a bomber out there, dumping chaff to disrupt our radar picture, and I'll bet he does have a radar of his own."

"What's chaff?" I had to ask.

"Shredded aluminum strips," he said. "We've been using it in Europe. You get a bomber to deploy bags and bags of aluminum foil clippings out ahead of our bomber formation. The air-defense radars see it and nothing else. Somebody's given the idea to the Japs."

"Bridge, Combat, the interference is spreading across an arc, from three three zero to zero three zero, true. We've lost contact on the bogeys."

The commodore leaned down to his own bitch-box. "Tell *Westfall* to come up on her air search. You guys go silent. Watch your surface-search radar for low fliers."

"Combat, aye."

"We'll wait three minutes," he continued, "and then switch, your radar up, *Westfall*'s down, and then we'll call *Westfall* in toward us at max speed. You ready with that star shell?"

"Yes, sir."

"Start firing star at max range in"—he looked down at his watch while he did the time-motion problem in his head—"four minutes. Set for highest possible airburst. Tell the gators what we're doing, and how close the bogeys are."

"We can't see the bogeys," I pointed out.

"Then do a dead-reckoning plot—start the star shells when they're fifteen miles out. I want the stars to blind them, not us. Bosun mate, I need coffee."

I relayed his orders to Sky One and then sat back in my chair and stared out the glass-free portholes. With that gash across the front of the pilothouse, they looked like Oriental eyes staring back at me. There was a fair amount of moonlight, not terribly bright but sufficient to reveal our little armada of gray gunships. My eyes were fully night-adapted, and the nearby small ships looked pale white in the moonlight. I wondered if we'd be able to see the suiciders; I had little doubt that they would be able to see us.

I marveled at the commodore's calm demeanor. This had become a technical fire-control problem, as far as he was concerned. Move the ships here, fire the star shells there, and then sit back, have some coffee, and wait to see how it all came out. I tried to remember if he'd actually ever been subject to a kamikaze attack on a destroyer. It was one thing to watch one come in on a carrier. When they came for us small boys, it was a lot more personal. Outwardly I tried to match his apparent calm, but inwardly it wasn't working. Even with two destroyers, one the Japs might or might not yet know about, along with a gaggle of small-caliber AA guns from the gators, we were still looking at six to eight suiciders, who apparently knew where we were, if maybe not how many we were. I wasn't sure if a Jap radar operator could tell the difference between a destroyer-sized return and that of an LCS. Either way, it took a major effort on my part to sit there in my chair and appear to be as confident as Commodore Van Arnhem.

Our five-inch swung out four minutes later and began slow, measured salvos of star shells. We'd alerted the gators so no one would panic when the five-inch began to speak. That chaff cloud had really clobbered the air-search radar, confirmed by *Westfall* when they came back on the air and we went down. We simply had to assume the suiciders would keep boring in. Somewhere out there in the dark *Westfall* was also closing us. They'd take a station two miles away, just outside of the ring of amphib gunships.

The first star shells burst way out there at eighteen thousand yards, ten miles, and hung in the air under their parachutes just like they were designed to do. Then Combat reported that the kamis had burst out of the chaff cloud at twenty-five miles and back onto our radars. They were already low, and they immediately split up, four going east, four going west, each section executing a wide circle around our little formation. Combat kept the gators informed as to what was happening, and I heard director fifty-one training around up above, straining for a lock-on. The commodore stopped the fireworks show and told us to load up with the real stuff. I wondered if the kamis were circling because they were trying to regain some night vision. They might also be trying to figure out what they were looking at when they could see. They were used to attacking a single destroyer, accompanied sometimes by one or more gunships. Now there was a crowd.

"Bridge, Combat. They're low and still circling, at about twelve miles now. Nothing on the air search, but they're all showing up on the surface search, so they're on the deck."

The commodore ordered the entire formation, such as it was, on a course of due east at 12 knots. There was no point in going any faster or we'd leave our bevy of gators in our wake. Combat reported to the air-raid control center on the light carrier *Cowpens* that we were being attacked, although that was mostly pro forma. There was nothing *Cowpens* or any of the other light carriers could do about it.

Then suddenly, from eight points of the compass, they all turned in and began their attack. We couldn't see that from the bridge, of course, but the radars picked them up immediately, and warnings went out over both radio and sound-powered circuits. *Here they come!* I was about to jump out of my chair when I realized there was nowhere to go. In daylight I would have been out on a bridge wing, maneuvering the ship to make sure the maximum number of guns could cover any black dot coming at us—but at night?

I thought I heard director fifty-one stop its search and steady up on a bearing, but before I could even think, our two remaining five-inch mounts, fifty-two just in front of the bridge and fifty-three aft, opened up in a rapid-fire chain of gun blasts. The forties joined in moments later, and then the twenties. The night erupted into lines of tracer fire, sheets of fire from the muzzles of the twin five-inch mounts, and the scream of airplane engines. I was dimly aware that all of the amphib gunships were firing with everything they had, but at what, I couldn't see. Then there was a familiar boil of flaming avgas sheeting across in front of us, followed by a second one on the port quarter. I was literally deafened by all the shooting. The muzzle flashes from both the five-inch and the new forty-millimeter mount forward illuminated the interior of the pilothouse like heat lightning, revealing faces and hands in a flickering electric arc light like a movie theater projector gone wild. I actually saw the commodore, still seated in his chair, holding a cigarette to his mouth for a deep, glowing drag, with his eyes closed, his other hand clamped onto his coffee mug.

There was *nothing* for me to do, and that still astounded me. My officers and crew were doing what they'd been trained to do, and the din of gunfire, the eye-stinging flashes from the gun muzzles, the clouds of gun smoke streaming through our broken portholes, and above it all the scream of airplane engines driven beyond their mechanical limits overwhelmed my brain until I just sat there like some kind of head-bobbing mental patient, nodding and rocking out on the lawn of an insane asylum. Then I heard an approaching airplane engine, its scream rising like a locomotive's whistle as it comes at you, followed by a hail of what sounded like rivets smashing all over the bridge and against the sides. There was a great whooshing sound, and then a ball of fire appeared on the opposite side as the kami went into the water. I had to work my jaws to get my ears to pop as I tried to gather my wits.

Then it was over. Just like that: over. I blinked my eyes as I realized Combat was calling me on the bitch-box. I tried to reply, but nothing came out but a squeak. I cleared my throat, hoping no one had heard that, but how could they—we were all deaf. I tried again.

"Captain, aye."

"Radar is showing no contacts," Jimmy said. "I think we got 'em all. *Westfall* had one hit his fo'c'sle, but they said there was no real damage."

"Very well," I said. "Now: look out for chapter two—make sure they didn't have friends at high altitude waiting for us to focus on the low-fliers."

"Combat, aye." I was still trying to gather my wits. I'd never seen a fireworks show like that in my entire Navy career. The concentration of twenty- and forty-millimeter fire from our dozen gunships had made our five-inch fire seem insignificant. I looked at the gyro repeater. We were still headed east, and I assumed we were still at 12 knots.

We should turn around, I thought, head back toward station, figure out what we were going to do with *Westfall.* The commodore had some decisions to make. I looked across the pilothouse as the GQ watch standers tried to clear their ears and regain some sense of what was going on. The commodore was still in his chair, but the back half of his head was missing.

THIRTEEN

I closed my eyes and took a deep breath, then started swearing.

"Captain?" someone was saying. "The commodore . . ."

"Yes," I said. "I know. Get me damage reports, now."

Chief Smith, my JA talker, spoke up. "They didn't hit us, Captain," he said. "That last one came in strafing, but . . ."

"But what?"

"It was high, sir. He went over the ship."

"I heard what sounded like a riveting gun," I said. "Maybe not high enough?"

"Combat, Bridge. *Westfall* is requesting instructions."

The skipper of *Westfall* was senior to me. Hell, every commander, USN, out here was senior to me. He was really asking the commodore for instructions, not me. Unfortunately, the commodore was no longer with us.

"Tell him to take the next picket station to the east of us," I said. "Is that chaff cloud still up?"

"Yes, sir, but it's dissipating. I think. We hold no air contacts."

"Very well," I said. "Get Lieutenant Commander Canning out here, please. And the doc."

"Sir?"

"The commodore has been killed, Jimmy. The pilothouse got strafed. We need to get a report out."

Al Canning came out of Combat like a missile. He went immediately to the commodore's chair, took one look, and then sank down to his knees. He was mumbling something that sounded a lot like "Fuck, fuck, *fuck!*"

My sentiments exactly.

My last image of him alive was with that cigarette, glowing from a serious inhale, and the mug of coffee, held casually off to one side, in case the ship heeled unexpectedly and spilled it. Doc came out of the charthouse passageway, saw Lieutenant Commander Canning, and hurried over. His medical bag was already open, so we'd taken other casualties, it seemed.

"Bridge, Combat. *New* bogeys, inbound, bearing two seven five, range forty miles, composition two to four, coming straight in, on top in six to eight minutes."

"Alert *Westfall* and the gunships," I said. "Send out orders to turn ninety degrees to due north, to course zero zero zero, speed twelve. Both air-search radars up this time. We'll do the same deal we did before: star shells ahead of them at nine miles. Tell Sky One."

"Combat, aye."

By the book, I should have called *Westfall*, told

her skipper that he was now the senior officer present, and requested orders. The truth was, however, that we weren't a real, formally constituted task unit, and by the time we got that news over to *Westfall* we'd have our hands full with these new suiciders. We'd deal with this new attack, and then I'd happily hand over to *Westfall.*

I took another look across the dark pilothouse. The doc had thrown a surgical drape over the commodore's head and shoulders and sent his assistant for a body bag. I called Doc over to my chair.

"Other casualties?" I asked.

"Signalman First Emory was killed by cannon fire, and Radioman Third Benitez took what looks like a twenty-millimeter round through the knee. Took his lower leg right off. He's on a tourniquet now until I can do some cleanup work. And, of course—" He bobbed his head in the direction of the commodore's chair. We both hung on as Combat executed the formation (such as it was) turn to the north so that everyone's guns would bear. The OOD and the JOOD were out on the bridge wings making sure all the gators had gotten the word that we were turning. Director fifty-one was already bumping and grinding on its tracks, searching west for the incoming raid.

"Bridge, Combat. Bearing two seven five, range thirty miles, and they appear to be lining up in a column of some kind."

"Any signs of a controller aircraft out there, beyond the bogeys?"

"Negative, but that chaff cloud is still out there. He could be hiding in that."

"Where's *Westfall*?"

"Three miles east of us, matching our movements."

"Captain, aye." I wondered if the Jap radar could see through that chaff cloud. I got out of my chair and went out onto the port bridge wing. Director fifty-one's big antenna was in the nutating mode, jerking that pencil-lead-thin beam out into the darkness, looking for anything. Our little fleet of gator gunships was roughly in formation around us, emitting huge clouds of diesel exhaust as they plowed through the calm seas. There was enough light to see them, but not enough to make out their hull numbers or other small details. I knew that CIC would be talking to them, giving them range and bearing to the incoming suiciders minute by minute. They wouldn't be able to do anything at all until they actually saw the first kami. We, on the other hand, would have that entire column under radar-directed fire from the moment it crossed the eight-mile range ring. I hoped *Westfall* would simply join in when her guns could bear. My brain wanted some coffee, but my eyes kept seeing the commodore's coffee mug, still clutched in his lifeless hand, empty now, just like him.

Director fifty-one stopped nutating, indicating they had a lock-on. I looked aft and saw mount fifty-three swing out to port, elevate, and then open fire with the first star shells. I missed being in CIC, where I could see the entire picture—where all the ships were, where the enemy aircraft were—and manage the stream of tactical radio orders going out to our minifleet. As exec, I'd become spoiled, having the whole picture displayed in front of me. As captain, though, I was duty-bound to stay out here in the dark, if only to order maneuvers to avoid collision or clear the firing arcs for the gun batteries.

This time I didn't look out to the west to see the star shells because I wanted to keep my night vision for as long as possible. Mount fifty-two trained out to port now, followed by the quad forty sitting on mount fifty-one's roller-path circle. I stepped back into the pilothouse just as fifty-two let go, rapid continuous, shooting VT frag now, as was mount fifty-three. Fifty-two's muzzles were only about twenty feet in front of the bridge wing, so I stepped back away from the doorway to avoid all the smoke and blast. There was a twenty-millimeter guntub down below the port bridge wing, and I knew its crew would be flattened on the deck with their hands over their ears because of fifty-two's muzzle blasts. I was waiting for fireballs in the distance. I thought I heard *Westfall* shooting, too, but it was hard to tell over the booming racket of my own guns.

Once again, I got that helpless feeling. The five-inch gun battery was blasting away, the guns being laid in train and elevation by electro-servo motors responding to orders from an analog computer down in the bowels of Main Battery Plot, which in turn was taking inputs from the ship's gyro and the all important fire-control radar mounted up on top of director fifty-one. Tracking circuits were tracking; magazine crews five decks below me were humping projectiles and powder cans into the ammo hoists; the hoists were elevatoring the rounds to the mounts; sweating gun crews were extracting smoking powder cans from the breach and ramming new shells back in, slamming shut the breechblock, and closing the ready key. *Blam-blam.* Drop the block and do it all again, quickly.

First fireball! It looked to be way out there, an early casualty of another deadly object doing its job: accelerating from zero to twenty-six hundred feet per second in one tenth of a second, the safe and arming interlocks opening up electrical pathways as the shell spun and arced high up over the water, its tiny transmitter buzzing out a cone of energy fifty feet in front of its nose, its receivers waiting for the first millivolts to rise in its sensors, indicating that there was a *thing* within fifty feet of it, a capacitor then firing a jolt of electricity into the fuze, the fuze firing a bolt of lightning into the warhead, the warhead exploding into a million red-hot steel fragments that burst outward, following that same cone that the shell's radar had been peering into, and tearing a suicider out of the sky.

As the last star shell blinked out, I put my binocs on that fireball and caught a glimpse of dark gray objects flitting past and just above the dying kami, illuminated by the avgas fire streaming from his riddled wing tanks, but only for the briefest of seconds. They looked tiny, and for a moment, they looked like they weren't headed for us. They were going to go *past* us? I'd counted four, maybe five shapes out there, but as I was trying to make sense of what I'd seen, the forties opened up and thinking was no longer possible. Mount fifty-two was training away to the right, toward the bow. Then all the gators got into it with their forties, and the night lit up with tracer fire and muzzle flashes all around us.

They *were* going past us.

Westfall. They were going for *Westfall*, all alone out there, six thousand yards to the east. Oh, Christ, should I have ordered him to close us?

Another fireball lit up the sky, this one fairly close, and I had to close my eyes for a second at the intensity of the flames. The burning kami flew into the water and exploded with a blast that had to have been caused by an underslung bomb. I thought I saw one of the gunships heel over on her beam ends from that explosion, but then my attention was drawn to *Westfall* as, to my absolute horror, four kamis, one right after another, in perfect column formation, flew right into her amidships. One hit the deckhouse just below the base of the forward stack, but those other three, *still* in perfect line formation, flew through the storm of twenty- and forty-millimeter tracer fire coming right at their faces, tearing off wings and tails and igniting banners of flaming gasoline along their flanks, and crashed into her port side. The first one exploded upon impact, blowing an immense hole in *Westfall*'s side right at the waterline. The second flew into that hole and exploded, causing the ship to bulge amidships as fire came out of every crack and crevice in her hull, and then the third followed the second into what was left of the ship's middle, exploding out the starboard side of the mortally ruptured destroyer in a sheet of fire, followed by yet another bomb blast that went off right on the surface. For one horrifying moment, two of *Westfall*'s main engineering spaces, the forward fire room and the forward engine room right behind it, were fully exposed. They looked like two flaming steel ovens, and I realized I could see right through her.

I was dimly aware that our guns had stopped firing, and so had those of the gators. We were all transfixed by the spectacle of *Westfall* collapsing in the middle, her bow and stern going up into the air in a flaming V only moments later, and then sinking out of sight in a boil of steam until there was nothing left to be seen of her. I felt sick to my stomach as the darkness drew down around us again. I was conscious of seeing some of the gunships breaking out of our circular formation and heading for the spot where *Westfall* had plunged, but, with my ears still ringing from all the gunfire and my heart pounding with the realization that there had been nothing—*nothing—Westfall* or any of the rest of us could have done about that kind of an attack, I just stood there.

The Japs had figured it out. No more onesies and twosies: bring a crowd, line 'em up at 300 knots, and then dive the whole column into any given ship. The guns might get one, maybe even two, but then the next two, or three, or four, would all hit the ship in the same place, cut in her in two, and put her and every soul aboard down in less than a minute.

My legs started shaking. I needed to sit down.

As my hearing returned I heard voices around me, talkers chattering about what had just happened, and the OOD calling into CIC for contact status. The bitch-box was totally silent, as if it, too, were too shocked to speak. I leaned over the microphone screen.

"Combat, Captain. Any more bogeys?"

"That's a negative, sir," Jimmy said. "That chaff cloud is still up, but it's beginning to disintegrate, we think."

"Very well. Detach all but three gunships to pick up survivors from *Westfall*, then give the OOD a recommendation to resume our assigned picket station. Get an op-immediate off to Fleet. Make sure they know there's only one picket destroyer left on the line."

"Combat, aye."

The docs had removed the commodore's body and that of the signalman topside. We would have to conduct a burial at sea first thing in the morning, after dawn GQ, assuming we weren't dealing with kamikazes. I glanced over at the unit commander's chair and saw the messenger of the watch swabbing the deck with a disinfectant solution. That's what we've come to, I realized. One moment a senior officer; the next, a bloody stain on the deck that needs disinfecting. Marty appeared at my elbow.

"We need to figure something out," he said. "We need to figure out how to stop an attack like that."

"I'm all ears, Marty," I said, "but I'm fresh out of ideas."

"How about a V-formation," he said. "Take all these gunboats and station them in a V-formation opening to the axis of attack. That way, every gunboat gets a shot at the line of planes."

"And if they change the axis of attack at the last

moment? Come in from a different direction? At least an AA circle gives everybody a chance to shoot."

He looked crestfallen. "Marty," I said, "keep thinking. You're absolutely right—we have to come up with something, or we'll . . ." I couldn't finish the sentence. I didn't have to.

He nodded. He was as tired as I was, which reminded me to think about my people instead of sitting there, quivering in my own fear. I called Combat and asked Jimmy to come out to the bridge. I told him to put his XO hat on and see to the crew. I needed a damage assessment, a casualty report, and then a plan to let people get some sleep while still keeping the ship reasonably ready to repel any more attacks. It was going on 0300, and I was desperately hoping the Japs had gone to bed for the night.

We couldn't assume that, however. We were just one ship, the *only* ship on the picket line. That fact wouldn't be lost on any long-range Jap bomber out there at eighty miles, looking in on what was left of the American picket line. *Hey, home base, send out another ten* kamis, *you can't fail. Then when the fleet returns, there will be no more early warning.*

I tried to collect my thoughts as the bridge team secured from GQ. I knew that something was wrong with my logic. *It's called fatigue, stupid.* Something about the fleet returning from their northern strike run. Of course they'd send replacement destroyers, establish a new picket line, maybe send up some AA light cruisers, dedicate a big-deck to the picket line CAP support mission. All of those things. Or would it be none of those things?

"Captain, you need coffee, sir?"

I glanced at the frightened-looking seaman apprentice standing at the arm of my chair with a mug of what looked like asphalt. He was the same one who'd been swabbing the deck a few minutes ago. His hands, which smelled faintly of disinfectant, were just barely trembling.

"Looks like your hands are shaking."

"Just a little bit, sir."

"Mine are, too," I said. "But we can't let anyone see, can we."

"No, sir. Can't do that."

"Two sugars, son?"

"Absolutely, sir."

"Good. Everything's gonna be okay, then."

FOURTEEN

With coffee in hand and all my bulky battle gear still wrapped around me, I took a turn about deck. There seemed to be more ambient light now, which meant whatever cloud cover we'd had was beginning to lift. I had no trouble finding my way down ladders and through all the guns massed amidships. A lot of the gun crews were asleep at their stations, with one man keeping awake and manning the sound-powered phones. I could hear the talkers whispering as I left one gun mount and walked aft toward the next one. Heads up.

I was amazed to see that most of the brass had already been policed and stowed in the shell case lockers. The forties had fresh clips poised above their loading slides, and the twenties were similarly loaded up and ready to go. The after quad-forty platform gun crews were still working at picking up all the shell casings. I could smell the burned grease fumes coming off the gun barrels, which remained too hot to touch. The gun captains acknowledged my presence, but there was no impetus for small talk. Everyone had seen what happened to *Westfall*, and at least the senior people knew that there was no defense against a line attack like that. I was walking around mostly to show my face, and also to distract myself from my own feelings of nauseous fear at watching *Westfall* break in two and sink like a hot rock.

I went down the port quarter ladder to the main deck and threaded my way through the depth-charge K-guns and out onto the fantail. Both doors on mount fifty-three were open, and their crew was also picking up brass powder cans. My chief master at arms, Chief Lamont, was back there, pretending to supervise but mostly staring out over the black sea at where we'd last seen *Westfall.* I joined him by the after depth-charge racks. We nodded at each other but did not speak. There wasn't anything to say, really. Mount fifty-three's twin barrels were burned black halfway to the mount's face. I could feel the tremble of *Malloy*'s twin screws beneath my feet and hearthe whine of the steering engine responding to small helm commands from the bridge.

"Are we It now?" Chief asked, finally.

"We're It," I replied. "Fleet's coming back tomorrow, so I expect some reinforcements."

"When tomorrow?" he asked.

"Don't know, Chief. Halsey hasn't been confiding in me lately. We might be breaking up."

The chief grunted. "Those gators do any good work for Jesus back there?" he asked.

"They say they've recovered between sixty and

seventy people; we'll get an accounting when they rejoin."

"Out of what, three hundred thirty people? Them's tough odds, Skipper."

"I've spoken to the gun boss," I said. "We need everybody to start thinking how we're gonna deal with an attack like that. Everybody with an idea, however crazy, needs to speak up, enlisted, chiefs, officers. Everybody."

He nodded. "Aye, aye, sir," he said. We stood there for another few minutes staring out at nothing but our minimal wake. Then I pitched the remains of my cold coffee into the wake and headed back forward, trying to ignore the leaden ball in my stomach.

We got word that Halsey and the carrier fleet were in fact on the way back to Okinawa the next morning, having savaged as many airfield and outlying airstrips as they could find within five hundred miles of Okinawa. They'd used mostly fighter sweeps, coming low and fast off the sea and strafing everything that looked like a plane or even a revetment. They'd be back within fighter range of Okinawa at around 2200 tonight. The air-raid coordinator was predicting we would have CAP overhead at about the same time.

I'd seen Lieutenant Commander Canning, the commodore's operations officer, going into the unit commander's cabin after dawn GQ. I'd followed him in and sat down on the bunk couch.

"I'm gonna miss him," I said.

"We all will, Captain," he said, sitting down at the other end of the couch. I assumed he'd come in to gather up personal effects. "I really wanted to tell him not to come up here when he said he needed to do that. But . . ."

"Kinda hard to tell a commodore not to sail toward the sound of the guns, isn't it."

He nodded.

"Tell me about his family," I said. "Georgia, right?"

"Married, two grown children, both girls. Women, I guess. One's in business, of all things—finance, I think. The other is disabled in some fashion. He never said what. His wife came from a Southern family and lives on the family plantation. He called it a farm, but I got the impression she considers it a traditional plantation. Anyway, they apparently made an arrangement when they got married: She would live there, on a more or less permanent basis, and he would come home when he could. He gave me the impression that she's really old-fashioned. Kinda like the wives during the Civil War, who took over management of the plantations while 'the colonel' was off to war. I think he thought it was quaint, but he said homecomings were wonderful."

He put his head in his hands, closed his eyes, and sighed. He looked old and tired, like too many of the officers in this bloody campaign. I realized he probably *was* older than I was, maybe two classes ahead of me at the Boat School, and yet he was a staff officer and I was in command. I wondered how he felt about having to call me Captain.

"The admiral will do the letter, won't he?" I asked.

He nodded again. "Or his chief yeoman," he said. "They weren't friends, as best I could tell. Admiral Chase can be a prick sometimes." He opened his eyes after he'd said that, then looked over at me to see if I thought he'd been disrespectful.

"I've never met Admiral Chase," I said, "but he's pretty quick with a blast, from what I've seen."

"You have no idea," he said with a rueful smile. "Jimmy Enright said we'd do the burial at oh nine hundred?"

I confirmed that, the kamikazes willing, of course.

"Can you do me a favor, then?" he asked. "Can you, um, retrieve his academy ring? I'd like to include that with his personal effects, if possible."

I nodded. "I'll take care of it," I said.

"Thank you, sir," he said. "It's the most personal memento I can think of to send home. The rest of it—" He gestured at the commodore's two bags, not yet fully unpacked. "It's just uniforms, shoes, that kind of stuff."

"I'll take care of it personally," I said, getting up. "Right now, in fact."

I called the doc and told him what I needed to do. He said he'd be ready in fifteen minutes. When I got down to sick bay, he had the commodore's body partially exposed on his stainless steel examining table. In repose, the commodore's face looked relaxed, almost if he were about to smile. I tried not to look at the back of his head. The fast-patching team had come to the bridge to plug all the new twenty-millimeter holes. On the starboard side there were some deep dents, too. Flattened in one of those dents was a bloody twenty-millimeter projectile. Whether or not this was the one that killed the commodore we'd never know, but it seemed possible. Zeros carried a twenty-millimeter cannon in their nose, but the disturbing thing was that this shell had U.S. markings on the base of the projectile. Commodore Van Arnhem had probably been killed by one of our own shells, most likely fired by one of the gator gunships in that last melee. The chief shipfitter had brought it to me and shown me the markings. I remembered saying something brilliant like "Oh, shit." He'd nodded and left it with me. I considered keeping it for about ten seconds, then pitched it over the side.

I looked at my watch. Just after dawn GQ we were going to bury the commodore and the young signalman at sea. I planned to leave the ship at GQ before the ceremony on the fantail. That way we'd have all the guns ready in case the Japs decided to crash the proceedings.

"I need his left hand," I told Doc. He lifted the arm out from the rubber bag and exposed the hand. I removed the commodore's Naval Academy ring and his wedding ring and put them down on the steel table. Doc then repositioned the arm into the bag.

"Now I need some scissors."

"Sterile?"

I just looked at him and shook my head. He went to his desk and produced some regular scissors. I cut off a hank of the commodore's gray hair and then asked for something to put it in. Doc unpacked a sterile urine sample bottle and handed it over. I put the hair in that.

Doc gave me a what-are-we-doing look.

"The commodore is—was—married to a Southern lady," I said. "Lives in Georgia on the family farm. If I get out of this war alive, I mean to make sure she gets his rings and a lock of his hair."

"I understand the rings, Skipper," Doc said, "but hair?"

"It's a Southern tradition, Doc. During the Civil War, husbands bound for battle would leave a locket with some of their hair in it as a keepsake for the ladies on the home front."

"If you say so, Cap'n," he said.

"I say so, Doc."

"Yes, sir. I'll get him ready for committal, then?"

"Yes, please."

As I went forward to put the items in my desk safe, it occurred to me that no one was doing anything like that for the signalman seaman who also died. I made a mental note to find Jimmy Enright in the next couple of days and show him how to do the condolence letter for the signalman.

I made two decisions then: I would not tell the family that their husband and father had probably been killed by so-called friendly fire, and I would take these things to his widow personally. I owed him that much. I also needed to find a more suitable container for the lock of hair than a urine sample bottle, I thought. I almost smiled. Van Arnhem would have laughed.

I passed through the messdecks, where the cooks were already working on lunch. Mooky Johns, the chief cook and maker of fine fat-pills, saw me and waved, his black face already covered in perspiration from hot ovens and warming griddles. I waved back and kept going forward, toward the wardroom and my cabin. The items in my pocket seemed to weigh more than they should.

The interment ceremony was brief, as it had to be, given our station. Thirty minutes before it began, the doc had come to escort me back to the fantail. Per Captain Tallmadge's tradition, the signalman chief was waiting, and he told me about the young man now asleep in the rubber bag. I listened carefully, hoping I'd remember all this, his hometown, his achievements in the division, and the fact that he played a mean harmonica. I thanked him and went back to my cabin to change. The signalman went first, then the commodore. Two flags were folded after the weighted bags had been sent overboard. Jimmy Enright had come up with a nice touch: When the commodore's remains slipped down the slanted planks, Jimmy got on the 1MC, rang four bells, and announced, "DesRon Five Oh, departing." A seaman and a commodore, plummeting together into the darkness of the deep ocean. War was indeed a great leveller. We stood there for another minute or so to let each man on board pay his respects and contemplate his own mortality.

After we secured from the burial, I called a meeting of the department heads in the wardroom to brainstorm a tactic that might give us a chance against the line attack that killed *Westfall.* Marty had brought his fire-control chief and both gunner's mate chiefs, Chief Lamont and Chief Christie, along. Lieutenant Commander Canning also sat in.

I sat at the head of the wardroom table and listened to a parade of ideas, some reasonable, some pretty silly, but all of them earnestly trying to come up with something that might keep us alive. After thirty minutes I finally put up my hand and silenced the table.

"It seems to me," I began, "that the five-inch are good for knocking an approaching suicider down from a max of nine miles into about three miles. They're the only guns we have that can place a VT-frag shell right in front of an approaching Jap plane and, hopefully, kill him."

I paused and sipped some coffee. "But that's a band of six miles. If the Japs are coming in at 300 knots, that means the five-inch have a minute and a half, at max, to do their best work. After that, from three miles in, or six thousand yards, the five-inch are running out of range. Their shells leave the barrel unarmed to protect the ship. They then have to arm, turn on their transmitters, and start looking for a return signal. At three hundred knots, the target covers five miles a minute, which is four hundred forty feet a second. What I'm saying is that the five-inch are good for about two minutes of effective work, all in. After that, the problem moves to the forties. A minute later, it's the forties and the twenties. Agreed?"

Nods all around.

"Okay, let's count barrels. If the Japs come from dead ahead, we have two five-inch barrels and, as a result of battle damage, four forty-millimeter barrels and four twenty-millimeter barrels. Right?"

More nods.

"If they come from dead astern, we have two five-inch barrels, *eight* forty-millimeter barrels, and four to six twenties, depending on the angle of approach. Here's my point: Heretofore, we've always presented one side or another to maximize the number of barrels firing at the incoming Jap. The problem with that is, if we don't get his ass, he hits us in the side and opens us to the sea. For those of you who saw *Westfall* die last night, you saw one open her up, and two more tear her in two, because three out of four hit her on the side, in the same place, in rapid succession.

"Here's what I think: If we present the side, either side, to four kamis coming in a line formation, we're done for. We might get one or even two, but two more will fly through the forward engine room and break us in half. Whereas, if we present the front end or the back end to a line formation, they can tear up the entire superstructure above the main deck, but they can't open us to the sea. Since we have more barrels pointed aft than forward, I'm thinking we show them our sternsheets and take it from there."

"We give up two quad forties amidships if we do that," Chief Lamont said.

"I know," I said. "If we still had mount fifty-one, I'd point the bow at them. But here's the thing I keep coming back to: The five-inch aren't that useful. At long range, nine down to three miles, they're the *only* thing that can hit them. After that, they're of no use, because their shells won't have armed before they're flying right past the targets. The five-inch have stopping power, I'll admit, but it's the forties and the twenties that can tear these line formations apart. I'd rather get hit with fragments than a whole Zero, with bomb—and not in the side."

There was silence around the wardroom table. We'd been presenting our broadside, as it were, to all the attacks we'd seen. With this new tactic, that wouldn't work anymore. The side was what they were after. Send three, four, hell, ten suiciders, and there was no way out for the target destroyer.

"Gonna be hell on wheels for all the gun crews topside," Chief Christie said.

"Yes, I know," I said. "So what can we do to protect them better than we've been doing?"

"Tell 'em to jump right the hell over the side when the second kami shows up over the fantail?" Lamont offered.

"Why the second?"

" 'Cause we'd have shot down the first one,

Captain," he said. There were some grins around the table, but they were halfhearted.

"That's what's different now," he continued. "They're *gonna* hit us. We can shoot down as many as we can, but those numbers you just talked about, three hundred knots, they're gonna hit us."

"And I'm saying it's better to get hit along the length of the superstructure, as opposed to three or four of them breaking us open to the sea."

"That superstructure you're talking about," the chief said. "That's where *we* are."

"That's where I am, too, Chief. I'm not arguing that they're gonna git us. I'm simply recognizing that they don't necessarily have to *sink* us. *Westfall* was gone in sixty seconds with most of her crew. Look, we can't survive what they threw against *Westfall* unless we keep them from opening up the hull. We need them to tear up stacks, director columns, life rafts, the mast, but *not* the hull. Now, let's talk about protecting all the people in the path of these things."

"Yeah, sure," the chief said. "Like I said, we gonna jump over the side?"

"Yes."

That produced a moment of stunned silence.

"Look, we make sure every man topside has a kapok life jacket *and* a flashlight clipped to that life jacket. We brief the gators: If we get one of these line attacks, there are going to be lots of our people in our wake. Look for those lights when it's all over. Pick 'em up. I'm serious. The gun crews see that there are a bunch of kamis coming down to hit us along our whole length? Jump. Go over the side. We have fifteen amphib craft around us. Go over the side, wait until the main event is over, and then turn on your light. Whatever happens on board, you're going to be safer in the water than on the oh-one level where three, four, five goddamned kamis have crashed, with all their gasoline and their goddamned bombs."

Marty raised a hand. "You're serious, sir?"

"Yes, I am. We cannot survive what they did to *Westfall* last night. No lone destroyer can. I believe they'll be back tonight with the same program. They had a controller out there last night, and he had to have seen what happened. I'm talking about saving as many lives as we can, given what's probably coming."

I looked around the table at their incredulous faces.

"I know what you're thinking," I said, "and I'm not saying we're going to abandon ship at the first sign of a night attack. If they come in the conventional manner, one, two, diving at us from wherever, we stay on station and we shoot them down.

"But if our radar sees that they're coming in line formation—four, five, six of the bastards—then

I'm going to point the stern at them and blow the ship's whistle. You hear that, get your people to safety. You don't *have* to go over the side, of course. Mount fifty-three's crew can open the emergency hatch to the upper handling room and drop down there. Quad forties on the oh-one level aft? Get down to the main deck, get inside the superstructure, and from there, down to the second deck berthing spaces. Midships forties? Same deal—get down to the main deck and get inside."

I paused to think. "I know this sounds like heresy, but I'm telling you, here's what I saw happen to *Westfall* last night. Those bastards came in three-second intervals, and no one, *no* one, had the first chance in hell of living through that. All their guns—and, unlike us, *Westfall* still had *all* their five-inch—were ineffective against that. Fact of life, people: The guns are ineffective against that. I'm trying to save your lives, so don't fight me on this. We'll shoot at them for as long as the guns can do good work for Jesus, but after that, you hear the ship's whistle blowing, execute the survival plan. Get below the main deck, and if you can't do that, go over the side."

Every man at the table was staring at me, and it was Jimmy who asked the salient question. "The bridge team," he said, "and CIC. What do they do?"

"Drop down to the wardroom," I said. "We'll

give it our best shot, which is the five-inch opening up to start hitting at eight miles. But if it's a line formation, at some critical point, I want all hands to get down, get down into the ship, because the oh-one level and probably the main deck are going to turn into a sea of fire. As bad as that is, it's better than turning to shoot at them and exposing our flanks."

There was a long moment of absolute silence. Then one of the other chiefs had a question. "You think Halsey's *not* going to send reinforcements?"

"Who's this Halsey guy?" I asked. "Has the Big Blue Fleet *ever* given the first thought about what's going on up here? We're on our own, gents. It's time to think clearly. Tomorrow, there may be a dozen new tin cans coming up here. Tonight? It's just us chickens, along with our gator gunships. We're on our own here. Let's stay alive, shall we? Somebody needs to welcome all those reinforcements."

After that meeting, I called Jimmy, Mario, Marty, and Chief Lamont into my cabin. They were all obviously disturbed by what I'd said out there in the wardroom. They sat together stiffly on the bunk-bed couch; I sat at my desk.

"Guys, are you with me on this?"

"Absolutely, Captain," Jimmy said. "I get it. There's no defense against the line formation attack."

"Marty?"

"I'm uncomfortable with abandoning the guns in the middle of a fight," he said. "But yes, I get it, too. There's no point to having a hundred fifty men glued to their gun stations if four kamis are going to use them for a landing deck."

"That's the point, gents," I said. "I'll fight this sumbitch to the bloody end, but I recognize an impossible situation when I see one. Go out there to your people and figure out a plan. Practice an escape route. Make sure everyone topside has a working flashlight tied to his kapok. Jimmy,let's get the COs of the gator gunships aboard. I want to talk to them personally. There's no reason for them to be operating in the dark. And another thing: Jimmy, retransmit the message we sent out last night about *Westfall* and the picket line. It's possible they never got it."

"Aye, aye, sir," Jimmy said. "One thing: I'd like to comb the GQ station bill for CIC and the bridge. There's no need to have *all* those people up there for a nighttime attack. I'm thinking people like the Freddies, if we don't get CAP. The quartermaster, bosun mates, signalmen . . . ?"

"You're right. We'll go to a normal GQ posture, but if an attack shapes up we can begin stripping down the supernumeraries. Mario, thin out the damage control teams topside. Consider this: If the superstructure is wiped slick, what gear would you wish you'd gotten off the main deck and down below?"

"All the fire hoses and P-250 pumps, for damned sure," he said. "Although that means having gasoline tanks inside the ship."

"If we take a couple of kamis tonight, three twenty-gallon fuel tanks won't make much of a difference," Marty said.

"Okay," I said. "Those are the details I need you guys to work on, before sundown. We can't plan everything, but we can sure as hell think about it today. I need to talk to the gunship skippers now. If Halsey's been raising hell in southern Japan we may have a quiet day while they regroup. But they will regroup, and I don't think we'll see any reinforcements for us up here until dawn tomorrow."

"If Halsey and the big-decks are all north and west of us today, why do they need a picket line at all?" Marty asked.

"Kerama Retto," I reminded him. "We're the only warning the gators and the freighters will get if the Japs take advantage of Halsey's absence and decide to firestorm the anchorage."

"Damn," Chief Lamont said to no one in particular. "No damned slack in this man's outfit."

When they left I found Lieutenant Commander Canning waiting outside my door. I invited him in, half expecting him to be profoundly against what I'd been proposing. He surprised me.

“That made a lot of sense, Captain,” he said. “Perhaps if we’d been embarked up here and not pushing beans and bullets down in KR one of us would have thought of it.”

“Maybe,” I said. “If you’d lived long enough. Besides, if there were ten ships up here instead of just one, we could design an AA formation and eat ’em up.”

He nodded. That remained the crux of the problem: never enough destroyers. “They have to fly two-hundred-some miles to get at us down here,” he mused. “What’s it going to be like when we’re ten miles offshore of the main islands?”

“That’ll work both ways, I think,” I said. “Ten miles is well within battleship gun range. Maybe those gray elephants will get to contribute something besides a nice flag cabin for once.”

FIFTEEN

By 2200 we'd all settled in for the much-dreaded night watch. I'd gathered all the gunboat skippers aboard *Malloy* to talk through tactics and what we might expect tonight following the sinking of *Westfall.* One of the possibilities was that there'd be *no* attack, because the kamikaze forces had launched a major raid against the carrier formations during the early afternoon, once again breaking their attack pattern. Not all the planes that had come out had been kamis—there'd been torpedo planes, bombers, fighters, the works—and while the fleet formation's CAP had cleaned house, there'd been a lot of damage done. More than ever, I was convinced our message about *Westfall* had been lost or at least overlooked in all the excitement.

The gunship skippers had been a mixture of lieutenants, lieutenant commanders, and even a few seasoned warrant officers. We were down to eleven, as I had sent some back down to KR with *Westfall*'s survivors, along with one of our three LCSs to give them some protection en route. I didn't have to tell them about what had happened to *Westfall*—they'd all seen it just as close up as we had. We'd kicked around several ideas about what to do with the gunships if another line attack materialized, and decided that the best approach was to put them into roughly two columns behind us, aligned with the axis of attack if there was time, and then make the kami column fly between those two columns and the resulting valley of death that all their guns could create, if only for about thirty seconds. Only the LCSs had radar, so for the most part, the gunboats would simply be shooting in the same direction they saw our tracers going in the dark. Better than nothing.

The skippers had been in full concurrence with our plans to abandon the topside gun stations once the radar-controlled five-inch ran out of shooting room. They were well equipped to get astern of us if we were disabled and pick up any jumpers. One warrant bosun made a suggestion: Have each of the crewmen stuff a Dixie cup, the sailor's familiar round white hat, in his trousers pockets, and put it on once they were in the water. The white fabric made it a lot easier for rescue boats to find them in the dark.

It was definitely a surreal meeting, sitting around the wardroom table and talking about the best ways to find men floating in the water at night and how we were going to deliberately abandon the weather decks if the column formations appeared again. I knew there was something sacrilegious about a destroyer's commanding officer talking about doing anything but fighting the ship until she sank beneath his feet, but all I had to do to stand firm was conjure up that vision of hell I'd seen last night when we all were able to see right through *Westfall*'s broken back.

Earlier that evening, after chow, I'd walked the decks and talked to the various gun crews, making sure they understood we'd fight if we could, but if they heard the ship's whistle blow, that meant we were about to be overwhelmed. As tired as they all were, I sensed that they were fully focused. They, too, had seen what had happened to our sister ship.

The bridge was quieter than usual, partly because we'd secured some of the less important watch stations. I was ensconced in my chair. We had an officer of the deck, a junior officer of the deck, one man instead of two to operate both the helm and lee helm, and a single messenger of the watch. My JA circuit battle talker, Chief Smith, was down in the chief's mess but would come up when we set GQ. The doc had established three additional first-aid teams throughout the ship, men who were capable of tending to immediate bleeding or burns in the spaces around them without having to wait for Doc and his assisting corpsman to get there. The chief engineer had set out firefighting hoses inside at strategic locations near hatchways to the weather decks so we wouldn't have to wait for a repair party to make its way from the designated repair locker to the scene of a big fire. We'd pulled all the fuzes out of the topside depth charges and struck down a major part of the ready-service ammo for the forties and twenties. They'd only have enough to shoot for about ninety seconds, but there wouldn't be ammo lockers exploding and decimating the weather decks once they were drenched in flaming avgas.

As I sat in my high-backed captain's chair, it occurred to me that these were some of the measures we should have been taking all along. Instead, we'd followed doctrine: everything loaded to the gills; repair parties mustered at their lockers in three separate locations below decks; most of the canvas firefighting hoses mounted and neatly folded, regulation-style, out on the weather decks, where a topside fire would consume them in seconds.

I called into Combat and asked if we had CAP yet. Negative. There were no night-fighters available. The Japs had come out again just after dark to treat Halsey to Bettys carrying baka bombs, so all the night-fighters were up protecting the carriers. I almost told Combat to inform the fleet air-raid reporting net that we were down to one ship on the picket line, but that net was a plain-language circuit and we knew the Japs monitored it constantly. On the other hand, I thought the Japs already knew.

The night was about as clear as it had been last night, with a light breeze from the northeast. The moon, unfortunately, was out and providing altogether too much light for my comfort. Our two radars were having a good night, though, and the Freddies could even see some of the fleet formation's high-altitude CAP about a hundred miles away to the northwest. The carriers would be some fifty miles behind those CAP stations, headed toward Okinawa. I hoped they'd be able to see and jump on any kamis headed down our way. I'd heard Jimmy telling his CIC crew that with the fleet between Okinawa and Japan itself, there'd be no reason for them to come down and attack the picket line tonight. It sounded like whistling past the graveyard to me, but what the hell—if it provided a smidgen of comfort, it was worth the try.

"Bridge, Combat. We just detected a snooper, bearing zero eight five, range sixty miles, heading west-northwest."

"Captain, aye," I said. East of us and heading northwest?

"And, Captain, it looks like he's laying down one of those chaff clouds, like last night."

That made more sense. Northwest of us was the bulk of Halsey's carrier formation, headed southeast with a ring of night-fighters stationed in air-defense sectors all around the carriers. Any snoopers or kamis headed for us on a direct line from Japan would have given that formation a wide berth—to the east, apparently. Now their controller was setting up an arc of radar-jamming chaff counterclockwise from east to northwest. That would make it impossible for any of the carrier radars to see what was happening along the Okinawa picket line, and blind our radars as well. Pretty damned shrewd. I felt the figurative jaws of a vise closing on us.

"What's the true wind?" I asked.

"From the north, ten knots, variable," Combat said. We were approaching the end of the north-east monsoon season. Soon there'd be no wind for about three weeks, and then the southwest monsoon would kick in.

"How about up at CAP altitude?"

"It'll be stronger than that, Captain. As much as forty or even fifty knots. If we had CAP we could tell you precisely . . ."

"Right," I said. "So that arc of chaff is going to drift in toward us, then."

There was a pause. "Yes, sir. We can't tell what altitude he's dropping at, but we're assuming twenty thousand feet."

Drift in toward us, masking whatever aircraft that patrol bomber out there had under his radar control. They could loiter out there at the far end of our air-search radar range until that all-obscuring chaff cloud was in to, say, thirty miles, then launch at us at 300 knots, or more, if they were diving from altitude.

"Alert our gators," I said. "We have probably a half hour before the Japs make their move. Conventional attack, everybody stays put. Line attack, you know what to do."

"Yes, sir, we do."

"Combat, compute a predicted track on that snooper. I'm going to assume the kamis are with him and will come from his predicted position in the cloud. Give me that bearing, and then we'll start steering in the opposite direction and set the gators up along that axis."

It took them five minutes, and then they recommended we come to course 170, almost due south, to point our stern at the expected threat axis of 350. I could be all wrong, of course, and they might offset to come at us from due east, but the snooper was still spewing his chaff cloud, and I was willing to bet his suicide group was tucked in close to him. I couldn't see the gator gunships, but I knew CIC was directing them to form a two-column formation parallel to our movements. I was taking a chance: If the kamis came from some other direction, we could change course immediately, but that gaggle of gators would probably dissolve into chaos.

I asked for some coffee, and the messenger jumped to get it. I knew everybody was scared of what might be shaping up. I almost wanted a cigarette, and that image of the commodore taking a deep drag on his cigarette leaped into my mind. We'd lost one of the good ones last night, and I'd been unable to suppress a tear or two when we'd slipped his body over the side. It had been comforting, actually, to have a senior four-stripe captain onboard. I'd been all too ready to revert to the role of XO. Now that I'd been the captain for a short while, though, I was beginning to get used to it.

I looked at my watch. We had maybe twenty minutes before we'd know what they were going to do. I remembered that the commodore had had a bottle of Scotch down in his unit commander's cabin. I was tempted, sorely tempted.

Strangely, however, the fear that had coiled up in my guts before wasn't there tonight. Was that because I had resigned myself to the knowledge that there really wasn't anything we could do about another line attack? Or was it a modicum of confidence that we'd made the best preps we could and now we simply had to wait to see if any of it worked? I noticed then that Chief Lamont had come up to the bridge. He was standing near my chair, strapping on Chief Smith's sound-powered phone handset. I raised an eyebrow at him, and he said simply that he and Smith had traded off.

"Bridge, Combat. Fleet staff has just come up

on the HF net," Jimmy said. "I'm guessing they finally got our message, because they want us to retire to KR immediately at best speed."

Best speed meant turn toward KR, come up to 27 knots, and get *Malloy* the hell out of there. The problem, of course, was the gator gunships. The best speed they could do was 10 to 12 knots, and that was downhill with a following sea. Besides, a fifteen-minute head start south wouldn't make any difference to a column of Zekes doing 300 knots.

"It's a little late for that, Jimmy. These bastards are gonna jump us in fifteen minutes."

"What should I tell them, Captain?"

"Tell them attack in progress, we can't abandon our gators, so we're gonna stay and fight."

There was a one-second pause before Jimmy's reply. "Yes, sir," he said. "I'll tell 'em just that."

Jimmy had sounded more enthused about my reply than he'd been about our preparations for imminent immolation. Well, I thought, just you wait, Jimmy, boy. Just you wait.

I heard a chuckle behind me. Lamont was laughing to himself.

"What?" I asked.

"Fiery words for posterity," he said in a pronounced Scottish burr. "I have not yet begun to fight, et cetera? John Paul Jones was a Scot, you know."

“And a great pain in the ass,” I said.

“Comes with the territory, I believe,” he said.

“I love the accent, Lamont, but, c’mon, where were you born, really?”

“Would you believe Hoboken?” he admitted. We both started laughing.

I looked out the bridgewing door at the gray shapes of the gunships as they scrambled to get into their V-formation. I decided to go back into CIC. I wanted to see that radar picture.

Once in Combat I stood behind the two big scopes the Freddies used to control their CAP, when we had them, that is. The chaff cloud occluded almost the entire top right quadrant of the screen, and it had drifted in to about thirty-five miles. I asked where the bomber was, and the radar operator pointed at a slightly brighter pinpoint of green light at the northwest edge of the arc. If there were fighters or suiciders with him, they reflected too little energy to be visible. For that matter, they could be anywhere in that broad band of green fuzz on the screen, awaiting their radio vectors to come find us. As I watched that tiny pip at the leading edge of the green arc, it disappeared.

“If that thing’s turned around and flown back into the chaff cloud, how long before he gets to the middle, or about due north?” I asked.

One of the radar operators worked a handheld

circular slide rule. "Eight minutes if he stays at two hundred knots."

I nodded. If that was the case, we had eight minutes before we'd know what was coming. "How close will the chaff cloud be in eight minutes?"

"Right at thirty miles," Jimmy said from the other side of the main plotting table. "But the cloud will also be thinning out. That stuff doesn't stay up forever."

Thirty miles. If the kamis popped out at thirty miles, going 300 knots, they'd be on us in six minutes, tops. That should be more than enough time to vacate the upper decks, because the entire crew could get to their GQ stations in less than two minutes. Line formation. That's what we were waiting to see.

I waited, mentally searching our plans for any big holes. Then I told Jimmy to compute a radar search sector centered on what we assumed would be their line of attack, and pass that to Sky One to begin a director radar search. The sooner we picked up the first suicider, the sooner the five-inch could go to work to thin them out. Our main gunnery computer usually lagged the target if it was going really fast. That meant that the computed gun orders would put shells behind the target. By now, however, our fire-control radar operators knew how to deal with a straight-in, slant-diving approach: add in an up-spot of a hundred feet in elevation and a drop-spot of three hundred yards in range. That would put the bulk of the ack-ack in *front* of the approaching plane. If it was VT fuzed, that gave the tiny radars the best chance to detect something coming at them. If it was a mechanically timed fuze, it should explode in front and just above the approaching plane, filling the air with shrapnel for him to fly through.

At four minutes, I had Combat send out a message to all the gunboats saying that we were expecting an attack very soon and confirming the bearing we expected it to come from. Admittedly, that was a big assumption on my part, but you had to start somewhere.

Of course, as it turned out, I was wrong.

One minute later, a blob appeared on the inside edge of the chaff cloud at 330, thirty degrees to the *left* of where I had thought they'd come from. Well, no, twenty degrees. Was it worth it to try to reform our two-column formation? I made a quick decision: Stick with what we had. If there'd been a division of destroyers out there, then I might have tried it, but the slow, clumsy-handling amphib support ships would have turned the maneuver into a cluster-fuck at the worst possible moment.

"Composition?" I asked, staring down at the radarscope.

"One," the operator said. "One large, from the size of the video, but one."

All right then, I decided. So tonight the bomber was coming. Perfect target for the five-inch. The two remaining LCSs each had a five-inch, but they were not radar-controlled. I'd instructed them to open fire upon my command at a pre-designated range, elevation, and bearing, if only to add volume to the ack-ack barrage. I didn't care who shot this guy down, so long as he went down.

"Sky One reports lock-on, single target, opening fire in thirty seconds at max range."

Opening fire with *one* twin five-inch mount, I realized. If I turned the ship, I could get two mounts to bear and double the firepower. If I did that, though, we'd be running over gators within ninety seconds. Holes in the plan? Here was one, a big one. Had I outsmarted myself? And just one suicider? All that chaff, for *one* suicider?

Mount fifty-three opened up in rapid-continuous fire, and I could dimly hear some other five-inch guns firing on either side of us.

"Main Battery Plot says this thing's coming in at three hundred fifty knots," Jimmy reported. "Big target."

I tried to remember which of the Jap bombers could make that kind of speed. Our time margin to decide was dwindling rapidly, but it was clearly one plane. Surely they could—

"Sky One reports fireball, but Plot says it's still coming!"

The forties opened up then, and with a burning target in sight they ought to be able to tear it up pretty good. The five-inch were still cooking. I wanted desperately to turn the ship and bring the whole battery to bear, but I'd trapped myself by putting the gunboats on either side. The good news was they had opened up now, and, even from within CIC, the noise level outside was rising satisfactorily.

I left Combat and hurried out to the bridge and then to the port bridge wing. I could see our portside gunners all looking aft, and then I saw a fire in the sky, bright red and yellow flames trailing something big as it bored in at us. The closer it got, the more lines of tracers converged on it, and I could see pieces coming off. A second later it roared overhead, a big gray four-engined bomber, big as an American B-17, three engines aflame but the fourth howling at redline, the red meatballs on its wings visible from the light of its own flames. I caught no more than an instantaneous look, but I could see the nose had been torn to pieces. It looked like there were human remains dangling out of the wreckage of its front end, flopping in the slipstream as it went over at just above masthead height and then nosed down into the sea about a half mile ahead of us.

The guns stopped. My God, that was too close, and much too big.

"That was a Liz, Skipper," Marty called down from Sky One. "Long-range land-based bomber."

"Good shooting, Marty," I called back. I looked out at the gator fleet, and they were all there, no doubt whooping and hollering at shooting down such a big plane. I realized then that if we'd turned, we'd have plowed over half of them.

"Bridge, Combat, bogeys, *bogeys,* five, maybe six, inbound, fast, low, bearing three four zero, range twenty-eight miles. Line formation!"

"Bosun mate," I yelled, "sound the ship's whistle."

Our steam whistle, which had been remounted to the mast after we lost the top of the forward stack, sounded a series of urgent blasts as director fifty-one wheeled around to look out over our starboard quarter and then began nutating urgently, looking for that lead kami. I was dimly aware of the sound of thudding feet as the designated people cleared out of Sky One, the signal bridge, the midships gun nests, and finally CIC itself. The director stopped, twitched a couple of times, and then stopped again, locked on. A moment later, mount fifty-three opened up again. Ninety seconds. That was all the good they could do.

I yelled at everyone on the bridge to lay below. I didn't have to say it twice: We were going to catch hell, no matter how well the after five-inch did, and they all knew it. There was no panic.

They knew the plan, and they hustled out of the topside spaces quickly but efficiently. Once everybody bailed out, the bridge was suddenly very quiet. Except for the continuous blamming of the after five-inch mount, we were suddenly the *Mary Celeste*, plodding through the dark Pacific Ocean, while six suicidal harpies screamed through the night thirsting for our blood.

I went back out to the starboard bridge wing this time, to watch the show. The muzzle blasts from mount fifty-three were a comforting sight, yellow-orange spouts of flame followed by actual smoke rings. Out to starboard, our remaining LCS was shooting its five-inch in the general direction of the incoming kamis. The LCS hadn't been issued the new VT frag rounds, so they were setting fuzes by hand and hoping for the best. The range was still too far out for me to see any ack-ack detonations, but I knew that wouldn't last. Composition five to six. We'd get a few, but . . .

Finally I saw a fireball, a big one, as the VT frag tore one out of the sky. Then a second one. Those down-spots were working.

Marty's voice floated down from Sky One. "Fifty-three is abandoning the guns," he yelled. "Kamis are at six thousand yards."

Six thousand yards, three miles. Be here in thirty seconds. Right. Get out of there.

"Lay below, Marty," I yelled back over the sound of the nearby LCS's five-inch. The poor gators had no idea how close the Japs were, but there they were, blasting faithfully away into the night.

"I'll go when you do, Skipper," he shouted back, as his director crew scrambled out of their steel box and scampered down the ladders to safety.

Fifty-three fell silent. I thought about running but then decided not to. If my plan worked, the kamis would wreck our superstructure, but our hull would remain relatively intact. As long as *Malloy* floated, however much our top hampers had been savaged, we could make it back to KR. We, or whoever was left alive.

Something nudged my arm. It was Lamont, holding two mugs of coffee. "Two sugars, I'm told."

We never heard them. One moment there was silence on the bridge except for that lone LCS banging away in the general direction of trouble. The next moment the ship lurched as a suicider crashed down on the fantail and slammed into mount fifty-three before exploding in a ball of flame. The next one did the same thing, skidding up against the after forty-millimeter gun platforms before flipping sideways and off the ship into the sea. In one surreal instant, I got a clear view of that lone LCS, blasting away into the night at targets that had long flown through the notch she was shooting at.

The third one missed, amazingly, howling past the starboard side, straight and level, turning hard to starboard, catching a wing in the sea, and then cartwheeling into the water in a huge explosion.

The fourth one came in from a little higher, hitting us at the base of the number two stack and exploding literally all over the ship, with pieces of the plane slicing the air near my face with a murderous hissing sound. I saw the ship's boats go flying off the 01 level as if they were made of balsa wood, just before the plane's engine smashed into the pilothouse. Then his bomb went off. I think. I wasn't there anymore.

SIXTEEN

When I was a little kid, my family would go down to the Mall in Washington and watch the Fourth of July fireworks from the Capitol lawn whenever we were back in town. I can remember grudgingly watching the show while waiting for the big finale, because that's when the sky really lit up, the whole sky, *bang, bang, bang,* going on seemingly forever, with me cheering it all on from between my father's knees.

Bang, bang, bang. Then voices, which I could barely hear through my sticky-feeling ears. One of my eyes didn't seem to work. I opened the other eye and saw flashes of light, then closed it right back up again. It felt much better closed.

Bang, bang, bang. "Anyone in there?"

Opened that eye again. More flashes of light, more banging. I was flat on my back in what I immediately dubbed a captain sandwich. There were flat plates of steel beneath me and more on top, squashing my nose sideways, and so close to my one operational eye that I could see striations in the blackened paint from a long-ago paint-brush. My arms were spread out on either side, and they both, I suddenly realized, were probably broken.

More banging. I tried to respond but only croaked.

The banging stopped. Again someone called. "Say it again."

I got out another croak, but that was all I could manage. Arms really hurting now, couldn't feel my legs at all, other than pins and needles, which in a way was probably a good thing. The lights went from flashing this way and that to steady. I croaked again.

"We hear you," a voice called out. "Lie still. We're gonna get this shit off you. Just lie still."

No problem, I thought. I couldn't move anything except that one eyelid anyway. There was steel pressing up against my cheek so hard that I couldn't really make my jaw move. I tried to take a deeper breath. No go. I drifted off for a while.

I woke up to more lights now, the sound of machinery, and then a crackling, buzzing sound from outside the pile. Welding? Was someone welding? I tried to move, and a wave of pain overwhelmed me. I elected to try that drifting maneuver again. When I woke up it was to the fact that some part of the pile of steel had moved, increasing the weight on my left leg to the point where I think I called out. Big mistake. I fainted again. Things were much better in the dark.

When I came to there was water flowing past

my pinned body. I didn't think we were sinking, but I couldn't really tell. The lights were still there, and there was more machinery noise, machinery I couldn't recognize. Then there came a veritable wave of water that swept through my little pocket, high enough to wash over my face. It felt good, tasted salty, and, fortunately, immediately subsided before it drowned me.

"You still with us?"

I still couldn't move my jaw, so I gave it another croak.

"Awright, we're about to lift this edge. We're gonna take it up slow. You holler if we're making it worse, okay?"

Double croak. O. K.

The steel moved. A crack of white light appeared in the direction of where I thought my feet were. It was just a crack, but as they lifted, it grew wider until I could see actual daylight, and then three round faces in total black silhouette peering in at me. I could move my jaw now.

"Thanks," I said.

One of the faces disappeared, and then I heard him shouting. "The captain!" he yelled. "We found the captain. He's *alive*."

You got it, sunshine. Now get me the hell out of here.

It took another hour of painstaking lifting, rigging, hauling, and rerigging, but finally they were able to rope my feet and begin pulling me out from under what I later found out was the remains of the pilothouse. Bright sunlight greeted me, along with some gasps from the onlookers. I felt a sharp sting in my right thigh. It felt good to be free from all that metal. It was even better to see that we were still afloat, that I wasn't imagining all this, and that we were surrounded by at least five destroyers. Well, finally, I thought. Fleet's figured it out.

My head felt like it had changed shape, and my arms wouldn't work at all. My left leg was one big red bruise from groin to ankle, and my ears were filled with crusted blood. Both my eyes were black, and my nose felt twice its size. I hurt in places I didn't know I had. Other than that, Mrs. Lincoln, I asked myself, how'd you enjoy the play? My khakis were soaking wet, and there were a lot of people standing around in that incredibly bright sunlight staring down at me. I finally recognized Doc as he leaned over and asked where it hurt. I was able to grin back at him, if crookedly, but then my friend, that dark curtain of cool oblivion, returned. I don't think I got to tell Doc much of anything as the shot he'd given me did its work.

It was afternoon when the morphine began to wear off and I came back to the world of the mostly conscious. I could tell that the ship was moving, and pretty well, too. There was a strong smell of stack gas everywhere. That was when I realized I was out on a weather deck and not in my cabin. I discovered Marty sitting next to me, sound asleep. I hoped. His khakis weren't wet, but they were wrinkled as if he'd been swimming for a while. Doc appeared.

"How you feeling, sir?" he asked.

"Shot at and missed, shit at and hit," I said, quoting the old CPO expression.

He nodded. "Want more dope?"

"Can I have some water instead?"

His assistant handed him a coffee mug with water in it. I drank it down too fast, choked a little, and wished I hadn't done that. My ribs all complained at once when I coughed.

"*Now* you want some more dope?" Doc asked, after seeing the expression on my face.

"First tell me what happened."

A man began calling out in pain somewhere nearby. I realized I was one of about a dozen men laid out on mattresses on the main deck, forward.

"I got him," Marty said.

Doc nodded, got up, and hurried over to a man who was very, very badly burned. Doc already had a morphine vial out.

"We made it, I take it," I said.

"Yes, sir," Marty said, "we did, thanks to you. There's nothing left of the deckhouse except the front windscreen of the bridge. Forward of that, we've still got mount fifty-two and that quad-forty kluge. Aft of that, however, we're ready to install a flight deck. Everything's smashed, burned, or gone over the side. We think we took four kamis, but the last one had a crowd-pleaser slung on his belly."

"Casualties?"

"You're looking at them, Captain," he said. "Thirteen. That's all—thirteen. It's goddamn amazing, is what it is. Main plant is in pretty good shape, although we're hand-steering, and the stacks are a problem. We're headed south to KR and the tender. We have *Waddell*—she's a Gearing class—for an escort, and there's five more tin cans up on the picket line."

I couldn't see the extent of the damage because we were all laid out on the forecastle, just under mount fifty-two's barbette. Behind the gun mount was the facade of the bridge, standing there like one of those ruined monastery churches in England. Behind that, where there should have been the director barbette, the mast, and number one stack, there was only blue sky.

"So it worked," I said, realizing now that I was very tired and probably about to go back under.

"It absolutely worked," he said. "I didn't want to do it. Just seemed wrong, against all naval tradition, but you were right. Worked like a charm, and there's three hundred or so guys want to thank you for it."

"You were still up there on Sky One when that last one hit," I said. "How—?"

“I did the most perfect swan dive I ever made, right off the port side. I was underwater when that big one went off, and I felt it, too, but the gators had my ass drying off in a small boat within five minutes.”

“Where’s Lamont?” I asked.

“Right over here, Skipper,” Lamont called out. He was lying in a Stokes litter, legs bandaged and splinted up to his belt. “I hit the deck, but then it hit me back.”

“Hoboken,” I muttered. He must have heard me.

“What can I say, Captain. Gotta be born somewhere.”

Good, I thought. Lamont was okay. I was still alive. *Malloy* was still alive. Good. I’d meant to say that out loud, but apparently it was naptime in the city again.

The next morning I awoke in what I recognized as Commodore Van Arnhem’s cabin on the tender. I was in a real bed with real linens. Sunlight streamed through several portholes, which still had their glass. I looked around and wondered why they’d put me here. There was a picture of someone I assumed was the commodore’s wife on his desk, a very handsome lady wearing what looked like a costume from a Civil War drama. Behind her stood a younger woman who was a real beauty. His daughter, perhaps? Weren’t there two?

I missed the guy, even though our acquaintance had been all too brief. I still had his rings and that lock of hair back in my safe, assuming my cabin was intact. I wondered if I'd have the nerve to go through with what I told Doc I was going to do when this was all over.

There was a soft knock, and a Negro steward stuck his head around the edge of the door. When he saw that I was awake, he disappeared and then returned with a tray of coffee and a fat-pill. I realized I was really hungry. I sat up and gasped. "Shouldn't have done that," I mumbled as my eyes rolled backward and I passed out again. Never got the fat-pill, either.

There was a doctor beside me when I came back to consciousness; the steward was long gone, but the coffee tray was still there. Better yet, so was the fat-pill.

"There you are," the doctor said.

"Have to stop doing that," I said.

"You have to learn to move really slow," he said. "You have no single serious injury, but your whole body was compressed under several thousand pounds of steel, from what your exec tells me. Slow, careful movements, with deep breathing before you move. Got it?"

I nodded, which made my jaw hurt.

He poured some coffee. "Two sugars, they told me."

I smiled. "Where's my ship?"

"Right alongside," he said. "There's a four-striper from Halsey's staff waiting to talk to you. You up to it?"

"Am I up to it?"

"Slow, deliberate movements, deep breathing before you do anything," he repeated. "I don't see why not. You've got some painkillers in you, for which you should be duly grateful. Let's get you semivertical."

That took five minutes of slow, deliberate movements and more deep breathing than I'd done in years. Every muscle in my body had something to say about it, none of it very nice. I finally got some coffee in me, along with a few bites—make that heavy gumming—of that fat-pill. Their baker was decidedly better than our Mooky. Then the fleet staff captain came in, followed by Jimmy and Marty.

"Captain Miles," he said, coming forward to shake hands. "I'm Captain Bill Waring, assistant fleet operations. We're very glad to see you're still with us, especially after I saw your ship."

I loved that royal "we" the fleet staff people liked to use. They were all sharing in the power and the glory of Admiral Bull Halsey when they used that "we."

"I'm very lucky to be here," I said. "Forgive me if I'm a little slow. The doctor said that slow, in my case, is good."

"Quite understand, Captain," he said. He was

tall, hawk-faced, and probably thirty pounds under his peacetime weight. There were dark circles under his bright blue eyes, indicative of twenty-hour days on whatever battleship Halsey was currently riding. He was, nonetheless, much aware of his importance.

"As I said," he continued, "I've seen your ship. The official report is one four-engined bomber, who missed, and four kamis who did not miss,and thirteen total casualties on board. I would really like to know how you managed that, sir."

His calling the most junior commander in the fleet "sir" was the same kind of address British commanders used when talking to their subordinates. You, sir, come here, sir. How dare you, sir. You insolent *dog,* sir.

Well, maybe that was overstating it a little. I was predisposed to dislike the fleet staff because they had left us in an impossible situation on the picket line, and I really wanted to divert the conversation for a moment to describe *Westfall*'s demise. Well, why don't you? I asked myself. It's the perfect lead-in to what you had your people do, right?

"Captain?" he asked.

"I apologize," I said. "I've had rather a bad night."

"I can come back, Captain," he said immediately. "I fully—"

"No," I said. "Let's get this done while it's fresh in mind. Jimmy, Marty, back me up here if I forget anything important, okay?"

They both nodded, and then I told Captain Waring the story of *Westfall* and how we'd prepared to prevent suffering the same fate. If I left out something important, Jimmy and Marty jumped in with salient details. It took a half hour, and when I was done, I was exhausted. To his credit, Waring saw that.

"Thank you, Captain," he said. "That's pretty amazing."

"I have a question for you, Captain Waring," I said. Jimmy knew what was coming and assumed a blank expression.

"Yes?"

"Why the fuck did Halsey, who came out here with seventy-seven destroyers, leave us up there with just two?"

Waring was clearly thunderstruck. Nobody, but *nobody,* questioned Bull Halsey's decisions on anything at all.

"You're obviously distressed," he said finally. "You've been through a harrowing experience. You—"

"Fuck that," I said. "I want an answer. All those dead on *Daniels* and *Westfall* deserve an answer. All those dead on *Billingham* deserve an answer. Dutch Van Arnhem deserves an answer. You have over a dozen big-deck carriers, another two dozen light carriers, hundreds upon hundreds of aircraft, dozens of cruisers, destroyers, battleships, for Chrissake, and you left us to die up there? Why? To give you fifteen minutes of early warning? What the *fuck,* Captain? Are William F. Halsey and that huge staff of his so very, very precious?"

Jimmy Enright was giving me a look that said, *Please, please, stop,* but I didn't care anymore. *Malloy* was wrecked. They'd probably tow her out off KR and open the seacocks, as they had done with too many Okinawa picket line destroyers. Small boys, the fleet people called us. Battleship admirals puffing out their bemedalled chests and trumpeting severely consequential orders: Small boys, harrumph, form on *me.* I knew I was a one-off, as the British term went. A young, nondestroyerman lieutenant commander sent from a carrier, for Chrissakes, to be exec in a destroyer, who had then become captain thanks to the Japs and a decided lack of volunteers out there in the Big Blue Fleet.

Captain Waring stood up and gave me a look that said my career no longer existed. "When you are feeling better, *Captain,* there will be a board of inquiry to determine how your ship was so badly damaged after you abandoned all your guns. Good day, gentlemen." He left the cabin. I looked at Jimmy and Marty.

"Screw 'em if they can't take a joke, right?"

I asked, quoting the commodore. Then I went back to sleep.

The next two days produced a feverish delirium for which I was not, thankfully, present. I was vaguely aware of white coats and sharp things sticking in my arms. On the third day the fever broke, and I was able to both eat and drink something. My body felt like I'd been steam-rollered, which the doctor said was pretty much what had happened. Jimmy and Marty came in and gave me a sitrep on the ship. Since the hull was intact and the engineering plant functional, the tender's shipfitters were going to erect a temporary pilothouse and two stacks, again, and then send us back to Pearl. After that, BuShips—the Bureau of Ships—would make the ultimate decision to either scrap her or rebuild. Then they had to leave because one of the battlewagons was going to come alongside the tender for some urgent repairs, and the three destroyers moored to her other side had to be ready to adjust mooring lines when the sixty-thousand-ton behemoth actually approached. That was something I'd like to watch, I thought before I drifted off again.

That afternoon, at around 1500, two corpsmen who I decided were secret Jap sympathizers forced me to get up and then helped me to get a bath, a shave, a change of hospital gowns, and even a bathrobe. I was given a sumptuous meal of Cream of Wheat and canned peaches. I was really hungry but found I could get only about half of the gloppy mess down before my stomach said, *Enough, awreddy.* My two torturers told me that was good enough and ordered me not to puke. Then they left.

As I finished the banquet, the light streaming in from the starboard portholes darkened perceptibly as something very large and dark gray slid along-side the tender to the accompaniment of much police-whistle blowing and lots of shouting from linehandlers. I actually felt the tender move forward and then back about fifty feet. Then a stentorian voice came over somebody's topside 1MC speakers, "Moored, shift colors." An hour and a half later, there was a knock on my cabin door and in came a commander in the cleanest and starchiest work khakis I'd ever seen.

"Afternoon, Captain," he said brightly. "Are you up for a visitor?" Not waiting for my reply, he stepped back, and in walked Admiral William F. Halsey Jr. himself. I blinked a couple of times and then wondered if I was supposed to stand up. Halsey came toward me making a gesture that said, *Stay where you are.*

He looks so old, I thought. He *was* old, by naval officer standards, somewhere in his early sixties by then, visibly worn down by years of fleet command and his own bête noire, shingles. His face was set in a permanent scowl, even when he smiled, or tried to. He and Spruance had been alternating command of the U.S. Pacific Fleet. When Halsey had it, it was called the Third Fleet. When Spruance took it, it was the Fifth Fleet. I'd often wondered if the Japs really thought there were two fleets.

The aide pulled up a straight-backed chair, and Halsey took a seat next to my bed. He put his left hand out, and the aide handed him something. Halsey then opened the box and pinned a Navy Cross on my bathrobe and then shook my hand. I hadn't seen a photographer slip into the room, but I did see that flash. Halsey's famous scowl twisted sideways.

"There you were," he said, his voice gravelly, "all ready to chew my ass, and now look. I pin a medal on you and you don't know what to do."

I nodded. I did not know what to do. Halsey was apparently used to that. I was aware that there seemed to be a lot of people in the passageway just outside the cabin door. A five-star admiral does draw a crowd, I thought.

"That is for the way you saved your crew up there on the picket line that I'm not supposed to care about," he said. "Captain Waring came back and told me what you'd done, and said. Then I got a look at *Malloy* before I came to see you. Thirteen wounded, no dead, that's goddamned amazing, Captain."

"Thank you, sir," I said. "There's no other way

to deal with a line attack like that, except get your people out of harm's way."

"And you had everyone lay below to second-deck spaces?"

"Yes, sir."

"Except yourself, I'm told."

I shrugged and winced. A mistake, my aching body told me. "It was too far to go," I said. "Besides, I wanted to see if it worked. The fourth one did the most damage. Some of them come with bombs, you know."

"Yes, I do know," he said. "That's why *Missouri*'s in here, to get a gun mount taken off. A kamikaze got through and smashed one all to hell. Captain Waring said you wondered why we left you guys so exposed up there."

"Yes, sir," I said. "Tethered to one spot like that, no mutual support from the other picket stations, we're sitting ducks. Once the Japs figured out the line attack, we became dead ducks."

Halsey nodded. "Here are the facts of life, young man," he said gently. "Carriers will bring the war to the Japanese homeland. Carriers and long-range bombers. Destroyers will *not* bring the war to Japan. We're about to take Okinawa. This will be the last island campaign before the really big one. Three airfields, that's all we want here, and they're *not* for the bombers—they're for the fighters who will escort the bombers.

Fighters are like destroyers: fast, useful, but they will not bring the war to the Japanese home islands—the bombers will. The picket line gives us fifteen minutes more warning than we can get on our own. In fifteen minutes, we can double the number of fleet CAP in the air, but only if the fighters are already up on the flight deck, armed, fueled, and ready. The fifteen minutes we get from you guys is the difference between a sky full of defensive CAP and a sea full of burning carriers."

"Yes, sir, we understand that, but you have so many destroyers—if we had ten tin cans up there instead of just five, we'd lose a lot fewer ships."

"You just proved that statement is no longer true, Captain. The line attack. Your exec diagrammed it out for me and my staff down in the wardroom an hour ago. It's unstoppable, isn't it. You said so yourself."

I nodded.

"Then I have to keep as many tin cans with my carriers as I can, in ever more crowded concentric rings. We are in as much danger from collision as we are from kamikazes these days, but we have to cut that line of kamis down to just one before they get to a carrier. You see, you're just finding out about the line attack. We've been dealing with it for weeks."

I blinked again. That was news.

"Now, some more facts of life: Destroyers are

there to protect the rest of the fleet. Necessarily, that means you're out there on point, as the Army guys like to say. You are *always* going to be exposed. Some of you protect us with guns, others with long-range radar. It simply makes more sense to expend a few destroyers up on the picket line in order to save one—even *one*—carrier from having to go back to Pearl for repairs. *Malloy* was your first tin can assignment, wasn't she? I think they told me that when I signed your promotion papers."

"Yes, sir. I'd been in—"

"Carriers, right? Bet you weren't too concerned about destroyers back then, were you, other than to make sure you had 'em all around you."

He had me there. I'd never given them a second thought. Halsey was grinning.

"Dutch Van Arnhem commended you in a message before he died," Halsey said. "Makee-learn XO suddenly thrust into command and doing stuff no one else had done up there and staying alive. Funny what dire straits can evoke in the way of improvisation."

He stood up. "Congratulations on that medal. You earned it. Get well and then come with us to Japan. *Malloy*'s going to limp home. You're going to command the next tin can that needs a skipper. And don't ever criticize me again, or I'll bite you."

Another grin to show me all those teeth, and then he was gone.

SEVENTEEN

As things turned out, my newly sculpted body let me down. Connective tissue problems, recurrent infections, hearing problems, a skull differently shaped from what I was born with, and extensive damage to the biggest organ in my body, my skin, got the best of me. One of the corpsmen tending to me said I looked like a walking (sometimes), talking Peking duck. I tried to glare at him, but my eyelids wouldn't work. I got my first look at myself a day after Halsey's visit, and I suddenly admired the admiral's self-control. For a long while, my skin looked like vellum. Halsey, being a victim of shingles, must have sympathized.

Malloy was escorted back to Guam and then to Pearl by two destroyer escorts, and the crew, captained now by newly promoted Lieutenant Commander Jimmy Enright, fought an insidious flooding problem all the way back. At Pearl they dry-docked her and discovered she had a cracked keel assembly along a hundred and fifty feet of her hull, probably caused by that big bomb on kami number four. The net result was that the BuShips rep at the Pearl Harbor Naval Shipyard recommended a strike. She was cannibalized for every spare part that was still usable, defueled, and then scuttled fifteen miles off Diamond Head in fifty-eight hundred feet of water. Jimmy Enright, Mario, and Chief Dougherty personally opened the sea chest clean-out valves, and she was gone in twenty minutes.

I was sent to the big naval hospital on Guam for treatment and rehabilitation, after which they sent me back to the even bigger naval hospital complex in San Diego known as Balboa. There a tropical medicine specialist found the fix for my skin problems, and I was officially discharged from the hospital and then medically retired in the rank of commander, USN. I walked out of the hospital into the eternal San Diego sunshine with no place to go, no car, and no nearby friends or relatives that I knew about. I got maybe a hundred yards before I had to sit down. Being semicrushed under the weight of the *Malloy*'s pilothouse structure had done far more damage than anyone had been aware of, and I knew I was lucky to be alive. Being eased out of the Navy, albeit kindly, with good medical care and a pension, was equally crushing. I hadn't realized how much my entire adult life had been defined by the Navy.

I had been moved to an ambulatory ward in late July. "Ambulatory" covered a whole spectrum of cases; mostly it meant that you no longer needed constant treatment, but rather, time to heal. It was staffed by an office full of smiling sadists who insisted that each day you walked just a little longer, and when you were done with that, you got to go play in the rehab room with the same kinds of things Torquemada used to refresh the Faith and set the answer to an occasional question. After a couple of weeks I realized that if I did these things voluntarily, the sadists would leave me alone. That's when I discovered a room in the ward next door that contained what was left of Pudge Tallmadge.

I'd taken to reading the name tags outside the patient rooms as I hobbled through the wards in my pj's and bathrobe, clumping along with the assist of two canes at first, and then one. I'd read the name, kept going, stopped, and turned around. The door was cracked open, and there was a woman whose face I recognized sitting in a chair by the window, reading a magazine. I knocked on the door.

"Yes?" she asked. The likeness was remarkable. I'd seen her picture on the skipper's desk every time I'd gone into his inport cabin. She was probably forty, a little on the plump side, with a sweet face and hair beginning to go gray.

I stepped in. She put a hand to her mouth and then apologized for her reaction. "You look terrible," she said. "What happened to you?"

I tried to smile, but my facial muscles weren't quite following orders yet. The resulting grimace probably frightened her. I introduced myself, trying not to mumble, and said I'd been exec in

Malloy under Captain Tallmadge, who was lying there in the hospital bed, eyes closed, looking positively serene.

"Oh," she said. "Yes. Connie Miles. Right. My God, what happened to you? Where's the ship?"

"The ship is asleep in the deep," I said. "It's a long story." I looked over at the captain, which is how I would always remember him. The captain. His eyes opened briefly, staring vacantly into the middle distance. His hands were resting com-fortably on his chest, and his mind was long gone, from what I could see. She saw me looking.

"Oh, don't mind him," she said. "He's resting. Now tell me, what became of *Malloy*? He loved that ship."

Resting, I thought. Well, I guess that was one word for it.

"May I sit down?" I asked, suddenly conscious of the fact that my legs were trembling. I'd learned not to let that go on for very long.

She jumped out of her chair and led me to it. Then she left the room. She came back a moment later with a second chair, pulled it close to mine, and sat down. She asked me to tell her the story. Everything.

So I did. I kept glancing over at him, but he simply lay there, eyes closed again, breathing in, breathing out.

"They wouldn't tell me anything," she said. "I

got a telegram that he'd been injured and was being sent to Guam, and from Guam, here. I got here from Maryland just about when he did. I expected . . . injuries, but this is how he was. They said they didn't know when, or even if, he'd come out of it."

She seemed resigned to his mental state, as if this was just a matter of time before he woke up one day and called for coffee. "What happens next?" I asked her.

"They've told me that they will train me to take care of him—bedsore management, one of the nurses called it, and, of course, hygiene. Then I'll take him home to the Eastern Shore. Soon, I hope."

I hadn't noticed feeding tubes or IV lines. "He can eat?"

"I put a spoon to his mouth, he takes it. I can get him up, take him to the bathroom, and his body seems to know what to do. Better than a coma, they tell me."

"Well, then there's hope, Mrs. Tallmadge," I said. "If he can do all that with your help, then one day he's going to look around, see that he's safe, and come back out."

"That's the plan, Commander Miles. That's the plan."

I realized then that he was in capable and strong hands. I knew a doctor had probably sat her down and laid out the possibilities, and she hadn't flinched. One of the advantages of a good marriage, I thought. I made my manners and told her to contact me if she needed anything. She asked where. I realized that I had no idea, so I took down her address and telephone number and promised to contact her from wherever I eventually landed, probably in Washington, D.C.

A week before that, the hospital administrator had informed me that the Navy was going to medically retire me. There'd be a pension, but after only ten years of service not much of one compared to the stipends given to officers who served the traditional twenty or even thirty years. My personal effects from *Malloy* had arrived in a cruise box from Pearl, along with a big black-and-white, framed picture of the entire crew, assembled on the 10-10 dock at the Pearl Harbor shipyard, and signed by every one of them on the back. There was a second picture, taken by Marty, of *Malloy*'s stern standing straight up in the air before making her final plunge. I ended up throwing most of the uniforms away since they hung on my somewhat emaciated frame like old laundry. I kept the crew picture and gave the other one away to the local Naval District Public Information Office.

Mrs. Tallmadge had asked where she could contact me. My mother was still alive and retired in the D.C. area. Having no job, no car, and no skills applicable to anything out there in the civilian world, I'd probably have to go home, regroup, and start over. The only good news was that I had almost four years of paychecks saved up in the Riggs Bank of Washington, so money wasn't going to be a problem, for a while, anyway. I knew that eventually, when the Japs finally gave up, there'd be a huge wave of people just like me coming home. The newspapers were already commenting on the influx of veterans coming back after VE-day, and there'd been editorials speculating on what the country was going to do with them, and for them.

I did have one more thing to do before I walked away from all things naval, and that involved going to a small town in Georgia. I still had trepidations about making that trip. It had sounded like the right thing to do when I went down to sick bay that morning, but now I wondered. How would a widow and a family react to a perfect stranger appearing on the front steps bearing something so terribly personal as two rings and a lock of hair?

Amazingly well, it turned out, and with grace and dignity besides. I'd taken a train from California to Atlanta. The train took four days to make the trip, during which I spent a lot of time just looking out the window with my mind in neutral. I rode in a normal Pullman car and not in one of the two cars allotted to recovering soldiers and sailors, each with its own small medical team. I hadn't been back to the continental United States since early 1942. Any leaves I had taken had been at R&R sites in the Pacific. It was pleasant to just look out the window and reacquaint myself with America. It looked pretty good.

Before leaving San Diego I'd sent off a letter addressed to Mrs. William Van Arnhem, care of the post office in Monticello, Georgia, telling her I was coming to bring her some of the commodore's personal effects. I spent a day in Atlanta resting up after the train trip, having arrived on August 6, 1945, the day we dropped the big one on Hiroshima. Based on the radio news, the war might be ending sooner rather than later. The next day I put on a coat and tie, packed my two bags, and hired a car and driver to take me to the booming metropolis of Monticello. Hiring a driver was a bit of an extravagance, but I hadn't driven a car in years and doubted my ability to find my way around the southern countryside. Not to mention that I was still pretty weak from my time at Balboa.

When I got to the tiny town of Monticello, and it was indeed tiny, I found the post office, introduced myself, and asked if a letter to Mrs. Van Arnhem had come through. The postmistress, a peppery lady of uncertain age, wanted to know who was asking. I told her that I'd sent the letter and now needed to take something to Mrs. Van Arnhem. "Oh," she said. "Yes, she knows you."

That apparently was the key: She knew me. How, I didn't know, but the postmistress gave my driver, a middle-aged black man by the name of Homer, directions to the plantation, known locally as Blue Pines.

I expected to see Tara looming majestically up on a hillside when we turned, as directed, into a long, tree-lined lane across from a large red barn. Instead, the one-lane sandy track wandered for at least a mile through fields of drying feed corn. The trees along the road were not stately oaks but some unidentifiable and distinctly scrubby specimens of little character. The house, when it finally appeared, was a two-story farmhouse with a wide front porch and a green metal roof. No columns, huge brick chimneys, or second-floor verandahs, and definitely no clusters of happy black people humming gospel songs as they loaded bales of cotton onto horse-drawn wagons. Clark Gable was not much in evidence, either.

Oh, well, I thought. This was probably what real plantation houses looked like. I hadn't seen any blue pines, either, but there were two vintage 1939 cars parked to the side of the house under the only oak tree I'd seen since arriving. It was just before noon, and the place seemed to be entirely deserted. For a moment I thought about simply turning around, but meeting Mrs. Tallmadge had strengthened my resolve.

"What do you think, Homer? Anybody home?"

"They be out directly, suh," he said. "Country folk gonna take 'em a look before they come steppin' out when strangers come."

He was right. A minute later the front door opened, and the woman whose picture I'd seen framed in the commodore's cabin stepped out onto the front porch. She was maybe five foot two and dressed in what surely did look like period clothes, as she had been in that portrait. She looked older now; a death in the family will do that to you, I told myself.

I got out of the car. Homer said he'd just wait outside if I didn't mind, so I walked up to the front steps. I was escorted by two friendly, tail-wagging dogs who'd appeared out of nowhere. I had to take one step at a time, but without a cane, finally.

"Mrs. Van Arnhem?" I said. "I'm Commander Connie Miles. I had the pleasure of serving with your husband, the commodore. I hope you received my letter?"

"I did, Commander, I did," she said in a lovely and cultivated Southern accent. I thought I saw someone else move behind one of the heavily curtained front windows. "Dutch told me about you in a letter just before he died. He said you showed great promise. Won't you come in, please."

I walked up the steps and took her hand briefly, and then we went inside.

“Have you come far, Commander?” she asked over her shoulder. The front hall was much cooler than the front yard. There was a living room to one side, a dining room on the other, and an ornate stairway dead ahead. Judging by the floors, moldings, and the thickly plastered walls, the house had to be nearly a hundred years old.

“From the other side of the world,” I said. “In a manner of speaking.”

“Yes, that must be so,” she said. “Dutch could never tell me where he was at any given time; the censors, you know.” She showed me into the living room, where we took seats. A Negro maid appeared with a tray service of what looked like iced tea and sugar cookies. Had she been expecting me? Of course, I realized. The postmistress.

“We were together at an island called Okinawa,” I said. “Which is only a couple hundred miles south and east of the Japanese home islands.”

“Did you know about this new bomb, an atomic bomb I think they called it?”

“No, ma’am, but from what they’re reporting, I suspect the war against Japan will end pretty soon, hopefully without the need to invade. The Okinawa invasion was bad enough.”

She nodded. “We listen to the evening news, of course, but the radio correspondents seem to always have a very optimistic slant on how things are going.”

I smiled. "That's called propaganda, I think," I said. "But in fact, Okinawa has been taken, and now the Army Air Forces are systematically pulverizing the home islands. I am, however, well out of it."

I explained my medical retirement after only ten years in the Navy, and she displayed some sympathy. "Does it bother you?" she asked. "That you must leave the Navy? It was everything to Dutch."

"Yes and no, Mrs. Van Arnhem," I replied. "The Okinawa campaign was very hard on the Navy, and I myself will be a long time healing, I think." I told her in relatively sanitized terms about what had happened to me and the ship. My ship. One of his ships. That thought stopped me for a moment, and she looked at me with sympathetic eyes.

"I am very, very tired," I said. "Rising to the rank of commander in ten years would have been impossible before the war, and in my case, it happened less because of any personal merit and more because of circumstances."

She nodded. "Dutch talked about that, before he left for the Pacific. After Pearl Harbor, he said, there would be big changes coming to the fusty old Navy. I would love to hear more, Commander, especially since my Dutch is not coming home."

I hadn't come there to talk about myself, but

this charming lady had managed to put me at my ease. I almost felt embarrassed.

"He was buried at sea?" she prompted.

"Yes, ma'am, he was," I said. "As the captain, I officiated. It was a formal burial ceremony, or as formal as we could make it. He'd only been aboard for a brief time before the attack. He was on the bridge in his unit commander's chair when the attack came."

She nodded, almost absently, and looked off into the middle distance. A cloud passed over the sun outside, and the room dimmed for a moment. Too much, I told myself. She doesn't want to hear this. Her husband's well and truly gone, consigned to the depths of the Pacific, that great eater of sea-going men and their presumptuous little ships.

"You said you were going to bring me something," she said finally. "The Navy returned some of his personal effects—uniforms, his sword, some hats." She looked at me inquiringly with sad eyes.

I took a deep breath and nodded. From inside my coat I removed a silver cigar case. It wasn't entirely appropriate, but I hadn't had much time in Atlanta to find anything else. I handed her the case, which she opened. Inside were his Naval Academy ring, his wedding ring, and an antique flat silver locket with an oval of glass in the front. And inside that . . .

I think she first focused on the rings. She smiled a smile of sweet sadness, and yet it was as if she were welcoming the rings back home, back to their rightful place. Then she saw the locket.

She gasped and almost dropped it, but then she picked it up with trembling hands and stared at it, her eyes welling up. Oh, God, I thought. I shouldn't have done this. What had I been thinking?

Then she pressed the locket between her tiny hands, closed her eyes, and began to weep. I felt like I should say something, anything, to comfort her, but I recognized that this was a very private moment, a homecoming vastly different from that of the two rings. This was between them. I wasn't even there.

After a few minutes she composed herself. "*You* did this?" she asked in a shaky voice.

"Yes, ma'am, and I'm very sorry to have upset you. I thought—"

"Oh, no," she said, cutting me off. "Thank you, thank you, *thank* you. How did you know?"

I took a deep breath. "The captain"—I was relieved—"told me that the commodore was married to a very traditional Southern lady. As I recall my history, a locket, with a lock of hair, was an old custom in the South. Since no part of him was ever coming back, I just thought you might appreciate it."

"My. Dear. God," she said. "You have no idea."

Actually, looking at her face, I did. For once

I'd done something completely right. I felt good enough about it that I forgot about my aching bones for a few minutes while she sat there clutching that silver locket and rocking gently in her chair.

"Tell me everything, young man," she said at last. "What he was like, how he looked, what happened at the end. Everything. I haven't seen him for three years, you know. Tell me everything, *please*."

We spent the next few hours in that living room, sipping on sugary tea, with me telling her probably more than I should have about our time on the Okinawa picket line. Toward the end I began to run out of steam, which was when she took a really good look at me. Then things happened quickly. Homer was dispatched back to Atlanta with, I found out later, a ten-dollar tip. My two bags and I were hustled up to a guest bedroom, complete with a four-poster bed, an armoire, and a huge wooden fan stirring the air above. I was firmly instructed to take a long nap. As I was stowing some of my clothes, the maid who'd brought the tea knocked discreetly on the door and delivered another tray, this one with some fancy crustless sandwiches and a cold beer. Navy family, I remembered. Libations would be available in the parlor at six, dinner at seven, and I was, of course, spending the night. I didn't argue.

I came down at six much refreshed. I would

have probably slept until the next morning except that I'd heard female voices out in the upstairs hall. When I got downstairs, wearing the same coat and tie but with a fresh shirt, I got a surprise. A much younger woman was there on the sofa beside Mrs. Van Arnhem, and I recognized her face from that portrait on the commodore's desk. Turned out her name was Julia, and she was, as I'd thought, their daughter. She'd arrived from Atlanta while I was sleeping off my cross-country trip.

Julia looked more like her father than her mother, with dark brown hair, sly brown eyes, and a very pretty face that would not have been out of place in *Gone With the Wind.* While her mother affected the mannerisms and dress of the nineteenth century, Julia was very much a denizen of the twentieth, if her stylish dress and sophisticated way of carrying herself were any indication. Her lipstick was vividly red, and there was a cigarette case on the coffee table in front of her that I was pretty sure did not belong to the lady of the house. She had elegant, slim legs and looked as if she knew her way around an after-hours nightclub. She gave me a frankly appraising look when we were introduced, which immediately had me wondering how well I'd scored. Given that I was twenty-five pounds underweight, with the remains of dark circles under my eyes and a way of moving that probably resembled a large but injured insect, I suspected not very well. This young lady looked like she regularly feasted on handsome, rich playboys up in Atlanta, assuming there still were any rich playboys, that is. I realized then there was a lot I didn't know about the United States of America in late 1945. I wondered if I was going to like it.

After supper we migrated to the living room for coffee. Julia offered me a cigarette when she lit up and seemed faintly disappointed that I didn't join her. Her mother excused herself after a little while. Julia promptly got up, went to a small sidebar I hadn't noticed, and poured a couple of cognacs for us. I asked her what she did for a living.

"I'm in the finance department of a large bank up in Atlanta," she said. "Investments, putting commercial deals together. That sort of thing."

"The only thing I know about finance is that it went off the rails in 1929," I said. I remembered the pay cut the Army and the Navy took in the mid-1930s as a result of the Depression that followed.

She nodded. "It's making its way back," she said. "Especially in Atlanta. That city is going to boom one day, and I wanted to be in place when it does."

"Are there that many women in finance?" I asked.

"There are now," she said. "Well, not very

many, but more than none. The war did wonders for women's opportunities in business. It'll be interesting to see what happens when all those men come back home."

"You think women will be pushed out?"

"I think that the competition is going to be really fierce," she said. "That's why I plan to start my own company this year. It'll depend on how many clients I can poach from the bank when I leave, but I want to have it in place when everybody starts looking for work. How about you? What are you going to do once this horrible war ends?"

"Damned if I know," I said. "Actually, I've been medically retired, so I'm really out of the Navy now. They say I'm physically unfit for active duty after Okinawa."

She nodded. "What will you do for money, then?" she asked.

The financier, I thought, getting right to the point. "I've got almost four years of paychecks saved up," I said. "I'm not married, so I just banked it. I'll be okay for a while, I think."

"That's good, because unemployment is going to go through the roof after the war. The economy's going to contract hard until the politicians get another war going somewhere. Europe is devastated. That's going to take a decade to fix, and somehow we're going to have to find a way to get the Germans back to work.

They're the only ones who really do work over there, you know."

"Sounds like interesting times ahead," I said. "I may just sit them out."

She gave me a strange look, seemed to make some kind of decision, finished her cigarette and her cognac, and then looked at her watch. "I've got to get up early tomorrow and get back to the city," she said. "But right now I'd like you to meet someone. I'll be right back."

I sat back in my comfortable chair and looked around the parlor, with its twelve-foot-high molded ceilings, real if slightly shabby wall-paper, and furnishings from what looked like the 1880s if not earlier. What do they do way out here in the sticks, I wondered. There'd been crops in the fields, but who was tending to the farm if all the men were gone?

"Commander Miles," Julia said, coming back into the room, "I'd like to introduce my younger sister, Olivia. Livy, this is Commander Connie Miles, of the United States Navy. He brought back Father's rings, and the locket."

On Julia's arm was a vision, dressed all in white. Olivia was probably late twenties, slim, taller than her sister, with gorgeous blond hair and one of those faces that make perfectly intelligent men walk into lampposts. She was hanging on lightly to Julia's left arm, and then I saw why: Those gorgeous blue eyes saw nothing at all. Olivia Van Arnhem was blind.

"Olivia," I said, rising to my feet. "A pleasure to meet you."

She turned her head in my direction and I tried not to stare at her, then realized, I could if I wanted to—she couldn't see me. Julia could, though, and she gave me a sympathetic look that seemed to say, *A terrible waste, isn't it?* She steered Olivia to the big sofa and sat down beside her, not holding her up, but close enough that Olivia would know she was right there.

"Commander," Olivia said, in a soft Southern drawl, something Julia had dispensed with. "You did a wonderful thing, bringing that locket. It meant the world to Mother."

"I was almost afraid to bring it," I said. "The longer I thought about it, the bigger intrusion it seemed. But . . ."

"Yes," Olivia said, "but we're very grateful you did. I can still remember the day that car came up the drive and those two officers got out. Mother went stiff as a board, and that's how I knew why they were here. She'd been so confident, you know. He was a senior officer, a commodore, and so less exposed to danger than younger officers. Or so we all thought."

"He was a little bit safer when he was down in the fleet anchorage," I said. "Being a commodore. But then he came north to the picket line when things got really tough. I think he knew I needed help, and I was very glad to have him embark. Now I wish he'd stayed at the anchorage."

"The picket line," Olivia said. "The anchorage. Commodore. I don't really know what those words mean, Commander. You must tell me about them."

Julia looked again at her watch and then stood up. "Livy," she said, "I've got to get to bed. I'm sure the commander can get you back to your room when you tire."

Olivia smiled at a secret thought. "Come back soon, Jules," she said.

Julia gave me a little finger wave and went upstairs. Olivia gestured for me to join her on the couch. "Bring one of those cognacs, if you'd be so kind."

I did, wondering how she knew we'd been having a cognac, and then I remembered the stories of how the other senses of the blind become much more acute. I sat down next to her, steered the glass into her hand, and clinked mine against hers. She smiled again and took a sip.

"When I tire," she said, repeating Julia's words and shaking her head. "I'm blind, not a fucking invalid."

I choked on my cognac, and she started laughing.

"Gotcha," she said. "Now you must call me Livy."

• • •

That's how I ended up spending the rest of my life in the wilds of middle Georgia. Okay, semiwild, although the farther one gets from Atlanta, the thinner becomes the veneer of civilization in the biggest state east of the Mississippi.

I stayed the next three days there at the farm as their guest, during which Livy and I spent almost all our waking hours together. I'd read about things like that, but never, especially after the nightmare of Okinawa, expected it to happen to me. Livy had not been born blind; her affliction was the result of a riding accident when she was sixteen, involving a fairly serious head injury. She was very functional around the house and adept at getting around the grounds, since she'd grown up on the family plantation. I once commented to Livy that it must be interesting to be a member of one of the first families of Georgia. She'd laughed at me. She did that a lot, but it was always a sweet laugh. "The so-called first families of Georgia were all snuffed out in the Civil War," she explained. "We're all descendants of the Carpetbaggers."

The point was, she was as secure and mobile as she could ever be right there at home, and, like her mother and unlike her sister, she was probably never going to leave it. By that time, of course, I was madly in love, so this posed a decision for me. It took me a good five minutes, and we were married after a "suitable" courtship of six months, to prove, as I later found out, that there was no whiff of scandal in the form of early babies in the offing. Not that Livy would have cared; nothing frightened that woman, not even when I would have a bad night and wake up shouting unintelligible orders to a bunch of ghosts.

I have not forgotten, nor will I ever forget, those ghosts, those brave souls and small fighting ships whose lives and futures were so harshly extinguished in that crucible called the Okinawa picket line. The ghosts—from the white hats to the commodores, and even those demented and much-damned young Japanese pilots, the kamikazes—have long since been transmuted into a variety of glorious life forms at the bottom of the deepest sea. The ships, broken, burned, shredded, and mangled, are finally at peace, as the cold dark heart of the Pacific rusts them back into the elements from which they were created.

We did the best we could. From time to time I find myself missing the smell of fresh coffee on the bridge, or Mooky's fat-pills. The rest of it has gone down in my memory like the ships of the picket line. That saddens me, until I look over at Livy. Then it's sunrise at sea again, the very best time of the day.

AUTHOR'S NOTE

My father was a division commander (commodore) of destroyers at Okinawa in 1945. I wish I could say that he told me all about it. He did not. He wouldn't speak of it. It was simply that bad.

The Navy had suffered casualties during the island-hopping campaigns leading up to Okinawa, but nothing like what happened there. In fact, the Navy killed-in-action (KIA) casualties exceeded the ground-troop KIA numbers. Considering the meat-grinder nature of the Okinawa land battle, with hundreds of thousands engaged, that is truly significant.

Navy losses were driven by the ferocious Japanese kamikaze assault. The Americans knew the kamikazes were coming, but drastically underestimated the scale of the impending attacks. Allied and naval Intelligence had estimated that there were no more than five hundred or so aircraft available to the Japanese for kamikaze attacks. The real number was closer to five thousand, resulting in Navy losses of 34 ships sunk and 368 damaged out of a combined Allied fleet of approximately one thousand five hundred ships and other craft.

As usual, I've taken some liberties with the historical sequence of actual events in order to simplify the story, but, for the most part, what I've written fairly accurately describes the horror of the radar picket line and the quiet heroism of the destroyermen who stood their ground. The fifteen to twenty minutes warning they gave the fleet at sea and the logistics ships at Kerama Retto was crucial. The proof of that came when the Japanese decided that they needed to make the radar picket line itself a priority target.

I've long believed that the Okinawa campaign played a significant part in the decision to drop the atomic bombs on Japan. The sheer scale of the fighting, the horrific casualties, and the ferocity with which the Japanese defended what they considered to be Japanese territory gave a clear indication of what would happen if the Allies invaded the home islands. The B-29 campaign and the atomic bombs marked a shift in the Pacific war strategy, with bloody amphibious assaults being replaced wherever possible by machines and brand-new technologies. The Japanese high command knew they could not hold Okinawa, but they were determined to make the Americans bleed for it, and perhaps think twice about an invasion of the home islands. Ironically, I think they succeeded with that.